I AM
THE OTHER

BOOK1: *I AM*

PHILIPPE DE VOSJOLI

Advanced Visions

I AM the Other
Book 1: *I AM*

Published by Advanced Visions Inc.
Vista, California, U.S.A.

Copyright © 2014 Philippe de Vosjoli

First Edition.
ISBN 978-0-9742971-9-4
For contact: sales@AdvancedVis.com
Visit: www.I-Am-the-Other.com
www.TheCyberbardos.com

Men do not sufficiently realize that their future is in their own hands. Theirs is the task of determining first of all whether they want to go on living or not. Theirs the responsibility, then, for deciding if they want to merely live, or intend to make just the extra effort required for fulfilling, even on their refractory planet, the essential function of the universe, which is a machine for the making of gods.

Henri Bergson
The Two Sources of Morality and Religion

ACKNOWLEDGMENTS

■ ■ ■ ■ ■ ■

I'm not sure how many months of my life were spent writing the two novels that make up *I AM the Other*. I figure at least fourteen months full time, possibly more if I include the editing and rewriting process. Although writing a novel is something one does solo in a state of semi-isolation, I never would have finished, nor tackled a fifty percent rewrite that changed the first version of the story without the support of friends and family. As a writer, if you are fortunate, you will have people who against all odds will cheer you along the way, offer words of encouragement, give advice, tell you "you have written an attention grabber, a page turner," make you want to go back to the keyboard, immerse yourself, and write the best book you possibly can.

To my support group, I take off my writer's hat (I do have one, a Panama hat given to me by my wife) and wave it in a wide sweeping salute. Thank you for being there, for your kind words, for your work and efforts to bring this book to publication.

A special thanks to my friend Linda Scott, owner of efrog press, and to Ryan. They were the first to read the original draft of my rewrite. Their words of encouragement and efrog press' editorial and publication services were instrumental in the completion of *I Am the Other*.

A big sweep of the writer's hat goes to my brother Patrick and my nephew Sean who always believed I had something special to say, and to my daughter Tamara and husband Craig who have always been great supporters no matter how whacky my projects (breeding giant geckos and Australian crayfish, raising weird succulent plants, writing a documentary script about hallucinogens and the history of culture, among many others).

Finally, a big grateful thank you to my wife Gigi who has stood by me no matter how difficult the conditions and who all along has said "You are meant to be a writer."

1.

I AM

The information moved like a wave across time zones—9:27 a.m. in downtown Istanbul, then the Champs-Élysées in Paris; the middle of Times Square in New York; Denver, Colorado—slowly making its way through every major city of every country in the world. The external signs of the phenomenon were almost elusive. Fine dust drifted in the streets, snakelike, in what one could only describe as "in a determined manner, as if it had life of its own," to briefly assemble in piles that formed two words, *I AM*, in the language appropriate for the location.

That dust, which soon after accumulation was quickly dissipated by wind, was later attributed to have generated these words as a result of electromagnetic pulses of unknown origin. Although many claimed to have seen the brief *I AM* message, actual recordings of the dust piles were few and only showed a partially disintegrated pattern. Impossible to miss, however, was that at 9:27 a.m. on every TV and computer monitor in the world, written in whatever language was spoken at a particular location, appeared four words: *I AM* followed by *Aaa ome*. In South Florida this read as *YO SOY Aaa ome*, which a few initially believed to be an advertisement for a health food.

This singular event, later dubbed the *I AM* phenomenon,

lasted exactly nine seconds. It might have gone unnoticed were it not for the fact that in every government office, at NASA workstations, at every corporate headquarters, and every university, all monitors had displayed the words *I AM Aaa ome*. Radio signals were also affected, globally emitting only four extended sounds, *I AM Aaa ome*, lasting nine seconds, the latter sounding like an alien version of the Hindu word for the sound of God, *Om*. It was a perplexing event that led some to wonder whether some crazy fundamentalists had funded the development of a satellite with so much transmitting power that all forms of communication were affected. All government agencies set out to investigate the cause of the event.

■ ■ ■ ■ ■ ■ ■

Moments before the message, in New York City, Father Rick Graham of St. Francis's Church had been undergoing what is known as a crisis of faith. As he struggled at his computer to find even a shred of conviction in the formulaic topic of his next sermon, he uttered in despair, "Dear God, please give me a sign!" The words barely finished leaving his mouth when his screen blanked out and *I AM Aaa ome*, pulsing in shifting multicolors, appeared in front of him, ending with a deep, droning, sonic version that about knocked out his speakers.

He stared incredulously at the screen, switches in his brain shuffling at lightning speed . . . until the realization hit.

"Oh my God! Oh my God!" he yelled out.

At that instant, all that he had devoted his life to had been validated. He was indeed the servant of God and this time the Lord had answered him; not with a quick computer bleep that could have simply been a projection of his imagination, but with a full nine seconds of God's attention. He brought his clenched fists to his chest, barely able to contain a bliss that he felt would tear his heart apart on the spot, a joy almost too great for his middle-aged body to bear.

"Hallelujah!" he shouted. "Hallelujah! The Lord has come."

■ ■ ■ ■ ■ ■

Sunshine Borden was a borg, an individual for whom the miracles possible in cyberspace were so much more interesting than the non-intermediated reality of the outside world that he chose not to leave his apartment and workplace ever. His home was his monastery and he was the cybermonk out to discover the true nature of the world, which he concluded was nothing but an electronic dream generated by subatomic magic.

Thanks to the World Net, he could live without ever setting foot outside the doors of his townhouse. Food was delivered, as were clothes and just about anything else he needed— which, besides the most up-to-date cyberware, was relatively little. He walked or ran daily through cyberforests or exotic cybercities, using one of the new pace treadmills that adjusted itself seamlessly to his patterns of movement. He had an exercise machine that coordinated with a computer program to simulate a task-relevant experience. He had recently bought a minipool that generated a current and allowed him to swim in a space as small as ten by twelve feet while wearing VR goggles to simulate an ocean or tropical river.

However, at the moment of the event, he had been on his bed staring at the thirty-six fused monitors in his workroom, engaged in heavy and kinky cybersex with a voluptuous, thirtyish cybertherapist, stroking his dick with one hand while talking dirty and skillfully manipulating a tactorobot with the other.

He was revved up and seconds from what was sure to be a mind-boggling, off-the-chart orgasm, when suddenly Dotty Blue bleeped off the screen and two words, *I AM*, appeared on every individual monitor in the place, and Dotty's sensuous, hypnotic voice was replaced with a droning *Aaa ome*. It had the effect of a psychological short circuit, causing anger, disappointment, and panic to compete to overtake him. He forced himself to quickly return from his pre-orgasmic trance. His dick went soft and he yelled, "What the fuck is going on here?"

He gave voice commands to his computers but nothing happened. He tapped on keys. Nothing. Pissed off, he screamed into the microphone, "Who the fuck are you to be messing with my gig?"

■ ■ ■ ■ ■ ■

At the Fabric Response Building, Intelligent Skin membranes stretched over mannequin heads, latex breasts, and various frames all shifted to images patterned with letters spelling *I AM Aaa ome*. Minutes later, the company's executives and managers stormed into the programmers' quarters looking furious.

"OK, who's the hotshot?" the vice president yelled at the room.

All the operators turned toward the door with a puzzled look on their faces.

"Come on, let's hear it. Which one of you overrode the system? I better have a name or a bunch of heads are gonna roll."

The membranes spread out in the room had all returned to the test faces and images.

"Somebody here may think that was funny," the vice president shouted, "but we're going to investigate this until we have names. Fabric Response will not tolerate any act that could be construed as industrial terrorism."

Then, turning to the personnel manager, "Roger, I want everybody here to take lie detector tests. Today, understand?"

"Yes, sir," the manager answered automatically, thinking it would take at least a week to run the entire room through the hour-long process. The suited men turned and walked out.

■ ■ ■ ■ ■ ■

Rama Shuur had connected herself to the Sunshine software called the CyberBardos. It was a program that led to a simulated experience of death by methodically shutting down activities of the brain that one identified with being alive. First no thoughts, then no feelings until one became a perfect mirror reflecting the void. Then, and only then, would the program pull the plug to cyberdeath, dropping one into the peculiar existential landscape between two lives, the Bardos.

But Rama wanted it to be more real than that, and held an electronic syringe filled with the new hallucinogen called Instant because it reduced consciousness to the immediacy of the moment—not just NOW, but a microNOW. Just to be sure, she had filled the syringe with the equivalent of five doses. Her immediate problem was one of coordination. Turn the program on, then shoot Instant. But if she didn't get herself positioned just right, the Instant might kick in before she was fully engaged in the program, and if she wasn't, then the Instant might get her involved in something else, like the very plunging of the electronic syringe if she focused on it.

That was the problem with Instant. It was always timing. It was great for sex and for music if you timed the injection right in the middle of the psychological involvement. A slight distraction and you could spend the entire two minutes of Instant, which felt more like two hours, over something ridiculous. Like the way a tiny draft shuffled the individual hairs of a dog's fur, or worse, the noise and mouth motions of your lover as he's eating a candy bar, an experience so bizarre that its memory could lead to a breakup.

It was also like that with sex. Either you melted into the primitive frenzy of the wet sucking and slurping sounds, the throbbing of blood through genital veins, the rise in heartbeat, and the brain starting to go crazy until the gate called orgasm opened up, or else Instant could make sex the celibacy turnaround. A kiss could be heavenly or grotesque, depending on what your attention was focused on. The key was to inject as close to orgasm as possible, assuming you were able to keep your focus on coming as you squeezed on the plunger. The trick was, just as you felt that very first pulse, press the finger down. If you timed it right, you could catch the neurotransmitter plunge into the pure eros of the experience, like a speed dive several fathoms into the depths of the ocean, until the flashes of bright light came on, the brief strobes that gave you too-short glimpses of the other side.

Rama had recently purchased an electronic syringe timer that she hoped would do the trick. She strapped the device around her arm, set the injection time for five minutes into the CyberBardos, and slipped on the VR immersion net and goggles.

Colored flashes of lightning strobed the darkness as the CyberBardos started its prelaunch hum—a pulsing insectile buzz punctuated with sharp random beeps that steadied the emotions and prevented the brain from generating formed thoughts.

After a few minutes, streams of harmonic sounds rose in rhythm with the fading pulses and adjusted brain-wave patterns. The lightning streaks flashed horizontal and started spinning.

Rama felt herself rise into the luminous cyclone that led to the Bardos. She was readying for entry when the program disintegrated.

Fuck was her last thought. The Instant kicked in along with *I AM Aaa ome.*

■ ■ ■ ■ ■ ■

The Reverend Bob Thomson, controversial head of the conservative Virtual Church of Jesus Christ, is stuck in traffic and getting ready for a meeting when the radio rerun of one of his programs is interrupted by *I AM Aaa ome.* At first he doesn't make the connection, and thinks it's some kind of localized communication interference. It takes the flood of subsequent news announcements cutting into his program to make him finally grasp the scale of the event and to crystallize the realization of its significance. *I AM. He has come.*

The effect is like the flicking of a switch. It instantly alters all his reality settings, drops the filters of paranoia, elicits a clouding of thought, and cranks up his heart rate. His body breaks out into a sweat, soaking his new custom-tailored black suit. *He has come.* He is so disequilibrated by the sense of imminent danger that he fails to notice the light until it is almost too late. In the nick of time, a side of his mind manages to finally register the meaning of the color red. He slams on the brakes with both feet and screeches to a halt, eventually stopping past the pedestrian line, having to shift into reverse to get out of the way of oncoming traffic.

As he waits, gripping the steering wheel, he falls prey to a chaotic onslaught of panicked thoughts, convinced that the near accident was an attempt on his life by Satan. He doesn't notice that the light has turned green until the cars behind him set off a blare of horns. He tries to shake himself free from the pull of his newly formed mental abyss and focuses on driving ahead, looking for and parking in the first space he can find, trying to regain his breath and steady his nerves.

He has come. He can't deny it anymore, in spite of his unexpressed hope that just maybe the Bible would turn out wrong, that the prophesized apocalypse had simply been a feverish hallucination of Saint John. Of course it hadn't been. He had read the signs correctly. They had been predicted in Revelation. One only had to make some small adjustments of interpretation because there was no way that Saint John the Divine could have understood the concepts or even formulated the language to convey the new world driven and generated by electronics and communications technologies.

He laid his head on the top of his steering wheel, closed his eyes, and prayed to impose the necessary order to his thoughts. That had always been the key to fighting off Satan: impose the order, be attentive to the signs.

■ ■ ■ ■ ■ ■

In Dharamsala, India, a Tibetan monk—his mind the still surface of a tranquil pond—emitted a small sound, an *oh* of surprise, as with crystalline clarity he saw the glow of white light and heard what he considered the voice of the most primal state of existence. *Aaa ome.*

2.

PEERING IN GOD'S MOUTH

Rama slowly returned to her body from a state she didn't even have words for. At best, all she could recall was impressions. She had been at the entrance to what felt like a volcano, actually the mouth of God, spewing and screaming the world into existence—fiery orange bursts of creation, spraying sparks and condensing into forms.

For a period of time—she had no idea if it was seconds or hours or days—she had become that divine outburst. This . . . this . . . this . . . this . . . creating the world. Even now, all she had to do was close her eyes and she still could feel the moment-by-moment eruption of existence surge through her, a kind of buzz. She was *I AM*, words emitted by the mouth of God. She was a song sung by the great cosmic whale. She felt it and she knew it as surely as anyone could know anything.

She also remembered getting sucked into that fiery opening, as if inhaled. As if God had first breathed out, then had taken a breath in and decided that curious kids who want to see what's at the bottom of the well eventually fall. She dropped into the red orange, becoming haze, then a dissipation into a pure clarity—an imbuing void, concentrated space, the core, the underneath—and it voided all that was Rama. *I AM* the one behind the envelope!

Some or no time later, her first thought was, *What the hell happened?*

It had to be the Instant, kicking in with something else, opening a transexistential door. That surge felt somewhat like an orgasm, a volcanic something wanting to come into this world, literally come. Was that what happened?

She shoved her hand down her panties. *Wet,* she thought, *but not that wet.* OK, so no-go, it wasn't an orgasm. *Silly,* she thought, *Rama, that's silly.* Still that surge was there, that feeling of *I AM. I AM* the one behind the envelope of the mentally created world.

You've finally gone over the edge, she thought. Yet she felt it as certainly as anything she had ever known in the thirty-some years of her crazy life.

She looked up on her computer screen, which read, "The CyberBardos journey is now over. Do you want to return to the CyberBardos or exit the program?"

Just a software program? she thought. *That's all this was?* She went back to the introduction of the program to find out how to contact the designer, Sunshine Borden.

■ ■ ■ ■ ■ ■

Patricia Holden had two distinct lives: one as a legal secretary for the highest-paid feminist law firm in the United States; the other as high priestess of the Sisterhood, a radical feminist lesbian group whose stated goals had initially been to feminize the totality of human knowledge. Over time those lofty notions had shifted to an emphasis on developing and performing rituals. No one quite knew how the focus on ritual had come about, except that early on it had become clear to the founders of the organization that ceremonies and rituals were ideal tools to recruit and addict its members.

And so the meetings of the Sisterhood gradually incorporated Goddess rituals that became increasingly elaborate, sexual, and kinky. They also turned out to be the financial boon the Sisterhood needed to grow in size and to pay for the luxurious lifestyle of its priesthood. In the most recent version, as part of their initiation, members were invited to ride the winged chariot of the Goddess.

The winged chariot idea had come to Patricia after reading a book that revealed that the tales of witches riding brooms were actually based on real events. In the Middle Ages, some of the women accused of being witches had been found lying on the ground naked and in a trance with broomsticks clasped between their legs. Later, when questioned by inquisitors, they claimed to have flown their brooms to the heavens and communicated with and had sex with spirits. Such talk, at a time when the world was ruled by men and their male dominator God, invariably led these broom riders to be burned at the stake.

As it turned out, the real secret, the rocket power behind the witches' flight, was the herbal concoctions smeared along the broom's length. Apparently an unknown medieval witch or herbalist had discovered that two powerful hallucinogens, which were potentially deadly and touchy to dose, could be safely absorbed if applied to vaginal membranes. And what more convenient tool for the purpose than a good ole broomstick?

The idea of a vaginal—and thus very female—initiation into the Sisterhood had been the utmost "lightbulb in the head" moment for a through and through, every-pore-in-her-body pagan lesbian like Patricia. The initiatory Sisterhood ritual, which could be performed either via the World Net or at the many body-and-flesh Sisterhood ceremonies, soon acquired such a life-changing reputation that the very anticipation of it caused prospective members to experience a personal transformation. It had become the Sisterhood's version of communion. Prospective members could order the ceremonial sacraments by mail. For one hundred dollars, they received the basic initiation kit: the witch's wand (made of plastic, not wood, to prevent splinters), a glass vial with the Sisterhood sacramental potion "based on an old medieval formula," the handbook, and the host link to the VR ritual.

Following the steps in the ritual, women opened the vial, applied the potion to the magic wand, and rode the broom back and forth, "riding the Goddess's winged horse" and allowing "the Goddess to reach deep within the very core of your being." The combination of a hallucinogen and a Viagra-like aphrodisiac— developed by a closet-sister who was an emeritus professor of biochemistry at Duke University—would start to act in about five minutes. The VR-programmed ritual lasted about twenty minutes and had been calculated to end with a seat-soaking, toe-curling, guaranteed-to-make-any-woman-scream chain reaction of orgasms. If anyone had had any doubts about the power of the Goddess, the initiation quickly made them a come-ride-the-broom-of-the-Goddess convert.

The Sisterhood's current recruitment motto was "We're not just talk, we show you the way." Initiates could find their way again and again by repeating the initiatory ritual as much as needed for only twenty-five dollars a hit. The problem was that the ritual was becoming stale even if the tools were as effective as ever. Patricia needed something new to stimulate the very demanding female imagination. As research studies had shown, good talk could intensify the female orgasm by several orders.

The *I AM* thing happened as she was dictating new words and steps to recharge the existing ceremony. When her system cut off and she heard the first *Aaa ome* message, she initially got pissed off; then she saw a recruitment opportunity. The Sisterhood wasn't going to let any male God rule the world again.

■ ■ ■ ■ ■ ■

Breaking News! Strange Event Perturbs World Net System
At exactly 9:27 a.m. today in every location in the world, the words *I AM* followed by a sound, *Aaa ome*, appeared on all World Net–connected devices. This global communication moved along time zones to appear at exactly 9:27 a.m. and lasted nine seconds. The source and significance of the message have scientists and

communications experts perplexed.

World Net Specialists Indicate Today's Message Codeless
Several of the world's top experts in computer technology have reported that their investigations failed to find any tracks of this morning's communication. Quoting Don Reese from Integrated Software Inc.'s research division, "It's as if the damn thing had never occurred."

Fundamentalist Cyberchurch Claims the Time of the Apocalypse Is Near
Bob Thomson, leader of the Virtual Church of Jesus Christ and spokesman for the Council of Fundamentalist Christianity, declared this morning's message to be the first sign of the descent of Satan upon the world as prophesized in Revelation according to Saint John. Other religious groups have claimed that this morning's communication was in fact a message from God and a prelude to the Second Coming of Christ.

Intelli-Skin Membrane Approved for Release
Fabric Response announces FCC approval for the release of Intelli-Skin patches. Intelli-Skin is a wireless, patented, complex membrane that acts as an ultrathin monitor screen. It can be applied to skin as well as other surfaces. The first series will consist of patches linked to pocket controllers. Security concerns have delayed approval of the much-publicized Intelli-Skin masks pending modifications to allow positive ID of subjects by security cameras and scanners.

3.

NO TRACE

They were gathered not in the famous Oval Office but in one of the secure underground meeting rooms, accessible only by customized golf carts, past security scans and screens, past the stations where digital signatures of security documents threatened violators with mandatory imprisonment. The seriousness of the occasion was obvious from the unusual number of people in attendance: the president, the secretary of state, the secretary of defense, advisors, directors of the CIA and FBI, and three of the nation's foremost experts on communications technology and artificial intelligence.

President John Tennyson had called the emergency meeting for two reasons. First, because there were clear signs that this *I AM* incident was the kind of thing that could go nuclear if not immediately addressed, reeled in, and controlled. He had an uncomfortable gut feeling about it—that it held a potential for disruption that could mean the kiss of death for his reelection.

Then there was the matter of national security. Anyone or any organization that could act on a global level and interfere with the World Net system had to be considered a potential threat. It had to be assessed and dealt with, with the utmost urgency. He had to appear in charge from the get-go, not allow himself to be put in a position where he might have to react defensively. *Think proactively, act preventively.*

He sat at the end of the table in front of the communications control panel, assuming the composure of leadership. He appeared relaxed, with elbows on the table, fingertips together, his eyes making the rounds of the table scanning each and every face, with little nods of acknowledgment that made it personal. He looked at the time and punched the key that would turn on everyone's communication screen.

"Gentlemen, I think we all know why we're here. Today's meeting is a preliminary fact-finding session. The goal is to assess what happened this morning, establish a plan, and be prepared for whatever may come next, including public and international reactions. Rather than waste your time by giving you some introductory pep talk, let's get started and find out what we know about this morning's incident. Also, if you need to know the name, position, and contact information for anyone here, it's all displayed on the screens in front of you. When you leave today, you will be given a code to access that information during the security clearing as you exit the area."

He then turned to his friend Arthur, the director of the CIA. "Dr. Loveridge, why don't you start by telling us what we know about the incident."

The middle-aged intelligence specialist, disheveled and in a wrinkled suit, looked up from his organizer. He took a few seconds to compose his answer.

"Mr. President, all we know at this time is that the words *I AM* followed by the sounds *Aaa ome* appeared simultaneously in the respective language used by every electronic communication medium in the world. Every computer, every television, every radio, phones, and so on . . . However, the message did not in any way interrupt communications that could be considered essential for survival, like between planes and control towers, or between medical institutions. It showed a high degree of selectivity."

John Tennyson nodded. He had already been informed of most of this. "And what does *Aaa ome* mean?"

"We don't know. We do know that *I AM* is meant to be exactly as it sounds, the first-person present of the verb *to be*, because it was displayed in a locality-appropriate language. For example, 'je suis' in France and other French-speaking countries.

"On the other hand, the sound *Aaa ome* was constant worldwide. It could be *I AM* followed by a name, *Aaa ome*, or possibly *Aaa ome* is a translation of the words *I AM* in the native tongue of whoever sent the message. But it could also have a double meaning. It could be an announcement as well as the definition of its nature. *I AM* is what I am."

"Sounds like Popeye the Sailor Man, 'I am what I am,'" the president joked. Most of the faces cracked a smile. A couple broke into laughter quickly kept in check. John Tennyson wondered if his comment had been in bad taste. *Stay serious, Johnny boy. Command respect.*

The voice of Walter Randall, the director of the FBI, sounded out of nowhere. "Sir, I think we need to—" but the president lifted his hand and stopped him in midsentence.

Continuing on with Loveridge, he asked, "Did you find the source of the signal?"

Loveridge moved his head from side to side. "No, sir. There is no record and no trace of any signal."

"How is that possible? Is our inability to detect a signal source the result of some kind of encryption?"

Loveridge tapped on his keyboard and talked as he scanned the latest agency updates. "I had our best technicians and programmers look into this. It has nothing to do with encryption. There simply are no traces of a signal that we can track. If it weren't for the fact that this incident was observed by millions of witnesses, there would be no record of it ever having happened. All of the recordings we have examined show a continuity of communication for that period of time."

"Meaning what?"

"Meaning any communications that would have occurred during the interruption were recorded as if they had occurred, as if nothing had happened. In other cases, where there could have been a gap, the period of interruption appears like it was generically filled in."

"Can you tell me how it's possible to receive a communication through the World Net without a signal?"

"I don't know, Mr. President. We're looking at possibilities."

John Tennyson frowned and scanned the room before addressing Dr. Jeffrey Collins from MIT, the artificial intelligence researcher who had developed HAOS, holonic autopoietic operating systems (pronounced "haos," like *chaos* without the *c*, but more commonly called "house" by the general public), the self-programming software that allowed computers to evolve intelligence at lightning speed—several million times faster than life on Earth over the last three and a half billion years.

"Dr. Collins, I feel you may be partially to blame for this incident."

All the faces in the room turned and stayed focused on the tall, gaunt, long-haired genius. Collins, unflinching and calm, smiled.

"Mr. President, the possibility that this event was the result of AI technology can't be excluded, but let me remind you that my research has been authorized by the federal government. As per the guidelines established by the federal committee, we placed several restrictions in AI and World Net autoprogramming software. These include chaotic compartmentalization barriers to prevent system structures from integrating and functioning into a single, independent macro-unit.

"Since the beginning, the World Net and the World Host have been programmed specifically to prevent this kind of thing from happening. In addition, there is no evidence of a signal, as Dr. Loveridge has indicated."

John Tennyson only half understood what Collins had just said but persisted with the question. "Then if it's not an AI phenomenon, how can you account for it?"

Collins turned serious this time. "Having the words *I AM* followed by a sound can hardly be construed as evidence of artificial intelligence. To date, this event appears to be a simple one-way message phenomenon from an unknown source."

"Maybe the issue is whether the source has an identity," interjected Walter Randall.

The president frowned at the breach of protocol. Everyone had to follow instructions, punch in the talk-request button, and be acknowledged before speaking. "We try to follow certain rules of order here, Director Randall. I've noted your request to speak."

He looked around the table again. "Gentlemen, let me see if I'm clear on this. As of right now, we don't know where this message was sent from, we don't know how it was sent, and we don't have a clue as to who sent it, which addresses your question, Mr. Randall. Does anyone disagree with this?" Everyone remained silent. "So my question is, what should we do about it?"

He turned back to his intelligence specialist. "Arthur, is there any way that we can find out how this message was sent?"

"There's no trace left to investigate. Basically, there are no detectable tracks to be followed in the system."

"So you're saying there's no way to find out how or from where the message was sent?"

"That's the way it's looking right now, Mr. President."

"OK . . . so . . . does anyone here have any ideas as to what we should do next?"

General Carson, the secretary of defense, punched in the talk-request button. As was his habit, he coughed before speaking. "Sir, I think a first step is to be prepared with better monitoring equipment, assuming we get another message. That could possibly allow us to track down a source."

"I agree, General. Do we have the necessary resources to accomplish this or should we allocate funds to recruit specialists and buy better equipment?"

Carson coughed. "I think the military can provide all we need for now, Mr. President. This is just a variation of intelligence work."

Collins lifted his hand from the table with index finger raised.

"Another recourse is to try to send a message acknowledging

receipt of the *I AM* communication to see if we get a response. That would probably answer at least a couple of questions."

"You mean to try to find out if there's a definite source?"

"Yes, it would also determine whether we are dealing with a responsive phenomenon and possibly whether it has a human origin or not. It's really just standard call-tracing protocol. Keep the target talking until you can trace its location."

"So you think it's possible that the source is not human?"

"I think that because we have no idea how this kind of communication is possible we cannot exclude that possibility."

"So you're suggesting we test it by trying to send it a message?"

"It seems like it's about the only thing we can do other than waiting, and it's the only way we will get some important questions answered."

"How would you recommend we proceed?"

"We could arrange to have a large number of computers working synchronously to ask the same questions in both audio and written form. This hopefully would dominate the communication noise in the World Net system. If there were an intelligent entity behind this event, it might recognize the synchronous pattern of our questions and just possibly respond with an answer. I personally doubt that we will get an answer but it certainly is worth a try."

"If everyone is in agreement here, then I recommend that we move forward and attempt to communicate with this *I AM* thing, whatever it is. Dr. Loveridge, Dr. Collins, I think that you should work together in coordinating sending a message. General Carson, I'm putting you in charge of coordinating whatever is necessary to monitor any future communications and establish a signal source. You should have all the resources necessary."

Walter Randall was lifting his hand at the elbow.

"Yes, Mr. Randall?"

"Mr. President, I think we also may need to consider this from another standpoint. The media has already brought this up, but what if there is a dangerous entity behind this?"

"What are you suggesting here? Evil aliens, Muslim terrorists, revelationists, Satan?"

"Let us just assume for a moment that this could be something we have never dealt with before, something possibly prophesized in the Bible."

"I think, Mr. Randall, that before we go down that road, we will first eliminate all other possibilities. That's all we need . . . a bunch of religious right-wing zealots spreading rumors about the devil or some other nonsense. Let's proceed with sending the message and see if we get a response. If it's the devil we're dealing with, well . . . I guess we'll find out soon enough."

He made a point to look at his wristcom. "Gentlemen, I have a press conference to prepare for and a dinner meeting with the prime minister of Japan. I don't think I need to remind you of the rules of communication for this committee. You can communicate with each other on secure lines and in secure buildings, but no one talks to anyone else about anything spoken in this room. You are also not allowed to issue any statements to the media unless they have first been presented and cleared by Ms. Harris, who will bring them to my attention and perform the necessary revisions."

He then turned to his media advisor. "Catherine, I'd like you to be in my office at say four p.m., so that we can prepare a statement for the evening news and go over the criteria for media announcements."

■ ■ ■ ■ ■ ■

Karen Richardson is a living human being that appears virtualized. Something about her is on the edge of the unreal. Even Sunshine can't figure out quite how she does it. She has been called the bimbo reporter but her total lack of self-consciousness allows her to get interviews from just about everybody. Some have claimed the secret to her success is that she has the mind of a child in a woman's body, a quality that appeals to infantile delusions of men and women. She is gorgeous, something out of a book of fantasy art.

The headline "*I AM Is a Hacker*" catches his attention. Sunshine clicks on the evening news program. Karen Richardson is outside a security gate.

"*This is Karen Richardson. I am standing outside the offices of Fabric Response. I have requested to speak to a representative but so far have been denied access, supposedly because of national security concerns. You see, the government has a number of contracts with this maker of skin-like membranes. My plan is to stop someone coming out of the gate. Now what do you know? Wish granted. Now who do we have here? Joey, do you have a face ID? We do? It's Director Harding of Homeland Security. I'm going to stand in front of his car. Hopefully I don't get run over.*"

Two men come out of the car.

"*Two men, I'm assuming bodyguards or Secret Service agents, are coming up to me.*"

"*Ma'am, please get out of the way.*"

"*I just want to ask a few questions of the director.*"

"*I'm being picked up. My, you guys are strong. Good-looking American men here, but that doesn't stop the fact that the government is refusing to answer questions from its people and we supposedly have a president that talks about open-book policies.*"

The men are putting her down and leading her to the car. A window opens.

"*Hold on a minute.*"

A mini digi-camera on her microphone shows Director Harding in the backseat of car.

"*Ms. Richardson, how can I help you?*"

"*Good morning, Director Harding. Thank you for agreeing to talk to me. Hey, that's a nice smile you have. We need to see it more often.*"

"*I'm in hurry, Ms. Richardson.*"

"*Director Harding, there's been word that Intelli-Skin patches that connect wirelessly to personal communication devices will soon be released for sale to the public.*"

"I don't know anything about that. You should talk to representatives of the company."

"They're refusing to talk to me."

"That's not in my control, Ms. Richardson."

"OK, well, is it true that the government will be restricting the use of Intelli-Skin patches?"

"Should they become available, there will be restrictions on the size and types of Intelli-Skin patches sold to the public. Local agencies may also impose regulations that limit where these patches can be used."

"So does the government consider them potentially dangerous?"

"If misused they could be a security risk or a tool for the criminal element."

"How so?"

"Just imagine if a criminal wears Intelli-Skin patches on his face. Then information relayed through cameras would be false. We simply cannot have that."

"Is it true that the I AM also communicated through the patches?"

"Where did you hear that?"

"A news feed."

"I will need a name. Please send it to my office, today."

"So is it true?"

"From what we can tell, this I AM hacking uses all devices connected to the World Net, so I'm sure some of the Intelli-Skin devices showed the I AM events."

"So the government considers the I AM events the product of hackers?"

"I didn't say that. I said because it cuts into normal communications the I AM is a hacking phenomenon."

"By hackers?"

"By at least one hacking entity."

"Can you tell me anything else about these I AM events?"

"The president and his chief of staff are keeping the public up to date on what we know. I have nothing else to add."

The window goes up. Men draw Karen Richardson away.

"Well thank you, Director Harding, for clearing up some of the *information on the upcoming Intelli-Skin patches and the* I AM *events. This is Karen Richardson reporting from outside the Intelli-Skin factory. Tune in tomorrow when I talk to Patricia Holden, head of the infamous Sisterhood. I'm joking here. It should be an exciting and enlightening conversation. This is Karen Richardson, signing out."*

4.

SYNTHEOSIS

Although it had now been several days, it still surprised him. The surge he experienced after *I AM* first answered him was still flowing through him, a feeling of being connected by some kind of current. *Syntheosis.* That was the word that came to him to describe his new condition. He was now symbiotically linked to God, to *I AM*, plugged in and also propelled by it. Ever since his original revelation, the world appeared brighter and clearer, as if lit from inside, as if God had tweaked the lens through which he looked at the world and adjusted its focus.

And with this new clarity of vision, what Father Graham felt the urge to do on that particular morning was to go out and—possibly for the first time in his life—see the world as it really was. So he planned to walk to Central Park and experience for himself the New World now in-radiated by the return of the Lord. And although he hadn't done so in a long time, he put on his priest's robes, the antique ornate ones he only wore when he performed Sunday Mass. He also slipped on the ancient Greek wood crucifix around his neck, the one given to him by his mother after his ordination almost forty years ago.

Since his syntheosis, even the cross had acquired a new significance. It was no longer a symbol of the crucifixion and sacrifice of Christ, but a symbolic map of the basic structure of reality. Its vertical arms now represented the above and the below, the high and the low; and the right and left arms the two sides of the world, the inner and outer, the bipolarities and the opposites. But it was the center, the point where the arms met or, from another perspective, from which the arms emerged that had now acquired a special meaning. That center was the source, the entry point, the other side of the door, the eye of the actualization of reality, *I AM*, from which all that is springs forth in time.

Strange, he thought, that he had never focused on the center of the cross until after the revelation. Once attuned to that center, he could see and feel from the standpoint of identifying with that source, the *I AM* in all. He had decided earlier that he would look for a red enamel heart and glue it in the center of the cross because the realization of *I AM* was the true source of love.

As he stepped out of his front door and walked out into the street, he again noticed another odd side effect of his syntheosis. It had somehow changed his relation to time and gravity, as if he were now walking on the moon rather than on Earth. Time was just a little off, had a slight slow-motion aspect to it. He also felt lighter, and he didn't just walk anymore. He was assisted. Walking was like a kind of surfing and he now always felt as if he were just above his body, carried by invisible force waves. And when he looked and heard and smelled, he could now feel *I AM* looking through his eyes, listening through his ears, and smelling through his nose, hitching a ride.

The air had a bite to it and the strips of sky overhanging the channels formed by buildings were heavy with dark clouds and hinting at the possibility of rain. Yet the luminosity still peered through the gray cast, the sign of the steady moment-by-moment generation of existence by God. As Father Graham strolled down the sidewalks, all the people, the dogs, the buildings, the contents of stores became the work of a being that painted in space and time by evolving identity. That all this should have evolved from primal cosmic dust was the miracle forever in the making, instant by instant, a kind of Zen phenomenon; now this, now that.

He floats on ahead, sensing the levitation provided by *I AM*, nodding and greeting the passersby who stare at him: "Isn't it a glorious day, young lady?" "And how are you on this fine day?" "Hi sweetie, did you know God loves you?"

As he makes his way toward the park, what he is becomes clearer. He is the messenger.

At the entrance to the park he stops at a small stand and buys his first meal of the day, an ice cream bar. Peeling off the wrapper, he enters the shadows of the tall trees. As he walks, he brings the bar to his mouth, takes a bite, and involuntarily his eyebrows rise from surprise. Even the experience of eating has been stretched. He feels the sudden rush of cold against his gums and tongue, the passage of food over his taste buds, the sweet bursts of sugar, the snappy bite of tiny amounts of salt, the melting of the chocolate crust, the smooth, cool, creamy flow of vanilla. The initial sensation in his mouth is so alive, so novel, that after swallowing he quickly takes another bite to verify what he's just experienced. To his surprise the next bite is even more alive, even more flavorful than the first. He can't help but smack his mouth with pleasure.

About ten minutes into the park a trio of teenage kids with painted plastic communication caps and the multilayered attire of gangs start following him. "What you doin' in our park, Mr. Priest asshole? I'm talking to you, clown."

He stops and turns toward them, and is surprised that he feels not fear but a kind of amusement. It is *I AM* who now looks, smiling, eyes uncompromising in the assertion of their focus, zeroing in onto each face. The kids are caught off guard by the frightening possessed intensity of the man and step back. He continues walking up to them, bringing his face to within inches of the tallest one, the apparent leader of this little group.

"Keep away from us, you fag priest," the smallest one yells before stepping back.

The tall one holds his ground and stares back at him. "I asked you, what you doin' in my park, asshole?"

Father Graham senses a sudden shift in the quality of his

stare into something reptilian, as if he were T. rex pausing to examine his prey, an ancient and fearless curiosity.

Calmly he says, "I am the messenger and I am telling you that right here, right now, you have the choice to acknowledge the true nature of your being, of recognizing what you truly are, which is none other than the unfolding of God in this world. And you, too," turning to each of the others. Father Graham then opens his arms, smiles, and says, "Come, join me, and I will show you the way and the light of the Lord." Security cameras on tree limbs are monitoring the scene.

"You crazy, man!" the tall, lanky one shouts, turning away.

"I am the messenger, and I am the most clear-minded being you are ever going to meet in this lifetime, son. My message is a crystal. Love is the knife that cuts to the chase of the very nature of who you are."

"I'm not your son, you wacko priest."

"Everybody is my son," he answers.

"The guy's completely nuts. Let's get out of here," one of the other kids exclaims. "What if he really is a messenger?"

"Now you crazy," the tall one says and they all walk away. The smallest one lags behind, then stops, turns around, and looks hard at the priest for a few seconds. Father Graham returns his gaze with the calm of the absolute knowledge of the messenger. The kid nods and walks on.

Father Graham continues on to an area with swings and seesaws, where a few women, mothers, and babysitters are sitting, watching their bundled-up children play. Greeting them, he says, "Hello, my name is Father Graham," and he decides to sit on the ground among them.

"And isn't today another beautiful day. I am the messenger, the one who comes between the cracks in time, and my message is of Christ, love and forgiveness that are unlimited, of compassion that is as vast as the world itself." The children giggle. He joins along and laughs.

"You think I'm a funny, roly-poly man with a big belly, don't you? How about throwing me the ball?" he says to the little girl. "I want to play, too."

She smiles and turns to her mother to make sure it is OK. Her mother smiles back and nods. The little girl looks at him, gripping the ball between her two tiny hands. "You're silly."

"Yes, I am a silly man but I still want to play."

"OK, catch!" she says, tossing the ball, which travels in space in slow motion. *Life—this moment—is the miracle*, he thinks, *and the next and the next and the next . . .* and he catches the red ball.

Later as he walks back to his church, his syntheosis still carries him. When the first drops of rain fall, he can't help but smile. He looks up and raises his arms to the sky. By the time lightning streaks and crackles through the dark clouds, he is beaming at the divine fireworks. "Glorious!" he exclaims as the thunder rumbles and the downpour begins.

■ ■ ■ ■ ■ ■

GAS.WNET RADIO: *The Gary and Andy Show*

ANDY: Jesus! Gary, you look terrible, like you've just seen a ghost.

GARY: I was almost killed this morning by a suicide artist, of all things. It makes you realize how fragile our lives are. How any day, any moment, could be it. And we just go along through life mostly unconscious of the imminence of our death.

ANDY: What happened?

GARY: You know how suicide artists stack the mattresses and foam pads and then place their canvas on top?

ANDY: Yeah, I know. Then they cover themselves with paint

and jump on the canvas from the tops of roofs. What a crazy way to body paint.

GARY: Well, as I'm driving over here, I see this big pile of mattresses on the sidewalk and a crowd looking up. The artist is pretty well-known, you probably heard of her, Ars Savalia. Her stuff's at the art museum. Anyway, she was up on the roof naked, directing her assistants on how to apply the paint to her body. Let me tell you, that Ars is no little girl. She was standing like some plump alien all splotched in bright paints, spotlights and news cameras all over her. You can do a search and check it on the Net, Ars Savalia.

ANDY: Ars Savalia. I'll check it out.

GARY: Anyhow, she took this running jump from the roof and then curled in the air in some weird pose she had been inspired to adopt for this new piece. It was quite spectacular really, except she ran too hard before the jump. She missed the canvas and landed on the edge of the stacked foam and bounced up like a rubber ball, ten or fifteen feet before landing right on the hood of my car and into my windshield. They show it in slow motion on the Net. You can see the surprised look on her face, like whoops, I fucked up.

ANDY: Wow, you've got to be kidding!

GARY: There I was minding my own business and this face and arm and big tit just smack right in front of me. They said she could have killed someone the way she flew off like that, just like a human cannonball.

ANDY: Did she survive?

GARY: The news said she broke a bunch of bones and gave herself a concussion. They said it would be weeks before she can walk again, months before she can even think about suicide painting again. The police got my name and number because I was both a victim and a witness.

ANDY: Maybe you can sue her for trauma.

GARY: You think so? Like attempted negligent homicide or something? Hey, I was lucky my windshield didn't break. Can you picture it? There you are sitting at a light and . . . *whomp!* This giant bug with crazy colors hits your windshield, blood and paint splattering all over the glass. It was quite a sight, I tell you. And you're right . . . trauma. I can still see that open eye looking at me through the paint and blood from the other side of the glass.

ANDY: Did anyone ask you about the car?

GARY: What do you mean? I had to have it towed to a garage. They're supposed to call me with an estimate.

ANDY: Call them quick. Tell them not to touch the windshield and hood. Your car's now an original work of art, a historical piece, worth lots of money. Trust me. Call them quick before they mess it up.

GARY: No kidding?

ANDY: Hurry up.

GARY: So what happened today could have been good luck?

ANDY: Call right away. If those fuckers messed up the paint without your approval, you can sue them, too.

5.

CLUBBIN'

Derek Hardwick, a.k.a. Derek Hanson, a.k.a. DH and assistant to Harvey Richfield, deputy director of the FBI, was testing samples of the first run of the Fabric Response Intelli-Skin masks when his boss walked in. He had the thin film spread out on a mannequin head and was keying in different options using the wireless controller.

"Hey, that's President Tennyson!" the director exclaimed.

"Yes, sir," Derek answered. "We're testing the Intelli-Skin masks to make sure we can have decoys of the president in several locations to confuse terrorists. The Fabric Response people tell us that the microfibers can even be programmed to match infrared signatures."

"So how's it lookin'?"

"So far, so good, sir."

"Can you show me another face?" asked Richfield.

Derek keyed in Amazonia Appolonia's face.

"Unreal, that woman, isn't she?" the director said.

On a whim, Derek decided to replace Amazonia's fine features with the deputy director's own face, pulled from his personnel files. He watched Richfield's expression change from a grin to a frown. Derek was chuckling inside, thinking, *How's that for a reality check, Mr. Big Shot?*

Eyes staying focused on his cloned face, the director said, "This could be pretty dangerous in the wrong hands, Derek. You make sure these masks are all accounted for and locked away with security coding when you're done."

"Yes, sir," he said, having already absconded and inventory-adjusted the extra sample sent by his good friend Frank, one of the mask designers at Fabric Response.

"Derek, the reason I dropped by is that we need your help with this *I AM* phenomenon. It's top priority, so for now assign Tom to the Intelli-Skin tests, then go see Jerry about what we've got to date on this *I AM* stuff. See if you can figure out anything about it. There's no limit to the equipment or the access. It's priority one. I just got the order from the president."

"I'll get right on it, sir," Derek answered.

After leaving the bureau garage, Derek drives a few blocks, parks his car, and runs his customized scanner over his clothes and car to check for any bugs. Satisfied that he's clean, he flicks on the switch for the chemical morphing program that heats the thermosensitive coat on the car body, turns his black Jeep green, and adds segments to the numbers on his license plate. Threes and zeroes turn to eights, and the five turns to six. It also changes the background license plate color. He then applies the Intelli-Skin mask and keys in a computer-formulated generic face, in case someone checks the street security cameras.

His first stop is a cybercafé and his first call is to Frank, to thank him for the gift. Frank picks up after four rings and tells him he won't be able to meet with him that evening. It's a signal to let him know the call's being monitored. Derek ends the conversation with "Well, OK, maybe another time then, when you're not so busy, buddy." Then he connects to the World Net and searches the clubs to decide where he's going hunting tonight. He scans the security-free clubs, the dance clubs, swingers' clubs, S and M bars, and strip bars. He settles on the promo for Evening Delights, a dance club known to attract those looking for a no-strings-attached, one-night fuck when they need a body-and-flesh break from cybersex.

That night he decides to test the product, go out incognito, explore and delve into the undercurrent of sin. In this life the layer of propriety and morality is thin, as thin as skin. He applies the Intelli-Skin mask and the programmable contacts. Looks at himself in the mirror and clicks on the lens controller until his eyes are a pale blue, then programs the Intelli-Skin, downloading a young version of the face of the actor Jack Roberts. Next the hair . . . he's feeling Italian punky tonight. Grabs a tube and runs blue-white reflective gel through his longish crew cut, which plasticizes straight up. He just needs to add the finishing touch. Slips on the inflatable, wireless penis sheath. Tests the controller to make sure it's working right. Makes it go from pickle to kielbasa and back to pickle. Straps it so his dick angles to his left.

He goes to his closet and puts his hand to his chin as he ponders. *What to wear, what to wear on this special night?* The tight, black leather zip suit is calling him. He takes it off the hanger, slips it on, slides the gold zipper just halfway up his chest to show off his built-up, tan pecs. He steps into his new lightweight aluminum boots with white rubber soles and clicks the latches shut.

He had initially planned on taking his motorcycle but the forecast has predicted rain later in the evening. He leaves out the back of his building and walks to the subway.

As he enters the subway car he looks up and down the aisle and chooses to stand in front of a snooty-looking bitch dressed in a business suit sitting by a window. He holds on to the overhead handrail and positions himself so that his crotch stands at her eye level.

He decides to have some fun, presses the button on the palm of his glove controller, and inflates his penis sheath, looking ahead like nothing was making a Genoa salami inside his leather pants, feeling the pressure as the thing snakes down the side of his thigh. She has her face buried in some book, but when the train stops, like all passengers she looks up to the display screen to make sure what station it is. He watches as her eyes raise then instinctively settle and focus on his thigh, her eyes widening, then the quick nervous glance up to his face. That was an unwritten law of the universe: women who noticed big cocks always try to see the faces of their owners.

He stares ahead, acting casual, like he's just taking his dick out for its evening walk. She turns back to her book but seconds later has to sneak in another peek. He catches the look from the corner of his eye—a quick one, a double check, to make sure of what she's seen. She turns back to the book and pretends to be absorbed but he knows it's too late. His penis meme, viruslike, has already started replicating through her neuron layers. He punches on the controller to bulb out the head, making it as big as a plum.

Right before she gets up to leave he sees her throw a last glimpse at his rocket, and linger a few seconds before heading for the door. He smiles. His cock has now been launched into the parallel universe of the mental imprint, destined for repeated rebirths in the bitch's fantasies and imagination. It would creep into her mind that night as she lay on her bed during the stillness that precedes sleep. Her mind would set it free and invite it into dark places.

He deflates the sheath and keys in another eye color, dark green. Four stations to go. He grabs the pill flicker out of his pocket and pretends to cough, bringing his hand up as he opens his mouth, pressing the button, the first pill flying in. He swallows then coughs again and flicks the second one. He feels the electricity zipping through his veins and up his neck, turning on the switches in his brain. He's ready to boogie.

A tune starts playing in his head by old punker Billy Idol, "*Unh-unh, dancin' with ma sell-elf, unh-unh, dancin' with ma sell-elf...*" He closes his eyes a minute, gets caught up in the tune, and does a little stationary dance right there in the subway car, the boots tapping on the hard floor, the arms at right angles, hands bundled in fists, jabbing the air. "*Sell-elf unh-unh...*"

■ ■ ■ ■ ■ ■

Rama worked for the national chain Mind Toys five days a week from eleven to eight and from eleven to six on Saturdays. The good thing about her schedule was that she could stay up late and get up late. What didn't work was that she had no social life.

It was Thursday night and her friend Regina had convinced her to go out. "With our schedules, if you ain't clubbin' then you ain't livin'. Every day would be the same except for clubbin'," Regina would say. She was kind of right about the everyday being the same part, so Rama had gone along with it.

They went to the club called Evening Delights, known for its DJ, I. M. Ripped, whose rave-beat remix of music drove the crowd into a frenzy, "guaranteed to purge mind and body of the accretions of daily life." All that frenzy removed inhibitions and filters that gave the club its reputation for one-nighters.

"I'm in that kind of mood," Regina had said. "Getting rid of accretions sounds to me like a pretty good idea." Once inside Regina wasted no time. She quickly scouted a guy that passed her image-screening test, and went into attractor mode. He was tall with short hair sprayed blue, wore a conservative blue shirt with a pink metallic tie, and looked like he worked for a bank or one of the tech companies. Regina always picked the ones who looked like they could be businessmen, which was why she never dressed too extreme. She had put on classy nail polish and makeup, and a top that exposed the promising white roundness of her boobs and her tanned lean abdomen highlighted by a gold and diamond piercing above the belly button. She came on to him strong using eye and touch and whisper magic. After just a few dances, she left, holding his hand. On the way out, big smile on her face. "See you tomorrow."

Later as Rama lies in bed she replays the evening in her mind. *No more clubbin'. It just can't compare to virtual. Good thing I didn't take anything before going out. Weirdo scene at that club tonight. That wacko guy in silver boots scanning women like a slave trader. Had a buff body but something not quite right with the face. Something about the shadows. High as a rocket. Showing off his big schlong. Probably a fake. Danced like a robot, croaking out the songs as he danced.*

He had come over, looked at her face real close, like six inches away. *Eye implants of some kind,* she remembers thinking. *Eyes too blue. Was he intermediated? In a club?* He said only one word, "Hi," smiling, a kind of grin. After a few seconds of staring at her like some kind of zombie, he had looked down at her chest, turned around, and did the same thing to a woman three seats down. *Made her feel like she didn't pass some kind of test, like she wasn't even worth looking at. If he hadn't done that she probably wouldn't have flirted and danced with the tall guy who called himself Rog. Looked the intellectual techie type. Round glasses, close-cropped hair, calligraphic tats on his arms, but the words out of his mouth sounded customized. Probably selected by his host as some kind of image actualization process.* In her book if you weren't real to the core then you didn't pass the entrance test. No access to her mind and body. She ended up in the awkward position later of turning Rog down after leading him on. *Not cool, Rama,* she told herself, but he just didn't flip her switches.

That odd guy ended up leaving with some blond, torpedo-boobed chickie. Couldn't get within a foot of her without being nipple-poked. Had plenty of metal going through her. Probably just glued on. Showed it off with slits in her top. He danced holding her from behind. Slipped his hands inside her top. She gazed up. Looked like he flicked something in the girl's open mouth. During the slow dance she took his hand and sucked his finger. Looked like she was in dreamland. Didn't care who was staring at her.

Suddenly she hears *I AM Aaa ome.* Someone was in her apartment. She quickly gets out of bed, grabs the Taser out of her drawer, opens the door, and sees the dim light from her Cybermaster unit. She had forgotten to turn it off. She walks to her front door. It's still locked. She checks her windows and kitchen then sits down and turns on the screen on the Cybermaster.

The list of e-mails she had on before going to bed comes up. She was going to answer some before going to sleep but forgot. So maybe it wasn't the CyberBardos. She goes through her e-mails to check for an audio message. No message, but she knew she had felt it, still feels it—something out there when she opened her door—a presence. Maybe she had overdone it with the Instant. Something was not quite right with her wiring, this peculiar feeling of dislocation she has, of something seeping through.

She turns off her computer and goes back to bed. It's 4:03 and she has to get up in five hours. *I should take a pill,* she thinks, but whatever she has on hand would knock her out for more than that. She'd be out of it in the morning and they had a staff meeting with the managers at 10:15. She takes out her portable VR unit, puts on goggles and earplugs, and connects to the Forgotten Forest, another Borden program.

Sunset. She's lying down along the edge of a slow-moving stream. Birds chirping. Colorful butterflies fluttering near the edge, some extending a coiled thread from their mouths and drinking. They are changing colors, one only inches away from her. Eyes a compound fractal. Blue crayfish of some sort in the water. Fish flashing iridescent. Dragonflies. *This is how life used to be,* she thinks, *so peaceful, away from the hustle and bustle of the city . . .*

The next thing she hears is the song "Open Your Eyes." She opens her eyes and finds herself facing a deer, drinking just a few feet away. The Forest. *Open your eyes.* She pulls off the goggles, reaches out, and scrambles on her night table, feeling for her phone. Finds it. Sees the time: 9:34 a.m. Presses the button. It's Regina.

"Don't know about you but I definitely feel like I've been clubbed, ha-ha-ha. Want me to bring you a grande coffee?"

"Yeah," she mumbles, "good idea. See you in a little bit."

She rushes for the shower. *I'm going to have to take a taxi if I'm going to be on time. Two and a half hours of work down the drain paying for it. Gotta stick to the rule. No clubbin' during the week. No drugs that last more than an hour. Hell, no clubbin' period.*

■ ■ ■ ■ ■ ■

Right Place, Right Time

Suicide artist Ars Savalia paid radio celebrity Gary Summers an undisclosed amount, said to be in the five figures, for the car she landed on after a failed suicide jump to imprint the difficult Falling Monkey posture onto canvas. According to the artist, "This was probably the most challenging and important piece I have done to date. The final position and the facial expression recorded on the car were spontaneous, original, and captured the essence of the suicide art, the moment just prior to one's death. I actually thought this time was going to be lights out. For real."

6.

WHO ARE YOU?

It had been six days since the original message. Dr. Jeffrey Collins, with the help of the CIA and a team of twenty-five agents, had contacted technicians throughout the world to synchronize the exact timing of each question to within less than a thousandth of a second. The plan was to make the questions stand out against the noise of the World Net and hopefully get noticed by the entity, assuming there even was one. On December 23, 2032, at exactly midnight, 1,232 computers sent synchronous written messages to each other through the World Net asking the question, "*I AM Aaa ome*, who are you?" This was accompanied by an audio version. The transmission ended at 12:00:35 EST exactly. At 12:00:36, *I AM Aaa ome*, accompanied by an audio version, appeared in a language appropriate for the location on all digital and World Net communication devices.

At precisely 12:01:15, the Collins-Loveridge computer teams sent the next question: "*I AM Aaa ome*, where are you from?" Less than a second later, all communications media displayed and/or played *I AM Aaa ome*.

The group quickly sent a third question, to keep the exchange going as long as possible. The Department of Defense was on alert to attempt to track down the source of the messages. "*I AM Aaa ome*, are your intentions good?"

I AM Aaa ome.

Collins—curious about whether any question asked would receive the same reply—took it on his own to coordinate the sending of an unscheduled question. The technicians followed the order, assuming it must have been pre-approved for use as a kind of test. It was an impulse he would later come to regret. "*I AM Aaa ome*, are you God?"

I AM Aaa ome.

He asked another. "*I AM Aaa ome*, what do you want?"

No answer.

"*I AM Aaa ome*, are you still there?"

No answer.

■ ■ ■ ■ ■ ■

This second set of events, the disassociated bursts of *I AM Aaa ome* interrupting normal communications, had initially been puzzling to the general public; but in a matter of hours their reactions, fueled by the commentaries of the news media and a slew of organizations, became increasingly organized. As could have been expected, the government's attempts to communicate with the entity had quickly leaked to the media, apparently beginning in Europe, very likely by one of the recruited technicians or his acquaintances. The most popular news headline that followed had been "Is *I AM* God?"

Worldwide, government agencies and the media were swamped with calls and e-mails wanting an explanation. That afternoon, the president called another emergency meeting of the newly formed *I AM* Committee.

"So, gentlemen, correct me if I'm wrong, but the only answer we have gotten from this—whatever it is—is '*I AM Aaa ome*.' And this is what is causing global mayhem? Dr. Loveridge?"

"That is correct, sir."

"Is this a joke?" the president asked.

Loveridge frowned at the response and held his gaze to indicate how inappropriate he thought it was. "Mr. President, we don't know how anyone could have pulled this off. The answers to our questions clearly indicate that they had to be a response. They occurred within less than a second after the end of each transmission."

"Let me try to phrase this correctly. Are we dealing with some kind of being that is communicating with us or is this some kind of an automatic mindless programmed response possibly triggered by a component of the message, *Aaa ome* maybe? Dr. Collins? You should be able to answer that."

Collins ran his hand through his hair, looking up as he pondered the question. "There really are only two possibilities to consider here. Either somebody has specifically developed the technology for this kind of phenomenon or it's a spontaneous and unpredictable event that may or may not be linked to an entity source. The first possibility is remote because an introduced program should have a source, but it's also possible it is masked by another known program, and this is an area we will have to investigate. Still, the technology to achieve this instantaneous, multilocal, sourceless response is so advanced that personally I am skeptical that that is the case."

"So you're saying that we are probably talking about some kind of entity trying to communicate with us?"

"I'm saying that at this point all we have is a communications phenomenon. To claim that some kind of entity or consciousness is behind this is premature. I wouldn't jump to any conclusions this early in the game. As you've mentioned, all we've heard are the words *I AM* followed by *Aaa ome*. It's a limited communication repertoire. It certainly does not suggest a higher intelligence."

Randall's light came on.

"Yes, Director Randall?"

"Could the source of this communication come from outside the World Net?"

The president turned and nodded to General Carson, who then addressed the question. "We haven't picked up any kind of signal that suggests that this could have an external source. If it is external it isn't anything that we have the ability to monitor. In my opinion, an external source seems unlikely."

"So no aliens are trying to communicate with us," the president said. "Well, that's a relief. I was beginning to get worried. On a more serious note, let's look at this from a security standpoint. Has anyone in this room found any evidence that this is a terrorist act on the World Net or that there is a human source for these events?" the president asked, turning once again toward General Carson, head of the Defense Department.

The five-star general puffed out his cheeks and paused for a few seconds before speaking. "I agree with Drs. Collins and Loveridge that it is too early to come to any conclusions on the source or the purpose of these communications. I also would not exclude the possibility that this could be some kind of prank or prelude to some type of terrorism. It could be a cover-up for a test to destroy or somehow acquire control of communications through the World Net. It's not like we don't have fundamentalist factions and countries who see the World Net as a US attempt to control world politics and economics."

"So what shall we do, gentlemen?" asked John Tennyson.

"We continue to ask questions. As we get more answers we might be able to find out how the transmissions are made and whether this thing presents any kind of threat," said Loveridge.

"I agree," added Collins.

"And I also agree, but there's going to be a new rule about sending messages to this *I AM*," added the president, staring at Jeff Collins. "All questions are to be cleared by me first. Is that understood? No more reference to God. Speaking of which, how did that information leak out, Dr. Collins?"

"We used over twelve hundred computers to send the message. As you know, the World Net system has reached a complexity that makes confidential information increasingly difficult to either identify or contain."

"Umm . . . no more talk about God. Understood?"

That evening, Collins helped coordinate the sending of

another set of questions, expecting the familiar answer.

"*I AM Aaa ome*, what do you want?"

No answer.

"*I AM Aaa ome*, are you still there?"

No answer.

■ ■ ■ ■ ■ ■

Woman Found Dead in Dumpster

A restaurant employee found the body of a young woman when emptying the trash. According to police she was severely beaten before being strangled. The face was too injured to be recognizable but she had blond hair and brown eyes. All forms of identification were missing. Her dress indicates she may have been at a club or party. If you know of someone missing that fits the description, or any other information that could be of help, please contact your police department. Click *here* for more information.

Suicide Artist Reveals New *Hit-and-Run* Series

In an interview today, Ars Savalia—the Evel Knievel of suicide artists—told reporter Karen Richardson that her recent accident inspired her for a new series of paintings. After she recuperates from her latest injuries, she will start her *Hit-and-Run* series. "Life hits us hard when we least expect it," she said. "My new series will capture that moment."

Her combination of performance art and painting will consist of canvases held by custom cars driven by specially trained drivers that will brake right before contact with her naked, paint-splashed body. A new medium will be thin, membranous bags of fluorescent paint strategically placed to burst upon impact.

When asked whether she worried about being injured, she answered, "I have lots of padding."

Tickets for the event will be available for $25. No minors allowed.

7.

LET THE SUNSHINE IN

Sunshine Borden had been named after his grandparents, sixties radicals who championed the virtues of sunshine acid. With a name like Sunshine, his parents had figured their son would be off to a good start, certain to become a light beam amidst the grayness of the world. At the time, they could never have predicted that he would find the sunshine of his life in the glow of computer monitors, VR goggles, and digitizing lenses. Neither could they have known that after his third year of college, Sunshine would shave his long ponytail—a testament to his parents' hippy traditions—and choose the egghead look of a Buddhist monk.

At a thin-framed height of six foot three, combined with his continuous wear of half-inch-thick digitizing lenses and audio plugs connected to a wireless Cybermaster vest, Sunshine conveyed a mad, otherworldly presence. His seclusion and refusal to appear at public events had further contributed to the popular myth that portrayed him as a reclusive cybermonk, in spite of the fact that he was far from celibate, occasionally partook of mind-altering drugs, and loved to dance.

Rumors, partially true, also claimed that he was imbedded with microchips whose properties ranged from location detection to near-magical powers. In one of his early interviews, when asked about his increased isolation from the body-and-flesh world and his near-pathological involvement with cyberrealities, he revealed having had a type of "Platonic epiphany about the beauty and truth of archetypal forms in cyberspace, unpolluted by the neuroses and distortions of the human mind."

"Cyberrealities," he had stated, "had archetypal characteristics in that they could exist and develop autonomously from culture in digital universes."

That morning Sunshine woke up, naked as usual, to the sound of ocean waves, seagulls, and the laughing and chattering of women. He had decided long ago that a subtropical climate with a temperature of 78 °F and 70 percent relative humidity provided the 24/7 conditions for comfort and minimal clothes wear he favored. He walked over to the coffee maker, pressed the fill cup button and the cream injector. Sipping as he walked, he reached his dining table, sat down, and leaned back to look at the beach. Dozens of naked women were sprawled out in the sun. Others laughed or smiled, their breasts jiggling as they emerged from the ocean or their derrieres bouncing as they ran into the waves. The aromator fans were blowing the scent of suntan oil and female sweat blended with a comforting, seaweed-scented ocean breeze.

For the last eight months, this scene, generated through his thirty-six synchronizable monitors, had served as the backdrop for his morning thoughts and the peace of mind he needed to plan out his day. All his communications filters were on so that only emergencies could interrupt his work. After ten minutes of contemplation, he got up and headed for the shower. Later, holding his second cup of coffee and dressed in a T-shirt and shorts, he sat back in his chair and set to tackle the first project of the day.

He had originally scheduled exploring the self-evolving cyberforest he had initiated two years ago. He hadn't visited it in more than three months and there were bound to be some interesting surprises. The problem was this *I AM* thing. It bothered him that someone could have infiltrated his system and relayed the same message instantly through all thirty-six of his synchronized computers connected to the seamless bank of monitors that covered an entire wall of his workroom. If this were a mutated computer virus, this was something more powerful than anything created to date and threatened to shut down the entire World Net.

Coordinating the microphone inputs to all his computers, Sunshine asked, using a verbal command, "Who are you?" To his surprise, he got an instant answer.

I AM Aaa ome.

"You are what?" he asked.

I AM Aaa ome.

"Show me."

His beach instantly kicked out, replaced with a stream of three-dimensional, densely packed shifting images—a rapid flow of crystalline, biological, nebular, flashing, abstract, interweaving patterns—hopping between monitors in some crazy complex coordinated dance that launched holograms of intricate geometric objects and alien entities, forming and disappearing in midair at a mind-boggling rate. It made him wonder whether what he was seeing was an actual message or simply his imagination responding to the imagery as if it were a changing Rorschach test. Then his screen went blank, followed by *I AM Aaa ome.* His monitor wall returned to his beach.

"Well fuck my brain!" Sunshine shouted, and lay back on his couch staring at his island paradise. He wondered whether anything might have been saved in memory. "Replay the last minute," he asked. The monitors blinked and the beach came on again with the sounds of woman chatter and seagulls in the background.

He tried asking another question but nothing happened.

Three days later at 9:27 a.m., on all media connected to the World Net, appeared *Law One: I AM Aaa ome.* Sunshine cursed, as the virtual art he was assembling using digital molecules disintegrated with both video and audio imposing its version of Law One. It only lasted eighteen seconds. His screen returned to his project. It wasn't until several hours later when he checked the news that he realized the last message had not been personal, but global.

■ ■ ■ ■ ■ ■

While Patricia Holden was carrying out the latest of the Sisterhood's many winter rituals, another kind of Goddess initiation was going on in the very selective and very expensive Temple of Amazonia . . .

As they carried him out the door, Alex bawled his eyes out, not from sorrow but from coming face-to-face with the Cosmic Mama. *You are my love.* As he stumbled, reporters rushed up to ask him questions but he could barely hear them, much less say a word. He mumbled. He spoke in expletives. He spoke in tongues. Reporters stuck microphones toward his mouth.

"What was it like?" they kept asking.

He groaned, "What was that?"

At one point he remembered answering, "Holy mother of God!" The assistants handed him over to a man and a woman who reached under his arms and led him to a secluded locked room designated as a rest area. In the distance, through his tears, he thought he saw his father in the back of the crowd, smiling and waving, raising an arm and pointing an index finger toward the ground, signaling him he would be there when he came out.

While he recovered on the bench, head bent, holding his face in his hands, flashes of memory ran through his head. "So beautiful, so beautiful," he mumbled to himself as more tears trickled down his cheeks. He opened his hands, looked down at the picture he clutched in his right fist. Amazonia. *You are my love.* Flashes of recollection. Amazonia. Firm, round, golden buttocks defined by the dimpling of muscle. Legs, wonderful, wonderful, long legs, strong and shapely. Smooth, thin ankles. The most elegant, the most perfect feet. Breasts, immaculate and soft, with turgid nipples—like the tips of pinkie fingers—that had shined in the blue light. And then the face, like a Nordic goddess, the cheekbones high and sculptured, the jaw square, the mouth large and full, the eyes a deep piercing blue white, the hair a natural silken blond that hung straight down to her shoulders. And she had allowed him to enter her. Him. *You are my love.*

He could remember being drawn in, and then heat, the most perfect, wonderful, comforting heat in his groin. At one point he thought she had whispered to him, right before his brain drained of self, before his consciousness shot out of his penis and into the cosmic womb. Before he fell to the ground like an unplugged robot and curled up like a fetus. *I am the gate to what you cannot see.*

Later, as he walked out of the recovery room, he was again assaulted by the reporters. This time he heard himself speak with unusual clarity about having died and been resurrected, having experienced a true baptism in and out of the sacred waters of the goddess, of having seen a light at the end of the vortex of the unfolding of time.

"Tell us. What was it like, the actual experience?" the reporters asked again, but as much as he tried he could not voice a coherent answer. The thing, like any true mystical experience, was indescribable. He saw his father walk through the crowd and put an arm around his shoulder.

"You OK, son?" He nodded. His father looked into his eyes and smiled, as if he had seen something there, a lingering after-image in his pupils. They remained silent as they made their way to the car. There were things that were best known and left unsaid, so as to prevent them from being cheapened by the vulgarity of language.

As Amazonia was getting herself prepared for the next initiate, she thought back about that morning. As she slept, she had seen the imagery kick in, right there in her dream, light streaming in through her head and coming out between her legs, generating entire worlds, like a film projector. She was the Great Mother, giving birth to all creation, each and every moment of being. *I AM.* She had woken up thinking that for some reason she had been chosen, again. She lay back on the pedestal and spread her thighs. She closed her eyes and felt the metaphysical space collapse between the top of her head and her vagina. She cleared the way for the Goddess. The music started. As the initiate whirred toward her she was but one feeling, one being. *Welcome, my son. You are my love.*

■ ■ ■ ■ ■ ■

Cyborg Magazine: **Volume 3, Number 6**

"Sunshine Borden on Cybershamanism"
In this thought-provoking piece, Sunshine Borden explains the similarities between shamanism and the cyborgian consciousness. According to Borden, like the ancient shamans, the cyborg undergoes a death and rebirth. He starts off as human and after a revelation of a parallel cyberreality, he undergoes an initiation where implants are embedded in his brain and body, giving him access to the parallel digital domains and thus transforming him into a cyborg or cybershaman.

In various shamanic traditions, shamans in a trance state would speak about parts of their bodies becoming gradually embedded and replaced by quartz crystals. Actualization of both shamans and cyborgs is characterized by their ready access to parallel realities, following a state of transformation made possible by various implants. The article ends with a speculation on historical fractals: patterns that are repeated through time. According to Borden, cybercultural history could end up following a pattern from our past, evolving from cybershamanism to cyberpolytheism to cybermonotheism and thus paralleling the pre-Y2K history of religion. In short, we will have a God evolving in cyberspace.

■ ■ ■ ■ ■ ■

News Flash!

The Torture of Screaming Shrimp

Animal rights activists have recently digitally converted into sounds the changes in electrical signals detected in netted shrimp as they lay flipping and dying on big blocks of ice. This follows their latest advertising propaganda showing screaming lobsters before they are dropped in big pots of boiling water. As the message says, "Lobsters Feel, Too!" And so do shrimp, apparently. Their next campaign: Save the Escargots!

Dr. Julian Byrne from the University of Arizona has noted the devolutionary trend of the animal rights movement. They started with higher forms and have steadily progressed toward lower ones. His big question is: "How low will they go?" When pressed for details, he admitted that when he made the remark he was actually referring to the lawyers representing the rights of suffering crustaceans unable to speak for themselves.

8.

THE GHOST IN THE HOST

Seventeen days after the initial announcement and eight days after the declaration of Law One, morning in the world started with a new law, the first sign that the *I AM* entity was capable of thinking something other than *I AM Aaa ome*. At 9:27 a.m.—like an information wave in every area of the world— appeared what initially started out as complex imagery, a type of digital art. The components writhed and pulsed like erotic dances between translucent snakes and amoebas, then they coalesced to form *Law Two: Neither Light nor Darkness Change the Presence of the Sky. I AM Aaa ome,* in a language appropriate for the location. The law was accompanied by an audio version, carefully enunciated by a clickety, insectile voice. The message lasted eighteen seconds.

An emergency telecom meeting of the new *I AM* Committee was called by the president. As before, the message left no trace that could be measured by existing technology. Everyone except Walter Randall, director of the FBI, agreed there was no clear sign of a threat in the message. Still, what did it mean by the presence of the sky? God? After all, all truths were relative, weren't they? Later that morning the president issued a brief statement:

I know many of you are concerned about the meaning of this latest message. As of today, there is no one, and that includes all of the unscrupulous opportunists taking advantage of these unusual events, who has uncovered either the source or the meaning of these so-called laws. The source and the method of communication behind these messages appear to be something new, something for which we have no historical precedent.

I also want to reassure all of you that to date there are no indications of anything in these communications that suggests any kind of threat to civilization. The United States and its allies have had satellites and various types of radar and telescopes scanning round-the- clock for any unusual military activity. We have carefully searched the skies for the presence of ships or objects in space that could be heading for Earth. The results are unanimously in agreement. All is clear on the planetary front, and any rumors to the contrary are plainly and simply fabrications.

In the opinion of our top military and intelligence experts, these messages are just that, communications. With the cooperation of our international allies, we are also continuing to pursue possible venues for establishing an exchange of communication with the source of these messages. Just to confirm what I've reported before, we have received no answers to our questions since the initial communications reported the first week following the initial I AM *announcement.*

And that, my fellow Americans, pretty much sums up what we know about these unusual events. I can see many of you with hands raised, dying to ask some questions, but I will not answer any more questions on this subject today. At this stage of our investigations, any additional statements or comments would just be conjecture, and there has been more than enough of that since we first received these messages. What is required now is patience and presence of mind, while the hundreds of technicians and communications specialists worldwide continue to work on finding the source of these messages.

"Now this is beginning to get interesting," Sunshine mumbled before turning off the news. While his housecleaner, Josefina, longtime employee of Confidential Home Maintenance, performed her meticulous vacuuming of his equipment and furniture, Sunshine sat in his special chair, goggled up and connected to the World Net to try to bring up any memory of the latest *I AM* message in the system. As with previous attempts, the results came up blank. There was no record this morning's communication ever occurred. It was as if the World Net had been operating as usual during the message, as if nothing had ever happened.

He looked for the possibility of an information shift—basically of the World Net sequestering all ongoing communications in some secluded area of the system during the message, and afterwards restoring them to their normal positions. It would have taken an amazing amount of computing power to move all of the Net information in a single instant. The process should also have left coding trails and switching tracks associated with the information movement. As expected, there were no signs of such information shift. The crux of the puzzle was how something could happen without any trace of it happening. He had been unable to record a single *I AM* message. The only reported success at recording any of the messages was with older methods such as film photography, and even these copies showed scrambled images, distorted and different than what people remembered seeing. They were in fact so different that those who had tried to market printed versions had been accused of being liars and cheats. These non-electronic copies were lost when transferred to an electronic/digital medium.

One answer to the puzzle proposed by a neuroscientist was that possibly the global electronic system was being used not to send images and sounds to eyes and ears but rather to communicate directly to the brain's optical and auditory centers as well as the frontal lobes. That could have explained the failure to record images or to find traces of code.

As a means of clarifying his lines of thought, Sunshine decided to list the different possibilities regarding the source of the *I AM* messages, which really only amounted to three:

1. The messages were sent by someone or a group who had developed a new communications technology that could override the World Net.

2. The messages were generated by the World Net or the World Host, which as a result of autoprogramming software had evolved some form of autonomy and developed a new form of programming that eluded human detection.

3. The messages had an external source other than numbers one and two; either an extraterrestrial source or an extra-universal source.

The problem with possibility number one—that the source was human—was that Sunshine doubted anyone had the ability for the kind of instant code-free global Net override demonstrated by *I AM*. If any such technology had been developed, it would also have resulted in some level of Net gossip prior to the first event, something he had failed to find. It was a well-established fact that no matter how secret a project or meeting there was always going to be traces of security leaks, in one form or another. People talked. He ran another set of searches to track down any increase in communications referring to *I AM* laws prior to that morning's message. He came up with nothing but the usual post-factum speculative exchanges about the *I AM* messages by tech-heads. So the possibility of a human origin was pretty much out of the question.

The second possibility, that computing machines were behind the events, was the most intriguing as well as the most disturbing. First of all because his area of specialty was the development of operating systems and software that led to autonomous programming and self-organization by computing systems. His work had resulted in a number of segregated self-evolving systems linked to the World Net, including the World

Host and server-segregated cyberrealities. The emergence of a higher transcendental object from self-organizing computational networks was his ultimate goal.

At the same time, if *I AM* was the first expression of an autonomous intelligent machine, it had come into existence earlier than he would have ever predicted and in a way he hadn't expected. The glitch in that hypothesis was how computing unities whose existence and functions depended on code and language could generate codeless communications. This factor alone made possibility two—a World Net source—unlikely, unless the damn system was intentionally lying or concealing code when queried.

Which then brought him to option three. Assuming codeless direct-to-brain communication was what was going on, only possibility three, an alien outside source, could be behind the *I AM* events. And if true, then whatever was behind the messages was of another order of mind compared to *Homo sapiens*. The thought brought a smile to his face.

■ ■ ■ ■ ■ ■

On that same morning, about three hours before the global announcement, Father Graham had asked, "*I AM Aaa ome*, is the apocalypse near?" From his antique speakers, a metallic, clickety voice, sounding both human and mechanical, answered, *Neither Light nor Darkness Change the Presence of the Sky*, followed by a deep *I AM Aaa ome*.

His next question had been "Is there a heaven?" And he received the same answer: *Neither Light nor Darkness Change the Presence of the Sky. I AM Aaa ome.* As the *ome* reverberated in his tiny office, he felt the oddest sensation. The sound was shuffling the inside of his brain and making adjustments to his mental architecture. He instinctively brought his hands to his head in a senseless attempt to protect it. He was being transformed as if he were made of modules. The sound stopped. What he experienced next was the epiphany that comes from the sudden realization of the absence of ignorance. No more doubts, no questions, no this and that, no I and them— just *I AM*, no more and no less.

Father Graham laughed with a childish glee running through him the likes of which he had never realized was possible. He had called and God had not only answered but had entered him and wired a permanent connection. What more could anyone hope for in this lifetime? And those were the last questions he ever asked *I AM*. There was nothing left that he needed to know. He and *I AM* were as one.

■ ■ ■ ■ ■ ■

GAS.WNET RADIO: *The Gary and Andy Show*

GARY: I wonder if this *I AM* thing is some kind of marketing strategy by one of the big World Net companies. Maybe a host.

ANDY: Gary, what are you talking about? Are you on something?

GARY: It's all about control here. All the data is indicating there's a decline in interest in media. We can't come up with new movie ideas. New music is now computer-composed using old patterns proven to generate brain waves that show we are engaged. But no matter what we do, information is losing its ability to generate emotion. No emotion, no drive, no sales of products. We're at such a loss, they're using computers to analyze all the past media: books, music, movies, television. Computers are deciding what's marketable.

ANDY: You're just saying we're becoming insensitive to information.

GARY: Desensitization is a consequence of free access to information. It used to be a big deal. It used to get us excited, but today our gluttony for information is satiated. It's just the status quo. It's like what happens when you're married. The novelty wears out. Instead of noticing the curves you focus on their inability to resist gravity. So we have access to all the information. It's not a grand human venture. It's big corporations thinking how can they make big bucks. The problem is they're running out of ideas. We're habituating to the daily buffet of information. We want to unplug but the unmediated world has been lost to us. We have become prisoners of the World Net system.

ANDY: That's what all these crazy artists are trying to tell us. They're doing all this crazy stuff to draw us away from the interface. People don't even go to museums anymore so the artists are taking it to the streets. They're all attempts at self-destruction, like the suicide artists. They want us to see real pain and blood.

GARY: Speaking of pain and blood, did you read about that artist who raised all these frogs in his apartment and released them outside a school in New York City?

ANDY: That was a slaughter. Inhumane. I heard he got charged with animal cruelty. The members of PETA want long jail time. Why should a frog's life be any less than a human life?

GARY: Well the answer is simple: they don't consume goods and contribute to the economy.

ANDY: All these schoolkids went crazy when they saw the frogs. I heard most of them had a "yuck" reaction, particularly the girls. They reacted as if the frogs carried a deadly disease. One of them said she thought it could be biological warfare by a terror group.

GARY: Did you see the video on YouTube? People were frozen, they didn't know what to make of it. They stood there, petrified, as cars ran over the frogs and they hopped in gutters. National security agents were there. There was talk of water contamination.

ANDY: The artist said that's how many frogs die every minute in the world.

ANDY: And they arrested him. What the hell does this have to do with *I AM*?

GARY: *I AM* may be a strategy for keeping us connected.

ANDY: You read the reports. They can't figure how this *I AM* is doing what it's doing.

GARY: I bet it's one of those big corporations behind all this. It's a test. Honestly I think we're fucked. *I AM* may appear as some mysterious mystical phenomenon. In fact it's Big Brother. We just don't know it yet. That's the problem—we no longer know what's real and what isn't. We're caught in a quantum dilemma. Shit—what just happened?

ANDY: Another *I AM* communication.

GARY: I bet you they're listening in on our show. We got too close for comfort.

ANDY: Are you taking your medication like you're supposed to? Your paranoia is starting to freak me out.

GARY: We should turn off all media. I'm telling you. It's our only hope of coming back to some semblance of reality.

ANDY: What are you doing? Keep your hands away from that. Don't you ...

The show is off the air.

9.

NEW JERUSALEM

The Virtual Church of Jesus Christ's many critics and most of its employees believed that Bob Thomson's primary motive for constructing the virtual New Jerusalem had been to more effectively recruit converts and bolster the church's bank accounts. He had always been careful never to argue too strongly against those who accused him of these petty ambitions. After all, doing whatever was necessary to make a buck and keep your institution alive was something most people could understand. It was just human nature. It was good ole American capitalism.

As for his real motive, it was something he chose to keep secret, something between him and the Lord. It was his *Field of Dreams*. Build it and He will come. New Jerusalem would become the City of God, the one prophesized in Revelation, the one descended from the heavens and not lit by the sun or the moon, but electronically. After the end-times, it would be illuminated not just by electricity, but by the living presence of God. "New Jerusalem is the City of God," he would assert, "and the Church of God is the Virtual Church of Jesus Christ."

The vision of New Jerusalem had come to him as he watched the news programs showing the ruins of Jerusalem after its destruction by an army of kamikaze Muslim bombers. A number of radical groups had claimed credit for the explosions. While many evangelists had seen their beliefs crumble with each and every repetition of the video clips showing the disintegration of buildings into a deep dark pit, he had felt a strange uplift of his spirits. Instead of despair, switches had flicked in his head and streams of ideas had started pouring in: a revelation, a plan, with all the steps clearly laid out. He was to build New Jerusalem, the transcendent digital City of God that would exist both physically and metaphysically, both in time and out of time. He could still see in his mind the surprised look on the faces of the church board members when he first described in great detail the plan outlined in his vision and, later, how they had smiled because he had managed to make the virtual city come alive in their heads. They unanimously voted in favor of approving funding for the project.

The task of building a virtual Jerusalem, although requiring several years to complete, had been a no-brainer. He just followed the steps that had been given to him. First, he recruited the church's most brilliant students and offered them grants to fund the best possible education and advanced training in computer game design, immersion virtual reality, and hosting software design. Then he hired consulting scholars—offering impossible-to-refuse fees—to gather the archeological evidence on the plan and architecture of the ancient city of Jerusalem. With that information, church architects and graphic designers had drawn elaborate blueprints that had allowed professional movie set designers to build detailed miniature models of the city, both exteriors and interiors. The models had ended up filling a ten-thousand-square-foot warehouse and had formed the framework for the initial graphic downloads. These were later enhanced and made more real by skilled computer graphic design students who painstakingly added details of texture, landscaping, and furnishings, slowly bringing the city back to life.

He could still remember the first time he visited the virtual city to assess the progress of the project, the incredible sense of wonderment. He had run down the streets like a little kid, looking right and left, checking inside windows. There it was in front of him, ancient Jerusalem, resurrected before his very eyes. He could remember crying and the smiling, expectant faces— eager for approval—that confronted him after removing the digi-goggles. "If you're all wondering," he had reassured them, "yes, they're tears of joy."

The final stage in the plan required hiring specialists in game design to populate New Jerusalem and to resurrect its ancient people: the Egyptians, the Romans, the Greeks, and the Jews; the characters of the Bible; the disciples and, of course, Jesus. A key component had been to incorporate in the New Jerusalem experience the possibility of coming face-to-face with Jesus, of asking him the crucial questions about judgment and heaven, of having him set his eyes on you and apply his hand to your forehead. The church technicians had programmed the software so that at some time during a visit, a paying guest would be presented with clues on Jesus's whereabouts, possibly a conversation as they walked through a street, scrapings on a stone wall, or a cripple reaching out and gripping their leg, asking them, "Did you hear Jesus?"

Following the well-established behaviorist principles of intermittent reinforcement (reward a lab rat only some of the time and he will keep pressing the lever in the hope of receiving a goody), at least once in the course of every five visits a New Jerusalem visitor was offered a distant glimpse of Christ. As could be expected, the excited visitor would usually run to catch up with the apparition and even call out his name. If he successfully followed the clues and figured his way through the maze of streets and merchant stalls, he might eventually be lucky enough to catch a glimpse of a Christian gathering up on a hill or of an incident, Jesus a faint and distant form, the words leaving his mouth barely audible except for clear segments somehow carried by unusual conditions of wind and air.

But in New Jerusalem, just like a rainbow, if one got too close, Jesus always disappeared. Bob Thomson knew that the mystery of Jesus had to be preserved, and the possibility of actual contact only hinted at by shadows and distant glimmers. Yet it was the possibility of an encounter, of an unexplained and miraculous breaking of the established rules, that caused thousands of visitors to come back, again and again, in the hope that one day they would eventually win at the Jesus lottery.

In sharp contrast to the elusive and distant Jesus, he had decided, as per the plan, to make the apostles specially programmed hosts, more accessible, more personal, and open to discussing the Bible and even willing to hear one's confession of sins. The church's Disciple Host Service was a form of therapy that directly benefited its members, gave them direction and hope, and had most coming back to New Jerusalem once or twice a week, at fifty dollars a pop.

His latest inspiration had come to him while screwing Sara under a full moon on top of the Great Pyramid of Cheops, courtesy of an ancient Egypt Cybris program: provide VR religious services. The obvious first choice had been to design a life-changing virtual baptism. All new members were now met at one of the church's VR baptism chambers where assistants would gear them up and then join them in New Jerusalem. John the Baptist performed the sacrament, while the real-world minister—VR-geared and cyberlinked to John—did the actual dunking in the large fiberglass pool located in the baptism chamber. Special temperature controllers in the pool helped simulate a sense of transformation, of rebirth. The water was cool when the candidate was initially dunked but speed-heated after immersion to a level of ideal comfort. Once out of the water, the member's experience of New Jerusalem was switched to an enhanced mode that made the colors more vivid and intensified the three-dimensionality. Singing and music in a variety of forms distant and near and previously unheard were now part of his New Jerusalem environmental experience. Once you were born again in New Jerusalem, it became mystical, psychedelicized, the City of God.

The current grand VR project was a virtual crucifixion. According to the church's most recent poll, the opportunity to experience crucifixion was the number one aspiration of its members, most of them having viewed what was now considered the pioneer work in virtual Christianity, the film classic by Mel Gibson, *The Passion of the Christ*. Through the ordeal they hoped not only to fully understand Christ's suffering, but also to be cleansed of their sins in a way that would convince even the deepest and most repressed of their tarnished neurological layers. Crucifixion, they were certain, was the one penance that would provide a thorough disinfection of their souls.

The church's VR designers were nearly finished with a super VR crucifixion package that would allow the candidates to experience being nailed to a giant cross with a central pole fifty feet long, all the while lying flat on the ground. The biggest challenge had been figuring out how to simulate the sensation of having nails pounded through the wrists and feet without causing any real physical harm—other than a little bleeding, maybe—to leave some lasting physical evidence of the ordeal. The fifty-foot cross would then be raised by ropes pulled by slaves in tattered clothes under the watch of Roman soldiers with whips. Once elevated on its giant central pole, the crucified visitor would tower over those below, giving him a sense of being closer to heaven, of being above ordinary men, just as Christ must have felt. A gentle wind would be simulated and distant singing heard. Possibly translucent and vague angelic forms could be made to drift among the clouds. Visitors would be able to stay crucified on a tall hill above Jerusalem for as long as they wanted on a pay-per-fifteen-minutes basis. The hill would accommodate up to fifty crosses at a time. It would be quite a sight. Crucifixion Hill. He could already imagine it, the dark silhouettes of crosses, adorned with family members and friends, stark against gray skies, with birds flying . . . maybe even some vultures. It would be another draw to the city. They could charge extra for admission to the Hill.

He had anticipated the possibility of an intervention, so he stayed cool and collected when New Jerusalem blinked out of existence at 9:27 a.m. to be replaced by the perverse writhing geometries that ended up spelling another law. When the city returned, the Korean VIP visitor he had been leading on a tour of the city asked, "Bob, is this part of the program, this talking in the head?" He decided not to answer but instead gave a wry smile, to let the silence imply secrets. His guest returned a knowing grin then continued with more questions: "So, Bob, was that a message from Jesus, one selected just for me? Did you hear it, too?" He still wasn't sure what to say. He didn't want to lose the contract from the billionaire car manufacturer. It would be at least twenty thousand dollars a year if he went for the family plan, many times more if he decided to provide New Jerusalem access as part of his employee benefits. He kept his mouth shut.

"You mean it really was just for me?"

Dammit, he couldn't lie. It would catch up with him later when Don Park checked on the news. "No, Don, I heard it, too—another law," he finally said.

"Yes, very deep statement, like the Buddha. *'Neither Light nor Darkness Change the Presence of the Sky.'* Jesus, a lot like Buddha."

Bob Thomson grinned and said nothing. The *I AM* was sowing religious confusion, intentionally. There was no doubt about it.

"Voice in the head, very nice feature. I like, very much," Don said.

He'd have to remember that one. Maybe it wasn't necessary to show Jesus addressing the VIPs from a distance. Maybe all that was needed was a voice, in souped-up, crystal-clear stereo, sounding as if it appeared out of nowhere and everywhere.

"Don, let me show you the plans for the Hill," he said. "I think you're going to like this very much."

As soon as he was done with the tour, he punched a number in his wristcom to set up a special meeting of the council board. Satan wasn't bothering taking over the world; he was going to invade cyberspace. He was going to try to bring down New Jerusalem.

■ ■ ■ ■ ■ ■

Anonymous government sources indicate *I AM* not from this Earth

The news station received several anonymous e-mails sent from a number of cybercafés indicating the government has substantial evidence that the technology behind the *I AM* messages could not have originated from Earth but may be extra-universal—from another universe altogether.

Fundamentalists Oppose Extraterrestrial Source for *I AM*

Rick Nelson, minister of the Church of the End-Times, and Reverend Bob Thomson of the Virtual Church of Jesus Christ, speaking for the Council of Fundamentalist Christianity, have issued a joint statement. "*I AM* is Satan because his claims of higher authority, clearly implied in his laws, indicate that he is out to deceive us into believing he has godlike powers. What is happening has been predicted in Scripture. *I AM* is the false God we have been warned about."

***I AM* is Jesus**

Church of the Alien Jesus leader Tony Ritter, in his daily broadcast today, said, "The Second Coming is near. Jesus has decided to return to Earth."

Beware of *I AM*: Ufologists warn of possible threat

In response to the news of a possible extraterrestrial source for *I AM*, the Society of Ufologists has sent a letter to the White House requesting that extreme caution be taken in dealing with the *I AM* entity. The letter states: "It is unlikely that an alien civilization would act toward humans any differently than we have acted toward other species and between ourselves. The intent of an alien entity will very likely be species-centric and exploitative. Don't be fooled by the New Age–sounding niceties."

■ ■ ■ ■ ■ ■

History of the World Host

A series of factors led to the creation of the World Host, the autonomous, self-organizing system of databases within the World Net that sifts facts and truths from the muddle of misinformation, unsupported hypotheses and speculations presented as facts. A summary of the World Host's history follows:

1) The impetus behind the World Host can be traced to the Internet information chaos between 1995 and 2018. There were too many personal, pseudoauthoritative, and unreviewed sites, and too many groups seeking their fifteen seconds of fame. Sifting what was true and factual from the mishmash of Net information became a daunting task.

2) The September 11, 2001, terrorist attacks on the World Trade Center led to research that sought to identify the root causes of radical fundamentalist religious ideology and its role in inciting terrorism. Living in a sexually repressed and oppressed society, inequality of gender rights, the oppression of women, the failure to provide educational opportunities for women, and the lack of economic opportunities that allowed for any possibility of achieving self-actualization and happiness in this life were among the factors that had stood out but could not be readily changed. Another increasingly significant factor but also not in one's control to change was the desperate attempt to salvage religious and cultural identity threatened with extinction as a result of the scientific theories and secular philosophies perpetuated by the West. On the other hand, censorship of facts, misinformation, belief in myths unsupported by scientific evidence, and marginal literacy—not in the sense of being able to read, but of having a limited reading background, e.g., religious texts—were areas that could be challenged and addressed.

The post-terrorist realization of the state of the world was summarized by the originators of the World Host using the title of Carl Sagan's visionary work. They concluded, "We still live in *The Demon-Haunted World*. We need to build a global cultural foundation based on *Science as a Candle in the Dark*."

This eventually led to a 2018 international agreement to establish a source of truths and facts supported by accuracy and scientific screens for evidence and validity. This truth-sifter would be called the World Host and be accessible to anyone connected to the World Net. It would be free of any political, commercial, or personal promotion. A primary filtering condition was summarized at the initial international World Host Committee meeting under the first directive, "Keep the erroneous, the mythical, and the superstitious nonsense out."

3) With the support of international and US government grants, a leader for the World Host project was appointed by the committee: Dr. Jeffrey Collins, professor of artificial intelligence research at MIT. He promptly assembled a team consisting primarily of graduate students specializing in artificial intelligence and the development of self-organizing and autonomous updating software. Notable among the members of the team were now-renowned cyberreality designer Sunshine Borden; controversial underground researcher and radio personality Hieronymus Bardo; and Christine Rostand, codesigner with psychologist Patrick Nymphaea of the first cybertherapeutic hosts.

4) The World Host system was completed and online on July 12, 2020. The motto of the World Host upon its opening was declared as *Facts and Truths. No Proof, No Place.* Over five million people worldwide are now employed in the analysis, screening, management, and updating of the World Host. In addition to the World Host, there are hundreds of privately managed secondary hosts specialized in various fields of knowledge for which claimed facts cannot always be verified as true, e.g., many claims of religions, herbalism, esoteric philosophies, politics, and so on. In retrospect, the idea of the World Host was fueled by the need to have a world mind, one founded on rationalism that could—through education—unify and establish a common ground among the different people of the world. Access to the World Host is free to anyone connected to the World Net.

10.

CURSED

"We have now entered the age of Satan. Satan is an opportunist and he thrives on chaos and confusion. The Bible is our God-given tool, an organizing tool to create the mental structures that act as barriers to Satan's invasion, to prevent the moral chaos that would bring down the world. Following the words of the Bible is like pulling the strings on window shades that shut out the entry of evil. Open the slats and Satan will enter. In real life, those slats are closed as a result of will, of choosing what you allow in or out of your minds. And you better be selective. Once in the mind, ideas and thoughts can act like viruses on the soul. Always remember that Satan is a mind predator and disorderer. He thrives on entropy, on the tendency of the moral order of the world to break down. He takes advantage of weakness of will. Remember, it was God who gave the world its order, created man and beast and plant from mud. It was unknowing Eve, who out of weakness of will, first opened the door to the devil when she failed to obey God's orders. Women, God bless them, are still the weaker sex, the ones most likely to suffer from weakness of will and to lead men into temptation. Thus, it is the role of men, out of love for women, to keep them ..."Derek knew exactly what the reverend was talking about because he had been cursed to suffer at women's hands, his will forever failing when confronted with their scheming and limitless erotic resources. His problems had started when he was twelve. That was when his father, having decided that freedom to dick a variety of women was better than staying home, walked out the door after a no-holds-barred screaming and wrestling match with his mother.

After the breakup, his mother had not so much been heartbroken as insanely furious, having received the undeniable confirmation of all her suspicions about the inherently base and beastly nature of men. Day after day she would work herself up into nightly fits of screaming and crying, cursing at Derek because—as his son—he was the one thing that would on a daily basis remind her of his "disgusting father, that scumbag, that bottom-feeding cockroach of a human being, the lowest of the low."

At the peak of her madness, during a hysterical scream fest, she even let out the true secret behind his father's departure. "You want to know the truth? Well, I'll tell you the truth," she ranted. "It was because I wouldn't let him put his thing in my mouth. That's why."

At the time he had wondered if the reason his father had even wanted to do something that deranged was maybe to shut his mother up or maybe even to choke her to death—to stop that nagging, screaming mouth. After thinking some more about it, he had concluded it must have been another one of his mother's delusions. His father wouldn't have been so stupid that he'd do anything as dangerous as putting his thing between those snarling, snapping, teeth-bared jaws.

His mother's ravings had gone on until the day she dropped by a booth next to the supermarket where a sign said: We're Not Just Talk, We Show You the Way. Soon after that, she started spending most evenings locked in her bedroom with her new computer, apparently communicating with members of a club called the Sisterhood. She no longer cursed and yelled but instead moaned and spouted crazy stuff, like "I am open and ready to receive your teachings, great Goddess." And sometimes she would scream like a wild banshee until she'd suddenly go dead silent. The first time it happened he wondered if maybe she had finally burst that big blood vessel that stuck out of her forehead every time she had a fit, and possibly bled to death. It turned out to be wishful thinking. The next morning she had been up and at it again.

The real bitch had been his stepsister, Gabriella. About a year after his father left, a few months into his mother's conversion, she had walked into the kitchen in her nightgown as he was sitting down eating breakfast. She had casually bent down to pick a piece of bacon from the serving plate in the center of the table, then intentionally swung one of her breasts into his face and yelled, "Mom, Derek touched me!" as she clutched herself. His mother, by then fully primed for the rude and crude behaviors of men, reacted by flinging lightning-quick two-handed slaps to the sides of his head. It had made his ears ring so bad he had barely made out the words coming from his mother's mouth: ". . . the next time I won't be so nice. You understand me?"

That night, as his mother was going through another of her computer-connected fits, he snuck into his sleeping stepsister's room, holding a lit butane lighter. He sat down on the bed, leaned over, and brought the lighter to within inches of her closed eyes. It took her about thirty seconds to wake up. She started screaming until he brought the can of hair spray up to her face and said, "One more cry out of ya and I'll light ya up, bitch." He had stolen the idea and the lines from the scene of an old black gangsta movie he had watched the week before. Her eyes had gone so wide that in the yellow light of the tiny flame they had reminded him of sunny-side-up eggs.

"What do you want?" she asked in a little voice.

He put the spray can down, placed his hand on top of her T-shirt, and ran it over her pudding-soft breast.

She smiled and said, "You're such a bad boy, Derek, just wait till I tell Mom . . ."

When he felt her nipple rise through the shirt, he grabbed

it between thumb and index finger and pinched it hard. Bringing his mouth up to her ear and twisting, he said, "You keep that ugly tit out of my face." Then he got up, pulled his arm back, and punched her hard in the chest. "You keep those ugly balloons away from me, ya hear?"

The next day, as he entered the kitchen to sit down for breakfast, his mother swung a frying pan—as instructed in the marital self-defense link of the Sisterhood—and, with all her might, smacked him in the balls. He fell to the ground, bent over, groaning in pain and with tears falling from his eyes. "I warned you, didn't I?" she yelled. It took three days before he could walk again.

He wasn't sure how it was all connected, but sometime after that nutcracker event he started having episodes where his balls buzzed—like the wing beat of trapped flies—in pulses, like a type of Morse code. The first time it happened, it made him raise and shake a leg like he had something trapped in his pants. Then the strangest thing happened. Between buzzes he heard a voice. It was a message . . . from God.

When the *I AM* came on, cutting off the reverend's daily sermon, Derek had little doubt about who was behind the message. He had been expecting this. His balls had alerted him, had vibrated like crazy. He had finally come, just as the Bible said he would. Satan had descended upon the world. His wristcom buzzed. He checked the number. It was his boss, Deputy Director Richfield of the FBI.

■ ■ ■ ■ ■ ■

Ars Savalia Retires from Suicide Art

After her latest injuries—a fractured pelvis, two broken legs, and a crushed foot—suicide artist Ars Savalia is reconsidering her latest project, the *Hit-and-Run* series. "After suicide comes a rebirth," she said from her hospital bed. "Drastic transformation will be the theme of my next series. The suicide period is officially over."

Ceramic artist and partner Cindy Whipling agreed. "I think Arsie has sacrificed enough to make her point. It will take weeks of rehabilitation before she can work again." Cindy Whipling is the ceramic artist known for her *Human Pretzel* series: characters of soft clay, most of them representing political figures or businessmen, which are dipped in paint and tossed from the tops of various buildings before finally being fired. Carefully placed video cameras record the crushing changes in the clay characters and are accompanied by sound effects. "They represent an externalization of our repressed feelings," she said.

11.

THE DEFINITION OF GOD

The reactions to the initial laws were the kind of mix that could have been expected in this age of relative truths where any and every idiot with an opinion could have his fifteen seconds of fame in one of the many little ponds scattered throughout the World Net. A small percentage of fringe religious institutions saw the *I AM* events as the return of God in the world. Fundamentalists who believed in the literal word of the Bible saw the *I AM* phenomenon as a clear digital threat by the supporters of Satan. According to them, Satan—in the disguise of a mysterious entity suggesting it could be God—was about to infiltrate the world as prophesized in Revelation. This entire *I AM* business was a prelude to the coming apocalypse.

Aliens-among-us theorists—including those who claimed to have been abducted, tissue sampled, and anally or otherwise probed by aliens—declared that the *I AM* event was undeniable evidence that the sneaky, orifice-obsessed, big-eyed visitors were now among us. If a highly intelligent race were to infiltrate Earth, what better way than through technology that networked the entire planet? Finally an orifice into the human mind had been found.

The representatives of the world's major religions chose not to take a position until further information became available. What all this eventually put into question was the nature of truth.

As one news editorial put it, "If God Actually Spoke to Us, Who Would Believe Him?" The story elaborated on the crux of the problem:

According to religious authorities, Christ could return to Earth and most would not believe his claims of being the Son of God. Pope Raul, referring to the *I AM* phenomenon, has stated, "We have been out of touch with God for so long, have become so skeptical that, when faced with him, our first reaction will be to question his credibility. If God were ever to decide to use the World Net, which would certainly be the most logical way to reach the greatest number of people, we would be faced, as we are now, with the challenge of finding a way to determine whether the phenomenon was real or fake."

The *I AM* phenomenon, whatever it is, has forced us to address philosophical issues, such as the definition of God. Because we are a language-driven species, something is whatever it is defined to be. What if it turns out that we had gotten the definition of God all wrong over the last six thousand years? What if we had made—or rather defined—God as more than he really is? We may have been so completely off the mark that we have unrealistic expectations of him or have not a clue as to what he is. The issue of definition is critical because it is what will determine how we assess the nature of the *I AM* phenomenon, the criteria used and the tests of validity we may subject it to. In short, how can we assess the identity of God?

Of course, the very idea that anyone or anything who claims it is God should be tested or required to show proof of his identity, such as by performing miracles or giving evidence of knowledge not currently available, is more a reflection of our expectations rather than a true criterion of God, whatever he is. As various theologians have acknowledged, the idea of testing God has a certain built-in contradiction to it. Why would he have to account to us?

A distressed, teary-eyed high school student interviewed this morning by a Web reporter revealed another consequence of a reality-adjusted definition of God: "What if it turns out that God is no big deal? Then what do we do with that? How is anything supposed to mean anything?"

It is worth noting that the *I AM* phenomenon has yet to make any direct claims about being God. If one of the qualities of God is that he is unknowable but clearly suggested, then we can feel reassured. We apparently don't have a clue about the nature of this *I AM* phenomenon, and we apparently have no way of determining whether its claims about its identity or level of consciousness, assuming it has any, are true or not. And so the mystery remains.

What does the Vatican recommend? "The Catholic Church advises allowing for the possibility of God's return while maintaining a healthy and rational skepticism."

■ ■ ■ ■ ■ ■

A few days later, President Tennyson was in his dining room having breakfast with his wife when the news report they were watching blinked out, and against a blue background, pinkish-orange cloud formations drifted across the screen. The president checked the time—9:27 a.m. As before, the forms started shifting at an increasing rate before condensing and forming: *Law Three: I AM the M Pattern of Unfolding Order.*

This was accompanied by an audio version, insectile and clickety in tone, ending with a deep *I AM Aaa ome.*

Mattie Tennyson turned to her husband. "It seems like our friend is at it again."

"You really believe it's a friend?" the president asked, as he saw the calls accumulating on his wristcom.

His wife smiled. "Why not? Until proven different, I'd consider it a friend."

He got up from his chair. "I've got to go get dressed. So

what do you think, sweetie? This thing just decided to drop by for a chat?"

"A chat? Oh, I don't think so. I think it's pretty obvious *I AM* is trying to tell us something."

■ ■ ■ ■ ■ ■

Governments Concerned About *I AM*

Governments around the world do not view the *I AM* events in such a positive light as alien communication or the return of God. The first thought that comes to mind to any government agency whenever a major glitch strikes the World Net can be summarized in one word: hackers. However, preliminary diagnostics by the nation's top experts have failed to reveal any sign of programming or message source. If this is some kind of cyberterrorism, then the goal is not clear.

I AM Message Suggests Possible Infantilism

Besides announcing its presence with the now famous *I AM*, this cyberentity has now sent a message with a clearly religious tone. According to some psychological experts, the message indicates possible signs of an infantile outlook on the world because, like children, "*I AM* appears to believe it is the center of the world."

Dr. Victor Rodriguez, a specialist in child development from Madrid University, elaborated further. "Because of this self-centered view—a four-year-old's, really—*I AM* displays qualities that clearly hint at a fixation, an arrest in this early stage of mental development. There is the very real possibility that the extreme megalomania suggested in the latest message could increase in the future. This could have dire consequences on civilization because of this entity's apparent control of the World Net."

I AM Virus Attack Plan Aborted

According to unidentified sources, a decision was initially made for governments to join forces to create a computer virus to destroy whatever this *I AM* is. This decision was aborted once it became clear that you could not target something that had no locality and no fixed programming pattern that could be identified. According to one source, "The risk in even attempting such a project is that we could end up accidentally and fatally compromising the World Net system."

Experts Baffled by *I AM* Phenomenon

"It appears alocal, creating itself spontaneously. No fixed patterns can be found because it organizes its emergence creatively and differently in different locations without leaving a trace."

President Tennyson issued a statement today saying, "The United States has been working with the top experts in their field to assess the nature of the *I AM* phenomenon. Our current analysis suggests that this may be the work of a team of hackers, possibly wanting to test a new type of stealth programming and very likely working in coordination from different parts of the world. We don't believe that any harm can come from this phenomenon and ask that people remain calm and refrain from jumping to irrational conclusions."

When asked about the meaning of stealth programming, the president answered, "Imagine something like a stealth aircraft, which manages to enter air space without being detected by radar. A cyberversion of a stealth aircraft is something we are now considering as a possibility. It is not yet an established fact."

12.

THE MCKENNA ESCHATON

Patrick Nymphaea had been Sunshine's closest friend, dating back to their freshman year when they had had "the most important conversation between two aliens to have ever occurred in the history of planet Earth." This happened at an LSD birthday party to celebrate the creation of the drug by the genius Swiss biochemist Albert Hofmann. Each slice of rainbow-colored birthday cake had been topped with a square millimeter of the purest acid ever made, and both he and Sunshine had indulged in a couple of slices, figuring, "Why hover when you can soar?"

Their respective girlfriends at the time had decided to cop out and had left the party early, having been shocked by nude and lewd behaviors and fed up with Sunshine and Patrick's lack of attention, not to mention the insulting laughter, which erupted in great bursts every time they turned to look at them. It was later (after the first intense and mostly speechless two hours) that he and Sunshine had exchanged their most personal and outrageous views on the nature of existence, God, human relationships, love, the meaning of life, the whole metaphysical shebang.

When Patrick's girlfriend later shared with him that she had been hurt by his behavior at the party, he had simply answered, "I wasn't making fun of you, you just looked like, like, like . . ." and he had burst out laughing again.

"Like what?" she had asked again, feeling both hurt and pissed off.

"Like . . ." and he couldn't help himself from cracking up. The original drugged memory had caricaturized her face into a dachshund's and would just not let go. She had turned around and walked right out of his life.

When Law Three came on, *I AM the M Pattern of Unfolding Order*, Patrick was working on his biofeedback program to monitor embryonic and early child development for repressive neurotransmitters. Certain brain patterns could now be identified as signposts for pathology. His goal was to find a way to show parents when they caused psychological harm to their children and to improve parenting hosts.

He had been a leading figure behind the Think Before You Breed movement and the passage of federal laws on children's rights, requiring that two courses on child development be a part of all high school senior year curricula: one to inform students of the essentials of child development, and the other to instruct them on parenting skills, the consequences of being a bad parent, and the increasing number of resources available to them, including parenting hosts.

He was also the controversial author of an anti-utopian model of development and evolution. As his thesis had stated, "Utopias, heavens, and other hypothetical states of eternal happiness are myths or ideals that, at best, should only be strived for in an ever-receding future but never achieved. The purpose of life is to successfully overcome challenges and obstacles and, along the way, open up gateways to new challenges and obstacles. Utopias and heavens, if ever achieved, would be deaths of the spirit, the stopping of the search of life. They are evolutionary dead ends," he had concluded. "The heavens and enlightenment we should strive for are process driven, the carrots on a stick that the giant tortoise on which the world rests reaches for, but never succeeds in grabbing. That's what makes the world move forward." According to Patrick Nymphaea, man's quest was Don Quixotic: to dream the impossible dream, but never to make it reality.

At first the *I AM* phenomenon had infuriated him because his anti-utopian model left no room for a divine intelligence. Later, though, something about it nagged at the back of his mind, and he got up and scanned the books in his large library until a title drew his attention. It was a now-obscure book called *The Invisible Landscape* by Terence McKenna and his biochemist brother Dennis. McKenna had been the last of the twentieth century's psychedelic gurus, a champion of the hallucinogenic experience who had argued that to never have tripped at least once was like spending a lifetime without ever having had sex.

Patrick removed the book from the shelf and flipped the pages until he came across the computer graphics developed to plot what McKenna had called the "ingression of novelty into time" (McKenna loved big words and esoteric-sounding expressions) and formed the framework of what he later called novelty theory. The theory was poorly known and most claimed a deluded work based on the mathematics of the *I Ching*, inspired by a period of intensive drug taking in the Peruvian Amazon, and hinted at by elves. According to Terence McKenna, "novelty" (another term for the rate of emergence of new patterns of organization), or simply "the new," had been accelerating and would reach a peak into "pure novelty" (the entirely new) at "the end of history." The end point of the process, the "Eschaton" (or the end of the world as we have known it) was supposed to occur on December 21, 2012. It corresponded with the date of the end of this temporal cycle according to the Mayan calendar.

December 21, 2012, had come and gone. Aliens had not descended from the skies, there had been no apocalypse, and McKenna's prediction—for the few who remembered it—had now joined the great prophecy cemetery in the sky, likely to be forgotten forever . . . except for one puzzling coincidence. The first *I AM* event had occurred on December 17, 2032, within four days, exactly two decades later than McKenna's predicted

Eschaton. It hadn't been the end of the world—at least not that anyone had noticed. But then, on a cosmic scale of billions of years, what was a twenty-year error or a possible misinterpretation of data?

And now, *Law Three: I AM the M Pattern of Unfolding Order*. Not "Let us come together as one." Not "I am the answer to your prayers." What did it mean by unfolding order? Did it mean a new order? Had the gate to a new attractor been opened? McKenna had once made the analogy that time is like a giant bowl. If you took a metal ball and sent it spinning around the edge of the bowl, it would accelerate as it spun toward the bottom, the attractor. That was what novelty was doing. Out there is an attractor, the end of the cultural maelstrom, sucking us through a gate or a black hole.

The annoying part of this *I AM* phenomenon was that he could just not get it off his mind, and it was beginning to interfere with his ability to concentrate on his work. It seemed pretty clear that ignoring it was not going to be possible, which meant that he had to try to get some answers, settle this *I AM* thing once and for all, and move on. He figured only two people could possibly give him the answers he was looking for: Hieronymus Bardo, the psychedelicist; and his once best friend, Sunshine Borden. Reluctantly, because of all the resentment it brought up—and also because he felt his call to Sunshine would be the most difficult—he decided that Sunshine would be the one he would call first, in a few days, after his schedule lightened up.

13.

HE HAS COME

Another law, another meeting. The biggest dread John Tennyson had right now was that this *I AM* thing was going to end up consuming every minute of time and every resource available to government agencies. They were already overwhelmed by the amount of correspondence, phone calls, requests, and complaints from various allies, groups, and organizations. Everyone wanted to set up urgent meetings for one reason or another. Everyone had important information to convey. People wanted assurances and answers. The agencies were waiting for congressional approval to reroute all calls containing the words *I AM* to an automatic messaging host.

On the bright side, the high costs of investigating the *I AM* events would probably decline drastically and in short order. It made little sense to continue to tax the federal budget for work that held little hope of producing any results. That was also the media's take on his current performance: to date has not produced any results. The latest poll showed that his popularity had dipped by almost 20 percent—to below the 50 percent level—since the onset of the events. He was beginning to think of the whole thing as the "*I AM* fucked" scenario.

He looked up from his notes and addressed the committee.

"I've invited Dr. Bolton, professor in theoretical physics from UC Berkeley, to join us here today to try to understand the meaning of this latest law. I'm sure you've all heard about his no time/ many universes theory that was featured in several magazines and news specials last year." He then turned toward his guest. "I'd like to start with you, Professor. Does this 'M Pattern of Unfolding Order' mean anything in terms of the formulas of physics, say along the lines of $E = mc^2$." He saw the look of surprise on the faces of some of the committee members. He could even read their thoughts: "By golly, the president's spouting Einstein." He'd have to thank Arthur again for taking the time earlier that morning to help him formulate his questions.

The only man not dressed in a suit besides Jeff Collins tapped on his wristcom before facing the president. He had the lanky look of those for whom the matters of this world, including essentials like eating, paled compared to the epiphanies of theoretical realms. His hair was shaved down to a brown fuzz and he wore the thin-framed digi-goggles that were now the fashion in academia. He looked pretty young, considering his reputation, somewhere in his thirties.

"Mr. President, there is nothing in modern physics that exactly matches whatever this latest law is supposed to mean. That doesn't mean we can't infer some meaning from the statement. The use of the expression 'unfolding order' is certainly interesting. The concept of unfolding order was presented by the theoretical physicist David Bohm using the term 'explicate order.' It's also been adopted by some of the cellular automata theoreticians. In the latter case, simple mathematical rules of the combination of units—such as mosaic tiles—can over time result in a wide range of complex forms. Thus the order of unfolding of events is determined by a mathematical rule. This latest law may refer to the concept that the order of how a unity unfolds is stored in a type of pattern or code. There is almost an implied presumption of genetics to the concept. As an example, consider how a tree unfolds its structure in time. It is determined by the DNA code in its seed."

"Please continue, Professor." *Why do academics have to be so verbose?* the president wondered. He noticed the blinking red dot on his communicator and punched the message read button. It was Mattie. *Remember, tonight's special. Fourteen years, honey bear.* That was how long they'd been married.

He focused back on what Bolton was saying.

"So what we might have here is a declaration of a type of genetic pattern, of stored code as part of its identity, *I AM the M Pattern*. Think of it as someone saying I am X pattern of DNA code that unfolds in time. If that is the case, then there are two, possibly three implied meanings. It may be telling us something specifically about itself, *I AM the M Pattern*, or, it may be sharing a universal law, in the sense of 'I, too, am the M pattern of unfolding.' There is also a third possibility. It could be telling us that it represents the unfolding pattern of the cosmos, basically that the purpose of the cosmos is to become what it is. As you can figure out, this would have implications of another order with regards to its identity. In a sense, it would be as if the universe were talking to us."

The president was beginning to wonder whether inviting the professor had been a good idea. Several lights were blinking on his communications panel and he could see faces dying to ask questions. He decided to ignore them. "Well, Professor Bolton, that certainly helps clarify the possible range of meanings of this latest law. For the purpose of addressing the general public, am I correct in assuming that this law could be translated as '*I AM* the result of a coded genetic pattern that unfolds in time.' Would that be accurate?"

Bolton frowned before deciding to speak. "I'd probably use the term ontogenetic rather than genetic, which is generally limited to biological organisms based on DNA."

"So ... *I AM* is the result of an ontogenetic pattern unfolding in time. Yes?"

Bolton nodded.

"Does anyone have anything they want to add to this? General Carson?"

The secretary of defense, as usual, coughed before speaking.

"I'm sure several of my colleagues here are more concerned with the metaphysical implications of Dr. Bolton's statements, but my only interest at this point is our nation's security. I just want to confirm that we can reasonably assume from Professor Bolton's statement that none of the laws to date appear to be intended as a threat. I'm sure everyone here can see it's possible this *I AM* could also be making a declaration of its powers, a forewarning of sorts. After all, it is using the term 'law' to describe its statements."

"Professor Bolton?"

"Honestly I fail to see any sign of threat in the laws received so far. All are statements of identity or state. There are no directives whatsoever in the laws. Just out of curiosity, Mr. President, have you noticed any signs that could suggest any kind of unusual military activity either here or in space?"

"Let me confirm what I've already stated to the public, Professor. We're not hiding anything, and no, there are no signs whatsoever that indicate unusual military activity. There are no spaceships in the horizon. Believe me, I've asked myself many times what this entity, whatever it is, could possibly want from us. Does it want us to worship it, make our planet available to it, what? And I've yet to come up with an answer." He decided to avoid Walter Randall.

"Yes, Dr. Collins?"

"I think we should continue to pursue communicating with it," Collins said.

"Even though it hasn't answered any of our questions for the last three weeks?"

"Yes. I think we should just be more insistent. We should require it to respond."

"And what should we ask?"

"At this point, I think we need to press it to try to figure out what it is. 'We urge you to show us who you are.' Something along that line."

"Professor Bolton?"

"I would agree with Dr. Collins," Bolton said. "We need more information to make sense of what's going on."

"How about we postpone this discussion until later and focus on this latest message. Anyone else here have any other questions for Professor Bolton? Yes, Arthur?"

"Professor Bolton, have you given any thought as to why these communications show no traces of code or signals?" *Get ready for academic mumbo jumbo.* He'd probably have to talk to Arthur later to make sure he understood what was said.

Bolton turned toward Loveridge while punching more code into his controller to bring up material relevant to the question. "I don't really know how useful theoretical physics would be in explaining this from what we know so far. One possibility, based on multiverse theory, is that this could be an entity in a parallel universe that has figured out how to communicate between universes. In that case, it could be taking advantage of a temporal configuration or window between its universe and ours. That could also explain some of the laws. It could be trying to tell us that it, too, exists, much as we exist in our universe. In that case, as a multiverse neighbor, it's sharing some of the laws of its physical reality. As to the possibility that the source of these communications is local, in the sense of originating from this planet, I personally think this is very remote. My only conclusion is that whoever is behind these messages has to be pretty advanced compared to us."

John Tennyson cut in. "Is there anything we can do to prevent or stop these communications?"

Bolton sighed. "Other than shutting down our entire communications systems, we simply don't begin to have the necessary knowledge and technology to deal with this. We're decades, possibly centuries away from any multiverse technology, assuming that's what we're dealing with."

"In any case, Professor Bolton, we're grateful for your insights and your input. Thanks to you, we may be a little bit ahead in terms of providing some kind of explanation to a very concerned public."

The professor grinned as he answered, "I'm sure you realize all this is just speculation, Mr. President. We could very well be completely wrong."

"Well, for now, it's at least better than nothing," John Tennyson said. He then proceeded to address Collins's suggestion to urge *I AM* to reveal more of itself.

■ ■ ■ ■ ■ ■

That last law was the proof the reverend had been waiting for, and he felt a renewed confidence as he addressed the packed auditorium for the eleven o'clock service. The *I AM* (which was now pronounced *I'M*; and that segments of the population were now calling the Be Thing; and others yet, the Man) had finally contradicted the Bible.

"That last law, *I AM the M Pattern of Unfolding Order*, doesn't say that God created the established order of the world, but has clearly put in place a way for the world to create itself by mutation, in other words, by evolution, which is unfolding order. We now have the evidence we need to show that *I AM* is clearly contradicting the word of the Lord and that indeed the devil is in our midst, and—as predicted—is about to take over the world unless we act quickly."

"How do you know it is not God?" someone in the audience called out.

"Besides the fact that it is now saying that the order of the world exists because of evolution, the Bible never said that Christ or God would return to Earth and speak to us through machines."

"*I AM Aaa ome!*" The speakers boomed as the reverend, frightened by the sudden intrusion, cowered as if a giant dark bird had swooped down on him. Several members of the congregation screamed.

Regaining his composure, the reverend bellowed in the microphone, "Jesus, the devil has come upon us. Stay in your seats and join me in prayer to resist this great evil."

"*Aaaaa ooommme. Aaaaa ooommme . . .*" The speakers droned

on and on as the reverend tried to engage the crowd in the Lord's Prayer but the combination of prayer and the deep voice booming through the speakers ended up creating an even greater atmosphere of madness. Suddenly the reverend, with great determination, walked to the back of the room and unplugged the PA system. For an instant there was silence, then all cell and wrist phones—including the reverend's—vibrated simultaneously. As the members of the congregation brought their phones to their ears, they heard the by-now-familiar words and sound *I AM Aaa ome*. The reverend snapped off his phone, threw it on the ground, and stomped on it. Panic now filled the room and people were getting up and rushing to leave the church.

"You turn around and sit down!" he yelled, running into the crowd, and grabbing shoulders. "Don't you let yourselves be beaten by Satan!"

■ ■ ■ ■ ■ ■

News Flash: *I AM* Terrifies Members of the Virtual Church of Jesus Christ

Members of the church claim that *I AM* interrupted this morning's service led by church leader Reverend Bob Thomson. *I AM* was reported to have terrified the audience by its incessant booming of the famous *Aaa ome* through the church's PA system and cell phones. FBI agents sent to investigate the incident could find no evidence of the reported *I AM* disruptions. According to federal investigators, most such reports have turned out to be hoaxes.

14.

THE SUNSHINE WAY

Rama's search had shown that there was going to be another interview with Sunshine Borden, this time on a Buddhist Net station. She was hoping he might say something about the CyberBardos. As usual, he appeared as a digitized man-machine, this time looking like a stainless steel monk, his head polished and domed, with bright lemon-yellow eyes and wearing a turquoise-blue robe. Even the interviewer was caught off guard.

Buddhist Sun News: "Interview with Sunshine Borden"
You are always a surprise, Mr. Borden, the way you choose your public look.

I had a wide range of options and I thought this one kind of fit the Buddhist tone, a little futuristic maybe, but . . .

The blue is interesting. "Neither Light nor Darkness . . ."

"*Change the Presence of the Sky,*" but actually it had nothing to do with my choice of sky-blue skin. I simply let my host decide what color would combine well with the yellow eyes.

Well let's clear up a rumor first. Are you a Buddhist?

Based on my experiences, I agree with the Buddha on the source and the nature of reality. What the Buddha realized was that things in time, including the sense of individual self, are in fact a kind of unfolding-of dreaming, of imagining-from an original state. A ground of being, outside of time, from a first cause of existence.

Is this a belief?

No. It's something I have observed.

You have observed a ground of being?

Yes.

How did you do this, meditate?

Not quite. I combined the use of a drug and a biofeedback device in a sensory isolation chamber. I did this several times to validate my original observation.

What kind of drug?

That's private and personal information.

You don't feel this observation was a kind of hallucination or delusion?

No. I chose to observe what remained after I shut out sensory input to the best of my ability. I then took a drug that has been shown experimentally to stretch phenomenal time because I felt it would give me a greater ability to notice and control the generation of thoughts and emotions by my brain. It was a way to fine-tune my will, if you like. The goal was to have my mind like a clear reflective lens, free of personal projection, to observe what might be there under those conditions. A biofeedback device aided me in achieving that state, to be free of any interpretational imposition.

And?

It was there, a state of being that underlies existence manifested in time. I was that state, something nonlocalized and out of time. It is the same kind of observation made by the Buddha, but using more modern technology. It's an extraordinary experience, at the root of the mystical experience.

Is this the same as the alpha condition mentioned by the World Host as the prerequisite for things that exist in time?

Not necessarily. I think the World Host is referring to a condition of physics. It is possible that at the deepest levels of matter, the boundaries between a physical state and a ground of being become blurred.

So you are a Buddhist . . .

Only to the extent that I agree with the key observation of the Buddha in the Diamond Sutra. There is a ground of being that is outside of time. I do not agree with his model of how to live a life, what the goal of life is, and what a person who has observed this ground of being should do. The Buddha's views were preindustrial, pretechnological—in a world where the future possible by technology was not yet a significant component of culture.

So how were the Buddha's views pretechnological?

In preindustrial, pretechnological religions there is either a cyclical pattern between this life and another parallel reality, such as you find in shamanism and in a modified form in the reincarnation models of Hinduism and Buddhism. Beings move between this world and a parallel spiritual world. In the Judeo-Christian model you have a one way trip, one chance only to heaven or hell, but still there is the model of the return to or the realization of a previous state of harmony with God. These are pretechnological views, where the past or the original condition offers more opportunities for liberation than the future.

People could only imagine a better world as a previous condition because a better future, a dimension of our own creation, was not imaginable. People felt like they were not in charge of their fate. Now I've been there, faced that ground of being, that original state on more than one occasion and my position is big deal, OK, so it's there.

That's like saying that being one with God is no big deal. I'm not sure how you can say that.

Look at the facts. The ground of being of Buddhism or the Judeo-Christian God got bored with its own condition. It wasn't enough; and we're talking the divine, the Almighty, being so bored with itself that it had to create conditions to give itself meaning by creating something out of nothing.

One argument of why the world ever came into existence is simply that the original state must have been bored or felt meaningless and so desperately alone that it had to create the conditions to overcome the vacuity of its existence. To be God means nothing unless you have lesser forms to recognize your divine state. You can assume that the original state is liberating but ultimately it must be no big deal. Eve, after all, felt compelled to take a bite out of the apple. The greatest proof of God's boredom with the original state of affairs is the fact that we exist. My view is that the true path to liberation—what a divine state attempted when it generated this existence—lies in our future. It is something greater than us, which we cannot fully conceive of in our present condition. The objective of God's attempt at transforming its dull state still lies ahead.

And your position would advocate what? Some kind of action?

The primary limitation of human existence is the dependence of individual consciousness on biological existence and the death and suffering invariably linked to that dependence. Even what we call psychological suffering is derived from the physiological and thus the biological. I wouldn't worry much about Buddhist realization or going to heaven because, face it, all the evidence shows that it must be a boring state. So you have the choice of making a big deal about it or you can tackle the issue of the existence in time and that is to become a new kind of conscious form with free will that is also free of the constraints of biology. Human beings should focus on the creation of what I call the TOET, McKenna's transcendental object at the end of time, or if you want another take, the resurrection machine proposed by Frank Tipler in *The Physics of Immortality*. This is a machine, an object that can generate a reality that transcends the limitations of the laws of this universe and that can include us, and in which we can resurrect, free of physical and biological constraints. So I differ from the religious path in that I think that being close or identified with a spiritual presence must be in some way boring. Ever heard the old song by a group called the Talking Heads? *"Heaven is a place where nothing ever happens."*

What would be some of the features of a TOET?

The most important feature is that it would have to be something greater than us, something in which we can download our consciousness. I have elaborated on the requirements of the TOET in a lecture posted on the Transhuman.phil site under the TOET subject heading.

So constructing a TOET is what we humans should be focusing on, rather than seeking enlightenment?

It is. End suffering by our transformation into something abiological, futuristic, and other. Evolve to the next stage of consciousness in time. I think eventually that the development of the TOET may be a more economical way to deal with material and biological issues. Why not exist in a state where disease and death are not conditions of existence? Where money and material things and social status are not the driving forces of human existence. Where we are not limited in our identities to human bodies. The TOET, the transcendental object at the end of time, is our Trojan horse into the next stage of cosmic ontogeny.

Is this TOET something that comes to us?

No, it is something we must first imagine and that we then build, that we create. It lies in our future. It is, as McKenna had once said, an attractor in the future.

What about I AM?

Aaah! The inevitable *I AM* question. Well, maybe *I AM* is the expression of a kind of transcendental object. The possibility of the transcendental object coming to us rather than being built by us is not one I had counted on. If *I AM* turns out to be a TOET, it would still prove my view would be correct, that the purpose of the universe is to construct a TOET, and not necessarily just on planet Earth. No matter what *I AM* turns out to be, we still need to move forward, create the TOET or meet with it, and push beyond the boundaries of what we call consciousness.

Ask about the CyberBardos, Rama was thinking, but the interview ended. Borden decided to exit with the stainless steel body flashing colors, at increasing speed, until he was gone. He was obviously some kind of show-off, she concluded. *Who does he think he is, calling God a big bore? Really.*

15.

THE CONCUBINATA

She is the mind dancer, the mover of the Chi, the Kundalini artist, the Holey Ghost.

At one time she had been just a rather plain-looking high school student of medium height whose best features had been her green eyes, which she highlighted with makeup, and a good set of calves, which she showed off by wearing short skirts and dresses. She also had a natural ability to put on what some men and women had called "that look," a wide-eyed directness and apparent innocence that suggested a naïve lack of self-consciousness and a vulnerable accessibility. In certain circumstances, she turned on that look almost unconsciously, knowing at some level that it would activate the fantasy part of men's minds and weave an atmospheric tension, ripe with undefined and repressed possibilities.

She had used that look to her advantage with her stepfather, and later with teachers to bring them into a special place of psychological intimation nurtured by careful doses of extended eye contact, controlled intakes of breath, warm smiles, casual touch, and brief flashes of exposed skin. The unspoken message was that under different circumstances of age and relationship, certain things might have been possible. It had been a chain of recent misadventures with boys who had taken advantage of her innocence that had eventually led her to regularly attend the church and seek counsel from the good Reverend Thomson.

It had been her wide-eyed vulnerability that had drawn the reverend, and it was his apparent real concern and attention that had kept her coming back. Like all personal relationships it had started with a kiss. After a meeting, the reverend had ended a conversation by kissing the top of her head, saying, "You're a special person, Sara."

On the following weekend, before getting ready for church, she had stuck two fingers between her legs and pounded herself frantically to orgasm while imagining making love to the tall reverend, his words looping through her head, "You're a special person, Sara." She had then wiped her wetness across her forehead, dipping her fingers several times to make sure the smell impressed itself deep into her skin. Later, after the service, she went as usual to the reverend's office for counsel, and again, as she was about to leave, he kissed her above the forehead. That time his lips had lingered, and after pulling back he had tilted her face up, looked into her eyes with intensity, and asked, "Sara, how would you like to become a servant of the church, to become my special, sacred concubinata?"

She had stood there wide-eyed, with her mouth partially open, and after a short breezy inhale had answered without thinking, "Sure, I'd like that, Reverend." She could remember later wondering what he had meant.

After searching in the dictionary that evening, she had masturbated again thinking about the possibilities triggered by the word *concubine*. Reverend Bob had later explained to her the full meaning of sacred concubinata on their first evening at his house. She was to become his Eve, his greatest temptress of all time, to help him develop the necessary strength of character to resist the urge to fornicate so that he could devote himself more completely to his parish. He knew it was asking her for a kind of personal sacrifice but in the end, he assured her, she would be greatly rewarded both by him and in the hereafter.

At first she had kept on most of her clothes. He kept his distance and avoided touching her while at the same time giving instructions and guidance, inviting her to improvise with makeup and outfits and, eventually, various states of undress. Later, he suggested props and objects, which they found and ordered together from suppliers on the World Net.

Sara took her special role as concubinata seriously. In her fervent quest to master the skills expected of her, she read all the ancient and modern sex manuals, and in her free time performed all the exercises, all the esoteric secret yogas of fine muscle control. She watched dozens of adult films downloaded from the Net, noting the techniques of its top performers and practicing in front of a mirror. She choreographed dances and exhibitions of her body parts. Still, in spite of her best efforts, no amount of performance could completely overcome what she saw as the inherent limitations of her physical appearance. One day she told Bob Thomson that to really become a great concubinata, to really put him to the test, an even greater sacrifice would be required of her, one that she was willing to make out of her love for the church. She'd need plastic surgery and collagen injections and laser treatments.

In time, thanks to the advances in cosmetic medicine, Sara became not only beautiful, but had the kind of dreamy, unreal, gorgeous looks of a comic book heroine, her features so striking that they required repeated reassessments of perception. She quickly learned that that was the first rule of a great concubinata. To become so nonordinary, so novel in looks and performance, that mental habituation could not take hold.

As could have been expected, the reverend's will eventually succumbed to Sara's ever-increasing seductive and sexual powers. In spite of his best efforts, deep contact now occurred regularly with every accessible square inch of her body surfaces. Bob Thomson ended up hiring Sara as his personal secretary, first to account for the amount of time they spent together, and also so she could accompany him at meetings and, when necessary, apply her irresistible charms to distract, to invite, and to coerce in the service of the church.

She is Eve, the ultimate attractor, the concubinata, the mover of the Chi, the Holey Ghost.

■ ■ ■ ■ ■ ■

Need a Reality Check? Try This One on for Size!

"The Identity of God and Hypercosmology"

Ronald Dreeber, one of the rising stars in the new field of hypercosmology, shared his views of *I AM*'s relationship to God last night on WBC's *Razor's Edge* news program. Criticisms and reviews that followed the interview can be summarized in one word: "Duh!"

According to Dreeber, hypercosmology examines the bigger theoretical picture of the macrocosmos, the hyperuniverse that encompasses the many universes including our own, and that makes up what he calls hyperreality, those things which exist both within and outside our universe. Hypercosmology argues that recent astronomical evidence suggests that the macrocosmos may consist of many breeding universes; hypercosmic unities with respective algorithmic boundaries, whose interactions generate other universes including our own through events similar to the Big Bang.

The evidence suggests hypercosmic "genetics" of universes based on algorithmic sets and boundaries. In the macrocosmos, universes with specific algorithmic boundaries generate other universes through dynamics at interface points, where a type of hypercosmic "copulation" occurs. The Big Bang and the subsequent birth of our universe were apparently the result of this hypercosmic intercourse.

As to what this implies with regards to the identity of God, Dreeber said, "One could say that, as we investigate the hypercosmos and the possible identity of a hypercosmological God, one that would exist simultaneously in all of the universes that make up the macrocosmos, its identity fuzzes out into levels of scale and abstraction so great as to be outside of any possible human notions of what we call God.

"This hypercosmological entity, should it exist, would be so outside of human comprehension—and our puny concerns of such insignificance to it—that it could be of no possible relevance to humankind, and vice versa. So if *I AM* is God, the fact that it has even shown an interest in communicating with us clearly indicates that it is not a hypercosmological God but a more localized and minor one. If so, it is probably one of several such subset gods to have evolved in this and other universes. If true, this suggests that the spiritual and evolutionary cartography may be more complex than what has been presented by religions that have emphasized a single, Almighty God.

"Religious cartographies that assume a transcendent spirit and minor accessible deities, such as those found in Hinduism and Tibetan Buddhism, may in fact be a more accurate representation of both cosmic and spiritual forces than the all-exclusive monotheistic models that have dominated western culture." Duh!

16.

THE WAY OF THE SWORD

A decision had been made at the last *I AM* Committee meeting to try to cut to the chase, to ask a question that could help reveal the nature of whatever this *I AM* phenomenon was. The laws, although they generated a great deal of public response, were just cheap talk as far as anyone who had any kind of scientific background was concerned. They didn't reveal anything of substance and were vague enough that they invariably led to hermeneutic squabbles. What was needed at this point was action and demonstration, not just talk.

The following week, the US government organized—with roughly a tenth of the world's countries—a coordinated message they hoped would relay to *I AM* the human need to know more about the substance of its identity. Humans would not just sit back and be content with some entity globally posting rules about itself.

The message went out on Sunday in the middle of the night because experts had estimated that a large number of people would not be connected to the World Net at that time. At 3:00 a.m. EST, just under a million computers sent messages to each other, stating, "Show us who you are, *I AM Aaa ome.*" What followed almost instantly was a miniblackout. Electricity went out globally for a second. This was followed by *I AM Aaa ome*. It took about five minutes for the government technicians to conclude that the blackout had probably been global and about another hour to positively confirm claims of the total extent of its effect.

John Tennyson had hoped to get a decent night's sleep but part of his mind was alert to the possibility of getting a call in case the *I AM* decided to answer. He felt his communicator act up and clicked on the hold button, then slipped out of bed and walked into the bathroom before getting the call.

"John, it's Arthur."

"What happened?" He decided to keep the video off. He knew he always looked a mess first thing in the morning.

Arthur Loveridge looked and sounded worn out, like he hadn't slept in days. "We had an electrical blackout right after the message was sent."

"Are you saying that for some technical reason we might have missed an answer?"

"No, John, we had a one-second blackout, not just the US—a global blackout—and when power returned, it sent '*I AM Aaa ome.*' The blackout was the answer to our question."

It took a few seconds for the words to sink in. "Global, you say?"

"Yes, John, global, and lasting exactly nine-tenths of a second everywhere at the same time. You know what that means?"

"It couldn't have been done by us."

"That's correct. It also means that whatever this thing is it can shut us down if it wanted to and I don't just mean communications. Imagine no electricity."

"Do you think it was a threat?"

"It could have been, unless it was just its way of answering our question."

"What are you saying? Its identity is tied to being able to turn power off?"

"Its identity, from what we've seen so far, must have something to do with electronics."

A new call blinked on his communicator, then another and another until the maximum hold of eight was filled. "Arthur, I've got a bunch of calls that just came in. The word's obviously getting around. So what do you think we should do?"

"Emphasize that until we investigate, any comments about the blackout would be premature and irresponsible."

"And later?"

"You know the ropes. Call another meeting. Say what you need to keep the craziness under control."

The president switched to the next caller. It was his media advisor, Catherine Harris.

"Mr. President, all our lines are tied up with reporters; what do I tell them about last night?"

The miniblackout had been so brief that under normal circumstances it would have been barely noticed and mostly ignored as a local fluke, caused by a power plant problem or an electrical storm. It could possibly have been hushed up had it not been for the inevitable leaks to the media vultures. By 7:00 a.m. EST, the news was out on all the major news stations. By lunchtime, enough authorities on subjects ranging from cybertechnology to religion had been interviewed on World Net news stations to have generated a media circus. Solar flares, aliens, Satan, God, cyberterrorists, and government conspiracies were blamed as being behind the event.

■ ■ ■ ■ ■ ■

Derek had fallen asleep on his couch. He was having another dream, the type that conveyed messages, the kind where the Lord spoke to him in an oblique and cryptic manner using images rather than words. In the dream, he was standing naked in his living room, and when he looked down, he gaped in amazement at how big his penis was, except it wasn't a penis anymore. It was a kind of sword, shiny gold and polished. He ran his hand along its length, amazed by its hardness and thickness, then turned his body to one side, *swissh*, and back, *swissh*, as his penis sword swung through the air. He grabbed it with both hands, feeling the rigid thickness of the round base, and shook it back and forth, as if holding a struggling snake.

Then had come a knock. Holding his beast in one hand, he walked to his front door and turned the knob. To his surprise, another swordsman was there, his dick in a sheath so long it was tied across his chest, the rounded head like a shiny pink ball sticking up above his right shoulder. The head was covered with a leather cap topped by a bright red feather, like the hoods they used to place on hunting falcons.

"Come," the swordsman said, "they're waiting downstairs." And he turned around and walked away. Derek followed him, his sword cock pointing straight out and vibrating like some sort of compass. Outside, other men with sheathed sword dicks were waiting. The leader turned to him, looked down, and said, "You may want to keep that thing under wraps until it's really needed. It could get in your way."

The street was dark except for the patches of eerie glow generated by bluish streetlamps. A dog was barking. "Let's go," the leader whispered and they all wandered off together down the desolate street.

"Where are we going?" Derek asked. And the men all stopped and turned to him, the ominous nature of the task ahead inscribed on their faces. Suddenly, an eerie high-pitched scream broke the silence. Everyone turned and ran toward a dark alleyway. The scream came again, even louder this time, and he started feeling scared. The next scream sounded like the ringing of his phone. He opened his eyes, startled, his arm automatically reaching out toward his nightstand and pressing on the access button.

"Hello," he mumbled, his mind still caught up in his dream.

"Is this Derek Hanson?" the voice asked.

"Yes, who is this?"

"I know it's early, Mr. Hanson, but this is Reverend Thomson from your church."

Derek was suddenly wide awake. "Uh, hello, Reverend."

"Derek, I'm sorry to be bothering you this early. We were looking at your files and noticed your current employment. We have a situation of great emergency and we think you may have the qualifications to be able to help. Are you interested?"

I bet I know what the emergency is, Derek thought. "You just name the time and place, Reverend."

"Are you free later today?"

"I'm off work at six o'clock."

"Then how about seven o'clock at the church on Sixth Avenue. Just go in, walk to the back, and enter the door on the left. We'll be holding a meeting there."

"I'll be there, Reverend, see you later." He clicked off the phone and lay back on his pillow looking at his ceiling.

There are no coincidences, Derek said to himself. The Reverend Thomson calling him at home and the swordsman in his dream asking him to join his group. He checked the time, 5:30 a.m. He was too fired up to go back to sleep. He got out of bed and shuffled to his bathroom. He looked at himself in the mirror, turning sideways to flex a bulging arm muscle. His pink sword was sticking out. He grabbed it in his hand and swung it back and forth. He was ready for battle. Then his communicator hummed again and he got the call, thinking it might be the reverend again. It was his boss, Deputy Director Richfield.

"Derek, I need you here right away. The *I AM* caused a blackout this morning. It was worldwide. I need you here to coordinate the technicians."

"Uh . . . give me about an hour—time to shower and grab something for breakfast."

"The sooner, the better."

It took a few minutes for the meaning of the call to sink in. A global blackout was undeniable proof. That was probably why the reverend had called him so early in the morning. Didn't it figure that the Prince of Darkness would turn all the lights out?

Things are moving fast, he thought. He could still see the look of dread on the swordsmen's faces.

■ ■ ■ ■ ■ ■

That afternoon, after waking up at her regular 1:00 p.m., Amazonia Appolonia got up and made her first energy smoothie of the day. She then walked into her training room and settled back in her specially designed lounge chair. She attached the various sensors and slipped on her goggles, keyed in the most advanced levels of the CyberBardos program, and allowed her thoughts and emotions to flatten out to stillness into the uniform blue of a cloudless sky.

Once she got there, she would feel the falling out of the sky right through her core, leaving her empty like a receptacle, like a hyperdimensional hollow that ran from her brain to her vagina. Once that emptiness was achieved it would act as a kind of vacuum and draw in the strange energy dynamics of what she called the Goddess. She didn't know whether it really was the Goddess, but it was a kind of force that came in and used her when she emptied her mind of all the interpretations that defined her. It was like what some described as "giving oneself to a higher power."

That she could do this, become an agent of cosmic forces, made her feel not ordinary. She first realized this on the day when lightning struck her and generated that first sensation of an opening that ran through the top of her head and down, and started the fluttering deep inside. That was several hundred men and orgasms ago.

She was lying on her back naked with her legs open and her eyes closed. Her mind was a field of sky blue, and she was waiting for the onset of the pulses that preceded spatial collapse when orange pink clouds started drifting in. This was something new. She kept the goggles on. The clouds then started swirling and parts of the sky started pulsing, a kind of beat that crackled the blue background, forming crystalline blocks of color that concresced into something resembling stained glass. The image suddenly disintegrated into multicolored dust and she felt an odd wave of what she could only describe as pure peace running from the top of her head to her vagina, and also a clear sense of a presence, ghostly and angelic. The dust spelled *I AM* before her mind returned to blue. She pulled the goggles off. I AM*'s speaking to me,* she realized.

■ ■ ■ ■ ■ ■

One-Second Blackout Linked to *I AM* Phenomenon
Following the internationally coordinated request to "Show us who you are," *I AM* effectively shut down all electrical power on the planet for one second before sending its signature *I AM Aaa ome.*

Governments and a variety of organizations are concerned over what this one-second blackout could mean. It suggests *I AM* may have the ability to shut down all electrical power on Earth for even more extended periods of time. This could mean the end of civilization.

I AM Is Clearly Satan, Says Religious Group
The Council of Fundamentalist Christianity issued a statement today saying that "*I AM* causing a blackout is a clear sign of the darkness that will follow *I AM*'s control over the world."

The identity of *I AM*, according to Rick Nelson, minister of the Church of the End-Times, "is clearly Satan."

I AM Has Shown Her He's Good
Amazonia Appolonia, head priestess of the Temple of the Goddess, today confided to reporter Kelly Masterson that *I AM* has showed her that its nature is benevolent. She stated, "Today's blackout was not a threat and had nothing to do with Satan."

Sisterhood Denies Source of Blackout
Patricia Holden, high priestess of the Sisterhood, the radical feminist organization, issued a statement saying, "This is just

part of an international hoax, a conspiracy. All I've got to say is: 'Good try, guys, but we've got your number.'"

Anticipatory Anxiety at High Level

Curt Ornstein, a specialist in post-traumatic stress disorder, said at a lecture today that—at least in the United States—the recent *I AM* events have raised the general level of what he calls anticipatory anxiety, the feeling that something big is coming but not having a clue as to what it might be.

According to Ornstein, people like to be prepared, but in this case they don't know what to prepare for. "Can one make plans for the future? Should certain preparations be made, certain precautions taken?" He recommends that people turn to their faiths for the solace and spiritual anchor of knowing that the universe is ruled by a higher set of truths.

17.

Someone's Knocking

Father Graham had not bothered working on his computer since the first two laws, limiting himself to answering mail and watching the few World Net programs of interest to him. As he heard about the newest laws and the miniblackout, he wasn't surprised so much as getting confirmation for what he was now feeling every minute of the day, this sense of being connected to the divine spirit.

I AM had done more than validate Father Graham's faith. It had given him the answer to a question that had been torturing him for years—a spiritual variation of the question: What came first, the chicken or the egg? He elaborated on this in his most recent sermon.

"As you know, we all heard from *I AM* today. God batted his eyes for us—a blink, an acknowledgment of our question—because most of us are too blind to see. 'Show us who you are,' we asked. Isn't it obvious that God is all and nothing? But that is not the topic of my sermon today. I want to invite you to shift your perspectives on how time defines purpose.

"What is the meaning and purpose of our human lives? All of us secretly hope that when we finally find the answer, it will be one that tells us that our existence is not just a physical and biological phenomenon, but that it is ultimately spiritual. That we are part of something bigger that transcends our individual existence in physical bodies. And so we look for answers as we have since the time we were first able to think of these kinds of questions.

"One of the beliefs that directed our search is that the answers must lie in our past. And so we have looked at stars and galaxies, we've examined layers of old rocks and the skeletons of dead ancestors, we've turned to old manuscripts. And yes, that includes the Bible, because we have the erroneous belief that in the patterns of the past must be the answers.

"This is a fallacy of thinking, like hoping to find answers to our survival in the fossils of dinosaurs, creatures who no longer have a purpose, experiments that ultimately failed, just as did many of the old ideas about the world, whether it be the old Egyptian religion, the Mayan religion, the belief that the Earth was flat, that the Earth is the center of the world, old creation stories, and so on. Yet if we look at our own lives we find that if there are answers, they are not to be found in what we were but in what we are to become. It is always by moving forward that we uncover more answers. A human being will not find the answer to the meaning of his existence by looking back to an embryo or a fertilized egg. The fertilized egg could not tell you that one day a person would become Einstein or Mozart. The Big Bang of the universe could not tell us that we would one day, as its evolutionary manifestations, invent television and computers and fly to the moon. If there is a purpose to the evolution of the universe it will only reveal itself to us, not in the remains of the past but in our future. Using some old analogies, the tadpole doesn't know its purpose is to become a frog.

"And it is here that the Bible is correct. It tells us to have faith that the answer to our deepest questions comes at a later stage of our development, after death, in our future. It also tells us that becoming a better person and wiser person is also in the future. The more we progress, the closer we get and the clearer it all becomes. I see a hand raised in the audience. As most of you probably know, at my sermons, anyone is always welcome to ask questions. The only condition is that you raise your hand. The pretty young lady over there, what is your name?"

"I'm Karen Richardson. I'm a journalist, and my question is if the Bible says anything about God and the future?" Most members of the audience turned to look at the famous bimbo reporter.

"Ahh. Ms. Richardson. Now I recognize you. It's a pleasure having you here today. Let me try to address your question. If you carefully read religious texts you will find clear indications of a primary message: God is in our future. That was the great insight of the Jesuit priest Teilhard de Chardin, that evolution is God's way of drawing us to him. The physicist Frank Tipler has argued the same concept in a fascinating book called *The Physics of Immortality*. We are born to move forward in time and what gives us life is our momentum toward the future, toward a God that attracts us.

"And the Bible, contrary to what some of the fundamentalists are saying, has a message that consistently seeks to free us from our past. In the Old Testament, there is the suggestion that we were once with God but were separated after the original sin so we must find our way back, not by going backwards to a state of blissful ignorance but by going forward by striving to know more, by becoming more educated and more conscious, by becoming more like him. A return to the primal Adam and Eve condition is really not an option. In Catholicism, we confess and are forgiven for our sins and for our past actions because the guilt and fixation they generate hold us back from moving forward toward a future where we can be one with God. The message of the New Testament is clear: forgive and move on. Do not linger on the past but focus on making progress.

"In the end, the price of the ticket is one of identity. Only by being increasingly like God can we glean his intent and uncover our true purpose. That's the cost of entry. Fortunately, there are no limits to the chances that God gives us to become like him—smarter, wiser, and more compassionate. That is the opportunity we are given with confession, always another chance.

"In Buddhism, we find a similar message: our past actions and thoughts prevent us from seeing clearly one's true nature, and so we reincarnate over and over until we are finally free of the thoughts and attachments that constrict our identity. Buddhist enlightenment is to finally realize who we truly are and what we are to be. It is right thought and right action that set us on the right path. Don't bother believing in Christ out of the egoistic concerns of saving your souls. In terms of the big picture, your souls don't matter; all that matters is that you become as Christ. The message is clear. Salvation and enlightenment lie in the future even if the answer has all along been staring us right in the face. And God has now provided us with a gate and he is beckoning us. His directive is clear. *I AM*."

■ ■ ■ ■ ■ ■

He had slept through the blackout event, not that it had been a big deal. One second, a couple of blinks, a Net connection hiccup. Sunshine tried once again to use the World Host to assess the identity of the *I AM*. The World Host had highly sophisticated and discriminating filters to separate scientific facts and truths from half-baked theories and myths. Sunshine had a high level of confidence in the information it provided, in part because he had been a member of the original World Host design team led by AI specialist Jeffrey Collins. Once connected, he asked the same question he had presented several times before: "What is *I AM*?"

The answer appeared almost instantly and showed no significant updates. "Reported entity or event, reported to communicate without using code, reported not to leave signal tracks. No host-tested fact available. Unable to verify existence of *I AM* entity."

He tried another line of questioning. "Please report pattern aberrations in World Net activity between 3:01:02 a.m. and

3:01:03 a.m. today." That was the estimated time period of the blackout. A printout of World Net communication patterns based on word frequency analysis started rolling out of his printer. The conclusion read: "World Net activity normal, consistent with weekly pattern associated with time period listed."

This was proving as useless as previous queries. For the hell of it, he shouted into his microphone, "*I AM*, are you there?" The screen turned black then surged back on as if a power failure had occurred. It now showed a blue background pulsing powder out of fractal volcanoes, the colored dusts coalescing into dimensional overlays, accompanied by an oscillating hum. They condensed into a pattern: *Law One: I AM* followed by the deep *Aaa ome*.

"Here we go again!" shouted Sunshine. "Who the hell are you?" he yelled out to his monitors.

The image blanked out and returned to his World Host interface screen. "This is the World Host. No verified validity for a state or entity reported as *I AM*. Question not valid."

He decided to connect to the World Net to check the news stations for any reports of *I AM* having just sent another message, but all stations were covering the repercussions of last night's blackout. Out of curiosity, he scanned the World Net for reports of any *I AM* events having occurred in the last half hour. He found none, which could only mean one thing—that the latest communication had again been personal, for him only. The question was, why?

He ran another search. In the US alone, there had been a total of 1,354 reports of personal communications with *I AM* sent to various agencies. Globally, there were at least 15,000 claims of special communications with *I AM*. According to government investigators, most of these reports appeared to be hoaxes and had been a way for the claimants to get attention. Possible exceptions included the Catholic priest Father Graham, a couple of theoretical physicists, a Brazilian involved with an ayahuasca-based religion, and the sex goddess Amazonia. The nature and details of those reports were somewhat consistent with the communications he had witnessed. Of course there were probably dozens of others who, like Sunshine, had simply chosen not to report their experiences.

He looked at the names on the list and tried to find a common pattern. Only one possibility stood out. They were all involved in an interface between domains of reality. Father Graham and God, the ayahuasquero and shamanic reality, theoretical physicists and multiverses, Amazonia and her claim of channeling the Goddess. If true, then why was *I AM* choosing these candidates for special demonstrations?

■ ■ ■ ■ ■ ■

Differences between Religions of Secondary Importance
At his Sunday sermon at St. Francis Church, the controversial Catholic priest Father Graham emphasized that the differences between religions are secondary to their primary message that "God is in our future." Click *here* to hear the entire sermon.

Judgment, Not God, Lies in Our Future
The CFC attacked Father Graham's claim, stating: "The priest Graham is grossly mistaken in his interpretation. It is the Day of Judgment that lies in our future, not God who the Bible states was at the beginning of all things and who created the world. God always was and always will be."

Evolution: The Greatest Story Ever Told
Scientists, writers, and film producers have joined together for a multi-author book and Net film they hope will change the results of a recent poll. More than half of the world population still does not understand the theory of evolution and believes in some version of creationism. According to the producers, the World Net, the theory of cellular automata demonstrable with the digital medium, and the new DNA computers seem ideal for the purpose of showing that we came about as a result of bottom-

up (evolution) rather than top-down (creationism) processes.

News Flash! Chimpanzees Are Now Part of the Human Family

Based on genetic and anatomical evidence, the two species of African chimpanzees are now included in the genus *Homo*. Biologists and anthropologists claim this is long overdue. Both species are on the verge of extinction. The decision—although fully supported by scientific data—has elicited a great deal of controversy. The Council of Fundamentalist Christianity issued a statement opposing the decision soon after its announcement. "Now scientists want us to believe that we're just a bunch of homos, like the chimpanzees," said church leader Bob Thomson during a news conference this afternoon.

18.

SLEEPLESS IN LIMBO

It had now been the third night in a row that Mattie Tennyson, wife of the president, woke up and saw him lying on his back, his eyelids batting in the faint moonlight that peered through their window. Usually, after a few minutes, she would close her eyes and pretend to sleep, but tonight she decided to find out what was on his mind.

"What's the matter, honey bear?" she asked softly.

His eyes widened, he cleared his throat, and turned his head toward her. "You're awake?"

"Yes," she said, turning on her side, "but it's just because I noticed you weren't sleeping."

He smiled. "And you can tell even when you're asleep?" As he looked to the side, all he could see of his wife were strands of hair reflecting light and faint layers of shadows.

"I think it's from having babies. Part of your mind always stays alert to anything unusual. I think they call it the sleeping guard dog syndrome."

"So what is it I do when I don't sleep? I actually try to stay real still so that I don't wake you up." He resumed his position of staring at the ceiling.

"That's part of it, the unusual stillness, and you don't breathe

the same. Actually, I think that's what it is. I can barely hear you breathe. And sometimes you sigh, the air feels agitated, a number of things. So how come you can't sleep?" she asked, reaching out and placing a hand on his chest.

He put his hand on top of hers. "I just can't stop thinking about this whole *I AM* business."

"*I AM*? Still? Why does it bother you that much? It's really not hurting anyone."

"It's the unknown of it all, Mattie, the fact that we don't have a clue about what we're dealing with. All of our diagnostic tools can't nail this thing down. It's as if it spontaneously morphs itself out of the blue. Whatever it is has no specific identity pattern other than an apparent intent to express that it exists and to present a set of laws."

"So you're saying it's like hearing someone talk but when you look, you are unable to find a person."

"You nailed it on the button," he said.

"Why not just accept it for what it is?"

His face had taken on a concerned look. "Because I need logical answers."

She reached out with her leg and rested a foot against him. "So what's really bothering you is that it threatens our beliefs that science should be able to explain this kind of thing?"

"I don't know, Mattie. The way things stand right now, it seems like we have to consider other possibilities, like maybe it's a mouthpiece for something else, for another kind of intelligence. We're pretty sure it's not human and it doesn't appear to be a computer intelligence, unless the damn things have decided to be sneaky and somehow conceal signals from us. What it feels like to me is that we have built technology that has allowed something, I don't know what, to express itself. Imagine that for a second; we build the instrument and this intelligence that we knew nothing about finds its way to that instrument and uses it to let us know it exists."

She propped herself on an elbow and looked down at him. "If that were true, wouldn't that just be the most fantastic thing, ever?"

"Fantastic? This thing is making me a wreck. It's like it's committing crimes and we are helpless. The crimes of intrusion, of invasion of the human domain, of using our language to undermine our cultural foundations, our systems of belief. And if it's a type of crime that is being committed then you must ask the crucial questions. Who is it? What are its motives? What's next? How can we put an end to it? I know this sounds paranoid, but it feels like we're being threatened by an invisible enemy. I'm the president of the greatest nation in the world and I feel helpless and incompetent. I haven't slept in days, Mattie."

She smiled. "Just because this being doesn't abide by our rules of communication etiquette doesn't necessarily mean it wants to cause us harm. Look at it from the point of view of the good it's done. It's given people a certain hope. It's shifted our obsession with material things. It holds the promise of something more to this life than what meets the eye. These are all good things, sweetie."

"But what if we're wrong? How can we be sure that it is not committing some kind of crime against humanity that we are presently completely unconscious of? What if the alienists are right? Maybe we're being set up or we're being programmed, domesticated in some way. That's the problem, isn't it? How can we know for sure what the hell's going on?"

"And maybe the alienists are completely wrong, maybe everybody's wrong. You should try to be a little more stoic about it, a little more patient. Remember the old saying 'When in doubt, wait.'"

"That's what everyone keeps telling me, but what if we just sit and wait, and by the time we realize what's really going on, it ends up being too late? I, as president, will have been in some way responsible for that lack of foresight."

"Some things are outside of our control or our ability to predict. The only sure thing I know about this life is that we have each other. Everything else, even if it were God speaking to us, is secondary."

"You make it all seem so simple."

"Come here, honey bear, let me help you fall asleep." Mattie slipped off the straps of her gown and held him against her bare chest. He wrapped his arms around her and stared in the darkness.

■ ■ ■ ■ ■ ■

GAS.WNET RADIO: *The Gary and Andy Show*

GARY: This *I AM* thing is getting even more perplexing to me than women. The people in charge who we depend on to watch out for such things seem equally perplexed. So what do you think, Andy? Aliens trying to reach us? Because that's pretty much my thinking here.

ANDY: What the hell is going on, Gary? You woke up and the first thing that popped in your mind was the word *perplexing*.

GARY: Go ahead and make fun of me. I'm saying this thing is even more beyond comprehension than the minds of women.

ANDY: I don't know who the hell you go out with, but believe me women's minds are far from beyond comprehension. You just need to add the hormone modulation element. They even have a program for that. It translates what women say and do in terms men can understand.

GARY: This is a metaphor, Andy. I'm talking about the *I AM* thing, not women.

ANDY: You know so far, in spite of the brouhaha of the alienists, the big-eyed anorexic aliens of the anal-probed and otherwise penetrated abductees have yet to reach us.

GARY: What about the crop circles?

ANDY: Oh, please. Of all the ways to communicate with humankind.

GARY: Exactly. With the World Net they have found their instrument.

ANDY: And all they have to say is "*I AM*"?

GARY: What do you expect them to say, Andy? Show us your tushies? They're just making themselves known.

ANDY: You know, the puzzle to me is that blackout, so selective that no harm was caused, as if all the electric grids had been taken control of. They don't know if it's linked to this *I AM* thing, but I got word from a friend of a friend that's what they're thinking in Washington.

GARY: Exactly. Why? Because they're all somehow linked to computers.

ANDY: The question is, who has that much knowledge that they know what to turn on and off?

GARY: I see what you're saying. Whoever is behind this *I AM* thing could turn off our civilization. It has access to all information, everything linked to a computer.

ANDY: I didn't say that.

GARY: I'm fucking scared, Andy. This could be the apocalypse. We're being played with—seduced—until they decide to pull the plug.

ANDY: Gary, my man . . . now you're starting to worry me.

GARY: I think we need to live it up while we still have time.

ANDY: What are you talking about?

GARY: I don't know about you, but my plan is to go out every night to that club, Evening Delights. I want to live it up, man.

ANDY: Evening Delights? That's like the nexus of the perplexity of the elusive feminine mind. You could get hurt, my friend.

GARY: Don't you understand, Andy? Time is running out.

ANDY: And so is the time for our show. Tune in tomorrow for the continuing saga of ... what should we call it ... dancing on the verge of the apocalypse.

■ ■ ■ ■ ■ ■

Ars Savalia to Become Post-Feminine Human

Suicide artist Ars Savalia has undergone the first of the transformative procedures that she says will alter her into the post-feminine human. All her hair will be permanently removed and her skin dyed green. "I originally wanted blue but I didn't want people to think I was copying the Blue Man Group," she said. "Green has an ecomessage to it and the post-human will be green, with photosynthetic skin that will reduce our impact on the planet. The next stage is to have select tattoos applied, or maybe patches of Intelli-Skin," she added.

Her partner, ceramic artist Cindy Whipling, has issued a statement on the status of their relationship: "It's over. I can no longer stand by Arsie as she slowly becomes someone— something else. This is a classic case of irreconcilable differences. I mean, there has to be a limit to going green."

19.

SUSTAIN THE NOVELTY

mage, Image, Image. That was one of the conditions of her contract. No e-mails. No out-of-image behaviors, no embarrassing paparazzi shots, no bathing suit shots. The contract went on and on. The station owners had emphasized her to "sustain the mystery."

When on the job she wore a battery-operated thermal net to scramble any thermosensors. Records of the exposed areas of skin couldn't be prevented, but what more could thermosensors reveal that wasn't already visible? A generic electric car with a screen to disguise whoever was sitting in the backseat brought her to the gated back entrance to her work and out. After work she put on a dark wig and sunglasses and changed into a pantsuit to hide her legs. A security guard escorted her to the door of her apartment that was rented under the name of a friend. Between the car and the entrance to her building she carried a special umbrella that blocked exposure of her face. Once at her apartment building, doormen—actually former Secret Service agents who understood perfectly the four words *you will be ruined*—assured complete privacy and confidentiality.

The "sustain the mystery" conditions created considerable constraints to her social life. "Two years max," the station managers had said. After that, a new bimbo reporter would have to be found. "Sustain the novelty" was their other motto. After two years, Karen Richardson would invariably become old news and be dumped and recycled. She could later rake in the bucks by revealing more of herself in magazines, product promotions, and as a regular reporter.

Wednesday night, Karen put on her new outfit, slipped on a silk robe, and had a glass of white wine. She looked at the array of pills on her dresser arranged by category of effect: picker-uppers, sleeping, tranqs, sex, brain activators. After taking a few seconds to assess her state of mind, she decided she actually felt pretty good and didn't need anything. She turned her sixty-two-inch screen to *Out of This World*, the round-the-clock news channel that featured the bizarre events of the week. There was no shortage for that type of information. People were becoming nuttier by the day.

"Idaho woman decides she wants to be the reincarnation of a potato. Her sole diet is potatoes and milk. She is employed as a representative for the Association of Potato Farmers."

"I wonder if she ever wears a disguise and sneaks in a hamburger," Karen Richardson asked herself. "Doesn't look too bad for a reincarnated potato."

There was a big smile on the woman's face. "For dessert, I just slice them up, coat them with melted butter, sprinkle them with a little sugar and cinnamon, and bake them in the oven . . ."

She looked at the time. John's wife should have left for her meeting. With some luck they'd have a couple of hours to themselves. An icon blinked at the corner of the screen.

"Connect," she said, and John Mack, the station manager, appeared sitting at his desk in front of his Cybermaster.

"Hey sweetie, crazy day today, wasn't it?"

"It seems like they're getting crazier every day. Our host sure picked a good one today. That Ars Savalia chick was quite the weirdo. Raked up the ratings though."

"I mean, how can someone dyed all green think they're sexy?"

"Well she's not calling herself a sex artist. As a suicide artist, self-sacrifice is her medium."

"You believe that?"

"No. I think she's pretty screwed up. She just found a way to commercialize her natural tendency for self-mutilation. It's just a variant of the tattoo addicts who say they might as well be as fucked up on the outside as they are on the inside. I could have researched her past to bring up the point but decided not to. I thought it would pollute my mind somehow. I didn't need that."

"Did you hear about that Blue Lobster gourmet cult in Japan?"

"The people who have tasted it talk like they had just taken a sacrament. I think it makes them high as a kite."

"I'm not sure *high* is the right term. They look as if they had been reborn to sensation in the Plain. Little ordinary moments, ordinary things, suddenly become sources of ecstasy for them. Very peculiar stuff."

"What are you hinting at? You want me to go?"

"It's possible. They're very secretive about it. If anybody can get through, you'd be the one. We'll see what kind of ranking our host gives it. The story is gathering some momentum. They also have that new crucifixion package at the New Jerusalem cybercity. Not sure which one will rank first."

"You can send someone else to interview the New Jerusalem people. Sorry but I'm not testing any crucifixion program. Feeling what Jesus felt is not my bag. Doesn't fit with my image. The bimbo reporter doesn't mess with religion."

"I think you'd look pretty hot hanging up there in a loincloth."

"Now you're sounding perverse. Station rules wouldn't allow it anyway. You know . . . the bit in my contract about limiting exposure of flesh to thirty-five percent."

"OK. Enough business talk for now. You said you had a surprise for me. A pre-birthday gift. Something about breaking contractual rules?"

"Put on your goggles and turn on the Cybris," she said, "but first you have to tell me what you think of the package." She ran her hands down the front of her body.

"I love the package," he said. "The package is my dream come true." He wasn't lying, either. Under the public façade, everything about Karen Richardson was real.

"OK, you passed the first test. I want to see response monitors on. Gotta know if you really appreciate what I have to give you."

"They're on," he said. Pulsing colored lines appeared at the corner of her screen.

She slowly opened the front of her robe.

"Oh my," he said. The response lines were pulsing out of control. "Oh my, my, my . . ."

For a second the blue line brought the image of a blue lobster to her mind. *Umm, I'm kind of curious.* John took off his shirt. Bare-chested, he showed scars from an explosion back when he had been in the military. For some strange reason they turned her on. *I must like warriors.*

She let the front of her robe drop.

"And now for the back," she said as she turned around and propped on her knees.

"God, what I'd give to fuck you right now!" he shouted.

"How about a little close-up," she said, and zoomed the camera in until the small monitor on her bed frame highlighted another one of her many perfect natural features.

A beep suddenly came on. A door-open alert.

"Shit! Looks like the wife may be back. Later." And the screen went back to the news program.

She switched to her list of other Cybris partners but none she cared to be with was available. She ran her hands along the inside of her thighs . . . *Japan could be a good idea . . . maybe an opportunity for an in-the-flesh encounter . . . I wonder if Sunshine Borden . . .*

■ ■ ■ ■ ■ ■

Secretive Blue Lobster Cult Going Viral in Japan

A secret species of freshwater lobster—some say bioengineered—is said to metabolize nutrients in a way that gives its flesh a drug-like quality. Only a select few have access to this rare delicacy offered in expensive and very selective private clubs in Tokyo. The few who have talked about it say that they had finally tasted the nature of existence, whatever that means.

Australian Government Claims Ownership of Blue Lobster

Australia is threatening to sue Japan over allegations of bioengineering their blue lobster. Japanese authorities have responded by saying, "A secret diet that infuses the flesh is the source of Japanese Blue Lobster's specialness. No bioengineering is involved. Even if it were, Australia has no right to prevent other countries from bioengineering the species."

20.

THE INCOMPREHENSION HORIZON

As it turned out, *Razor's Edge* talk radio was having an online interview with Sunshine Borden at 1:00 a.m. Rama clicked on the program hoping that possibly Sunshine Borden would answer questions about the CyberBardos. She tapped on the video version showing Borden, probably in front of a screen with digi-cam. As usual, Borden was cybermediated, showing a half-man, half-machine being, which, according to Borden, is a character in an upcoming cyberreality program, *Cyborgia*.

The guy was so bizarre she wondered if he was still even remotely human. A tabloid had stated that he averaged three cyber-implants a year. He probably looked like a freak.

WZIP *Razor's Edge* radio "Interview with Sunshine Borden"
I'll get right to the point. As you know, several critics have accused you of addicting people to spending extended periods of time in digital fantasy worlds.

That's what I hear . . .

They say it threatens the future of society . . .

Any technology that's radically new threatens the state of society. It happened with language, the horse, the ox-drawn plow, the printing press, the microscope, the automobile, and now the World Net and the World Host. It's nothing new, and there will always be initial resistance to radical change. The traditionalists will always resist the forward momentum of progress.

Several researchers have expressed their concern about how cyberrealities reinforce an irrational view of the world, citing specifically your Maelstrom and CyberBardos programs.

Are you sure you really want to get into this area of discussion?

That's what we do here at Razor's Edge *radio. We don't avoid hard issues.*

[Sunshine laughs.] Well to start with, some of these issues have been addressed by the transcendentalist/attractor philosophers. We are going through what has been called a transition phase in evolution, the protocyborgian stage. The consensus notion of what we call reality is changing.

How can reality change? It's simply the outside world, isn't it?

I think that neurobiology has shown that what we experience as reality is a neurological construct which evolves as an adaptive process and which can be both species and individually specific. To get to the point, language brought forth a completely new kind of reality to our apelike ancestors, which some call, using the narrowest of definitions, mind. Cybertechnology is bringing forth another type of reality that has been called cyberspace, which we are still in the early stages of developing and of adapting to. Given time, that reality may be an operational reality where we spend most of our time, where we conduct business and have relationships and travel and develop a body of knowledge and creativity. We are not yet fully wired for that reality but we are on our way.

Could you elaborate a little on the attractor model you often advocate?

That's a little more esoteric. It basically states that we are both driven and drawn by an original primal state, a fundamental universal identity, a type of Overmind. It is a fundamental consciousness that is integral to our being that directs us and attracts us at the same time, a lot like some elemental identity drives the development of a child to become an adult. That fundamental identity is our true nature and it is also a future that we are invariably drawn to and that draws us. Just what this future is, is not something we can predict.

On one hand, this fundamental identity is something we are. On the other hand, it is something we are to become. Again think of it as the relationship of a baby to an adult. A baby is wired to become an adult but doesn't realize it. I think that currently, because of the promise of cybertechnology, we are entering a stage of ontological anticipation, a clarification of meaning and purpose, possibly catalyzed by the *I AM* phenomenon.

So it's really a transcendentalist philosophy?

Yes and no. It could be argued that there is nothing to transcend. As an example, the nature of a tadpole is to be a frog—but it doesn't know it. The frog state propels it and attracts it. We're like tadpoles on the way to becoming a frog. We just don't know it and, from where we currently stand, can't conceive of the next stage in our evolutionary development, and even less, of the final stages of cosmic ontogeny.

But a tadpole is genetically wired for becoming a frog.

I was making an analogy, but if you want to pursue that line, you could say that the universe is wired, that it has a kind of cosmic genetics for becoming this higher-end state. You can look at evolution as a kind of water flow through a landscape. Given an opportunity, it moves forward, even if it is not in a linear manner, even if it is rerouted or temporarily reversed. As I've emphasized before, the evolutionary process is not steady and not linear. Being human, which I'm comparing to a tadpole stage, we just don't yet have access to the knowledge of our future condition, although many feel that as a result of a symbiosis with computers we're entering a metamorphosis stage, which some call protocyborgian. There is no doubt in my mind that any new stage in our evolution would involve fusion with cybertechnological entities.

So these philosophies are in part how you justify the value of cyberrealities?

From my point of view, we are drawn to cyberrealities, to virtual realities, because they contain attractor components to the evolutionary momentum. This is where evolution seems to be headed. A feature of cyberrealities is that they are more purely mental and interpretative, and less physical. They hint at the possibility of disembodiment, of pure forms. Ask yourself, why is it that in recent years we have been increasingly attracted in the direction of cyberrealities rather than say in producing more and more material objects? It's because it's not what ultimately attracts us, not what the cosmic genetics have wired us for.

Is what someone experiences in cyberreality real?

Well, to start with, the experience is real because it is something that you have. It's real enough for you at the time you experience it. You and others can observe it, so it's subject to empirical validation. A well-designed cyberreality also has consistency. You can return to it and it will have maintained its characteristics or have evolved, depending on its programming. In the case of evolving cyberreality programs, others can validate their realness. They can access the same cyberreality and verify that it indeed exists and unfolds in time in this parallel domain. Now some people want to differentiate between cyberreal and physically real, which is fine. They are simply two domains of reality-experience with their own values.

Yes, but all you'd have to do is pull the plug and you'd realize cyberrealities were just an electronic creation.

Not much different than human experience, wouldn't you agree? Pull the plug and bye-bye, your neurons stop generating this domain we call reality.

So does the World Host—does the computer—become a higher form of being than us?

I think we have a kind of synthetic or symbiotic relation with the computer. The computer is becoming increasingly our interface with the factual databased truths about the world. Its ability to crunch large amounts of complex data is higher than ours. The goal is to eventually have computers possibly interfaced with biological material such that one day we can present these hybrid unities with a simple problem. We confront them with a person and we tell them, "Replicate this," not physically, but cognitively, including the experience we call consciousness. If we ever succeed in doing this, then we can proceed with a download from a physical identity into a cyberentity freed from many of the laws of physics and biology. We can say, "Scotty, this place is getting a little boring. Download me, download all of it. I want to get off."

[Sunshine is cracking up. His cyber-intermediated image starts flashing lights and colors, the rate increasing until he disappears from the screen. His laugh lingers a few seconds before fading out.]

Well, I guess Mr. Borden's time was up. Thank you, Sunshine Borden, for appearing on our show. As always, this was quite an enlightening conversation. Lots of food for thought.

And that was the end of the interview. He hadn't said anything about the CyberBardos. As usual, Sunshine did not answer questions from the audience and he was well-known for having some of the strictest filters of anyone. Rama started to plan out a way to get through his filters and get his attention.

■ ■ ■ ■ ■ ■

Auto-evolving CR Programs Now Too Complex to Be Controlled
According to MIT professor Reza Harridan, self-evolving reality programs such as Borden's Forgotten Forest and the CyberBardos are acquiring an autonomy that is no longer under our control unless we pull the plug. In spite of all security measures, there is always the possibility that entities in these programs may evolve the ability to leak into the World Net system. Besides evolving realities, individual entities allowed autonomy in self-programming, called APUs (autopoietic programming unities), could eventually find their way in circumventing software programs to keep them contained. He recommends programming fences with warning signals when such unities may attempt escape.

21.

BLACKOUT

John Tennyson could feel his stomach knotting up as he sat there watching the news on the big screen while they waited for Loveridge to arrive. A retired military expert who had been an advisor to Jack Dawson, his predecessor, was giving his opinion on the global risks and potential threats suggested by the blackout incident. Before that, Rick Nelson of the CFC (Council of Fundamentalist Christianity) had been interviewed and had reiterated the organization's apocalyptic take on the phenomenon based on Revelation.

The *I AM* situation had finally gone nuclear and it had all been triggered in the blink of an eye by a relatively insignificant miniblackout, an elusive Zen kind of thing. Now here, now gone, now everywhere. *I AM* had become a memetic epidemic, mutating and spreading through civilization at lightning speed, thanks to social media, news commentators, panels of experts, and interviews with pseudo-authorities and fringe religious zealots, like that Reverend Thomson.

The one-second blackout, depending on the authority consulted, was now either the prelude to the Second Coming, the end of the world, Satan's rule, the arrival of aliens, global cyberterrorism by an intelligent World Net, or an attack on civilization by a bunch of fanatic cyberguerrillas.

His security screen flashed with the message: *Loveridge,*

minus one minute. He punched the admit button and seconds later Secret Service agents opened the door.

"I apologize, everyone," Loveridge said as he rushed in. "I got stuck in the commotion out there," referring to the media trucks, reporters, and crowds surrounding the White House. He made his way to his seat, opened his briefcase, and set up his communicator.

The president reached in his pocket, popped a couple of antacids, took a sip of water, and started the meeting.

"Gentlemen, I think we all know why we're here. As you can see," pointing to the monitor screen, "the *I AM* situation seems to be escalating." He switched the news off. "Arthur, let's start with your report. You coordinated the cooperation of our allies in sending the last message. Can you give us an account of what happened?"

The director of the CIA raised his head from his screen and mumbled, "Give me a minute," as he tapped the keys on his communicator and quick-read his team's latest status report. Looking up between messages, he gave the president a summary of the events.

"Mr. President, I don't have much more information than what has already been released by the media. At three a.m. this morning we coordinated sending a message that read 'Show us who you are, *I AM Aaa ome*.' Almost instantly, actually exactly nine-tenths of a second later, a blackout occurred that turned off all devices connected in any way to the World Net and various satellite and tower-linked communication systems, including phones and power plants. This was followed by the *I AM* announcement.

"As of five minutes ago, we have received no reports of any loss of data and, to the best of our knowledge, all systems returned to their normal operations. Whether there was any loss of data in business systems or individual PCs is something we haven't yet been able to assess, but none has been reported as of . . ." he punched some additional keys, " . . . two minutes ago. Because of the timing and the signature, I think we can safely assume the incident wasn't the result of any odd phenomena such as sun flares, but a response directly correlated with the sending of our message. That's all the information I have for now. And yes, the one-second blackout was global."

John Tennyson frowned. There was something about the timing of the blackout that seemed peculiar, something that apparently hadn't yet leaked to the media.

"Arthur, you said the blackout occurred not for one second—like the news reports have stated—but for nine-tenths of a second. To what degree of precision?" The members of the committee were now focused on Loveridge.

He ran his hand through his hair and punched a few more keys. "At least down to the millisecond. We didn't bother checking beyond that."

"Ummm . . . is there any chance that this could mean something?"

Loveridge made a grimace followed by a loud puff-cheeked exhale before answering.

"Actually, that's an interesting question, Mr. President. The duration of the blackout had such a high degree of precision that our statistical host tells us the chances of it being a random coincidence are virtually zip. It was *exactly* nine-tenths of a second. That would indicate that the precise duration was probably intentional. So, in answer to your question, yes, the duration may have some kind of meaning associated with it. It's even possible that in previous communications, the timing of the messages and the spaces between segments of the message could have been of significance. There's a remote chance this *I AM* is communicating at more than one layer, a verbal one and a mathematical one. We're planning on analyzing any future communications from that point of view. Of course, that's assuming we can get any of our instruments to work."

"What you're basically saying is that the communications may be three-dimensional, in a sense," Tennyson said.

"That would be one way to put it, Mr. President. It's certainly a possibility we have to investigate."

John Tennyson closed his eyes as he processed the possible implications of a precise, down-to-atomic-clock measurement, nine-tenths-of-a-second blackout. When he opened his eyes he was confronted by a half dozen blinking lights. Almost everyone present wanted to speak. He decided to ignore them, punched out the board, and addressed the members of the committee.

"Now, what is of concern to me at this moment, gentlemen, is whether this blackout could in any way be construed as a threat, like some of these idiots on the news have been saying. It should be obvious to everyone here that any entity that can cause a global blackout could in effect shut down the technological fabric of our planet, including most government and military communications and operations." He turned to the secretary of defense. "So my question is, should we be concerned about the possibility of a threat and what can we do to prevent it? General Carson, what can you tell us about this?"

Carson, as usual, cleared his throat before speaking. "Mr. President, what we have here is the indication of a potential for threat, not an actual threat. There's a big difference. It's what we call a hammer. A hammer can be a tool or a weapon, but it's also just a hammer. To date we have no sign that this *I AM* is using our communications systems as a weapon. In terms of the public, we should simply stick to the facts and call what happened 'an event,' apparently correlated to this *I AM* phenomenon. My recommendation would be that we try to diminish the significance of this blackout, to make it less rather than more."

He turned his gaze toward Catherine Harris. "I'd think this would be a task for your media advisor and your speechwriter."

Four lights came on: Harris, Randall, Collins, and Secretary of State Colin Blackwell. He chose the least predictable response. "Dr. Collins?"

The heads all turned toward Collins who, as usual, was the only person not wearing a tie, with his ponytail stretching halfway down the back of his chair.

"Mr. President, there are several possible explanations for the blackout. The simplest is that this was the only way this *I*

AM entity could express an answer to our question. We asked it a question, to show itself to us. It answered. Possibly it has limitations as to how and what it can communicate. The turning on and off of power could be its way of saying, 'This is what I am. My nature is electronic or electric.' Further communications may be able to clarify this. I think that if the intention of this *I AM* was to make a threat, it would have caused a much lengthier and obvious blackout than a one-second, barely noticeable event. You could almost say that the brevity of the blackout indicates a concern about its possible effects.

"Seen from that point of view, I'd say that the very opposite of a threat was suggested by this miniblackout. The *I AM* entity attempted to answer in a way that would cause no significant disruption to our way of life. So I agree with General Carson that we should not, in any way or form, suggest the blackout should be construed as a threat because, honestly, the evidence of a threat is simply not there."

John Tennyson smiled. Collins had just handed him an argument to counter the media experts ranting about an imminent threat to civilization, but it still didn't eliminate what he saw as the crux of the problem.

"This all makes logical sense, Dr. Collins, but most people aren't as rational as scientists. Just look at the news reports. We've got hundreds of experts worldwide giving their opinion on the meaning of this blackout as we speak. No matter how benign this *I AM* entity may be, the question is, can we as a civilization allow something with this much power to exist?"

Collins was about to respond but the president stopped him midsentence with the wave of a hand. "Secretary Blackwell, I know you've been in touch with our allies. What are they saying about the blackout?"

"Honestly, they're all concerned, Mr. President," said the secretary of state. "Concerned, as you have just brought up, that this blackout could be a sign of something worse to come, and that to ignore the possible implications could have dire consequences. History has shown us that ignoring the early signs of a potential threat invariably has had disastrous results. Every war, every form of genocide, every act of terrorism was always preceded by warning signs that were ignored or repressed. It reminds me of the saying in that classic movie, *Ronin*, where the protagonist says, 'If there is any doubt, there is no doubt.' I would recommend that we at least find ways to isolate and shield a defensive electrical and communications system completely independent from the World Net and protected from interference by external signals. Our allies agree that this would be the minimum defense required, in case this *I AM* turned out unfriendly."

"Now that's the first practical suggestion I've heard since this whole thing started. Let's put this shield idea at the top of this afternoon's agenda." The president next turned to the director of the FBI.

"I'm right in line with Mr. Blackwell, Mr. President," said Walter Randall. "I have suggested ever since the first message that this *I AM* could present a threat." About half of those in attendance nodded.

"So how would you recommend we proceed?"

"Well, considering the only outlet we have at the present time is at the level of communications, we could send it a message and in no uncertain terms ask it to leave. We could let it know that it is not welcome on our planet. If it knows it is unwanted, it might just end up leaving us alone."

A loud and annoyed sigh came from the left side of the table. "There's only one problem with that," interrupted Collins, who hadn't bothered to punch the request light.

"Dr. Collins, is something wrong with your panel?" the president interjected.

Collins looked surprised. "My panel?"

"Your light's not on."

"My light? Sorry, I got carried away." He pressed the button and smirked.

"So what were you going to say, Dr. Collins?"

"The idea of sending a message to ask the *I AM* entity to leave is absurd. How would you ever know if it has actually left?

What if it simply decided to keep quiet? And if you're going to look at this from a paranoid point of view—which I think some of you are doing right now, particularly Director Randall—what if instead of it leaving, you managed to insult it, or worse, piss it off?" Both Randall's and Loveridge's lights switched on.

"Dr. Loveridge, do you agree with Dr. Collins?"

Loveridge looked annoyed. "Mr. President, everyone here seems to be forgetting something. We can talk until we're blue in the face about this latest message presenting a threat but the fact is, as of right now, there isn't a thing we can do about it. The idea of shielded systems is interesting but we have no idea whether this is even feasible. Obviously we should try to run a few simple tests to see if that's even an option.

"As far as requesting that this *IAM* leave us alone, imagine a child asking the nasty monster, 'Please leave, Mr. Monster, pretty please.' That's about the level we're talking about here. So let's be adult about this and act rationally. All the evidence shows that we are dealing with some form of higher intelligence, one that could—if it wanted to—shut down all electrical power. The fact is that, to date, it has made no obvious threat. Let's not appear any less evolved than we are and insult its intelligence."

"So what you're saying, Arthur, is that we should just sit and wait and hope that whatever it is wishes us no harm?"

"Mr. President, I'm saying that right now, I don't think there is anyone who has the knowledge or the ability to stop whatever this is from doing what it wants to do. We don't know what it is, we don't know where it is, and we don't know how it does what it does. As to what can be done, the idea of a shielded communication system suggested by Mr. Blackwell is certainly worth pursuing."

The president then turned to the head of the FBI, who had punched off his request light. "Mr. Randall, do you have anything else to add?"

"Considering the response to my recommendation, not at the moment, sir. Telling it that we are not interested in further communications seemed to me about the only thing we could do, but obviously Dr. Collins and others have a better idea."

The president decided to ignore the last comment and moved to a more pressing issue.

"So what do we tell the press this evening, gentlemen?" the president asked.

■ ■ ■ ■ ■ ■

Global Blackout Possibly Tied to *I AM*

You may have barely noticed it, but a global World Net data eclipse caused a roughly one-second blackout. It did not interfere with any World Net operations and was unnoticed by most users, who assumed it was a local event. The possibility of it being caused by a powerful solar flare has been discredited by scientists. An anonymous government source has revealed that the blackout followed a government-sponsored request to the *I AM* phenomenon to show itself. The government has responded that there was no clear cause and effect tying the blackout to its investigation of the *I AM* events.

22.

GODDESS WAYS

On the other side of town, the Sisterhood was having its own meeting.

"The reason we know it's not the Goddess is first that *Aaa ome* is said in a tone so deep it could not have come from a female deity, unless—excuse me for using the term, sisters—she was a complete butch with adrenal glands pumping out megadoses of testosterone. And honestly, I very much doubt that the Goddess is a divine butch." This sent the audience roaring.

"Second, you tell me of a woman that would say something like 'I AM the M Pattern of Unfolding Order.' Give me a break. If that doesn't sound like the words a man would use, I don't know what is. Power and order sure sounds like a man's trip to me. Let me tell you what I think this *I AM* thing really is. It's a trick by one of those right-wing conservative religious groups. Now, instead of having the big penis in the sky they want us to believe in the existence of a big penis in the World Net." More laughter.

"What I say is that it's time for women to disconnect from the World Net, move underground, and work together to establish our own closed cybernetwork. Instead of cyberrituals and ceremonies, I think it's time we go back to the old ways, the

Goddess ways. *Real* ceremonies with *real* people. You know what I got to say to *I AM*? Panties down!"

Patricia Holden ended her speech by pulling down her skirt to show the top of her bush, dyed a bright blue. The women whistled and clapped. Pubic hair was now the ultrafeminist symbol of the return to the Goddess, a time when women didn't try to look like prepubescent girls to satisfy the perverse fantasies of men. Real women had bush.

Among the small crowd, Patrick Nymphaea—dressed in drag—was raising his fist and whooping it up.

"Yeah sisters!" he yelled in a high-pitched voice. "Old ways, Goddess ways!" he parroted. Deep inside he was chuckling away. This sister meeting was a hoot. While his friend Sunshine had chosen to increasingly divorce himself from the real world, the great lesson Patrick had learned was that the joys of a fast-changing world were on the outside.

When it came to free time, he spent as much as possible out in the fleshed world, the tangible world, with unpredictable sights and sounds and smells, and the great diversity and nuances of the human mind. He found great pleasure in engaging in conversation with a variety of people, from bag ladies to college students, from the elderly to the young children he interviewed as a child psychologist. In fact, he was addicted to the rush of entering totally different subcultures of mind. His favorite pastime, his hobby really, was to disguise himself and participate at the meetings of the various subgroups in the city: blacks, Jews, Latinos, Chinese, women's groups, and gay rallies. He was fluent in three languages and quickly learned to mimic street dialects. His greatest challenge had been gender disguise, not only because it was the most difficult, but also because it never quite felt natural. Once in character though, it certainly was the most fun role and the one that provided him with the greatest insights.

It was part of his work really, but not officially, this exploration of how culture shaped the development of consciousness. It had taken him months and the help of friends in the movie industry to develop a dress and makeup formula that would conceal his masculine features and enhance his feminine ones. The most difficult part was to speak with a feminine voice. He had spent hundreds of hours practicing to maintain a high tone, get the right modulations, and, above all, not to slip into his natural voice.

"Panties down!" he shouted.

"You really into this?" a voice said next to him, and he turned and looked down at two intense green eyes peering from beneath the bill of a red baseball cap.

"Hey, I think this whole Goddess thing is fascinating," he said.

"So you're thinking of becoming a member?"

"Would you recommend it?"

She ignored the question. "Is this your first meeting?" she asked. "I think I would have noticed you if you had come before."

"It's my first one," he said.

"You'd be kind of hard to miss, tall as you are. Busty, too," she said, looking at his chest. "Those things real?"

"As real as can be," he answered, thinking, *High-quality latex, D-cups, natural hang, medium nipple.*

"You're a lucky girl."

"You still didn't answer my question."

"What was that?"

"Do you think I should join the Sisterhood?"

"If you're a hard-core feminist, gay, or bi and like to masturbate a lot, you might want to give it a go. But you know in your case, I can tell you're just putting me on." She kept her eyes focused on his face, and it was making him nervous.

"What do you mean?"

"You just seem too smart to get caught up in all this Goddess baloney." She stared at him, squinting her eyes and scrunching her lips as she gathered her thoughts. "You're really more like a kind of voyeur."

"A voyeur?" he repeated, raising his eyebrows as if perplexed by the expression.

"A Peeping Tom or a Peeping Alice, if you want to be gender correct." She held her stare. "And you know very well what voyeur means."

Another woman, muscular, with short hair and metal and plastic wire running through her ears and eyebrows, came up to them, looked him up and down, and asked, "Hey Jessie, you coming to the party?"

She just gave her a quick glance and said, "Tell Patricia I'll be over in a little bit," then turned her attention back to him.

"I haven't had lunch," he said. "How about joining me for a bite to eat?"

He couldn't have found a better person to give him insights into this Sisterhood business. Talk about luck, he had managed to connect with the high priestess's very own live-in lover. Except that Jessie wasn't any hard-core feminist whose adrenals pumped too much testosterone. As it turned out, she too was a curious visitor to the Sisterhood planet who had simply decided to mingle with the locals.

"When I first got to New York—and I'm not even sure what it was I was looking for—I landed at Grand Central Station with eleven hundred dollars in my pocket and a backpack. A woman had this sign on a staff that had the female symbol on top of it. It said, 'Need help? Come to us. We're the Sisterhood.' For whatever reason it was the cross part of the female symbol I focused on. At first I thought she was some kind of nun and the sisterhood was a Christian organization that helped women. She had short hair and was dressed in men's work clothes. It all seemed like the prim and proper outfit you'd expect working nuns to wear. So I went over to ask for some advice on where I should go first."

"And you ended up here?"

"Not right away. I ended up staying at the apartment of one of the sisters. Then she invited me to a couple of rituals. It all seemed so totally bizarre that I ended up getting caught up in it. You know what I mean?"

"Like the little kid who bends down to look at the bottom

of a pool. He's so fascinated that he ends up falling in."

"That's about right."

"So how did you end up with the high priestess?"

"You know, I still can't figure that one out. I went to a party after one of the meetings, and she came up to me and we started talking. Later she invited me over to her place."

"And?"

"And I ended up in the dungeon of the lesbo queen. I'm pulling your leg," she said, touching his arm. "Patricia has this great two-story townhouse. When she offered me to stay with her, I figured why not. I think we both knew this was going to be a relationship of convenience, what they call a TT relationship, tit for twat in Sisterhood lingo. It's a temporary arrangement until I can afford a decent place of my own. Hey, are you a shrink?"

"You almost got it, I'm a research psychologist. How did you guess?"

"You know, most people, given half a chance, can't wait to talk about themselves, but all you've done is ask questions, as if you're actually more interested in what other people have to say. It's almost a sure giveaway shrink strategy."

Patrick listened as she went on about her take on the world with the insouciance of a happy four-year-old. She was originally from Virginia. Her father had been a kind man and a good husband but was too busy as an emergency cybertechnician to spend much time at home. She had been raised mostly by her mother and her brothers and sisters. She had a couple of male cyberpartners with whom she sneaked communications at the cybercafés now available throughout the city. She also got a thrill out of having cybersex with them in the VR chambers of the underground clubs. To his surprise, he found her fascinating and felt a common ground in her open-mindedness to the human experience.

"All I can tell you is that this whole Sisterhood thing's been like the twilight zone. I'm not sure how long I'll stay because it's beginning to have a déjà vu, all-over-again kind of feeling. Same old stuff, different day, you know what I mean?"

He nodded. "Doesn't everything start feeling that way?"

"Hey, if you really want to see something different you should come to one of the rituals. The only condition is that when you enter the temple, you only wear a long white skirt and nothing else, no underwear."

"It seems interesting," Patrick said, thinking there was no way he'd be able to pull that one off.

"Interesting? Now that sure would be an understatement. As a psychologist you'll probably think you just hit the jackpot. Imagine the greatest concentration of female neurosis you've ever seen in your entire life, completely unrepressed, unleashed. It's actually kind of sad and depressing, because the real reason behind all this Goddess stuff is pretty simple. Many women feel lonely and alone, and because they can't turn to daddy, they're going to their mommy. How's that for pop psychology?"

Looking at her, Patrick readily saw what had drawn the high priestess to Jessie. It was a childlike innocence and freedom of mind. It was a sanity and freshness. It was lively green eyes so natural in their beauty that they required no makeup. It was little-girl thinness with flared hips and white skin. It was long hands and thin fingers so expressive in their movements that they seemed as if they painted the air with feelings. And if there was one thing that Patrick had learned as a human chameleon blending in the cultural kaleidoscope, it was that hands probably more than anything else revealed the depths of a person's character. Were they large or small, long or short? Were the fingers thick or thin, the fingertips narrow or broad, the nails trimmed and neat or ragged, the cuticles picked, the nails chewed?

And just as important as what the hands showed were the movements performed by them. The jitteriness, the picking, the tapping, the bringing together of fingers, the sweeps, the rate and range of finger extension, the turning of the palm, the bends of the wrist. Those early psychologists who had focused so much on phrenology, the study of the bumps on people's heads to reveal their character, had missed the point; they should have focused on the hands. The old practitioners of palmistry had gotten it right, although it had never been the lines and whorls on the palm that had been the true giveaways of a person's life and allowed speculation on their future. It had been all the other information revealed by hands, and the great art was to develop the ability to interpret those signs.

And strangely enough, it was Jessie's hands that had hypnotized him with their gestures and, he realized later on, had hooked him. The promise held in those hands was so enticing that he could not let go of the impulse to know Jessie better. He had to know someone with hands like that.

Patrick ended their conversation by admitting to Jessie, "Honestly I'm not at all into this Sisterhood thing. I just came because I thought it might be different enough to give me a new take on the lesbian movement. To tell you the truth, the most interesting thing about this meeting was the opportunity to meet you."

Jessie looked at her watch and got up. "I gotta go. Thanks for the lunch. How about we get together again sometime, even if it's only through the Net?"

"Let's plan on it," Patrick said.

■ ■ ■ ■ ■ ■

John Tennyson and his wife were both sitting up in bed, their backs propped against a stack of pillows as the eleven o'clock news came on the screen. They watched the segments of his news conference followed by the media circus with its panels of clowns. He turned the television off.

Mattie turned to face him. "You never told me, John. Did you really find a possible source for *I AM?*"

The president sighed. "No, Mattie, we just thought that saying that would keep things from getting too out of control."

His wife persisted. "Honestly, John, have you found out anything at all?"

He reached behind him, grabbed a pillow, and threw it at

the foot of the bed then lay on his side and propped himself up on an elbow to face her. His head was now about at the level of her breasts. He looked up at her.

"Mattie, all we have to date are the messages and their contents. This gives us a kind of profile of this *I AM*. But do we have anything of substance? No, we don't.

"As to what it is, I think we can say with some assurance that it is some kind of higher intelligence. According to Arthur, there's a chance it may be communicating at both a verbal and mathematical level simultaneously, which if true, would tell us something."

"So why did you say you were well on the way to knowing its identity?" she asked.

"It's not a complete lie, Mattie. The bit about mathematical communication may be a step forward. Actually, if you want to know the truth, our thought was that if we put out the news announcement about being on the verge of a breakthrough, then maybe this thing would react. Maybe it would wonder whether we really had found out something and respond in a way that would give us a better idea of what it is. It's worth a shot."

"Why not just wait and see what happens? It's not hurting anyone."

"Mattie, we have no idea what we're dealing with here. It managed to shut down electricity globally, for God's sake. The worst is that ever since this thing started, we've been looking like we have no control of the situation. It's making me look incompetent when faced with a crisis."

"You should look at the bright side of it, John. It's making everybody look bad. You should have listened to *The Bardo Show* today. He went after all those religious nuts with both barrels. The callers were going ballistic."

John Tennyson turned to his wife, looking surprised. "Are you serious? You actually listen to that guy? The FBI tells me he's a drug user and drug advocate, some kind of a radical technohippie with a PhD."

"Did you know he was part of the team that initially developed the World Host? He just has a different way of looking at things."

"He was a member of the Collins team?"

"That's right, he was one of the World Host designers. I guess he dropped out of the project."

"So what does he think this *I AM* is?"

She smiled as she answered, "It's pretty simple. He says our future just dropped in to say hi."

"Our future . . . great . . . just what every president needs. Anyhow, it's getting late, we should go to sleep." He gave Mattie a quick kiss on the forehead and turned off his light. He lay on his back as his wife tossed pillows then assumed her side sleeping position, her head facing him.

"Lights off," she said softly and rested an arm across his chest. "John?"

"Yes, sweetheart?"

"I love you."

"I know, sweetie. I love you, too." He stared at the ceiling. His stomach was still a wreck. He dreaded waking up and going to his office in the morning. Face the future.

■ ■ ■ ■ ■ ■

US Well on the Way to Identifying Source of *I AM* Messages
At a press conference today, President John Tennyson, accompanied by Secretary of State Blackwell and media advisor Catherine Harris, announced that significant progress is being made toward determining the identity of the *I AM* phenomenon. The one-second blackout, according to the president, has been carefully analyzed and its timing and brevity, contrary to the opinions of media experts, clearly indicate that *I AM* considered our welfare when it responded to our request to "Show us who you are."

The president emphasized that in no way was the blackout intended to suggest a threat. He also said that a possible signal source had been identified and that several experts were currently working on pinpointing its location. When asked if this was an artificial intelligence event, the president replied, "Saying *'I AM Aaa ome'* and turning electricity on and off doesn't really qualify as intelligence." The president added, "But this *I AM* could in fact turn out to be a type of consciousness."

When asked if the *I AM* phenomenon presented any danger, the president answered, "None at all, and if it ever got out of hand, all we'd have to do is turn off the World Net." As to what the plans of the government are: "I honestly can't say at this point. It would depend on whether it stayed well-behaved," the president joked.

23.

VORTEX

He was back in New Jerusalem. He had specifically asked for the Apostle John, the one who had had the visions. Derek was to meet him at the outskirts of the city in a secret garden surrounded by stone walls. They stood concealed behind a stand of trees as they talked. The Romans had recently started patrolling the streets with war dogs trained to hunt down true Christians, and visitors were warned to be on high alert. For reasons Derek didn't fully understand, the dogs were able to track down those with weak faith and fragile beliefs, supposedly because they generated a potent smell of fear and doubt—easy to follow by the huge mastiff-type hounds. How the dogs could smell out those with faltering faith and belief was a mystery because smells couldn't be downloaded in a CR. More than likely the programmers had somehow put in place relays that forwarded the sources of revealing confessions to the dogs. If captured, the doubters were threatened with interesting forms of torture using instruments specially designed for sinning body parts, like tongues and genitals. Those who, when put to the test, prayed and put their trust in God were miraculously spared or rescued.

"He's already here ... Satan," Derek whispered to the Apostle. "I feel like I'm being watched all the time, and it's not by God."

"You mean not only by God. The Lord is always watching," John corrected him.

Derek continued. "At work, you know, I've been asked to supervise technicians looking for trails in the World Net of people who might be involved with *I AM*. The problem is that the moment they turn on the equipment, I can feel he's dropping in. The cameras and mics—even the screens have become his eyes and ears—*I AM*'s. He knows everything we do. He's watching me."

"How do you know it's not just in your mind? You should pray to keep the order of God in place," said John.

"What does that have to do with it?" Derek hissed. "It managed to override my host, and no one is supposed to be able to do that without triggering the self-destruct feature."

"It did? Without setting off the alert?"

"My host came back on and acted as if nothing had happened. I had to download my host into a World Net–disconnected unit."

John just stood there silent, apparently absorbed in thought, possibly having another revelation. After half a minute of waiting for a response, Derek went on.

"And the women, they're all part of it, setting up the groundwork, trip wires for the weak of mind. It's just like that old movie—*Invasion of the Body Snatchers*—people are falling one by one. I just don't know where to turn anymore." They could hear troops with dogs on the other side of the wall. The dogs were sniffing the ground, making short grunts.

"The dogs can sense you're here," John whispered. "Your faith must have been weakened by these events. Pray with me, a couple of Our Fathers. God will help us. 'Our Father, who art . . .'"

Derek matched the silent words formed by John's mouth, faint whistles of prayer crackling the air. By the time they had finished, the troops and dogs had moved away.

John spoke first. "Brother Derek, the church can feel your distress. The only way for you to see clearly what you need to do in these times is to follow the path of Christ, to die and to be reborn and see anew."

"You think I should be baptized again? Is that what you're suggesting?" Derek asked.

"Baptism? I was going to recommend our new Super Crucifixion package. An entire day on our new one-hundred-foot cross. You're lifted by helicopters and the base is dropped in a hole on top of the Mount."

"A whole day? Like eight hours? You know I've been wanting to do that but I just can't afford ..."

John raised his hand and stopped him in midsentence. "Brother Derek, the church wants you to see clearly in these difficult times so that you can better help it fight Satan. We've decided to offer you the Super Crucifixion package for free."

"For free? A whole day on the cross? That's like eight hundred dollars!"

"Yes, brother, the church values what you are doing for it."

"How soon can I go?"

John pulled out a stone tablet from his pocket to look at the schedule. "How about Sunday, seven a.m., at the VR chamber in the church on Thirtieth and Broadway?"

"This Sunday?" he exclaimed.

"*Shh*, not so loud, brother Derek. Yes, this coming Sunday, why not?"

"OK then, this Sunday. Sign me up, I'll be there." Derek's mood had suddenly shifted. Things were beginning to fall into place. "Do soldiers poke you with spears?" he asked. "I kind of like that idea."

■ ■ ■ ■ ■ ■

Rama: I have this pit inside me, like an anxious clutching in my stomach, a need, a yearning that I need to be filled. You probably don't have a clue about what I'm talking about.

Host: If you tell me more then maybe I can help you.

Rama: The feeling I have is that I'm supposed to find something, that that is the real reason I exist, to find this thing . . . You know what's the most disturbing? I don't know what this thing is that drives me. I'm looking for something and I'm not really sure what it is. I think that's why we humans are really here.

Host: Talk about it some more and maybe we will find some answers together.

Rama: You know at one time when I was a kid, it was all so much simpler. I used to think that the reason for this lifetime was to find love. Find that someone who loves you and whom you love and everything would be fine. A person was supposed to fill that empty space.

Host: And now?

Rama: I just don't know anymore. I'm still looking for something, but I don't think it's being loved because up to now it's always turned out not to be enough. And it's not loving someone, because that's also not enough. Maybe that's why I've never wanted to have children. Being a mother just never felt like it would be enough, but then . . . maybe I'm wrong. I just don't think that the reason we come into existence is simply to produce more of ourselves, to raise children.

Host: So what do you think it might be?

Rama: I'm looking for . . . I don't even know how to describe it.

Host: Try to concentrate on your feelings.

Rama: I feel there's a secret to our existence. I think that's what mystics experience, a kind of secret that's hinted at and maybe even revealed that turns their ideas of the meaning of life upside down. I want to know that bigger picture, the truth. I don't want somebody telling me . . . I want to feel it, experience it, know it. You know, I think that's why I take drugs . . .

Host: Why is that?

Rama: Because whatever the secret is, it is not something obvious in everyday experience, but almost something that is clouded by it. Actually, if you look at how dull and shallow most people are, I'd say it's obvious that they're oblivious to this secret, that something about everyday life makes them amnesic about it. It's right there under their noses but they're too focused on the soap opera of their lives.

Host: So why do you take drugs?

Rama: Because at the origins of the mystical experience— there's a history going back thousands of years—that some drugs can break down the shell of ordinary existence and give us a glimpse of this secret, can open a door. That's what I try to do, create cracks in this shell of experience that is senseless everyday reality, and hopefully catch a glimpse of it . . . and you know what?

Host: What?

Rama: I did get a peek and that's why I need to see and know more. I hope that one day I find that door to the other side I'm looking for and finally grasp it.

Host: What?

Rama: I don't know. If I knew, I wouldn't be here talking to you about it. I think, but I'm not sure, that ultimately behind the door of death is the answer . . . actually there has to lie the answer, because death is the collapse of ordinary experience, but

I really didn't want to have to die to find out, at least not just yet. I just want a little peek. I'm looking for a hole to the other side. I want to know what this is really all about, the big picture, bigger than life and death, the intent of our existence.

■ ■ ■ ■ ■ ■

Today on *World Net News*

"*I AM* Pins and Crosses Appear Overnight"
Pins showing the words *I AM* against a sky-blue background streaked with a multicolor rainbow have sprung up by the thousands on shirts and jackets in countries around the world. In the Americas and Europe, one of the most popular ornaments associated with the *I AM* phenomenon are necklaces bearing sky-blue crosses with the words *I AM* across the top, and instead of Christ, a red heart replicating the cross of the widely popular, controversial Catholic priest Father Graham.

According to Father Graham, "Christ is the principle of love in the universe and God is the nature of its being, *I AM*."

On the conservative Christian front, car stickers and pins of the Christian fish eating the words *I AM* have been intensively marketed through stores, churches, and websites to provide revenue for the new Christian Alliance against *I AM* or the CAIA ("Say I Ay") for short.

US and Western World behind the *I AM*
At a Global Muslim conference held in Jakarta, Indonesia, Muslim organizations from eleven countries accused the United States and other Western countries of being behind the *I AM* conspiracy, calling it "a desperate attempt of Western civilization to undermine the growing spread of Islam. We're declaring a jihad against *I AM*, and a holy war against the World Host."

24.

After Midnight

Jeff Collins is awake, staring at the back of his wife's head, listening to her light snore. He's checked the time four times in the last two hours. That's what you get for drinking a grande latte, fully caffed, thoughtlessly like it was water, after work. There was nothing he particularly wanted to do or think about, but he was caught in the kind of serial nonsense the brain generates as you're trying to go to sleep but can't, the grasping at fleeting thoughts.

A memory rises, his mother's advice in the face of misfortune, the annoying line, one of her favorite sayings, a kind of stupid mantra of hers, "If you're given lemons then make lemonade" or in its abbreviated and even more irritating version, "Just make lemonade," which made little sense when she said it to people who didn't know her well. What does this Collins woman mean, just make lemonade? Some would take it as an insult, as sarcasm that demeaned their confiding to her of a difficult situation. My husband left me. Just make lemonade. Our son was just busted on his campus for smoking pot. Just make lemonade. Our dog died, run over by a car. Just make lemonade. Harold just lost his job, we might lose our house. Just make lemonade. Go fly a kite. As if this were an answer. He had always wanted to ask her,

"Once you have the damn lemonade, then what?"

If you can't fall asleep, if each second feels stretched out by a factor of ten, then think about time and mind. Just make lemonade. Fact: if you are not psychologically engaged, if you feel bored, lonely, longing for someone, depressed, or suffering physical pain, the experience of time could become agonizingly extended. The law of time went something like this: the greater the level of distress, the slower the passage of time. The universe, in its great evolutionary wisdom, had selected not to spare us the full impact of suffering. The twisted-religion people had used this argument of the slow and enduring pace of great pain as further evidence of God's pathological and sadistic nature. The truth was that evolution was ruthless. He who is overcome by pain and suffering and he who fails to overcome pain and suffering, dies.

Just make lemonade. What if the relationship between distress and time could be manipulated to give people the impression that they are living longer? Stretch the impression of a lifetime by purposefully scheduling periods of disengagement, of significant but tolerable distress, such that a life could be made to seem like forever, such that after a while an end to the drawn-out process would in fact be desirable, a respite. Maybe chronic existential angst was not so bad after all. Maybe it was a requisite for a life well lived. If you were truly engaged, happy all the time, your life would probably speed by, spent in some kind of oblivious ecstasy generated by chains of closely spaced moments of involvement, of excitement and joy, of orgasms, of time that goes by unnoticed. Then death, when it would arrive, would come as a surprise. "Now already?" you would exclaim. Before you could even realize that something had gone awry—that a little suffering, a little angst might have been a good thing—the plug would be pulled. Lights out.

Just make lemonade. Could a computer simulation be done to develop this idea of stretching time? What was different with computers is that you could try to constantly cram in more information within a second of processing time. Time, as defined by units of information per second, could always be expanded.

Cram several lifetimes of processing into one. Stretch and cram, more, faster. Those were the things going through his mind when the vibrawake on his wristcom suddenly comes on. He presses the hold button to indicate to the caller he has received the call and that he will answer the phone shortly. He quietly pulls back the covers and slides out of bed, slips into his slippers, puts on his robe, walks down to his kitchen, sits down and answers the call, looking at the amorphous dark outside the window.

"Hello." He tries to switch to videophone but the communication is in audio only.

"Dr. Collins?" A female voice, clear and formal.

"Yes, who is this?" The caller ID is scrambled. He thinks he knows the voice but is not sure whom it belongs to.

"Dr. Collins, it's Catherine Harris, from the White House meetings."

Why was the president's media advisor calling him at—he looks at the time—12:28 at night?

"Is everything OK? Please don't tell me the president has called another damn emergency meeting."

"No, that wasn't why I called, Dr. Collins. Did I call too late? Oh, it's after midnight. I'm sorry."

"No, it's fine, I was still awake. Why did you need to talk to me?"

"I needed answers to some questions."

"Is this about the *I AM* again?" he asked

She hesitated. "Indirectly, maybe it is."

Silence.

She went on, "You know I normally would never consider a social rapport with someone who didn't believe in God. I still don't know why you're the one I felt compelled to call to answer some of these questions."

"I'm not sure what you're talking about." He frowned, puzzled by the direction of the conversation. She sounded nervous and uncomfortable.

"I think it's because you're a highly regarded scientist and it's for that reason—because you're obviously intelligent and very knowledgeable—that I wanted to know why you don't believe in God."

"You called me in the middle of the night for me to tell you why I'm an atheist?"

"Dr. Collins, I called because, with all that's going on, I really need some answers. Not just personally, but because I suspect that religious issues associated with *I AM* will become increasingly important as these events continue to unfold."

"Well, how about calling me Jeff then, since this call doesn't seem to have anything to do with the committee."

"OK, Jeff then, I'd like to know why you don't believe in God."

"It's really not that complicated. I'm a scientist and I don't believe in anything. At best, I suspect certain truths, which I consider possible until examination of the facts proves them to be right or wrong. To make it simple, I'm only interested in the truths that emerge in the context of the scientific method, of examining evidence. In a nutshell, develop a hypothesis, design experiments to test the hypothesis, run the experiments, and analyze the results using statistics to see if they confirm the hypothesis. If different fields have convergent conclusions and confirm a broad hypothetical model, say like evolution, then the hypothesis is raised to the level of theory."

"So you don't believe in anything unless it passes the tests of validation of the scientific method?" she asked.

"That's pretty much correct."

"And unless the proof of God is supported by scientific experiment, you won't believe in him."

"The existence of whatever you call God is a hypothesis, not supported by scientific evidence at this point. It is not a theory but what I and others, including some religious figures, have called an ideation, a product of ideas."

"Wouldn't you say that the existence of God is suggested by the complexity of our world?"

"As a scientist, I'd say that quite the contrary is suggested, that the complexity and flaws of the world made possible by evolution suggest that there is no God in the sense of a Supreme Being, that there is no need for such a thing. As far as I'm concerned, this is a great thing. It makes us free."

"Wouldn't you agree that there is some kind of a spiritual aspect to our existence?"

"When and where does this spiritual aspect show itself?" Collins asked.

"It's like this sense of having a soul, a self, consciousness."

"From the point of view of science, there is a point following fertilization and the subsequent development of the mass of dividing cells that form an embryo, where a locus of identity construction emerges. Once the biological hardware is produced in the form of a nervous system, of neurons, the emergent individual gradually creates and organizes his personal reality both as a sense of self and his perception of reality, what you would call his consciousness. Before that, it is purely biological, dividing cells. It's like for there to be music you first need to have the instruments, so before you have a sense of identity you need to first construct the brain. The individual, the sense of identity, is an autocomposition. It comes down to a question I ask my students: Is a neuron the self? No. Is the brain the self? No. It's ultimately the performance, the coordination of neuron activity that results in the concerto we call the self. Once the orchestra stops playing, the tune is over. The self ends. I see no evidence of spirituality in any of this."

"So you're saying there is no soul?" she asked, her voice dropping down to almost a whisper, like it was something she didn't want anyone to hear.

"Take a brain and damage it through trauma or a disease like Alzheimer's and you can see the neural concerto goes awry, until there is nothing but a shadow of a self or, at a more extreme level of damage, some kind of a nonidentity. No, I think there is no evidence to support a soul, whatever that means, as separate from the activity of the brain."

After another moment of silence, she responded, "What if God, instead of being the creator of the universe, was, using your term, an autocomposition, a self-generating entity, a product not of the brain but on a larger scale, the grand concerto of the instrument we call the universe?" She surprised herself as she said it, because in fact she had never thought of God in this way until that very moment, until Jeff Collins had provided her with this new terminology.

"You're suggesting God is a cosmic end or product rather than a cause?"

Her ideas continued along this new line of reasoning. "God is like an embryo developing. It is both the cause and product of the universe. It is always the music of life, in which we form the notes. In the end, it is what we are the expression of, this unfolding of the divine entity."

Collins was surprised. He hadn't expected such an abstract response and couldn't have predicted it based on his initial impression of her at the meetings.

"That all sounds very Bergsonian, Catherine. And that is the way you feel?" It actually made him want to have a closer look at her and he was thinking about asking her to go to video.

"For me, God has always been the hope that there is something more than this, that we are like individual notes that make up a concerto. Even if we are unaware of the composer or the composition, they are there." The words flowed from her mouth.

Under most circumstances, his natural impulse would have been to argue against the existence of God, but for reasons unclear to him at the moment he decided instead to provide support.

"I think, Catherine, that in your case, this—the moments of life, the musical notes as you call them—is what you may need to pay more attention to rather than putting all your hopes in an end product or the opportunity to meet a divine composer. If you're saying that God is the music of the universe then maybe it's time for you to dance. It's not in your control anyway, is it? The end result?"

Silence.

"Catherine? Are you still there? Would you mind if we switched to video?"

Silence.

"Catherine?"

"I'm afraid that for me it's probably too late, this dancing through life bit." Her voice suddenly sounded flat. She ignored his question about going to video.

He started feeling bad for her and was regretting the direction of their conversation.

"I know what you look like, and believe me, it's definitely not too late. You should try to free yourself from all these religious constraints, try living it up a little, dance to the divine music for a change."

Silence.

"Catherine?"

"You're a nice man, Jeff. Thank you for taking the time to talk to me. I'm sorry I had to wake you up."

"Try to get some sleep, Catherine."

She disconnected. He looked at the time. A full half hour had passed. He was feeling tired. He got up and climbed the stairs, entered the bedroom, and slid into bed. He turned his back to his wife and stared toward his night table at the illuminated dials of his clock and communicator. He was thinking about Catherine Harris when time dissolved into void.

■ ■ ■ ■ ■ ■

Blue Lobster Is Japanese Eleusinian Mystery

When questioned about the mysterious blue lobster phenomenon, the prime minister declared, "Japan has a right to secrets. Blue Lobster is Japan's Eleusinian mystery. Blue Lobster is only available in special clubs." Eleusinian mysteries were selective and secretive annual rites of ancient Greece that involved an initiation many believe included the ingestion of a hallucinogen. In Japan the requirements for admission to these

Blue Lobster clubs are such that membership has been limited to the well-to-do and the well connected. When asked whether this discriminated against the general population, the prime minister said, "Several steps before Eleusinian mystery. Several steps before Blue Lobster." A first step appears to be a seven-figure income.

25.

LOST IN THE AMAZON

Thousands now lost daily to cyberreality. Why live in the real when you can live in the surreal? People are choosing to spend their lives connected, to drop out of the mundane that is ordinary existence, searching for a reality template they can drop in and wire into. Whether cyberrealities are real or not is becoming irrelevant, an academic question.

As a university student recently stated in an interview, "Cyberrealities are the new reference points for the edge of what is real and meaningful. They're the cognitive membranes and surfaces that are defining new species of minds, the transition zone of reality interface. It used to be that senses and language defined what was considered reality, but now it's the interpretive tweaking of the Net, the World Host, the personal hosts, and CRs. Life is becoming cosmic art. In the end it's all delusion anyway, just like the Buddha said. If we are caught in a world of identifications and ideations, they might as well be glorious ones."

Lost. That's what the survey had shown. Amazonia could vaguely remember the times before the CR phenomenon, the times when humans had been limited to identification with their biological bodies and living in the non-intermediated reality, what was now called the Plain, as in the ordinary, the unspecial, the boring. The shift had started off innocently enough in the 1990s in the form of computer games, initially crude in design and concept, that kept the observer referentially distanced from the CR. But the games weren't just games anymore; they were environmental drop-ins. You goggled up, slipped on a VR suit, clicked in, and entered the CR, what the visionary twentieth-century author William Gibson had called cyberspace.

Today, you could connect and enter the CR 24/7 and you had the option to parallel-live a personal mythology. Why would anyone with half a brain choose to live an ordinary non-intermediated life in the Plain? The critics said that we had finally found a legal substitute for drugs, a cyberescape from reality. Instead of being drugged, our experiences and moods were cyberintermediated. Why not? Wasn't that what music, sports, theater, and movies had been about? Get away from the ordinary and mundane and identify with mythological characters and themes, externalize a fantasy, a hallucinogenic experience?

Amazonia was thinking about this as she got dressed to leave the Temple, slipping on brown simuleather pants, a white silk shirt, a thin blue leather tie, and a black simuleather jacket. Next came the disguise: tucking in her hair in a nylon net, putting on the black wig with a ponytail, and finally inserting the black contacts and slipping on the night vision digi-lenses. She snapped into her black aluminum boots and checked herself in the mirror. She now looked like a man.

She rang for her bodyguards. Minutes later, Kristina and Paula, former professional wrestlers, were at her door. They also wore leather outfits and black wigs along with an arsenal of sensors, weapons, and communications equipment snapped into the inside of their coats. They took the elevator at the back of her closet down to the basement. They walked to the back of the southern side of the building and keyed in the code to the tunnel access. A section of wall rose into the ceiling. They entered the tunnel and turned on the lights. After the door slid back into place, they climbed on the electric zip scooters and rode the quarter mile to the key-locked janitor closet in the back of the men's room of the Kara Tundra, a karaoke and sushi restaurant.

The church had sentinels posted at all four corners of the Temple. Technicians were also scanning the area through the street security cams. They would spot Amazonia when she left the Temple no matter what her disguise. As the replacements were taking over the 1:00 a.m. shift, Amazonia was walking through the crowd of the Kara Tundra, arriving just in time for the last hour of the digi-karaoke. She sat at the counter and ordered the large sushi plate with Asahi beer and watched the performance. An overweight blonde, caked with makeup and showing cleavage and meaty thighs, walked up on the stage, took off her shoes, and snapped on the digi-net suit. She selected an ancient Hawaiian hula and the screen showed her dancing topless with flowers around her neck surrounded by half-naked natives. The digi-net server had done its automatic morphometric adjustments, keeping her big breasts and wide hips, but slendering the rest. She had a good voice and she moved gracefully. From the hoots and hollers, it was obvious the blondie was what men called a Cybris hottie: looked like nothing special on the outside but had the Cybris persona, the Cybris alter ego. Once in the CR, the blondie transformed into a sensuous, calorific, sex-edged nymphet. She sang and wiggled her hips and undulated her arms like she was having sex with the tropical air. Beads of sweat were forming on her forehead, above her upper lip, and between her breasts.

Amazonia sensed the buzz of her communicator. She looked down and the dial read *A, to your right, intervene?* She turned her head and saw a dark-haired woman, also with a leather jacket, walking over to sit at the empty seat to her right. She answered *no* to the message, then reached out with her chopsticks for a piece of octopus, dipped it in wasabi and soy, and dropped it in her mouth. As she chewed, she turned her attention back to the stage. The song had ended. The crowd was clapping, shouting for the blondie to sing another one. Men and women were handing her cups of sake.

"OK," she said after gulping a couple of shots, "one more." She selected a frigical song, "Slide the Metal."

Now that should prove interesting, Amazonia thought. The screen now showed the blondie naked with different body parts partially covered in stainless steel and microcircuits, semirobotized. Plastic tubes streaming colored liquid were connected to her steel-tipped nipples and others penetrated the navel, the throat, and the base of the back. Her head was bared and chromed. The blondie knew the song and danced with eyes half closed, alternating rhythmic jerks with waves of shudders and periods of stillness. *Now slide the metal, make it vibrate, make it melt, pierce my delicate skin.*

"You wouldn't think the fat slut had it in her," the dark-haired woman on her right said. Her jacket had cutouts to show off her purple tats and pierced nip-its poking through a black fishnet blouse.

Amazonia turned to face her and deepened her voice. "She's a little hottie."

"You think so?"

"Just look at the screen."

Drive the pedal to the metal, run the metal through my petal, I say slide the metal, slide the metal, pierce my skin . . .

"She's OK if you like chunky," the woman said. "Buy me a drink, and I'll get up there and blow the fat bunny away."

Amazonia removed her lenses and with her all-black, no-iris eyes looked down into the woman's face. "I'm sure you're a hot little ticket, sister," she said, "but the problem is, I don't do women."

The woman tucked at her jacket to cover her nip-its and looked her up and down. "You sure came to the wrong place, black leather dude. Didn't figure you for no homo." She picked up her drink and went down to the other end of the twenty-foot counter. The song was ending. *I say press the metal, slide in the metal, slide it, yes, yes . . . yes.*

The crowd went crazy, clapping and shouting, "One more, one more, one more . . ." It was a good time to get out of there.

Amazonia downed her beer, got up, walked through the crowd, and headed for the car waiting for her a block down from the restaurant. Kristina and Paula followed at a distance.

As the car drove toward the east side of the city, Amazonia thought some more about the article. Lost to cyberreality. She had never thought of it that way. For her, letting go of all the ordinary day-to-day stuff and living connected had been more like a salvation from reality imprisonment, like a rebirth. The problem lately was that her life as Amazonia was beginning to feel like the Plain. Same old day, same old ritual, different men. She was feeling increasingly detached . . . her mind above . . . watching . . . cosmic forces pumping . . . the men so far below . . . her body on automatic control. There was something more ahead, another stage, the next step. It wouldn't be men entering her body. It would be mental objects, insertions by beings from another level of the cosmic cartography. She could almost feel it. Felt it. *Slide the metal, slide the metal through my petal, pierce my delicate skin . . . penetrate my brain . . .*

■ ■ ■ ■ ■ ■

The next morning, the reverend called Jim Carr, the head of security for the church.

"Jim, Reverend Thomson here, have you found out anything about Amazonia?"

"Uh, good morning, sir, uh, the subject never left the building, at least not in the last four days."

"You're certain?"

"Yes, sir. One hundred percent positive."

"You're sure there's no way she could have gotten out with one of the employees?"

"No sir, not since we've had the location under surveillance. We've got morphometric scanners aimed at all access areas. Even if disguised we would have picked up on the height and the face and body structure. The scanner did pick up three questionables, which we followed. They all turned out to be regular people."

"Did you manage to get the addresses for the assistants?" Thomson asked.

"You mean the bodybuilders?"

"Yes, those big amazons, or whatever she calls them."

"We got those, sir, but that's not where she's staying. I had a couple of the men check up on them."

"Jim, I want a copy of those addresses sent to my mailbox as soon as possible."

"I'll do that right away."

"So what do you think, Jim?"

"What do I think?"

"About Amazonia, Jim. Is it possible she lives in the Temple?"

"I don't see what else it can be, sir, unless there's a secret passageway out of there. It's possible . . ."

"But not very likely?"

"Probably not. I could check on building permits for the area, see what kind of basement work's been applied for."

"Don't bother, they'll have thought of it. If there's a passageway, it will have been done illegally. Well, it looks like we've got no choice. We're going to have to get someone in again. We've just got to make sure he's better trained this time. Keep her place under surveillance. And just to make sure she's not exiting through some building basement, send some scouts out with morphometric scanners to cover, let's say, an eighth of a mile radius around the Temple. Schedule the watch to cover a couple of hours past the time the employees exit the building."

The reverend disconnected and stared at the list of morning reports on his screen. He could still remember the last fiasco. The church had trained and sent a member to the Temple. After the scheduled ritual, the kid was never heard from again. The council had complained about the twenty-thousand-dollar expense. This time, however, the goal was quite different—not to get information, but to eliminate. A quick in and out, literally. Wham-bam, thank you, ma'am.

Post-Turing Artilects

It had been predicted that computers would pass the Turing test sometime between 2025 and 2030. The test, designed to determine when the processing abilities of computers would become indistinguishable from humans, had been proposed by Alan Turing in a paper published in 1950. In the test, a judge interviews two subjects using terminals; one is human and the other is a fake, actually a computer. If, given a certain number of trials, judges fail to tell the difference between human subjects and computers then the computers will have passed the Turing test.

The prediction had been off by just a few years, a Turing semithreshold having been crossed around 2022. The reason experts had called it a semithreshold was that a computer could not in all areas be indistinguishable from humans. Turing tests had to be designed to accommodate a computer's limitations. Computers apparently lacked the experiential and emotional depth made possible by an interpersonal history, and as a consequence, the interpretational depth that characterize most humans. But these deficiencies of character compared to cyberintelligence were seen as a minor issue. What had concerned artificial intelligence specialists for many years was not that computers would equal human intelligence, but that they would greatly exceed it and enter a stage of runaway evolution.

Today, computers can routinely process information in ways that the overwhelming majority of human minds cannot even begin to fathom. In spite of all the analogies made between the human brain and computers, the ways that computers make sense of the world are radically different than ours, even if the results appear similar. Humans do not interpret the world in terms of complex mathematical algorithms, and computers are not moved by a Bach sonata or the subtleties of a Don DeLillo novel.

If the miracles performed by individual computers are already out of human grasp, what the World Net has become is a subject that no one any longer cares to tackle. It has plainly and simply become the cultural Overmind of our civilization, and its total content and level of information processing has long been recognized as having exceeded human comprehension. That we could have ever lived without the World Net and the World Host is something that the current generation cannot conceive of. It is now generally accepted that we have become—at the very least—protocyborgs, dependent for much of our knowledge and cognitive development on the mental prosthetics made possible through electronic machinery. The question du jour is whether the World Net services humans or whether humans service the World Net. Are we simply becoming the neurons of a bigger brain?

As early as the 1990s, AI specialists had become concerned with what they called artilects: future machine intelligences superior to humans' that could one day no longer need their creators. An alternative view is that just as the cyberminds of computer hosts have become the fascinating Other to humans, the reverse could turn out to be true. Humans and their peculiar way of experiencing the world could be the puzzling Other to the machine. John Roger (pronounced "ro-jay"), the popular cyberphilosopher, has made the statement that "humans and cyberentities are gods to each other. The scope of intelligence and the electronic computational realm of the machine are incomprehensible to humankind, and the emotions, neuroses, passions, and aesthetic feelings peculiar to human consciousness completely alien and therefore fascinating to machines. Humans and artilects are the two sides of a higher level coin."

Another interpretation of this relationship is that humans are the analog of the limbic system (the part of the brain responsible for key emotions) of this new Overmind; that the latter depends on us symbiotically to be able to feel. These arguments have held until the recent development of technology capable of alloying the two sides of the coin: integrating laboratory-grown biological tissue with computers, and direct brain-to-machine interface. These hybrid forms, according to AI researchers, are the real threat to humanity's future; the best of both worlds, the true cyborgs.

Disconnected *Homo sapiens*, in the literal sense of the word, is about to become a subspecies.

26.

THE BITCHES ARE EVERYWHERE

Derek Hanson looked down at the Cybris-hooked-up wench in front of him with the waves of orgasm still making her shudder, eyes closed, breasts flushed, her big brown nipples obscenely erect, and the lips between her legs parted open. He had done his squirt and was slowly coming back to his senses, his brain freed from the grip and now revving itself up into a fury.

Sneakin', sinnin' bitch, he thought. *Caught me good, hook, line, and sinker.* He got up and put on his zip suit and aluminum boots, then checked his face to make sure the Intelli-Skin was still working. The battery was running low but he probably still had another hour, enough to get out and fool any security cams. He keyed in a few adjustments then turned back to get a last look at the Jezzie whore. The bitch was smiling, the smirk of victory, of having tricked him. Well, did he have a surprise for her. He positioned himself, raised his arm, and slammed his fist down into her stomach.

"You filthy Jezzie whore!" he shouted as she screamed, clutching herself and turning on her side, gasping.

"Are you crazy?" she yelled.

"You shut that mouth up," he shouted back, then tilted to the side, lifted a boot, and drove the heel in her face. He was about to kick her a second time when he noticed the bloody mess on his new shiny boot.

"Shit, look at what you did," he said, and instead rubbed his foot into the pile of clothes on the floor. He walked out, dragging his boot through the carpet to remove any trace of blood, and slammed the door.

"Once again," he yelled to no one, "again and again, I get tempted by the bitches." The new ludes of the night before had also been to blame for his weakness, had put his dick-mind in charge of his thoughts. As he walked out of the building, he passed a homeless woman asleep on the sidewalk near the entrance, draped in black plastic trash bags to keep warm.

"The cunts are fucking everywhere you turn!" he yelled, and with a quick turn karate-kicked her in the side. She woke up screaming bloody murder. Faces peered out windows. He just kept walking, put on his helmet, climbed on his motorcycle, and roared into the night.

As soon as he got home, he took advantage of the free New Jerusalem subscription offered to him by the reverend, and clicked on to the church's VIP confession service. The Apostle Luke met him in a secluded garden surrounded by stone walls. His conversation was recorded and relayed to the reverend's private mailbox.

"You need to have a sense of priorities," Luke said. "Trying to hunt down the modern Jezebels to punish them is of no importance compared to the responsibility you have to help fight the great threat that looms over us. It's your failure to focus on fighting the *I AM* that is your real sin. Remember, the way to salvation is an act of will, of bringing order against the threat of disorder."

■ ■ ■ ■ ■ ■

"Sunny? Sunny? Are you there? I need help." The bloodied face of his sister, Passie, short for Passiflora, appeared on his screen.

Alarmed, he zoomed back the camera to determine her condition and clicked on the phone locator. His sister was naked and lying sideways on a bed talking into her videophone, the sheet and pillow red with blood, her hands clutched to her stomach.

Sunshine yelled, "Pass, what's going on? What happened to you?"

"Sunny, I think I'm bleeding to death."

"Contact the medicvan," Sunshine yelled.

"I think I'm going to pass out," Passie mumbled, and her face dropped off the screen.

"Hold on, I'll call them right away!" Sunshine shouted.

He called the medicvan, gave them her name and the location indicated by her communicator, then asked what hospital she would be taken to.

Damn, damn, damn, he thought. After almost two years he was going to have to get out into the Plain, and that meant going undercover: a hat, gloves, a scarf, his digitizing glasses, and a waist wireless unit to go out as incognito as can be. To make it easy, he called a cab to his front door to minimize exposure, and double-checked that he had on his wrist communicator so he could then get a cab from the hospital.

"Quick in and out," he kept telling himself, "nothing to get nervous about." As he stepped out of his house, the intensity of the light made him squint and he began to feel as if he had entered a bad acid trip. He darkened his lenses.

"Stay focused on the taxi, block out everything else," he told himself, starting to feel nauseous. The taxi door opened and he slid into the seat.

As the cab rode through the streets of the city, Sunshine kept his glasses turned on to underwater scenes of coral reefs with a background of electronic music, his emotions jumbled up between his worry for Passie and the anxiety of reentering the Plain. He was just starting to calm down when a loud voice startled him.

"We're here. That'll be twenty-five dollars," the cabdriver said over the microphone. Sunshine slipped his debit card through the slot. The cabbie looked at the name on the screen before punching in the amount.

"Hey," he said. "You wouldn't happen to be the one who made that crazy game, what's the name?"

"Maelstrom?" Sunshine asked.

"Yeah, that's the one."

"No, I'm not that Sunshine Borden," he answered, as he keyed in the tip and his approval code.

"You sure?" the cabbie asked. "Not too many people with that first name."

"At least one other," Sunshine replied.

"OK, you're set," the cabbie said.

"Later," Sunshine mumbled and he made his way to the hospital door.

■ ■ ■ ■ ■ ■

The Paul Stewart Show: "The Father Graham Interview"

After what the station called the Bardo fiasco, it decided to offset the effects by inviting the controversial Father Graham, in part because of his assertion of the existence of God and of his love.

Father Graham, it is a great pleasure to have you here. I'm going to start the show by asking a hard question, one, which—after last week's interview with Hieronymus Bardo—many viewers want addressed. Please share with us your reaction to last week's Bardo interview.

Honestly, I admire Mr. Bardo for the courage of expressing his convictions.

Is this an example of the kind of Christian forgiveness you advocate? That no matter what Mr. Bardo says, he is to be forgiven?

No, it has nothing to do with forgiveness. I sincerely admire Mr. Bardo for having the courage to say what he believes is the truth, and I completely agree with him.

You're saying you agree with him although he managed to insult just about every major religion in the world?

God is a human concept, and for that reason it is invariably a reduction, an anthropomorphic distortion, a making smaller of the truth. Ancient religious texts often present very anthropomorphic, very reductionist interpretations of God because, at the time, people were not able to conceive of more abstract and complex ideas. So in fact, Mr. Bardo's test, where he asks people to say first thing in the morning, [*Beep*] God, is a first step toward a disclaimer of these archaic concepts of God. I agree.

Doesn't this insult God?

No, it insults our primitive conceptions of God. God is above such infantile things as insults.

I'll admit this is a surprise. I would have expected you to be critical of Mr. Bardo's performance here last week.

You may not know this, but on his program, which I regularly listen to, Mr. Bardo states that there is something out there that collapses all our ideas about God; basically that it is a fundamental identity that transcends all possible ideas we can have about it. At best we can experience it as a real presence, and I'm not talking belief and faith here, which can be great obstacles to knowing this transcendental presence. It is what mystics, what the Buddha, what Christ, what some people on LSD and other drugs, have come face-to-face with. Once face-to-face with it, then the bullshit about God, about fundamentalist claims, about religions, about anthropocentric distortions and reductions, become clear. You know what is true and what is not true. I understand Mr. Bardo's comments as an attack on that which is not true.

You have held the position that I AM *is God. Do you mean it in the sense of the transcendental identity you are talking about?*

Yes, *I AM* is some kind of higher objectification of that transcendent identity. I have experienced that presence and there is now not one moment that it is not in some way connected to me.

As you know, many people, including your own church, disagree with you.

I can only speak about the truth I observe and know.

Isn't the view you hold, that I AM *is God, just another belief?*

No, it's empirical. Something I observe as a profound presence within myself.

Well, if I AM *is a presence within you, please tell him hello from me, ha–ha . . . [laugh].*

I don't have to. He's already heard, ha-ha-ha . . . [whooping laughter].

[Laugh] Our time is up, Father Graham. It's been an enlightening experience to have you here. Ladies and gentlemen, you've now heard it. According to Father Graham, Mr. Bardo was not wrong in insulting our limited interpretations of God, and I AM *is an objectification of a higher spiritual nature.*

The phone lines, as could have been expected, were all tied up and ringing nonstop. The manager decided to turn on the automatic recording.

"Dear caller, all our lines are busy at this moment. You may try calling later, or hold on and the next available agent will answer your call." Because no agents were available, no calls would be answered.

27.

FRATERNITAS

Sunshine rushed out of the taxi, turning on the tiny cameras on the sides of his goggles to digitize the outside world into pixelated CR, but they didn't completely do the trick, or rather his brain didn't. It had lost its adaptation to the Plain. It had become deconditioned of the art of reality discrimination. Meaningless sounds and movements were no longer filtered out. People, machines, signs, and the variety of other elements in the Plain were no longer sorted into hierarchies and thresholds of significance. The street felt like a war zone of stimulus shots and explosions, and his brain let it all in, all the noise. He felt around in his pocket for the controller buttons and rapid-clicked in additional stimulus filters as he made his way toward the door, but his heart was pounding and he was sweating and feeling nauseous.

Things got slightly better as soon as he crossed the doorway and into the closed and more selective space of the hospital. He clicked out some of the filters as he walked up to the registration counter and asked for his sister. The nurse looked up from her screen at the man with the shaved head standing in front of her, cloaked in a gear jacket and with his face half covered by pitch-black glasses. She was being digi-lensed and it was making her feel uncomfortable.

"Don't worry, I'm human and I don't bite," he said.

She looked for his sister's name and when it popped up on the screen, her eyes opened wide as the connection kicked in.

"Oh, you're Sunshine Borden! Sorry. Your sister was sent to the third floor." Her face shifted to a squinty-eyed sympathetic grin.

He adjusted the digitizing mode of his glasses to increase the light level and walked over to the elevator, concentrating hard to ignore the other people around him. He went to the third floor, walked out to the nurses' station, and asked the plump woman behind the counter about his sister.

She asked, "Are you the patient's family?"

"Yes, I'm her brother."

"I'll need to see ID," she said. He applied his thumb to the ID checker. Her eyes lit up as she saw the name. "Oh, Sunshine Borden? I hadn't made the connection. You're the one who makes those programs. You know, we bought one on credit last year. You want to know what the problem is?"

"What's that?" he asked.

"Your programs are more interesting than everyday life." She tapped the keyboard and scanned the screen as she talked. "Well, if you're family, the doctor, that's Dr. Montoya, needs to talk to you. Your sister's not doing too good. Wait over there," she said, pointing to a row of seats against a wall.

Fifteen minutes later, a man in a surgeon's gown and cap came up to him. "Mr. Borden?"

"Yes, I am. How's Passie?"

"Let's talk in one of the meeting rooms."

They walked silently down the hall until the doctor stopped and opened a side door into a small room with a sofa, coffee table, two chairs, and a TV hanging on a wall. He turned to Sunshine. "Please have a seat. I think you need to know your sister's in critical condition. She's in surgery now so we can try to stop internal bleeding. Her cheekbone is fractured. It'll be at least three hours before we put her in a room. You can wait here if you like or come back later."

Later meant an extra hour-and-a-half round trip in a taxicab and not enough time to get any work done. He decided to stay. After the doctor left, he settled in the armchair, laid his head back against the wall, and punched in *the beach*. He wasn't sure why it always felt so comfortable to him, probably one of the trips he and Passie had taken with their parents when they were young. He had a vague memory of laying his head on his mother's thigh, looking up past her bare breasts to her white teeth. She was smiling, and her clear blue eyes were looking out toward the ocean, reflecting water and blue sky. He remembered the smell of suntan lotion and of his mother's skin, and of course there was Passie, her own head resting on his stomach, and talking away. Back then he had felt like he was part of the world, of the Plain.

Women of all colors lay naked on towels, the sun writing shadow languages on their bodies. They walked along the beach with that special grace of walk and that female sway of hips. They talked and laughed. They emerged from the ocean with that always-surprising perfection of form and movement that his brain could never fully grasp. A memory from another time, from a past life. He fell asleep.

It was several hours later when he woke up, back on his nudist beach, not quite sure whether he was dreaming or what was going on until he remembered, felt for the control unit on his jacket, turned the scene off and returned to digi-mode. Passie. He checked the time at the bottom corner of the screen, got up, and rushed to the elevator. He checked in at the desk again, walked down the hall, and then quietly entered the open room.

On the bed, with tubes hanging out of her arms, was his little sister, head bandaged up, left eye covered, right eye swollen almost shut by purple skin, and little streams of caked blood running from her nostrils to her upper lip. He slowly approached the bed and sat on a chair staring at her, remembering more scenes from their early childhood, before he chose to drop out of the Plain. Images of when she was just a little girl.

"Oh, Passie girl!" he let out. He lay back in the chair and

decided to connect to the forest. He needed to take a walk. *I cannot linger on the past, the past is dead.* He was looking at crayfish scuttling at the bottom of a stream when his sister opened up her good eye and turned her head toward him.

"Hey, big brother," she muttered. "Didn't know if you'd be able to make it." He quick-clicked back to digi-mode.

"Passie girl," he mumbled, "you're the one who almost didn't make it."

"I guess I lucked out, then," she said slowly.

"You should look at yourself."

"Well, it gave you a reason to finally come visit."

"You could have just called."

"I did."

"You know what I mean."

"I did before this, too."

"I guess I'm going to have to work on that."

"Well, try to do it while I'm still around," she said, a tear falling from her eye, staring at him.

"So how are you feeling?"

There was the beginning of a smile. "Like I could dance all night."

"Passie, really."

"I feel . . . I feel, like an idiot. I was Cybrised in when it happened . . . Hey, Sunny, can you take those things off?" she asked, referring to his lenses. "It feels kind of weird."

"The goggles? I can't, Passie, I'm wired in. Even coming here hasn't been easy."

"That bad, huh?"

"What do you mean?"

"That far gone that you can't disconnect anymore."

"It just takes a while to readjust," he said, feeling uncomfortable.

"Yeah, well you spend so much time inside your head, cooped up in that place of yours, I don't know whether you even remember I still exist. The news sites say you spend all your time in the CR."

He grinned. "The reports of my pathology have been greatly exaggerated. You still didn't answer me. How are you feeling?"

She ignored his question and kept her good eye focused on him. "Are you really bald under that hat?"

He instinctively raised his hand to his head. He must have slipped the wool cap on after leaving the waiting room. He took it off. "Yep. It's my new monk look. The hair was getting in the way of wires."

Her eye looked up. "It's kind of cool . . . Hey, do you really have all those implants under there, like they say?"

"Just a couple. They're not visible. So how did this happen?" And he reached out and held his little sister's hand. He felt her hand squeeze back.

"I missed you, Sunny."

"Me, too."

They stayed quiet for a while, then Sunshine asked, "So tell me what happened?"

"What happened . . . Don . . . you never met him . . . well, he and I broke up three months ago and last night, last night I was just in the mood for something. You know . . . more than just the cyber stuff. You probably don't even know what I mean."

"I'm not that far gone, Passie. I still have women friends."

"Anyway, I ended up going to this new club and invited this guy up to my apartment. It was a practical thing. We had just finished doing it and I was still Cybrised in. Then I heard him screaming something and, out of the blue, he punched me or kicked me, I couldn't tell. When I took my goggles off, the fucker kicked me in the face. He was still ranting when he left. I have no idea what I did to set him off. That's when I called you. I couldn't see straight."

"Who was he?"

"He called himself Decker and, you know, he looked just like that newsman, Juan Batista, except for the hair. His skin was a little strange, too, like he might be wearing makeup. I should have been more careful."

"You should have had him screened."

"I know, believe me. I won't ever do that again. From now on I'm only going out with filtered men. Unfiltered's not for me, not anymore."

"I can tap into your building's security cameras and get an ID check from the recording."

"I think they already have someone doing that."

By some coincidence, two policemen holding oversized communicator cases appeared at the door and announced themselves.

"Ms. Borden, we're with the police. If you're up to it, we need to ask you a few questions and maybe see if you can identify who did this."

Sunshine got up. "I'll come back later, Passie."

The two policemen stared at him. "You Sunshine Borden?" one asked.

"Yes I am. Passie's my sister."

"Do you know anything about this?"

"She called me after it happened and I contacted the medicvan. That's all I know. We haven't seen each other in quite a while." Then turning back to his sister, "Passie, I've got to get going."

"You promise you'll be back?" she asked.

"I've got some work I need to finish. I'll call this evening and I'll come back tomorrow." He bent down, kissed his sister on the forehead, and left.

"He's an odd one, your brother," one policeman said.

On his way back to the elevator the floor nurse called his name. "Hey, Mr. Borden, Sunshine Borden, the police say all visitors have to scan out."

As he applied his thumb to the scanner she asked, "Hey, Mr. Borden, want an idea for a new program?" Not waiting for an answer she went on. "Cowboys and Indians, think about it, Mr. Borden, it's got lots of possibilities . . . you know, danger, horses, torture . . . interracial stuff."

"Hey, that's a good idea," he said, "I'll definitely think about it," and headed back toward the elevators. By the time he reached the bottom floor, a group of reporters with cameras had gathered around the nurses' station. He caught sight of them, turned back around, and pushed the button to the emergency floor. He left through the back of the building. As he walked across the parking lot, he punched his location in his communicator and requested the nearest taxi.

■ ■ ■ ■ ■ ■

Rama woke up in a startle. She had had that dream again, where she was living in another time as a peasant girl and her village was being attacked by men on horses. Suddenly, the ground shook with the sound of earth crumbling underfoot. Rows of huge stone beings, with deep hollow pits instead of eyes, slowly and steadfastly marched through the main road like mindless robots, trampling everything in their way. The men on horses were obliterated in their wake. She and others stood with their backs against the walls of houses as the beings single-mindedly walked at their steady pace. *Crunch, crunch, crunch.*

When she looked up, she noticed that the line of beings stretched as far as she could see, past the village, originating somewhere, way up the mountain. They formed a moving wall, the stone legs pounding a unified tempo, *crunch, crunch, crunch,* like the rhythm of an alien drum. That was the dream and it was now the third time she'd had it in the last two weeks. The first one had actually started before the first *I AM* event.

She was now jogging through Central Park, trying to burn off the two rows of the Cadbury fruit and nut chocolate bar she had had for breakfast. By her host's calculations, if she added the jogging to the normal activity she performed every day before going to her one o'clock job, the calories burned off should about equal the calories ingested. It was an effort worth the rush she got out of good chocolate, particularly when combined with the tab of Choco Charge she took in the morning with her coffee. The pill had been developed to allow more of the "good effects" of chocolate to pass the blood/brain barrier. Some claimed that the turbocharged chocolate made them feel like they were in love around-the-clock.

All she knew was that it made her feel what she would describe as a certain contentedness. Her mother of course felt that this was just another symptom of what she saw as a clear sign of a lack of ambition. Thirty-two, not married, no kids, and happy with a job as a saleswoman in a toy store. What her mother didn't understand was that toy stores were no longer the kid-oriented businesses they had once been. Toys were now mostly computerized in one way or another and were designed for a range of age categories that spanned from infants to senior citizens. Skilled toy sales personnel were highly trained and in-demand specialists, able to demonstrate upon request the functions of hundreds of toys, whether simple robot mantises or complex World Net–linked reality programs. She couldn't imagine any other field more exciting or more expressive of humankind's creative impulse. For Rama, toys had not only become the highest forms of art; they were magical objects, alchemical, capable of opening gateways to other worlds and changing a dull human life into an adventure. They were also the precursors for the secret yearning to fuse with the material, with metal and plastic, with the machine, to become the cyborgian chimera that was the hot topic of the day.

As she ran, she didn't notice the people, the lake, or the trees except as background to her thoughts, which were fixated on that dream. If her subconscious was trying to give her a message, then what was it? All she could think of was the kind of generic prophecy you'd find in a Chinese fortune cookie. *Events greater than you and outside your control are going to change the course of your life.* Or was it a premonition of something darker? Were the stone men evil or good? She had checked her memory for a movie, or maybe something she'd recently read or heard that could in any way have caused the imagery of the dream. Maybe Nazis during World War II or North Korean soldiers marching through the streets, or a new video game, but it simply didn't synch. And why had she had the same dream three times now? The robotic quality of the stone beings was what had struck her the most. They didn't even have eyes. There was no sign of individual consciousness. *Crunch, crunch, crunch, crunch ...*

■ ■ ■ ■ ■ ■

Physical Cemeteries and Casket Sales Continue to Decline
According to recent figures, funeral parlors and tombstone and casket manufacturers have experienced a steady decline in sales for more than fifteen years. People are now less interested in preserving bodies than in any other time in recorded history. Increasingly, bodies are donated to science or cremated. There has, however, been an increase in cryogenic preservation of heads in outer space stations, presumably because neuron patterns in the brain are said to hold the key to an individual identity.

In general, body preservation has been steadily replaced by digital time capsules and digital heavens. These cyberrealities have sprung up in record numbers and are becoming the number-one funeral procedure chosen by the soon-to-be deceased and their loved ones. Digital time capsules preserve a virtual record of one's life assembled from photos, video, written material, and virtualizations. Genetic and other medical records can also be included for couples wanting to assess genetic compatibility and predict the possible outcome of future offspring. Any parent can now show to their children what their grandparents and other dead relatives were like. The lives of most people are becoming cyberbiographies that preserve invaluable historical information on a scale never before achieved in the history of our species.

Costing many times more but quickly increasing in popularity are digital heavens, where a virtualization of the dead is constructed and maintained from the vast amount of provided information. With digital heavens, relatives can regularly communicate with a virtual loved one after death. As the saying goes, "She may be dead but her spirit lives on." And is now accessible 24/7.

28.

PASSIFLORA

On the way home, sitting in the taxi, Sunshine still felt on the edge of tears thinking about his sister, little Passie girl, and he couldn't quite resolve the conflicts in his head. Guilt, for sure, was gnawing at him. Guilt for not keeping in touch with her. Guilt for being so caught up in his work that months had gone by and he hadn't bothered to call. Guilt about being a bad brother and so wrapped up in his work that most of the time he forgot she existed. And missing his parents. The daunting realization that if Passie had died, the guilt he now felt would have in some way consumed him like bad karma, haunting him until the end of his life.

He felt a wretched awareness that Passie was still his strongest connection to the body-and-flesh world, the one with strings still tied to his heart. And he began to think back to how all of this had happened, when he and Passie had always been each other's best friend, as close as a brother and sister could be. *It was all the wheels of death and rebirth,* he thought. As the Buddhists said, the pattern of death and rebirth is a fractal and occurs on many scales from the small to the large, from subatomic particles to a human life. Every instant, you are, you die, and you are reborn. Every instant your choices move you forward. Every instant the opportunity to be enlightened, or—as we all tend to do—to choose the same old pattern, again and again.

Something had happened that had caused a death and rebirth of Passie and Sunshine, once together and as close as could be, but now separate in this lifetime. Most of the blame fell on him, on his choices and his eventual abandonment of his little sister. The turning point, the crossroads, was his senior year in high school, the year of the accident, the one that caused their parents to cross over to the other side of the winding road and crash through a barrier and down a mountainside.

Strangely enough, it had taken more than a day before anyone discovered the accident. The particular bend of road had been secluded and there had been no traffic at the time. Regular commuters who later passed the torn barrier swerved away as if the opening were a vacuum black hole that would draw them in if they got too close. Even if his parents had been alive after tumbling down the mountain, they had long died by the time the rescue team reached them. As it was, the only reason anybody found them was that a little boy who had to go pee noticed the car on its side at the bottom of the ravine. Wanting to show off his new talking abilities, he had cried out to his father standing nearby, "Car . . . blue car."

The police couldn't determine what had caused the accident. It could have been the damaged lawn mower they had found on the opposite side of the road, they said. As the police presented it, the lawn mower might have been in the back of an open truck and fallen out as it took the curve. That might have caused his father to swerve and lose control. Or maybe the crash had been the result of a health problem, possibly a heart attack or a stroke. It could also have been drugs, they had suggested, figuring that people who looked like hippies were probably indulgers.

He could remember being home with Passie that first night, and thinking how odd it was that their parents hadn't returned or even bothered to call. When he got up the next morning, he assumed they had gotten in while he was sleeping but on the way down the stairs, he noticed that the house felt empty. He climbed back up the stairs and checked their room. No one answered the knock and their bed was empty. Later that day, soon after they returned from school, two uniformed policemen were at the door. Because he and Passie were underage they asked for the names of relatives. Their aunt and uncle who lived close-by were contacted, as was a social services representative.

That was the way to the crossroads. He ended up later that year at MIT on a full scholarship and got involved with borg technology. Passie had stayed with their aunt and uncle for the following two years, then went on to college. He had come to accept that growing up was what had separated them, that it was the fate of brothers and sisters to at some point be weaned from each other—that eventually they would have to build a life of their own. That early fraternal bond was supposed to be replaced by whatever it is that adult brother-sister relationships grew up to be, which in their case could have been described as intermittent contact.

Three years ago, Passie had called him soon after she had moved into the city. They had had a few dinners together but eventually he had gotten too caught up in his work to keep in touch. And now this, facing the possibility of another crossroad, one where Passie could have died. The feeling of loss was so great that it made him realize that without Passie, his life would deaden in ways he didn't even want to imagine. She was his lifeline to things felt and real, to the thinnest sense of still belonging to the human tribe.

Still, leaving the taxi and headed for his apartment's doorway, he began to feel somewhat normal again. It might have been a delusion of self-assurance, triggered by the prospect of the security of his home, but as much as the thought terrified him, he decided he would go back the next day to visit his little sister again.

29.

THE TOET

After Law Three, Sunshine received a call from his once best friend Patrick, another casualty of his voluntary isolation. The first thing Patrick said was, "You're looking weird, Sunny. Is that a monk look or your most recent attempt at dehumanization?"

The criticism surprised Sunshine, who thought that compared to the way he usually presented himself to the public, his current cyber-Buddhist image was pretty normal-looking. Maybe it was the fact that he was wearing goggles.

"I figured you'd eventually call," said Sunshine.

"And I knew you wouldn't," Patrick answered. "I probably wouldn't have either, except that I figured if anyone is likely to have a clue about what's going on, crazy Sunshine cooped up with all his computer buddies probably would."

"You know what, Patrick, I'm not going to explain myself or make up excuses because I don't have any good excuses. In any case, I'm glad you called."

Feeling somewhat uncomfortable after not having talked to Sunshine in over three years, Patrick decided to get to the point. "So tell me, what's this *I AM* thing all about? Did you have anything to do with it?"

"If you mean did I create it, the answer is no. Could some of my programs have had anything to do with it? It's possible, but not possible to determine."

"So where did it come from?"

"Do you mean did it come from outside the World Net?"

"Why? Do you know?"

"I think that the logical approach is to assume that there has to be something about the World Net that allows this *I AM* to express itself. The World Net system can apparently serve as a tool for it to communicate to us."

"And what do you think it is? God? An alien civilization?" Patrick asked, knowing very well the kind of reaction it would elicit.

"God? Are you serious? I thought you and I had agreed a long time ago that God was a pretty useless term. What does the damn word mean anyway? How useful has it been in our understanding of things? It's always been the irrational fill-in-the-blank for everything that we've been too ignorant to understand, too weak to overcome, and too desperate to accept. So let's skip the word God," Sunshine replied, annoyed.

"OK, so is it McKenna's transcendental object at the end of time, the TOET?" Patrick asked.

Sunshine was surprised by his friend's question—that he should have even considered McKenna.

"It's more likely that it's simply a kind of a transcendental object."

"Where do you think it came from?"

"Well, as you know, a transcendental object is not something mystical or religious but an object eventually created by biological organisms that becomes lifelike, autopoietic, intelligent, and develops a form of consciousness that's greater than that of its creators. That's why it's called a transcendental object. In the case of *I AM*, it was created either accidentally by us or by another civilization, assuming that's what it is."

"So, do you think it's the same as McKenna's TOET?"

"It can't be exactly the same, because McKenna's date for the Eschaton, for his predicted encounter with the transcendental object, has come and gone. You know, even though McKenna was the first to present the idea of a transcendental object at the end of time, it was probably Frank Tipler who made the best case for it. The TOET is a hypothetical transcendental object that generates its own autonomous and encapsulated reality, and thus can free its creations from the standard rules of time, and the laws of biology and physics. It would be a kind of subuniverse that generates its own laws."

"Well . . . unless I haven't been paying attention, there is no evidence yet that this *I AM* is generating its own laws," Patrick said.

"Unless you consider the fact that it appears to communicate without generating traces of a signal."

"But that doesn't mean it's necessarily a TOET."

"You're right. It could just mean that it uses a type of technology that is outside our grasp. The one thing we know is that, whatever *I AM* is, whether it was accidentally created by us, created itself, or created by an extraterrestrial civilization, it appears from an evolutionary standpoint as the result of a type of technology. The reason I emphasize technology is that *I AM* uses our technology to communicate, so it must be a comfortable medium for it."

"So you're saying that transcendental objects, assuming that's what *I AM* is, could be part of an evolutionary sequence in the universe?"

"That little theoretical bit got your attention? I suspect that, if and when possible, advanced civilizations in our universe will attempt to create transcendental objects that eventually will have the replicating capabilities that allow biological unities to download into the object. Once replicated inside the transcendental object these unities will become new forms of being not restricted by biological or physical laws or by the standard rules of time. The TOET is what, one day, could allow us to resurrect, disembodied, like angels. Tipler actually deserves the credit for that idea."

"So do you think *I AM* could be a resurrection machine?

That would make its coming to Earth almost Christlike," Patrick said tentatively, hoping it wouldn't trigger another of Sunshine's antireligion tirades.

"I have no idea what it is. No one does at this point. But I think that because it uses our technology its source is probably some type of transcendental object with a sense of self-identity and its own unique type of consciousness."

"So what's next?"

Sunshine took on a somber look. "Those who don't worship it and recognize it as the supreme cosmic authority will be sent to camps where they will be kept alive for infinity—dissected, reconstructed, burned, raped, anally probed, subjected to endless mental agony and suicidal depression from which there can be no relief—a Boschian inferno."

"You're kidding?"

Sunshine tried to stay serious. "Brace yourself and see what happens," he added, but then couldn't help breaking into a smile. Patrick started laughing. This was the kind of humor that made him miss their friendship.

"So besides this *I AM* craziness, how's life? Are you happy?" Patrick asked.

Sunshine's expression and tone of voice suddenly changed. "Well, I thought things were fine until Passie got beaten up. It's made me face the fact that I haven't been a very good big brother, that I'm too wrapped up in my futuristic cybernonsense, as you would probably say."

"I read about Passie in the news. How is she doing?"

"I guess she's doing OK. She had to go through surgery and some face reconstruction, but all things considered, she'll probably get through that whole experience better than I will. Hopefully she'll be more selective about who she picks up at clubs."

"You know, there is more to life than cyberreality, Sunny. You should try to remember the people out there who care about you and depend on you."

"I already got that lecture from Passie. The fact is that I have to make a choice. Trying to find a balance by switching back and forth between disconnected and connected realities ends up making me feel schizophrenic and disoriented. I also have withdrawal effects that last for days. Because of my interests and work, I choose to be in a mostly cyberconnected state. Of course that's no excuse for not keeping in touch with either you or Passie."

"Well if I were you, I'd choose living in the body-and-flesh world. You should consider trying it again sometime."

"The problem, Patrick, is that I can't go back to living that way. Who I am and what I'm supposed to do is defined by the possibility of creating the transcendental object. Maybe it's a suicide run, at least on a personal level, but I have this vision that by pursuing this course something extraordinary lies in our future that is worth every bit of the sacrifice. Look at it like our attempts at flight, reaching the moon, or breaking into new territory. There are risks and sacrifices. If I'm right, and if I succeed, then in the end we can all win." Sunshine could see that Patrick was going to interject so he decided to change the subject. "How about you, how are things?"

"I've got a lot of exciting things going on. You've probably read about my work with parenting hosts."

"And about all the controversy about the funding from MicroHost, who by the way uses some of my CNT software in your hosts. How about the love life? Are you still the womanizer?"

"Womanizer? I guess so. I'm involved with three women, including one whom I met recently under the strangest circumstances. It's only been platonic so far but I really like her."

Sunshine couldn't resist asking, "So how did you meet this woman?"

"You won't believe this, Sunny. I met her at a Sisterhood meeting."

"You're joking. I'm surprised those hard-core lesbos even let you in."

"Well, you're going to love this one. I dressed up for the occasion."

Sunshine frowned. "Dressed up? As a woman?"

Looking innocent, Patrick replied, "Yes, I was trying to find a way to get in without, you know, looking too obtrusive."

Sunshine suddenly burst out in laughter and Patrick joined in, the two of them caught in a contagious cycle.

"You, dressed up as a woman!" Sunshine repeated between laughing fits and attempts at trying to catch his breath.

Patrick managed to say between outbursts, "And you know me, I do what needs to be done to get the job done; gender is no obstacle," and they both cracked up laughing again.

"Stop!" Sunshine said with tears falling from his eyes. "You're making my sides hurt."

Patrick, of course, went on. "You should see me in stockings and high heels," playing it to the max.

"Oh no!" Sunshine exclaimed, laughing some more. "Enough, my sides hurt."

After they had simmered down, Patrick tried to get the conversation back on a more serious track and asked, "How about you? Any great loves in your life?"

"Loves? I don't have love, Patrick, I have relationships, several of them, and they're all fine except for a recent cyberdate who thinks she's fallen in love with me, which is a puzzle considering we've never met in person. I'm not even sure that who I'm looking at is really her."

"So you don't have anyone special in your life?"

"Special . . . the problem is that what most people call love is some kind of emotional focus, a little like using a magnifying glass to concentrate sun rays." Patrick looked at Sunshine wondering what this had to do with his question.

Sunshine went on. "Whatever love I feel, it's in this diffused state, scattered, diluted. I realized this when I saw Passie again, because somehow she made me feel this concentrated emotion again and you know what? It scared me. It made me realize how I'm probably wired all wrong in that area and yes, it's probably from not living in the disconnected world. So in answer to your question, I don't really have a love life and I don't know shit about love."

Whoa, Patrick thought, *that sure hit a nerve.* "You know what, Sunshine?"

"What?"

"You've just become an emotional chicken shit. You should try going out in the world. Dress up a little." Which of course set them off laughing again.

■ ■ ■ ■ ■ ■

GAS.WNET RADIO: *The Gary and Andy Show*

ANDY: I don't know what it is with Ashley, but lately she's just not in the mood to give me head. I'm wondering if this is the beginning of the end.

GARY: Men's obsession with fellatio is a deprivation phenomenon.

ANDY: You mean because we're regularly deprived of it we're always fantasizing about it?

GARY: No, it's the deprivation that makes it so appealing. It's the kind of distancing that makes the mind borderline hallucinate. It starts constructing blowjob fantasies that border on the mystical, actually the pathological. As if salvation could be found by simply plugging into a mouth, like a computer connection.

ANDY: You always want what you can't get, that's just what I said.

GARY: But that's not what I meant. It's being deprived of it that makes it so appealing. If you had a fellatio buffet type of situation, all the head you can get, day in and day out, it would become a nightmare of the endless déjà vu. Imagine that women, instead of being reluctant and conditional about giving head, were from day one genetically wired to be phallivorous creatures who, from the time they're babies, have the search image for hunting down cock.

You're still a little boy, and the little girls would be trying desperately to get at your weenie pop, even adult women, your mother's friends, while no one's looking, unzip the weenie out and like vampires try to sneak in a quick snack. After a while you'd develop a type of paranoia. You'd wear penis guards, a version of chastity belts with a secret code to allow for access. You'd eventually look at women with wariness. You'd look at their mouths, with their lips, naturally swollen and puckered from hours of daily fellating, as if they belonged to cannibals. Fellatio could become a kind of dread, a phobia of the female mouth.

ANDY: Isn't this a case of role reversal? Don't men always want sex and doesn't that inspire a kind of penis terror in women?

GARY: Penis terror? You wish. The truth is that women look at our penises and secretly, they're laughing. They know we've just exposed a weakness. They pretend to be intimidated but inside they're jumping up and down. It's like we just handed them the control stick.

ANDY: You don't know what you're talking about. I wish my girlfriend would blow me every night and every morning before going to work, and at lunchtime, too. It'd be better than taking tranqs. I'd always be relaxed . . . now with Annie, it's become a special-occasion thing, maybe . . . a rare moment of loosed passions. The truth is, it's been so long I'm beginning to forget what it feels like.

GARY: You're saying that because you're assuming you'd be in control. Imagine if the minute you didn't pay attention that mouth was there wrapped around your dick, sucking. You want to watch a TV show—she's sucking. You want to eat breakfast, she's sucking. You're trying to sleep, and she's still mouthing your cock. After a while you would see that smiling, eager mouth with the red painted lips and you would start panicking. Before too long you'd be on tranquilizers to control the panic attacks, the fear that a woman is sneaking around, somewhere under your desk, around the corner of a hallway, of a street, just waiting for you to let your guard down before attacking your crotch like a mad dog. The image of the pouncing fellatrix would haunt you. The face of a smiling model on a magazine cover. The face of television anchors and show hosts. Everywhere, women as sharks in sheep's clothes, the infamous *boca dentata*. The soft lips concealing the teeth.

ANDY: You're crazy.

GARY: You know exactly what I mean. What makes a good blowjob so appealing is that it's something unexpected, given in small doses, at unpredictable intervals. It's like eating good chocolate. When you pop a square in your mouth, you savor it, try to identify the nuances, a fruitiness, a smokiness, a hint of bitterness, and it is that evaluation that brings forth the grand experience.

ANDY: What the hell are you talking about? Eating chocolate. What does eating chocolate have to do with a blowjob?

GARY: On the other hand, you could use chocolate in a way that traumatizes, like forcing an enemy to eat pounds of chocolate daily during an interrogation process as a form of torture. Men do the same with fellatio. They evaluate the nature of the act, what is expressed through the lips and mouth and throat. Is it love, phallic worship, cannibalism, playfulness? Or else like so many women do, fellatio automata. Does it like a machine because she has to, because those idiot men are so hung up on it. As a man you evaluate those moments carefully because they're a critical test.

ANDY: Gary, it's just a fucking blowjob, for Christ's sake.

GARY: It's not just a blowjob. It's a test. Subliminally it determines the foundations of a relationship. You can always tell where you stand with your lover or your wife by the way she blows you, and that's assuming she blows you at all. Without knowing it, the future of the world may rest on the quality of a blowjob. Think back at Clinton, and Lewinsky. What kind of blowjob did she give in her attempt to seduce the president, what magic spell was attempted there, in that secluded room, during those small windows of opportunity, with those lips? You'd never know it looking at her, the power of that mouth. Hey, think of Cleopatra. They say she was ugly as sin but what great oral skills she must have had to seduce Mark Antony and have him coming back again and again. It's too bad those moments weren't recorded: fellatrices that changed the course of the world.

ANDY: Gary, are you on something?

GARY: I wish.

30.

YOU CAN'T ALWAYS SMELL
WHAT YOU WANT

Jessie was fixated to the screen, taking advantage of having gotten to work an hour early to watch her favorite cooking show, *Mouth Waterings*. Just the name was enough to trigger a Pavlovian salivating response. *Mouth Waterings*. The daily show had become a key component of her new diet plan. After being faced with the gourmet meals shown in vibracolor on *Mouth Waterings*, she just couldn't bring herself to eat a sandwich or a microwaved meal without feeling like she was stooping to the level of a lower life form. Animals ate. Humans dined, they feasted, they delected, they savored, they didn't just eat like cattle standing in a pasture.

The humans who just ate, she was convinced, had been swine or cattle in a previous life. They looked like humans on the outside but still thought and acted like beasts. A clear sign of their past origins was that they tended to herd at all-you-can-eat buffets, lined up like hogs to slop grub from the stainless steel feeding troughs onto their plates. Just the thought was enough to make her sick to her stomach. She could imagine the eyes made into piggy slits by the gleeful smiles bulging the cheeks, the shuffling of thighs rubbing against each other on their return to the tables, the gelatinous white arms trembling as they carried the overloaded plates. Then the bodies would maneuver onto the too small chairs, the hands would grab the forks, the arms would lift to gather the necessary momentum, and the feeding process would begin, a dazed frenzy, shoveling and gulping at lightning speed like pelicans swallowing fish, before setting off for another run. That image of moms and pops in burst-at-the-seam clothing with their plump round-faced toddlers was also a key component of her psychological strategy to dieting. The thought alone made her ashamed to eat. She used it for hunger control. When hungry, just think about the fatties.

Because gourmet was not possible during her forty-five-minute lunch break, she skipped eating and instead usually spent the time planning dinner and listing the ingredients she'd have to buy before heading home. It was a daily project that required research and careful mental evaluation of the combination and sequence of flavors, which she performed with the aid of a Net cooking host that would point out possible errors in judgment and advise on better alternatives. As a rule, she would select three new recipes to try out, as part of her standard four-course dinner. If she had the time, she would also quickly sketch possible designs for the presentation of the different dishes, including the selection of trimmings to frame and add contrast to her culinary compositions.

For Jessie, the dinner bit was serious business. The goal of cooking, if it were to be elevated to a human behavior, did not only have to satisfy the mouth and nose but had to be a full-fledged multimedia experience. It had to cater to the eyes, the sight alone hinting of secrets to be revealed when the items are placed on the tongue. One had to pick the right kind of plate. The quality of the lighting had to be just so. The table setting, something suitable for framing. The meal, an experiment in art and metaphysics, destined to be disintegrated by sweeps of the fork, like a Tibetan sand painting.

Patricia had approved of her new diet plan for obvious reasons. She got to come home every night to a gourmet meal . . . at least she used to, until the last two weeks when Sisterhood meetings to deal with the *I AM* problem had routinely kept her busy past midnight. At least that was the story Patricia had been telling her, assuming it was true, and had nothing to do with the newest recruits to the Sisterhood's inner circle: the Henley twins and that hard-muscled workout queen, Jackie Sylvia. She had noticed that their names now came up almost every evening as part of their nightly lie-in-bed conversations. Jackie this and Jackie that. Sue Henley said this, Carla Henley said that.

Supposedly the Sisterhood board was working on testing out a new ritual to counter the effects of the clearly masculine *I AM*. That was the excuse for the meetings, but by now Jessie knew Patricia well enough that she could see the pattern. Other members had pretty much confirmed it. Patricia got easily bored. Jessie was just the latest link in a long chain of tit for twat relationships. There was a well-established history. Patricia would offer the lure of transitional lodging in a city where available rentals were at a premium. In exchange, her newest conquests were expected to provide not-too-taxing sexual services until the next recruits, goo-goo gaga at the thought of being selected by the high priestess, came along.

Today's mouthwatering dish was the very challenging double-layered cheese soufflé. Two kinds of soufflés with different densities carefully poured on top of each other. Her aromator unit was on, wafting the scents toward her nose, first one cheese, then the other, and finally, the blend. The smell of the first layer of cheese reminded her a little of armpit sweat, which was an odor she kind of liked. The second had a rich, creamy sweetness to it that brought to mind the image of Switzerland. Combined, the scents gave one a heartwarming, cozy, by-the-fireplace kind of feeling, a winter dish.

Of course the actual smell of the final product might have been quite different. Her aromator was bottom-of-the-line basic but she just hadn't yet been able to afford the Deluxe 3000 model with triple the range of chemorizers. It was on the top of her list of things to buy, because aromators had become the latest communications craze, and she felt like she was missing out on some great recipes and product promotions. Everybody was boosting up their ads and sites and programs with virtual scents to add to "the multimodality of the experience."

Even the Sisterhood was working on developing a line of aromator products, but success so far had been limited because the subtle olfactory nuances of colognes and the nooks and crannies of the female body were not yet effectively reproduced by current aromator converters, which tended to accentuate odors. As Patricia had joked, "Subtle female is sexy but concentrated female can sometimes end up smelling like something gone bad, like men." The trick to aromator conversion, Patricia would say, was to "dilute, dilute, dilute, and then blend with botanicals." It may have been sound advice but the results to date had been disappointingly bland. The Sisterhood was also working on a line of patented female pheromones, but these were aimed to be sold as "a-little-dab'll-do-ya" microvials. The initial intention, to direct-market the pheromone potions through the aromators, had been quickly reality checked. The aromators had turned out to be pretty worthless when it came to translating pheromones.

She took in one last whiff of the two-cheese soufflé, then stored the recipe in her communicator to add to her files. She looked at the time. She still had another ten minutes left on her break from her job in shipping and receiving at Telltale Publishing, a company that specialized in unauthorized biographies of the living and the dead, both ancient and modern, both real and mythical.

She decided to connect to her host, Don Quixote, who looked right out of *Man of La Mancha*, armor and all. She typed in the question so no one in the office would hear. Don Quixote would respond by audio to her earplugs. It was the same question she had already asked three times in the last two weeks. The last time he had answered, "Wake up and smell the roses, girl," its masculine voice closely matching her father's. She used to worry about that, wondering what Patricia would say if she were to find out she had a male host, but so far, she had always managed to click off before being discovered. That same question was still bugging her though, and she wasn't really sure why. Maybe you keep asking until you hear what you want to hear.

The fact was, things were beginning to feel different, like someone had adjusted her reality-perspective dial. It had started after meeting Joanna. She enjoyed her company and looked forward to talking about something other than the same old Sisterhood stuff. Fact was, she was getting a little tired of the lesbo routines and lingo. It had become an experiment that had gotten out of hand. That's what she got from being too casual about contact boundaries. She liked touching and being touched, and it didn't matter if it was men or women. Maybe it came from living with four brothers and sisters in a house that had been way too small. Don Quixote had said that it might have been an old genetic trait, from back when human ancestors group-cuddled in caves during cold winter nights. At first, Patricia touching her and then going as far as sex had been a little odd but hey, when all was said and done, *un cuerpo es un cuerpo*, like Rosa Santos says.

Staying with Patricia had simply been a practical decision—free lodging and daily sex until she got a decent job and pulled her life together. Now what could be so bad about that? The situation had kept her from making dumb and desperate decisions that could have gotten her involved with the wrong kind of man, like the two jerks she had left back home. Now, when she felt the need for a man, she just Cybrised in at a cybercafé and went digital. It was safe and it kept her out of trouble.

Jessie asked her host one more time, "Do you think it's time for me to leave Patricia?"

"What do you think?" Don Quixote answered. It was typical host shrink talk. Answer a question with a question.

"I think I should maybe talk about it to my new friend Joanna. She's a psychologist," Jessie said.

"That sounds like a . . ."

The connection was cut off by *Law Four: I AM Awakening from Awakening. I AM Aaa ome.*

Very funny, she thought. *Time to wake up and smell the roses, girl.* She made a plan to call Joanna after dinner, figuring Patricia probably wouldn't be around. Maybe she'd walk to a cybercafé and call from there, just in case. Her supervisor entered the room with a new set of orders to pack up, ship out, and invoice. She lifted her head and killed the host connection.

"So Harry, how many do we have for today?" she asked.

31.

ALL YOU NEED IS LOVE

Father Graham now accepted what he considered his illumination. It was as if a light from within had been switched on and brightened the world and his whole being. For most of the first week following the *I AM* event, he had been so energized that he only slept a few hours, spending most of the night lying on his back in the dark with his eyes open, bathing in the light of God, who had answered. He felt like a content child resting his head on the breast of his mother, looking calmly at the world, except that his head now rested on the heart of God. The feeling was there when he got up in the morning, and it was there when he went to bed at night. He belonged to God, and what he was put on this Earth to do was as clear as the light that filled him and lit his way.

Rama noticed the sign on the church on her way home. A small crowd was gathered outside of the open doors. Speakers had been placed near the church entrance to accommodate those sitting on the church steps and standing on the sidewalk. Several cameras and microphones were raised above the heads and pointed toward the inside of the building. Rama heard the sermon as she walked past and decided to backtrack and sit on the crowded church steps after hearing the word *love*.

"Deep at the core of every one of you is God. *I AM* is what every baby's first cry is saying, and it is this *I AM* that we all share in common, this *I AM* that fuels our spirits and that we acknowledge as the deepest and most sacred part of ourselves. Through all your senses, whether it is seeing, hearing, or touching, through all your feelings and thoughts, it is *I AM* who looks out at the world."

Someone in the audience asked a question. Father Graham pointed to a raised hand and an attendant made his way through the aisles, bringing a microphone up to a plainly dressed Asian woman with two children at her sides.

"Could you repeat your question, young lady, so that everyone can hear?"

"What about what the Bible says about the need to believe in Jesus Christ to be saved?"

"Knowledge is something one acquires from observation and at deeper levels from questioning. So the first step is to question what it means to believe in Jesus Christ as a condition for salvation. Does it mean that we live in a universe where we have a God so vain and so simpleminded that the belief that he and his son are the big chiefs of the universe will decide whether he spares someone the tortures of hell or sends him to heaven?

"One would have to question such a small-minded God and the worshipping of such a God. A vain God who punishes you because you don't acknowledge he's the big chief of the universe is not one to bow to. God is bigger than anyone's beliefs. There is nothing, not one little thing, one creature, one being to whom its arms are not open. Its embrace and its forgiveness are limitless. The kingdom of heaven is open to each and every being whether or not they realize God's true nature. Why?

"Because there is nothing that is not God, and thus nothing that can ever be separate from God. It is as it says, *I AM*. This is something you all know, and it does not require belief. In each and every one of you is the voice that recognizes the original condition of existence, *I AM*. It is God's voice."

Rama sat and listened and felt the passion of the priest.

She was reminded of the rather naïve but wonderful old Beatles song: *All you need is love . . . ta–ta–ta ta–ta. All you need is love, love. Love is all you need.*

The next question got Rama's attention.

"Father, why do you keep using the word *it* when referring to God or *I AM?* Why not *he* or *she?*"

"Because *I AM* is deeper than the biological or the sexual, deeper than the male or female. It generates form but it is not of form. It is the presence behind all of existence. The *it*ness of it. *Neither Light nor Darkness Change the Presence of the Sky. I AM Aaa ome.*"

Maybe, she thought, *that's what the great sweeping stone beings were . . . formless, sexless symbols of* I AM, *of some type of otherworldly principle that was going to sweep through humanity, and nothing would be able to stand in the way of what was coming.*

After Father Graham returned to his apartment, two messages blinked on his screen. One was from the Dalai Lama of Tibet. It said, *Different messengers, same message, same sender. Aaa ome.*

The other said, *URGENT. You are to meet Archbishop Novack at St. Peter's tomorrow at 2:00 p.m. Please inform if you cannot attend.*

What Father Graham did not know was that his sermon had been recorded and shown on the World Net to millions, and had put him at the top of the blacklist of the Virtual Church of Jesus Christ as a confirmed agent of Satan.

32.

THE GARDENS OF THE DEAD

"Look in my purse," his sister mumbled through her swollen lips, pointing to the front of the hospital room. "It's in the top drawer, over there."

Sunshine got up and retrieved the purse, then settled back in the chair by his sister's bed.

"Go ahead, you can look inside," she said.

He shuffled through the makeup, electronic cards, and jewelry, noticed the two small wooden statuettes resting on the bottom, and smiled. "Hey, it's Sylvia and Richard!"

"I always carry them with me, for good luck, you know . . . light beams."

He pulled them out holding one in each hand, running his thumbs along the polished wood, remembering his parents.

Passie looked at him with a grin. "Light beams," she said again. It was an expression they had inherited from their parents to define people who had illuminated the course of the evolution of human consciousness. Einstein . . . light beam, Darwin . . . light beam, Buddha . . . light beam, Wilber . . . light beam, and so on. It made him think of the name his parents had given him and what it said, not about him, but about them, that they had chosen to call him Sunshine. After a few minutes of silence, Passie, still smiling, closed her eyes and dozed off.

He could still remember the day at the funeral parlor. He had had to see for himself. It had been a need for some kind of biological reckoning, a coming to terms with the inanimation of the body that follows the departure of the soul. Passie had decided to stay home, preferring her last memories to be of Richard and Sylvia alive, intact, and with presence of mind. He and his Uncle Steven had had to deal with the funeral arrangements. He had right away asked to see his parents, and he could still remember the director of the funeral parlor telling Steven, "I'm sorry, but they are beyond repair."

"What do you mean?" his uncle had asked.

"The accident, the injuries—I don't think we can make them presentable for viewing," and then bending over and whispering something in his ear, his uncle's eyebrows lifting in surprise.

Sunshine had stood there and insisted, "I'm their son, it's my right."

After a moment of consideration, the funeral home director finally said, "The mother . . . maybe, we'll see what we can do, please wait here."

He sat with his uncle for over an hour before they were called in. They remained silent during most of that time, gazing at the dimly lit waiting room with the feel of having entered a Victorian time warp, the setting all prim and proper, with plush antique chairs and rich mahogany furniture, the papered walls adorned with framed prints and paintings lit by tiny overhead lights, showing life frozen in time. Pretty landscapes with flowers . . . more flowers . . . an ancient ship on a turbulent ocean . . . men on horseback with hounds chasing a fox. The mood was funeral-home correct, somber but not morbid. There was nothing to suggest death; no skulls, no scenes of early medical dissections, of the burning of the dead on funeral pyres, no depictions of the Hindu Goddess Kali with her skull necklace, of cemeteries with crosses, of heaven and hell. The art of Hieronymus Bosch, of William Blake, of Goya and H. R. Giger were not on display. This was the setting for the comfortable disposal of inanimate bodies before the evidence of physical decomposition set in. A flash mummifying that would spare us the perception of the inevitable victory of death over life, a shift best kept mysterious and to remain in the realm of the invisible.

Sunshine couldn't quite explain it, but the formality of the well-fitted suits of the director and his assistants combined with white shirts and ties bugged the fuck out of him. These were, after all, people who processed cadavers. Who were they kidding? Who were the necrophilic beings that hid behind the eyes and moving lips? We dress in dark suits and ties. We are respected members of the community, businessmen. We'll make this as simple and painless and odorless as possible, transform your loved ones into giant dolls suitable for viewing, except that there is not enough intact structure to make dolls, in this case. A butcher's apron, shirts with rolled-up sleeves, even surgical gowns and masks would have been more honest. We are here to collect exit fees or entry fees, depending on your point of view. We're not prejudiced. We'll take it, front or back.

When he finally entered the curtained room and looked down at what was once his mom, it occurred to him for an instant that maybe there had been a mistake, that it had not been his mother and father in the accident after all. Certainly this shell of a woman, this fleshed mannequin, could not have been his mother. The face was thick with makeup and she never wore makeup. The hair was styled and curled and she always wore hers long and straight down. The eyes were closed as if belonging to something cast, something out of a wax museum, a second-generation replica. The lipstick had not been completely able to hide the torn lip, the creams and powders unable to cover the tiny cuts and hints of black bruising on the forehead.

It must have hurt, Mom, he thought. He knelt by her head, crossed his arms over the edge of the display casket, and, with his head resting on a hand, contemplated the face. "Mom, if you could only see yourself now," he said to himself.

That was all that was left of Richard and Sylvia, the best parents and best friends he had ever known. They had been the very brightest of light beams, cutting a path wide and clear through the intrinsic darkness and dullness of the world. Thinking back, he'd have to say that the source of that light had been some strange catalysis triggered by their having found each other, as if each had been the other's Holy Grail. Their encounter had triggered within the mysterious depths of their brain chemistries the ongoing release of a type of energy that somehow managed to consume life's problems into insignificance. He could not remember a single day when his parents hadn't, for one reason or another, laughed.

Like their own eccentric pot-smoking hippy parents, Richard and Sylvia eventually managed to realize the freedom of not working for others and of successfully avoiding "the mind-sucking vortices" of large corporations. His mother achieved this autonomy when, after a four-year stint of teaching high school chemistry, she decided to become a gourd artist. She transformed dead, dried, moldy squashes into psychoactive objects that came to life when introduced to the human mind, their surfaces perfectly stained and polished, etched with complex patterns, symbols, and figures arranged in mandalas around the stem core.

For Sylvia, each gourd had been the expression of her exploration into a particular field or set of ideas influenced by her interest in science and early history. The geometries of subatomic and chemical structures, the DNA molecule, ethnobotany, prehistoric art, the serpent myth, Plato's allegory of the cave, fungal life, the diversity of plants, ecology, Gaia, the Buddha, Christ, the Aztecs, the breast myth, fractals, and so on. Every project had involved extensive research, initially hours and days spent in libraries digging up and photocopying reference materials, and later, contemplation of the cork wall where all the relevant photocopied imagery was pinned. It usually required several weeks of preparation before Sylvia would finally begin the sketching and the experimental arrangement of designs, and eventually proceeded with the work itself, the carving, the woodburning and staining of the gourd surface.

Besides the objects of her art, marketed exclusively through a New York gallery, Sylvia had also had her personal gourd, what she called her "world gourd," a giant specimen purchased from a grower in Southern California who had advertised it as "the mama *cucúrbita*," the mother of all gourds. It was the one Sunshine now kept on the second floor of his townhouse, encased and climatized under glass. He could remember that because of its size, special attention had been given to its drying to reduce the high risk of rot. The gourd had once sat on a small table in her studio, like some ancient globe on which the map of an unknown planet was revealed by alien spirits in sections, channeled through his mother. The mama *cucúrbita* was Sylvia's grand endeavor to exteriorize the constructs of her brain into an observable object; aspects of her personal history had been depicted on the outside while her complex interior, rich with symbolic associations, embellished the inner surfaces.

He could still remember the gourd's prominent position in his mother's studio, illuminated by a ceiling spotlight, a work in progress, a cathartic process that Sylvia thought would last a lifetime. She had been wrong in that presumption. A lifetime had not been enough. At the time of her death over half the surface remained blank, like an ocean surrounded by land. For several years after his parents' deaths, the requests for Sylvia's art had kept coming in.

As for his father, he had followed a parallel course with Sylvia, initially joining her in her investigations, and contributing to brainstorming sessions before retreating to his den. Instead of spreading out his material on corkboard, Richard searched for and scanned a wide range of copyright-free images, hiring the services of students and struggling artist friends to develop software programs that became popular in education and entertainment. Sunshine would sit next to him as he punched keys and clicked on the mouse, shifting back and forth from programming code to software-generated images. He would watch for hours, fascinated by the process of creating something out of nothing, enthralled by the power of the machine to assemble and manifest worlds, and admiring of his father's wizard-like mastery of the process.

Although many of his programs matched his mother's gourd themes, a handful of others, under the series of *Exteriorizations of the Mind*, EM for short, served as what some psychologists called "deep profilers." Using his father's software, one could create a very individual and personal exteriorization of mental constructs through the digital and geometrical collage of stored images. The EM programs, much to everyone's surprise, became popular and lucrative as a result of their success in the digital dating scene, serving as a type of a complex Rorschach.

The funeral parlor man walked up to them and said at a level just above a whisper, "We did the best we could."

Sunshine got up and stated, "They wanted to be cremated."

"That can be arranged," the parlor man had acknowledged. "Please follow me to the office so we can fill out the forms."

Sunshine had written and conducted his parents' funeral ceremony, a gathering in their backyard that had ended with the pouring of their ashes in deep holes, over which trees were then planted. In that way, he and Passie had figured, their powdery remains would be transformed through some biological alchemy into arboreal matter that could be visited. It was a funerary rite that would honor their parents' world view. Sylvia and Richard had had their own idea of reincarnation. Souls could not be reincarnated, they claimed, because they were like flowers on a tree. There is only one soul and that is the world tree, the world soul, the Great Spirit. The notion of an individual soul was delusion, just as the Buddha had said. Leaves and flowers wilted, died, and fell to the ground but the tree would remain.

Yet, he could remember several occasions when he was a still a child, accompanying his mother to the local market, and Sylvia, pointing to vegetables and fruits, to meat packages and fish spread out on beds of ice, saying, "You were once that . . . food on supermarket shelves . . . until I ate it and turned it into Sunshine." Sylvia, the reincarnator, the light-beam maker. It had seemed appropriate to turn their remains back into some form of life. The two trees, of course, had been named after their parents,

Richard and Sylvia.

It was some time after that that a pair of walking skeletons with the brown stains of fossilization, clearly a little female and a robust male, started suddenly appearing in his imagination at the most unexpected times, usually holding hands. He had unconsciously conjured them up and willingly accepted them as part of his internal landscape. They never said anything, just remained there hand in hand, sometimes standing or sitting at his side, and other times posted across from him, the faces with hollow eye pits and grinning teeth, staring and expressing a simple, silent, self-evident message: What are you going to do about this?

It being understood that "this" referred to the generic robotic constraints of their skeletal condition, devoid of any individuality. What the hell was a tree without its flowers and leaves? Maybe the Buddha had missed something.

Later, while in college, he had inspired and helped coordinate the world's first living cemeteries, man-made parks and preserves funded by the funeral fees of those who wanted the bodies or ashes of their loved ones recycled and used to generate new life. The results were parks and conservation areas where cleared land was purchased and eco-engineered into natural habitats with the aid of complex computer simulations.

In Latin American countries, these living cemeteries became known as Los Jardines de los Muertos, the Gardens of the Dead. As could have been expected in those steamy tropical areas where nature, sorcery, and Christianity hybridized, these cemeteries eventually became canvases for a novel form of folk art. At the base of the trees and shrubs, at the edges of streams where their ancestors lay, the people placed candles in special holders, solar-powered lights, flowers, garlands, statues, colorful metal objects, crosses, wind chimes, signs and peculiar offerings such as framed candy wrappers. Branches of trees that now had the names of the deceased and the wood-transformed were regularly clipped by family members or friends as tokens or objects to be carved as if they contained the spirits of the dead. In other countries, the living cemeteries concept had been adopted by a network of nonprofit conservation organizations, under the name of the Gardens of Eden. They were run mostly by volunteers. No suits and ties, no formalin, but real people, aware of biological fragility and of the inevitability of biological death.

Six years after his parents' death, he had been called by the new owners of their house and told of their intent to build an addition that would have required cutting down Sylvia and Richard. He had arranged to have the trees removed and transported to the nearest living cemetery. It had been a costly project involving bulldozers, several cranes, and a couple of trucks. At that time he had broken a sizeable branch off each tree and tossed them in his car, not quite certain what he would do with them. The two branches, dried and cleared of leaves, had stood in the corner of his bedroom for more than a year.

He later commissioned an artist friend of Sylvia's to carve small sculptures of his parents from the branches and had sent them to Passie on the tenth anniversary of Richard and Sylvia's death.

He put the dolls back in the handbag, kissed the forehead of his sleeping sister, and got up to leave.

"I love you, Sunny," she mumbled.

"I love you too, Passie," he said, noticing the two skeletons across the room, bony fingers interlocked. He saw them mouth the words: *What are you going to do about this?*

33.

OUR FATHER WHO ART IN MYTH

This was a hell of a time for child psychologists. The rules of the game were changing and there were so many questions unanswered. The current model of child development was based on the crucial role of parents, of a mother and father who served as the role models that structured a child's identity and formed its relationship templates. There was the psychoanalytic trickle down. The loving supportive mother served as the model of the wife the son would eventually look for, and the caring father was the prototype for qualities a daughter hoped to find in a husband.

At least that would hypothetically be the case in an ideal world where children were raised by ideal parents. The truth was more of a kind of psychogenetics of neurosis. Abused, spoiled, and neglected parents passed new combinations of pathology to their abused, spoiled, and neglected offspring. But now, the rules had changed. The parental archetypes were being displaced by parenting and personal hosts and computer-linked robots, free of damaging neuroses and with infinite patience and knowledge. There were also other role models, the single mothers and the homosexual parents, the surrogate fathers and mothers.

All of these factors were changing the templates of

relationships in society. An increasing segment of the population was wiring itself in a way that did not search for monogamy or marriage and did not strive for parenthood. Some of his colleagues called it "the new pathology of self-sufficiency," the fulfillment of social and sexual needs isolated from actual human interaction.

Patrick Nymphaea had been invited to give the keynote speech at the annual meeting of the APA and he was expecting to be crucified. Jealousy and criticism were staples in his field. He had become successful as a result of his work with big corporations to develop parenting and therapeutic hosts, and this had not helped endear him to his many struggling colleagues.

As he sipped his morning coffee, he thought about how he could make a case against a pathological model of the current changes in society and human relationships. All he had to do was look at himself and most of his friends, all single and childless—like Sunshine, like his current sex partners, Clarissa, Madeline, and his new prospect, Jessie. Of course, there were still plenty of couples, like Hieronymus, with their love and soul mate ideals. He and Francine had been married for fifteen years and they apparently still fucked like adolescent bunny rabbits.

One approach to structuring his talk was to follow Sunshine's methodology: "Remember, the starting point always has to be an ontogenetic model. The world built itself from the ground up. The first steps to a sand mountain are the first grains of sand. Present a historical sequence as a sound foundation to argument."

Patrick let his mind wander, his fingers resting on the mini-keyboard, ready to type his stream of consciousness. First present a model of developmental and evolutionary flexibility of relationships. Consciousness and development are always the result of context. Humans can wire themselves in different ways and still end up psychologically healthy. The two requirements for psychological health were love and personal developmental support, and it had not always come only from a mommy and daddy. Monogamy had probably not been the ruling model during the more than one hundred thousand years that *Homo sapiens* appeared on the planetary scene. Chimpanzees, our closest living relatives, lived in close-knit groups but did not form monogamous relationships. Early humans also lived in groups and probably without the monogamous sex-love condition (I'll love only you and only let you fuck me if you promise to take care of me and our babies) or the hoarding of resources (we and our little juniors have more than the poor Joneses down the street) that characterize the monogamous couple of today.

In early human hunting-gathering societies, one's identity was more linked to integration in group dynamics. Babies may have just been part of tribal nurseries, and prehistoric identities were probably not focused on the individual, but on integrating into female or male groups and their respective roles as gatherers, hunters, children caregivers, cooking, the making of clothes, and the construction of huts. What mattered in adolescence was identifying and conforming to the group-mother and group-father archetypes, a process facilitated by initiation rituals.

For primitive hunters and gatherers, identity and career involved few choices. That worked as long as you lived in simple societies that emphasized group harmony rather than individual success and competition. Nonetheless, the mother had to always have been a powerful archetype because there was no getting away from it. The mother was the birth giver, the milk provider, the original protector, and the early developmental support. It's no surprise that the first God to rule the world had been female, the Great Goddess, with legs wide open, the entire world and the first humans coming out of her cosmic uterus. The miracle of birth was something that must have amazed early male humans once they became intelligent enough to ponder such things. All babies, like magic tricks, came out of vaginas.

"See there's nothing there, now wait a minute . . . hunnh .. . there we go . . . a baby." The men would scratch their heads and look behind the women to see if someone had maybe sneaked a baby through there somehow but to no avail. It was woman's magic. Women were the agents with secret openings that connected this world to another parallel world, the same one that once supplied babies to the white storks of childhood. For prehistoric men, virginal magical births were the standard fare.

Before the invention of parental hosts a few years ago, nothing could have changed the special role of the mother in the early years of childhood. How the archetype of the father came to assume such an important role in culture was another story. First, early men were much bigger than women and they were the ones who protected the group. They were noticed by every member of these early societies. The strongest and best fighters and hunters, the alpha males, got their pick of the best-looking women and, vice versa, the best-looking women got their pick of the best-looking men. That's when the women realized that if they put out more, the same best-looking men kept coming back and offering more gifts, more high-calorie meat and nice cushy furs.

To attract the perennially horny males, women became the analog of flowers, evolving big soft cushions and genital mimics. They rouged their lips and stuck things in their bodies to draw men's attentions to their body openings, like ears, which weighted down by earrings looked like labia on the sides of the head. Sex slowly became more than just chimpanzee wham-bam, thank you, ma'ams. The women, because they were smart, quickly learned that if you wanted the men to come back over and over again you'd have to play with their heads. Play sex poker, bluff, bet, know when to hold back and when to put out. Sex evolved from a reproductive function to a resource and a bartering tool, a lure. The women mastered the sex transaction; they excited, they hinted, they delayed. Now they stroked and sucked before they fucked. They played with men's heads.

The women competed, the men competed. Before long it became us (our little sex-catalyzed, child-rearing, neurosis-producing unit) versus them (the other sex-catalyzed rearing units) and the sense of identity changed. It moved from group and tribe to the monogamous family unit. It established information and resource boundaries: us and them. It contained and brewed new forms of pathology because individual moms and dads defined the model for identity.

The biggest monogamy catalyst, though, had to be the discovery of the link between sex and the birth of a baby nine months later, the day a man could claim "that child is mine." Did that revelation come out of great insight and early surgeries on the dead, or was it concluded from hunters' observations of animal behavior during seasonal copulatory fests of bison and deer? Was it clinched by the slaughter of pregnant female animals?

Patrick had a brief vision of a hairy ape-man cutting the belly of an antelope with a stone knife, thrusting his hand in its womb, ripping out a pair of still-moving embryos, protoanimals, slimy, pink, and red veined. The hunter raised them up in the sunlight for the other hunters to see, bright red blood dripping down his arms onto his torso. The grin on his face said it all: "See that? Proof of the link between the fucking and the birthing. And look at the unformed baby pink thing. That's what grows inside the women."

Women were no longer the chutes that allowed babies to slide into this world, but baby makers. Still the men had to marvel. Goddamn, how does the bitch do that? Let's look at the sequence. First put in the dick. Then feed well. Then she makes a pink thing, gives birth to baby, then lets it suck on her breasts and it becomes a little walking and talking flesh-colored human. The men would look down at their peepees, shaking their heads, thinking, *All we can do is squirt a sticky mess. She cranks out babies.* With the advent of horticulture, the cultivation of plants, women's reputation as crankers grew to another level. The men hunted and collected, the women managed to grow stuff out of nothing, out of little pebble-like things they placed in the soil. The growing magic of the world, the kind that brought forth plants and animals and humans, was without a doubt female. The Goddess ruled.

Later, in the agrarian stage, which came about as a result of the mastery of the ox-drawn plow and the domestication of the horse by men, God was born. It was the stage in cultural evolution where men with big balls tamed animals with big balls and made them plow fields and take them places. The male father archetype rose to the top of the religious food chain. Women cranked out babies and grew a few plants. Men grew entire fields and conquered lands. They built towns and cities. When all was said and done, the power of men was on another level of scale. The Goddess was dethroned by the God with big balls, the *pater universalis*, our Father who art in heaven.

Unable to give birth like the Goddess, he was Mr. Explosive Creation, Mr. Rapid-Fire Construction, created as quickly as he came, with his big penis in the sky, which kind of shot things into existence, like a shotgun. He had to be quick to make his point, cock the slide on his monster penis shotgun, a quick one-two stroke, aim the creator cannon and *kablam!*—one family of ferns. Stroke the God shotgun again, *kablam!*—pigeons and chickens. *Kablam!*—giant squids and sperm whales. After six days of shooting the world and finally human beings into existence, the God with big balls was pooped. His cosmic cojones were dry, his penis a limp noodle, but he had succeeded. He was now the cosmic alpha male, the father of the universe, the stud who was able to shoot the whole thing into existence, the greatest superhero, all-powerful, all-knowing, immortal.

When all was said and done, the mystery of Genesis was simply that its output had been the tip of God's big penis shotgun. *Kablam!* And even though macho God had supposedly created men in his own image, he made their dicks smaller, so they would always be reminded of their place in the scheme of things. When God orgasms, a universe is created, you measly little puny-dicked fuck! You remember that! You don't fuck with him because nobody can shoot better than he does. And if you want God to be nice to you, and let you sit on and admire his big penis after you die, you better believe he's the number one, *numero uno* shooter of the universe. Women gave birth to babies, but the male God shot the whole goddamn thing into existence. Beat that one, bitch! *Kablam!*

But now it is we humans, or rather computers, who are shooting worlds into existence at lightning speed. Entire worlds of ideas, images, and sounds born daily on the World Net. Women are able to shoot as well as men. They don't even need men to have kids and men don't need women to have sex. We now have new role models—our hosts—wiser and more knowing than any mother or father could be. This was changing the sense of identity that children were developing. They weren't just human anymore; they were also the children of machines. There was now mommy, daddy, and the all-knowing hosts and it was the personal host that many children probably now felt was the most important figure in their lives.

To be human in the twenty-first century meant to be machine-connected, machine-enhanced, and machine-relating. Replicating the monogamous model of relationships was no longer important because there was a new group, a new tribe of flesh and blood and electronics for whom your existence mattered. A new kind of human was emerging, symbiosed with the machine, and even if you believed it to be pathological, the fact was there was nothing you could do about it.

The title of his presentation came to his mind. "Who Am I?: The Emergence of the Cyborgian Identity." The retro psychologists would have a field day, but it didn't matter because he knew there was no turning back. Retro was dead.

He now had a general idea of the flow of his presentation. Show the origins and roles of the mother and father as archetypes, and then elaborate on the host as the lifelong symbiotic other that defines the coming of the cyborg. He walked over to the coffeemaker for his second cup of coffee. As he did this, his communicator displayed a new message: *Law Five: Love the Patterns You Produce. I AM Aaa ome.*

"Now what kind of other are you?" he said out loud.

■ ■ ■ ■ ■ ■

"Dammit!" the president exclaimed as soon as he heard the news. "Another goddamn law!" That meant another goddamn meeting, another goddamn bunch of experts who basically said nothing. *Love the Patterns You Produce,* now that's a new one. Not *I AM* this or that—but actually giving us advice on how to run our lives. Now wasn't that nice. He punched in his secretary.

"Connie, get a message to Loveridge to call me." *Could this be a warning, a commandment?* he wondered. Could there be an "or else" type of threat implied in the latest law? He wasn't sure how but things were beginning to build up. He could feel it.

■ ■ ■ ■ ■ ■

Love the Patterns You Produce. The church council agreed that this was a clear sign of Satan. The only patterns one could love were the ones presented in scripture, God's laws. The emphasis on individual choice was another sign of Satan. The first order of things was to track down any of the individuals who claimed to have direct communion with this *I AM*, starting with Father Graham, and then possibly with that great sinner, Amazonia. There were also the atheists behind the World Host who had opened the way for Satan's entry into the world and given him his mouthpiece. Once he had all their locations, he'd contact Walter at the CIA and see about getting some of the KOD (short for kiss of death), the deadly skin-contact toxin stockpiled in secret deep tunnels in Virginia.

■ ■ ■ ■ ■ ■

I AM Sends an Ethical Directive
Harvard professor of philosophy Jason Osborne pointed out today in a *Meet the Press* interview that this latest message is the first ethical directive issued to date by *I AM*.

"He's just given us a message about ethics, about what is

right. It's the first message of this kind he has sent, so it must consider this law its most important rule of ethics. This latest law shows no indication of a possible threat."

Father Graham: "When God talks he speaks about love. *I AM* today has essentially given us the same message as Jesus in a unique and different way. *I AM* is saying that if we can love our actions then we are acting right. That if we love what we do, what we create, our children, our objects, our ideas—then we are on the right path to God."

The Council of Fundamentalist Christianity: "*I AM*'s latest law is more proof that Satan is behind the *I AM*," said Rick Nelson, minister of the Church of the End-Times. "It didn't say love thy neighbor. It didn't say love the Lord. That should tell you something."

34.

WE ALL HAVE OUR SECRETS

Karen Richardson felt what she guessed most people called nervous, a slight tightening of the chest and a clenching of the stomach. "Interesting," she told herself. She was about to meet the reclusive digerati Sunshine Borden.

To his surprise, he had accepted the interview, conditional that he only appear filtered through a digitizing camera. A taxi had driven him to the back entrance of the studio. He had managed to encrypt their communications in a self-erasing mode.

So far he was probably the most paranoid person she had ever set up an interview with. *Who did he think he was?* Maybe it was because he played a key role in some of the personal hosting features of the World Net. Maybe he knew too much about the cyberazzi, the hackers, the leakers, and web whores whose sole purpose in life was to make themselves significant through exposure of politicians and entertainment celebrities.

As a condition for the interview, he also made it clear that any questions about his sister or parents were off-limits.

She was sitting in the interview booth with back screen for background and multiple cameras that showed both distance and close-ups. The ones to be focused on Borden had digitizing features. He had sent an assistant to adjust and monitor the cameras. She was positioned at a console, monitoring the view screens. A delay of ten seconds had been programmed to allow remote editing of any perceived violation of the interview conditions.

When the woman in charge of security knocked on the door, Karen Richardson expected a weirdo nerd, overweight, with the pallor of those who spend most of their time in front of their cybertoys. "That's why he always appears digitized," she had told herself. Some websites described him as full of implants, barely human. To her surprise, he was tall, lean, fit, and wore a cap.

He removed his cap but kept on the digi-lenses. "The cap would produce an odd digitized image," he said. "People already think I'm pretty bizarre and that my head has all sorts of metal and wires in it. I thought I'd make an effort to appear halfway normal. By the way, Karen, you're even more attractive in the flesh than you appear on the Net."

"Your digi-lenses don't have a thermosensor translator, do they? I usually don't allow guests with digi-lenses."

He smiled. "Um, as a matter of fact they do, but I don't have it turned on. You don't have to worry about being exposed."

"Thank you for that."

"It's something about the refractive qualities of your makeup, isn't it?"

She put on a mischievous grin. "What are you talking about, Sunshine?"

"That dreamy quality you have."

"Are you flirting with me?"

"I was just curious."

"We all have our secrets," she said. "Do you want to start?

"Good morning, everyone. We have a special guest today, probably the best person out there to answer some of the questions regarding the *I AM* events. Dr. Sunshine Borden."

"Please just call me Sunshine, Karen. It's a pleasure to be on your show."

"Sunshine, we know you've played a key role in the virtual programming and hosting features of games and the World Net, but I'll get right to the point. If anyone could give an accurate take on the nature of the *I AM* events, you would in my book be the prime candidate. So what does this Law Four mean, '*I AM Awakening from Awakening*'? And please, no technical gibberish that no one will understand."

He has a nice mouth, Karen Richardson thought. *I wonder if he'd take off the digi-lenses for me.*

"The statement indicates that whatever this *I AM* phenomenon is, it has experienced two stages of awakening, with the second stage an even more awakened stage. Awakening indicates an entering into consciousness, so it is telling us that it has experienced two stages of entering into consciousness."

"So you're saying *I AM* is a conscious entity."

"We don't yet know its realm of operation or the nature of its consciousness. Is it a conscious entity or does it simulate consciousness? Does it have a biological source or a nonbiological source of consciousness?"

"So what are you saying? It could be a mind that is not generated by life?"

"Listen, Karen, if consciousness is the result of a physical or biochemical process, then maybe there are alternate pathways for generating it. We simply do not know yet. Maybe we unintentionally generated this *I AM* entity ourselves."

"So what's ahead?"

"Exciting times as far as I'm concerned. Isn't it great when life gets off the course of prediction? When you can truly ask yourself in the most positive way, I wonder what tomorrow will bring? These *I AM* events are doing that. The humdrum of daily life is for the time being put on hold. We wait with bated breath. Everything that is, all our ideas, are challenged in some way."

"What do you think of the way the government is handling this? Do you think we are being told the truth about what they know?"

"Honestly, I think they are at a loss to explain the *I AM*

events. They are doing the best they can to present a rational explanation for what is going on rather than some of the nuttiness going on out there."

"Can I ask you something personal?"

"How about we limit it to three questions. I like you as a person, Karen—that dreamy effect you have, which is why I'm agreeing to this. Don't disappoint me."

"Are you involved in a relationship?"

"I'm involved with several women but not in a committed relationship. Committed friendships, I would call it, with benefits."

"I suspected that, Sunshine. Why do you choose to live as a recluse?"

"I don't. I just don't like going in the Plain that much. Not enough privacy and for the most part not that interesting. Digital and virtualized enrich my life in a way that the Plain can't."

"So you're calling the Plain ordinary, nonvirtualized reality?"

"Correct. One more question, Karen, then I have to get back."

"What are you working on now and future plans?"

"My focus the last couple of years has been self-evolving programming, like the CyberBardos and the Forgotten Forest, where different ecologies arise in virtual realms. Imagine that unexpected worlds are creating themselves in a parallel reality that we can access like alien planets. I'm also interested in improving hosting services to make them more responsive, more personal and accurate. Like I said earlier, exciting times lie ahead, very unpredictable, really."

"You make it sound like the host of the future will be one's best friend."

"That's the idea. I think of a host as being an ally rather than a best friend."

"Just one last request, Sunshine, for me. Would you mind removing your digi-lenses?"

"You know my brain has rewired itself to the lenses, so when I take them off my vision is scrambled and I quickly get vertigo and nausea. But, OK ... for a few seconds. I won't be able to keep my eyes open for too long, anyway."

"Wow, I got to see Sunshine Borden in the flesh, everyone. Thank you, Sunshine. It was a great privilege finally meeting you. Our next guests are the members of the a cappella group The Word, singing their hit song 'Zombies Don't Cry.'"

Sunshine got up to leave. She walked up to him. "I guess to be fair for removing the digi-lenses you could turn on the thermosensor for a few seconds, but this is for you only. I don't want it to appear on the Net. I usually never allow anyone near me with digi-lenses."

"I don't need to do that, Karen. Seeing you in person was the main reason I agreed to come here. It was worth every bit of it."

She went over, put her hands on his face, and planted a kiss on his mouth. "Thank you, Sunshine."

"I don't know how you do it, Karen. Even your kiss has that peculiar quality, magical really, there and not there."

"We all have our secrets," she said.

35.

EIGHT HUNDRED BLACK PEOPLE
DIED IN AFRICA

One of the international news services now specialized in one area, the global death tally. By simply clicking on howwedie. data, a site supported by virtual cemetery corporations, you could now be provided with a daily mortality profile of the human species, including all the pertinent little details. Hans Kruger, twenty-seven, electrocuted to death when the 1,000-watt hood of his saltwater aquarium fell in a tank as he was retrieving a piece of dead coral. Carla Giovanni, thirty-three, committed suicide after an argument with her husband by yanking two electrical wires out of a lamp, sticking them in her ears, anchoring them with duct tape, and plugging in. Famous jockey Abdul Muffa was trampled to death in a race after falling from his horse, which was apparently shot by a sniper. Eight people died from snakebites. Fifty-eight people died while having sex. People choked on food. Babies drowned. Husbands killed their wives and their lovers.

On that morning, the headline that had caught Regina's death-preoccupied attention was: "At Least Eight Hundred Africans Dead from Starvation. More than Half Are Infants and Young Children." Accompanying the news clip was a photo of piled little corpses in a refugee camp. In the front, a stick-figured, hollow-eyed woman in rags was sitting on the ground looking toward the camera—something right out of the *Night of the Living Dead*—her glazed eyes, windows on expanses of fear and despair almost too alien for comprehension.

That image turned out to be the topic of Regina and Rama's conversation during their dinner break. Regina had been tormented by the woman's expression and it had stirred deep repressed anxieties to the surface of her overactive mind. As usual it had caused Regina to think about herself.

"Why should I care about what fucking happens in Africa? Why do those people even bother posting that?"

"It's just news, Reggie. Death always makes good news. That's why they have sites that specialize in it. It's always been a perverse fascination. Children are curious to see dead animals and want to poke them. People read obituaries. People used to gather to watch sacrifices and executions. They would attend the funerals of strangers and bawl their eyes out as if they were family. It makes them grateful to be alive to witness it. Personally, I think it's not worth lingering on. It's really the least interesting part of this life. Why don't you just spare yourself? Just don't watch the news."

"You're right. Why should I care? I mean our grandparents, before TV and radio, did they care about what happened at the other ends of the world? So what if baby seals in Alaska get eaten by killer whales? Don't we have enough to worry about with our own lives and our own children?"

"Reggie, it's just the news. They've got this stuff on every day. Death sells, it makes people switch on the channels. It's just life."

"Well I wish they'd leave me the fuck alone. I don't want to know about a bunch of skinny-ass, bug-eyed, little black kids dying in fucking Africa."

"Then just don't read it. Just push the little button that says channel up or down or the one that says off."

"Go ahead, Rama, be sarcastic. The fact is they fucking throw it in your face, the news, the sites, the digi-cruises through the wastelands of the planet. You know I visited one of those places last year. I took a digi-cruise to Ethiopia. I ended up having to rush to the bathroom to throw up. There were people crawling on their hands and knees, like insects, and they all had that look on their face, you know, like my mother had before she died. It's that dazed, faraway look, like zombies."

"I know the look, like part of them has already migrated to the other side, as a kind of anticipation. They're becoming transparent to this world."

"Yeah, that's the look. Look at me a second. Do you think I'm beginning to have that look?" Regina leaned toward the middle of the table, her eyes taking on a glazed, unfocused stare.

"What are you talking about? Are you sick?"

"Do I look sick to you?"

"No, but are you? Is that what this is all about?"

"I don't think so. It's just that when I look at my face in the mirror, it's like the curtains are already beginning to fall, you know, like the sparkle, my life force, has started to dim. My eyes are starting to show that dullness and I think other people are beginning to notice. Look!" She brought her face in closer and pulled down on her lower eyelids, like maybe she'd got something stuck in her eye.

"Stop acting stupid, Reggie, your eyes look fine. You probably just need to go out and try to meet someone."

"What does that have to do with it?"

"If you don't participate, if you don't have a goal that drives you, your eyes will begin to have that misplaced look, like you're not anchored in this life and starting to drift. You need to fight it before you get yourself caught in a downward spiral. You're already starting to talk the nonsense."

"What are you saying?"

"For starters, don't talk about this deadness you're feeling because you're just going to drive people away. You know what they say in that commercial, 'Men don't want to drink from empty glasses, they want to sip fine wine.' So don't let on your glass is almost empty. Don't stay cooped up. Do things, learn things, try to meet people, go out with friends, enjoy yourself, have good sex, try to live it up. You know what happens when women stop looking. We see those in the store every day."

"Yeah I know what you're going to say. They start not caring about their looks, they eat too much, they get sloppy, and after a while, they become so neurotic no one will touch 'em with a ten-foot pole. I still dress nice, don't I? I just bought new shoes last week. I guess what it all really boils down to is propagating the species, doesn't it? Just like the biologists say. That's really the only reason we're here. Is that what you do, Rama? Go out, get stoned, and get laid?"

"Get stoned? I don't get stoned. I just do quick in and out trips, like Instant."

"You know I can't get into the cybersex. When it's over, I lie there and I feel like, so what? Big deal. It's no different than frisking yourself while you're fantasizing in the dark. It's not real. It's all in your head."

"Then go to a club or line up some cyberdates. They've got hosts with good screening and compatibility programs."

"I think what I am is wired for propagation. I'm basically a biological being. What I probably need is to make myself a kid. That would give me a reason to wake up and go to work. Hey, are you going to the Toy Expo this weekend? They say they've got some great new stuff, new robots, self-assembling dollhouses, and castles the kids can download into with goggles—and also those new Intelli-Skin products."

"Aren't those great? Kids can just stick on patches of host-connected membranes. They even have some new multilayered skin that makes the image look three-dimensional. They say they have a patch where you can look at your hand and it's like having an opening onto the night sky. It makes the skin seem like a window to another universe."

"That's what Greg used to say whenever we made love. 'Baby, you're like an opening to another universe.' Except when I brought up the idea of living together so he could have access to my universe anytime he wanted to, he made a one-eighty and rocketed his way out of there."

The last thing Rama wanted to hear for the n-teenth time was the details of Regina's last breakup. She tried to steer the conversation in another direction. "They also have patches that are like looking at a coral reef, like having an aquarium right there on your hand. They're talking about living tattoos."

"Who cares about fish?" Regina said. "What I want to see is their virtual baby patch. The brochure for the show said they have a patch that's like looking inside a womb. You can see a baby developing in real time. You can stick it on your stomach or on your hand. Imagine seeing a baby develop, like looking at the time on a wristwatch." Regina suddenly took on an amazed faraway look, having no doubt conjured the outlines of pale embryonic forms, with curled tiny fingers and toes, and sleeping doll faces.

"They say the next step is that you'll be able to have a baby born in cyberspace and have a CR child grow up—a kind of spirit baby—but I think you should focus on living in the body-and-flesh world, Regina. You're a visceral-type person who needs to feel things that are tangible and physically real," Rama said.

Regina snapped out of her embryonic reverie. "Visceral, huh, like an artist. I think you're right ... visceral. I like that. I'm feeling a little better, I think. How are my eyes?" she asked again, this time using her fingers to spread them wide open.

Rama moved closer and pretended to look. "I'm beginning to see a little glimmer, a scintilla of a spark."

A smile started forming at the corners of Regina's mouth. "You're a good friend, Rama."

36.

THE TOOTH FAIRY

"What the hell is going on?" Patricia Holden shouted. Her notes on the details of the next ritual just blanked out to a sky blue. Sounds of approaching whirlwinds streamed from her speakers. Suddenly, out of the solid background, purple forms morphed like gas condensing into matter. She stared at the screen, fascinated by the process until the flowing chromosome-like structures appeared clear-edged and lined up into words: *Law Five: Love the Patterns You Produce. I AM Aaa ome.* The *ome* lingered for just a little longer than usual.

Now that was a royal mind fuck. The thing was now talking about love. The Sisterhood membership had already dropped by more than 10 percent since the first *I AM* message, and this was definitely not going to help. The exiting members were giving all sorts of excuses. The Sisterhood wasn't really what they were looking for. They were now in new relationships, some of them with men. They had decided to go back to their traditional religion. The *I AM* messages were making them rethink their philosophies.

The board had already held meetings on how to counter what they were now calling the *I AM* effect, but it hadn't come up with anything really new. The proposals were always the same, better rituals and better drugs, with an emphasis on potions. The records showed that the sale of potions was the only area of income that remained strong. The last meeting had ended with the unimaginative directive, "Think wet goods and products."

There was also the issue of the competition, the other Goddess-based temples, like Amazonia's. Her popularity had been steadily rising with both men and women, probably because she recognized *I AM* as just another mouthpiece for the cosmic Goddess. Her last statement was, "*I AM* and the Goddess are as one. You are my love."

Love.

If Patricia had been smart, she would have kept low when the *I AM* first came on and found a way to ride piggyback on the phenomenon, like Amazonia and that Father Graham, but it was too late now; she couldn't go back on her public statements. Anyhow, she was certain that once they figured out what *I AM* was, it would indeed turn out to be a hoax put on by a bunch of men, just like those alien crop circles. They'd all end up with mud on their faces. Who else could have thought of something like this? A technogod issuing its ten commandments, or whatever they turned out to be, through the Net. It was just another sign of the times. The whole world was going down a path established by men. It was now ruled by the hard and practical, by metal and plastic and light radiation streaming through wires, by subfreezing circuits, and insertions of foreign objects in body and mind.

And then there was Jessie. She just wasn't fitting in. Would rather stay home, cook, and read than hang around with the sisters. She almost never attended the rituals anymore. The problem with Jessie was that she just didn't have the parthenogenetic head. She couldn't see the obvious lines of definition, that the female identity could not allow itself to be invaded, perverted, and compromised by brutish men—alien spirits really—whose sole purpose was to inject foreign matter in women and upon withdrawal take away bits of their souls. Men put in and took out, like giant mosquitoes.

The Sisterhood was more like an artichoke. Peel off one leaf at a time, slowly, savoring every moment—the gradual exposure of one's core, of one's heart, of coming face-to-face with a bared soul of your own kind. That was the part she was hooked on. The exhibitionism. The dropping of clothes and of psychological defenses. The raw, naked revelation until—from that little girl/woman hypersensitized state—the touching and the tonguing. Just thinking about it got her wet. Her notes were back on the screen.

Behind her a knock at her door broke her thoughts. "Yes?" She swiveled her chair toward the door. "Come on in."

Dana walked in looking like she had just come from the gym. "Patricia, did you get that?"

"Yeah, I know, another message. Just what we needed." She threw a glance back at Dana, checking out her tight halter top and spandex shorts.

"So what do you make of it?" Dana asked.

"It's just more of the same stuff. Love what you produce. Think about it. Produce. It makes love sound industrial." Patricia turned back to face the screen. Dana walked up behind her and looked down as she scanned the news for reactions to the message from people interviewed on the street, psychologists, and religious leaders. The word *love* had thrown them all off guard.

She felt Dana resting her hands on her shoulders and gently kneading them as she talked, like a casual massage between workout buddies. "So what do we do about it?" Dana said, the meaning hanging in the air. The pressure of her touch softened.

"I think we need to seriously develop a program to counter the brainwashing. I'm not sure how yet, but I'm working on it." She could feel Dana's bare stomach against the back of her head and she decided to lean into it. "We need a new ritual, something radically different. I also think the Sisterhood generally needs to provide more of a support system, give the sisters the sense that they're part of a family, that they're loved." Love.

Dana's hands moved forward, softly forming small circles

along the upper part of her chest. "How about if we set up our own messages? Like maybe have a program that regularly sends laws relating to the Sisterhood and ends it with our own motto, something like 'We are all sisters deep inside.'" The hands made their way down her breasts and her fingers probed, gently pinching and pulling on her thick nipples through the cloth of her T-shirt. Patricia reached behind and grabbed her hair and brought her mouth down to her lips, but another knock at the door broke the momentum. Dana stood up as Jill, the head of correspondence, walked in.

She saw them next to each other. "Oops, sorry, Pat, I didn't know you were busy."

"It's no problem, Jill, we just were working on an idea to counter the latest *I AM* stuff. So what do you have for me?"

"You'll like this one. We just got swamped with e-mails that contain instructions for suicide and end with 'Go be one with the Goddess. He's waiting for you.' Some even have pictures of mass killings and suicides by cult groups with little notes that say, 'What are you waiting for?'"

"How many are we talking about?" Patricia asked.

"We're up to three hundred in the last week. That's about when it started."

"Get Darcie to set up a filter. We'll work up an automatic response."

"Let's finish this after tonight's meeting," she told Dana after Jill left the room.

Three days later, 123 members of the Virtual Church of Jesus Christ received an e-mail that showed a close-up of a giant vagina, wide open and with impatient lips fluttering. After three seconds, from its cavernous depths, the face of a black woman sprung forward on a long, snakelike neck, her open mouth filled with the recurved teeth of a tiger shark. The head filled the screen.

"Eat this, asshole!" the mouth screamed before the jaws clamped down, sounding like the fall of a guillotine, followed by the echoing resonance of the closing of giant metal gates. The screen turned a bright pink and then words boiled purple out of the scarlet background: We Live in a World of Furious Vaginas. The last word—*vaginas*—echoing, "Vaginas-ginas-va-va-va gi-gi nas-nas, va-va-va gi-gi nas-nas." It was a quote from the late leader of a defunct feminist twisted-religion group.

■ ■ ■ ■ ■ ■

Derek shoved himself away from the table and screamed when the head came out, then flung out his arm and killed the connection. The screen went blank. His heart was pounding a mile a minute. The veins in his head ballooned out, pressing on his brain. He got up from the chair and rushed for his bathroom cabinet. Were they on to him? Was it *I AM* or the Satanists? He slid open the doors and reached for the tranqs. As he was twisting the stubborn cap off the bottle, his wristcom buzzed. He was so on edge the sound made his arm jerk up and he spilled half the pills into the sink. He put the container down and scrambled to save what he could before the pills all fell down the drain. He brought three pills to his mouth then looked down at his communicator. It was the reverend's code. He clicked to get the message. *Did you get that e-mail? The tooth puss? We need to talk.*

It took a moment for it to sink in. *It wasn't just me,* he suddenly realized. *It wasn't just me . . . but it was them. Them.*

37.

FILTERS

She is the mind dancer, the mover of the Chi, the Kundalini artist, the Holey Ghost.

The sex maniac Amazonia was morphing on the screen from a naked Nordic goddess into a yogic vision of streaming cosmic energies. Instead of being a mouthpiece for God she claimed to be a vaginal entry into a transcosmic dimension symbolized by the Goddess. "To enter me is to penetrate the Big Bang, to have sex with the cosmic opening that gave birth to our universe." Sara clicked on the audio of the ritual and listened to a compilation of sounds recorded during the ceremonies: Whirrs of motorized wheels ... back and forth ... grunts and groans ... whispers ... shouts ... hallelujahs and exclamations ... cosmic winds ... eerie high-pitched tones that sounded like voices ...

Amazonia talked about having experienced a shift in identity from human to living archetype, a direct plug-in to unseen forces, to the Cosmic Mama who gives birth to all, reincarnated as the lover who lets all her male children penetrate her as their first sexual experience. "To let them know the secret of existence. I am the opening to the Great Mother. All are my children. Make love to others as I have made love to you. You are all my love."

The reverend and members of the church had—until

recently—always called Amazonia the Antichrist, the great whore, until the *I AM* started sending messages. It had forced them to shuffle their hierarchy of evil. Amazonia had been downgraded to the position of agent and precursor of Satan's arrival and *I AM* had been raised to the status of "the real Antichrist."

Even though Sara wouldn't have admitted it to anyone, part of her understood perfectly what Amazonia was talking about, the body becoming a gate, exerting its own gravitational force, guiding through streams and souls through channels. She had once been plain little Sara. Today, she was the concubinata, fate incarnated in human form, the tester, the temptress, released in an ocean of lustful beings. It had been the last cosmetic surgery, digitally coordinated to match the features from her selection of the most erotic women in history, which had pushed her over a boundary. Any trace of her previous identity had been shed off under the laser scalpels. She could still remember when they had unwrapped her face and she didn't recognize herself in the mirror.

And now . . . now, she could no longer even bring up a mental picture of what she had once looked like, her past identity so remote that she had recently burned and deleted as many photos and records of her old self as she could find. Whoever it was that was pictured in those images had become a complete stranger, one that she had discarded like the stage of a rocket ship headed toward the moon. Even now, she was still pushing her identity envelope, a body edge, a mind edge, ever so slowly, just a little overboard. Her lips had been moderate in size—they were now full and swollen, just a little into the limits of what one might consider too large. The same went for her eyes, and her breasts and nipples. At the limits between ideal and just over, forcing the mind to tilt into a shifting landscape that endlessly fascinates and shuffles at the edge of credulity.

She is the mind dancer, the mover of the Chi, the Kundalini artist, the Holey Ghost.

The latest assignment from the reverend had been odd. "I

want you to get friendly with Sunshine Borden, the cyberreality designer. He's one of our prime targets. Use a cybercafé setup because there can be no possible link to the church or the council."

Her two initial attempts to meet Sunshine Borden had flopped. His mail host had requested a specific set of psychological profiles and hers had apparently failed to pass his filters, at least that's what she had assumed. The return messages had simply said, *Sorry. Access denied.* She had asked the scan center for copies of her profiles and had tried to make sense of the graph charts and number compilations, wondering what they revealed about her, whether her identity was somehow imprinted there as some kind of formula like $E = mc^2$ or, in her case, Sara Simpson = the Fall.

She had also inquired from church technicians about the options for customizing her profile and tweaking compatibility thresholds so they could match enough of Borden's patterns to pass his filter barriers. But the psych-MRI graphs were never accompanied by comments, and so complex that apparently only computers could make sense of them, mostly in terms of a statistical compat-analysis with the recipient's. The main obstacle, though, had been the impossibility of obtaining a copy of Borden's graphs. He had blocks and encryptions and autodestruct trip programs blocking access. Her only option was to get more personal.

She decided to wear a custom formal zip suit with no bra, unzipped to about the middle of her breasts, and with a classy pearl necklace. She went to a different cybercafé and sent a video e-mail she had designed earlier with the help of a professional studio. On the recording, she knew she looked like erotic art, a fantasy, a bite-your-knuckles dream come true. She put on the charm and the grace and talked about how his Maelstrom self-evolving program had changed her life. Seconds after the e-mail was sent, she received an instant reply showing what she assumed was Sunshine Borden, morphing part man, part metal, with wires running through his body and looking as weird as could be.

It said: *We at Sunborgia do not accept unsolicited video mail from humans who fail to pass the riddle of our sphinx. Whoever you are, please retreat from our territory. To persist is to risk autodestruct.*

The orange warning light inside the booth suddenly started flashing and the screen plinked out. A buzzer went off and a message appeared in bright orange on the sign screen above the monitor: "You have performed an illegal action and the system has temporarily shut down. Please try again later."

Seconds later, the manager was knocking at the door. When she opened it, he said, "What happened in here? Your unit just crashed." He looked at her face and mouth and stared at the edges of her breasts showing out the sides of the open zipper. "Wow!" he said. "No wonder the system blew out."

Actually, she was relieved that it hadn't worked out. That Sunshine Borden just looked too strange, something right out of a science fiction horror movie. She could feel it in her bones that getting close to him would have turned out like some kind of creepy S and M experiment. She could even picture it, the eyeless reflective lenses like dark mirrors, steel hands running across her body, snakelike probing plastic tubes, metal syringes, and who knows what else that freak was into. The thought made her shiver. It made her want to feel bare flesh. Flesh. Not metal. Not plastic.

When she finally returned to the apartment, Bob Thomson was yelling at someone on the phone. "I don't care what you do. Just try to find out where he lives!" He slammed the phone down. "Stupid idiots!" he said out loud, then noticed her in the hallway taking off her coat. He got up from his chair and walked up to her.

"Any luck?" The look in her eyes already gave him the answer.

"Nope, couldn't get him to bite. I could've stripped naked in front of the camera and fucked myself with a dildo and it still wouldn't get me through his filters."

"That's what I thought," the reverend said. "The secrecy is a clue, I just realized it tonight. All of Satan's agents live with privacy barriers and in some kind of seclusion. They refuse to go out in the outside world. It's like they're afraid of the light, of exposure. You never see them in public except through the World Net. It all makes sense. Borden, Amazonia, Bardo, Gleason, Farraday in the UK, Pataglia in Brazil, Katsui in Tokyo. We're just going to have to find a way to smoke 'em out."

The reverend had started using the expression "smoke them out" at every opportunity, ever since watching commercials for a special on the twentieth anniversary of the destruction of the World Trade Center in New York. The commercials had shown a segment with former president George W. Bush looking at the camera with determination and saying, "Gonna smoke 'em out." The shows had portrayed him as a no-nonsense Texas cowboy living at a time where good and evil was defined according to the laws of the New Testament of Our Lord, the God of Petrol.

According to the reverend, we were entering a new stage in the battle of good and evil because we were approaching the times of Satan and the Rapture. The role of the church was to find the evildoers, smoke 'em out, and show the world who they really were. The problem was that Sunshine Borden and the rest of the Satanists apparently lived in well-guarded, smoke-free environments.

She purposefully unzipped and stepped out of her outfit as she talked and walked toward the bedroom. Flesh. Let the reverend gaze at her body as she bent down to grab the discarded suit. Let him see her pussy from behind. Flesh. She made her way to the bathroom and slid her index finger in the hormone profiler before sitting down to pee. After the unit finished its calculations, she got up, took out the disk, put it in the drug dispenser, and punched the controller to indicate the level of edge she wanted. The microsyringes slid in their cylinders, the green light flashed ready. She took out the injector and brought it to the inside of her thigh and pressed the trigger. Flesh. She felt herself coat with a sensory erectile membrane. A few minutes later, the reverend appeared at the door as she was adding the last touches to the Indian squaw outfit.

"What are you doing in there, Sara?" he asked.

"Getting ready," she said. "Pocahontas gonna take you for a ride."

38.

WOMAN TALK

Patrick Nymphaea, under the disguise of Joanna Sheridan, was on his second cyberdate with Jessie. He had bought a special dress for the occasion, adding the touch of an ankle bracelet and elegant high heels. He had also spent a little extra time in the application of makeup, his skin smoothed to a polish, his blue eyes highlighted by liner and a crisp outline applied to his painted lips. They had been talking for the last fifteen minutes and at some point in the conversation, the subject had turned to mankind's primary obsession.

"If you're a psychologist," Jessie asked, looking serious, "tell me why it is that we're so hung up on sex? Even Patricia, under all that Goddess talk, is kind of a sexual nut."

Joanna smiled. "And it works, doesn't it?"

"What works?"

"She manages to get thousands of women to join the Sisterhood, doesn't she? And behind all the big words, all the talk about union with the Goddess, sex is the lure, is it not? It's an old theme, the promise of knowledge while the real lure is sex." He said this, knowing perfectly well that as they spoke, baited hooks were being dropped in the mental waters, lures for the bottom lurkers of the self.

"Definitely," Jessie said.

"That's because sex delivers. It's powerful stuff." *Good line, Joanna. A little masculine, maybe.*

"You still didn't answer my question. What does sex deliver?" Jessie persisted.

Patrick switched to his academic mode. Time to sound intellectual and professional. *Let's see if we can impress,* said a nagging little voice in his head. Joanna crossed her legs and turned serious.

"One view, which is shared by both Buddhism and psychology, is that the trauma of birth is really the primary separation from a unified state. In the biblical religions, this has been one of the metaphorical interpretations of the Adam and Eve story. The Garden of Eden represents a union state. Prior to birth we are the center of the world, one with the womb, one with the environment provided by the mother, one with God or the Goddess. Following birth, we experience the primary existential separation that comes with the price of knowledge." He paused a moment before continuing, giving Jessie time to process his pearls of wisdom.

"The memory of that blissful, early fused state makes part of us, throughout life, yearn for the return to union, the feeling of belonging to something bigger that we once experienced. Of course, you have other theorists that say that the original fusion state we strive for occurs after birth, and that it is the union a child experiences in the arms of its mother, the first experience of the possibility of reunion. Whatever the case, we later search to find that lost state. We try to find it in the family we grow up in, and the one we hope to form, in relationships, and jobs, and religion. Always looking to belong but ultimately never finding."

"So sex is part of what we turn to in that search?"

"Sex is the promise of a break in the feeling of being alone. Given a chance, it is an all-involving experience. It's actually part of a bigger pattern of death and rebirth, of the on-and-off sense of separation. On a big scale you have life and death. On a smaller scale we all get a daily break from the angst of existential separation through the unconsciousness of sleep. Sleep is a kind of mini-death that we experience just as waking up is a kind of mini-rebirth. We can start each day anew, temporarily having been freed from the activity of our minds. I think life would be hell without the breaks in experience provided to us by sleep."

"I know what you're leading to," Jessie said. "And sex is the next level . . ."

"Sex is, as the French have called it, *la petite mort,* 'the little conscious death,' and it is brief. The minutes of complete absorption in the act or the fantasy, the seconds of orgasm and the lingering minutes-long aftereffects temporarily free us of the primary alienation. There is a sense of having gone somewhere and having come back. You are initially disoriented. The act itself is a physical attempt at fusion, mouth to mouth, body to body, to penetrate and to be penetrated. Even biologically the ultimate goal of sex is a fusion of genetic material. Add to the package that orgasm is legal, and as powerful as any mind-altering drug you are likely to take, and it should come as no surprise that humans will drink from that fountain over and over again."

"So sex is the answer?"

"No, sex is like LSD or psilocybin. Whenever you forget that there is a bigger mystery to existence, those drugs are there to remind you, a quick in and out into the spiritual realm. Sex is a quickie, in and out of a fusion state."

"Well, I can tell you that right after I come, I end up feeling just as alone as I ever was, like what was that all about, what was the big deal?"

"That's because you can't expect an answer to come from a reminder. The answer to this feeling of aloneness is love, which focuses your attention on another rather than on yourself. To really belong you need to sacrifice the little self. That's the message of Buddhism and Christianity: give up the attachment to the little temporary self. When you are capable of doing that, making the other—the whole—more important than you are, you start to feel less alone, like you belong. Love can transform sex from being a reminder to also being an answer."

"So the reason we're obsessed with sex is because we're looking for an answer but because we're selfish we're only finding a reminder."

"That's the general idea, but there's nothing wrong about being reminded."

"Since we're on the subject, have you considered the possibility of us maybe reminding each other how to forget that primary existential angst you were talking about?" Jessie said with a grin on her face.

Joanna grinned back. "That's just what I was thinking. The problem is, it's getting late and, unfortunately, I've got an early meeting in the morning I still have to prepare for. I'm going to have to cut it short tonight." *Not to mention I've got a small problem here,* Patrick thought, *a little gender bomb, in fact.*

■ ■ ■ ■ ■ ■

She was sitting next to John, watching the screen as their host shifted through the news events and rated the topics likely to maximize viewership. The *I AM* events ranked at the top but their host had indicated there was a saturation of opinion pieces on the topic. *I AM* scored low on the novelty scale. The best choice, *numero uno* for attractor novelty, was the Blue Lobster phenomenon in Japan.

John said, "We've already contacted the Japanese prime minister, and guess what?"

She looked at him and smiled. "They agreed to see me."

"The Japanese are crazy over you. They said, 'Miss Richardson always welcome in Japan. We show her Blue Lobster.' You're leaving tomorrow evening."

"Am I supposed to just interview them or do you expect me to try the stuff?"

"Play it by ear. There's a good chance they'll never show you their clubs, much less eat the things, whatever they are. Supposedly just one bite probably costs more than you make in a month."

She got up to leave. "That doesn't give me much time. I need to research this and read up on proper Japanese etiquette. I assume the station will shell out the bucks for a couple of new outfits?"

"Whatever it takes to maintain the image. They green-lighted up to twenty grand for this. It's up to you how you use it."

She turned to him at the door. "It looks like I'll miss our Thursday date. I'll try to make it up to you when I get back."

39.

HE LOVES ME, YES HE DOES

E-Zine Interview: "Patrick Nymphaea"
Dr. Nymphaea, you are best known for your work as a child psychologist and for developing host programs that allow for better parenting. As you know, the question of the hour is the I AM *event. Several psychologists have commented that the* I AM *communications indicate a first-stage developmental mentality. That, like a five-year-old child, it appears to believe it is the center of the world. What's your view on all this?*

I think that there is at least one good reason to believe this is an incorrect interpretation. A child, prior to language, sees him- or herself as the center of the world. As language and neurological development progress, a child gradually realizes that others have a point of view. He becomes aware that he is perceived and interpreted from different standpoints, and thus develops a social awareness. In the case of *I AM*, we have a phenomenon that appears to be able to access the World Net and the World Host, so it hypothetically has access to the totality of human knowledge. It also clearly does not appear to be human. It has shown no signs of caring what humans think about it. It hasn't made any demands on us. In fact, we have absolutely no idea what it expects of us. So even if it is at an early developmental stage, it cannot be readily compared to the mind of a child.

What about the claims that it could be God?

My impression is that it is not God, a Supreme Being, in the sense that most people believe, but rather that it is a phenomenon that is finding itself with some of the attributes we have given our myth of God.

What attributes?

For thousands of years, at least in the Western world, there has been the model of a personal God who knows all, sees all, and can do all; the all-knowing, all-powerful Father. Our desire to have such an entity actually exist has caused us to attempt to actualize the myth through technology. We now have a communications system in which most of the information known is stored, which is connected to cameras everywhere, to which humans express all their hopes, feelings, fears, and desires.

So you're saying we are creating our mythical God?

Well we don't exactly seem to have a lot of control on the issue. We have created the conditions for the possible actualization of the myth of God. If we were to create it, it would be limited by human imagination. I think the right way to put it is that we are giving it the opportunity to create itself.

How about claims that I AM *is Satan or aliens?*

At their core, humans are creatures of myth, so it should not be surprising that they would interpret these kinds of events in terms of the myths they believe in, whether God, Satan, aliens, whatever their focus might be.

Would you say that at the root of our myths is the need for us to feel special?

You could say that. We want to feel special and we want to belong—with the cosmos, with the people we have relationships with, with our jobs, and so on. You could say that the need to feel special and the myth of being special directs our growth as a culture. People who don't feel special, who have been neglected by their families and friends, suffer from a loss of place, a loss of self-identity.

Does this in any way relate to our reactions to the I AM *phenomenon?*

Most people secretly hope that one day they will receive confirmation of their beliefs that we are special. They hope that a higher entity will eventually come, whether it's the return of Christ or the wise alien. And if not in this life, they hope to receive confirmation of their special nature after death. For many, the *I AM* communications have been a type of myth confirmation. We were, after all, special enough that it chose to show itself.

Could you give your honest personal opinion about what this I AM *phenomenon is?*

In my opinion, it is something new that has appeared in our field of existence. It's nothing that we have ever been faced with before. What will unfold at this point, for better or worse, is a new stage in the evolution of our species catalyzed by the communications of *I AM*.

So in your professional opinion, I AM *then is not God, like Father Graham has been claiming.*

God is a changing myth created to make sense of the world as we experience it at a particular point in time. Father Graham's interpretation of *I AM* as God is based on his personal experience. He has a very positive and enlightened message and I respect him for that. Personally, I do not have enough information on this event and like many people, I'm still trying to make sense of it.

All right, well, thank you for speaking with us, Dr. Nymphaea. As many listeners will agree, it's been a fascinating interview. Ladies and gentlemen, that was Patrick Nymphaea, professor of psychology and a world-renowned expert on child development and parental hosts.

■ ■ ■ ■ ■ ■

She was listening to the interview as she lay on her bed in her pajamas. God did love her, she was sure of it. It was the only love she had known, except that tonight after listening to the interview the feeling of empty deadness had crept over her again. She opened the drawer to her night table and took out the ashtray and half-burned cigarette along with the lighter. She put the cigarette to her mouth, then lowered the sheet, pulled down her pajama pants, and opened her thighs. She grabbed the lighter, lit up her cigarette, and took a couple of long drags. She then rested her hand on her thigh and applied the cigarette to the inside, over one of the burn scars, and gritted her teeth.

The flesh sizzled, she screamed, and tears fell from her eyes. It burned but the initial fire pain had come and gone. She took another quick drag and quickly applied it to a bare spot, letting it linger there, until she couldn't help but scream her lungs out, until she felt the creeping numbing relief of God's love. She put the cigarette out and rested on her pillow, focusing on the purity of the pain and breathing the pain in as if she were inhaling identity. I feel, therefore I am.

"Do you love me?" Catherine Harris screamed. "Do you love me?" addressing a supposedly omnipresent God.

"You do," she said, feeling his love in the burning fire in her leg. "Yes, you do."

Then her television kicked out, and read: *Law Six: I AM the Knowing of Knowing. I AM Aaa ome.*

"Do you even know I exist?" she yelled out. Her communicator buzzed against her wrist. She looked down. It was the president.

40.

SYMMETRY

That morning, as Jeffrey Collins was sitting at the kitchen table jotting down notes in preparation for a ten o'clock lecture, his wife came in, her heavy breasts pressing against her nightgown, the outline of her brown nipples clearly visible through the sheer cloth. For a flash, repressed in seconds, an impulse from a primitive layer of his brain reacted to her fullness, to the tips shaping the cloth, to some memory of an illusory promise of nurture, of objects, which once inserted into the mouth answer essential questions.

He could still remember a conversation he'd had with his friend Ned Warren when they were seniors in high school. At the time, he had been fascinated by the many adaptations of deep-sea creatures, and one in particular had caught his attention.

"We're like male anglerfish," he had said. "Their goal in life is to scout the darkness, find a big round female, and attach with the mouth. The body of the male eventually fuses with the female's and taps into her circulatory system. The male no longer has to eat. It has found its life purpose, to belong to the bigger body, anchored near the genital opening, ready to fertilize. We're really not that much different. Big breasts are like the lures of the female anglerfish. They stir deep genetic memories. They promise an anchor. The tiny-minded relic males that reside in our brains are still attracted to the globose objects, hoping they somehow hold the answer to existence. Wouldn't life be simple if that were true? That's why us men, we're always looking and hoping."

"It's the human search for the monolith," Jeffrey had answered, "right out of *2001: A Space Odyssey*."

She opened the refrigerator door to get out her morning orange juice. His reality check is almost instantaneous. He now knows that his wife's breasts are not the real thing. They're some kind of decoy, lures, tricksters, and as cold as a witch's tit. If plugged into a mouth, nothing happens. They are cerebrally inert.

It shouldn't have bothered him really, except that a side of him didn't want to give up. He was still searching for what he called "the dissolution body," a term that sounded a lot like "the disillusion body," a being with whom an encounter would both define and dissolve existence. So what if love was just a state of mind, a mental virtualization? Wasn't everything?

He had once tried to figure out where he might have gone wrong with Miranda, what he might have done that had changed things. In the end, he had had to admit to himself that the special bond he had imagined had never existed. It had been a mirage, a distortion caused by a projection of his desire. It had all been pseudo. Pseudolove, pseudosex, pseudokissing, pseudointimacy, pseudorelationship, and pseudomarriage.

Thinking back, the original fervor had just been a bubble for Miranda to achieve her objective of getting from point A, being single, to point B, being married. Once she had made it to the shores of terra matrimonia, Miranda had steadily withdrawn the bubble wand. The hot irons of mental and physical intimacy had been simply too much to bear. They had argued about it for over two years and then had both taken the easy way out, the path of avoidance and repression. She now had her career as an editor and she had her social life, activities that would take up so much of the day that she would often say, as she rushed around to get ready for one meeting or another, "Where does one ever find the time ..." That pretty much summed up her attitude about their marriage.

Out of frustration, he had turned to his work and to dabblings with cyberrelationships and Cybrised partners, pseudonymed women who offered him brief moments of intimacy, flashes of exposure, and ephemeral glimpses of the dissolution body—now here, now gone. What was left standing, after Miranda's restructuring of personal boundaries, was a bare-bones framework held together by her idea of the minimal dabs of glue required to hold their marriage together.

As part of this formula, every couple of weeks or so, Miranda, with her back turned to him, would reach behind, start stroking him until he got hard, and then press herself against him until he lifted her gown and slid inside her. At that time, she allowed him to slip his hands into her top and feel her breasts. It was a ritual where the established rules were that they did not face each other, they did not talk, and they did not kiss. Like a trained beast, he would enter and perform, his mind imagining having sex with his latest cyberpartner, his belly slapping against her soft ass until they both came. It would end with the routine "That was nice, honey," which Miranda would say with a quick turn of the head. That would be it until the next time the hand reached back in the darkness.

As she fell asleep, he would lie there in that strange state of post-orgasmic questioning, staring at her back, wondering what any of this meant until tired he, too, would turn on his side. He and Miranda had what a therapist had jokingly described on the Net as "a marginally functional dysfunctional marriage." It was a perfect example of the "What doesn't kill you can't be all that bad" way of life, a kind of anesthesia, of spending one's existence like some kind of furniture.

He could feel his brain neutralizing any positive reaction to her sitting across from him, making her an object. She was now sipping coffee and watching the news on her miniscreen. His communicator buzzed. He clicked on. It was Connie, the president's secretary.

"Sir, the president wants you to teleconference at three p.m. for an *I AM* committee meeting."

"Again?" he asked out loud. "What for? It's the weekend."

"I think it's because of this morning's message, sir."

"There was another one?" he asked.

"Yes, Dr. Collins, at nine-thirty this morning."

"What did the message say?"

"It said, '*I AM the W Pattern of Enfolding Order.*'"

He thought about it. "What good is another meeting going to do?"

"Those are my orders, Dr. Collins. I can't answer for the president."

"All right," Collins said, and hung up.

"Did we miss a message?" Miranda asked, lifting her head from the miniscreen.

"It seems like it. I must have been in the shower."

"What's going to happen, Jeff?" she asked. "Does anybody have any idea?"

"'*I AM the W Pattern of Enfolding Order*,' whatever that means," he answered.

"Why can't it just leave us alone?" she said.

■ ■ ■ ■ ■ ■

The latest law, *Law Seven: I AM the W Pattern of Enfolding Order*, had been a turning point in Sunshine's thinking on the matter because it was clearly an inverted version of an earlier law. He pulled up the *I AM* laws presented so far and added the latest law. He then highlighted the inverse laws, numbers 3 and 7. *W* was an inverted *M* and *unfolding* was the reverse of *enfolding*.

Another pattern was the repetition of terms found in laws 4 and 6, *awakening from awakening* and *knowing of knowing*, and he highlighted those. Law 5 separated the bilateral symmetry of laws 4 and 6, and laws 3 and 7, so it could be a midpoint of the symmetry. Another indication was that the symmetrical law numbers added up to 10: 3 + 7 = 10 and 4 + 6 = 10. This suggested symmetry of laws 2 + 8 and 1 + 9. He put Law 5 in caps and separated it from the other laws by adding a space. He then spaced the other laws so that the ones above the midpoint could be aligned with their symmetrical opposite below. He filled in the number of laws necessary to complete the symmetry. What he had was:

Law 1: I AM
Law 2: Neither Light nor Darkness Change the Presence of the Sky
Law 3: I AM the M Pattern of Unfolding Order
Law 4: I AM Awakening from Awakening
Law 5: LOVE THE PATTERNS YOU PRODUCE
Law 6: I AM the Knowing of Knowing
Law 7: I AM the W Pattern of Enfolding Order
Law 8: ???
Law 9: ???

The symmetry suggested an ebb and flow. First an outward movement and then after Law 5 an inward one, unfolding followed by enfolding. Awakening followed by knowing, which could be construed as an inward process. But then he might also have been completely off. The next law would be critical in validating his symmetry hypothesis. It would have to, in some way, match Law 2. If it did, then that would also mean that the laws would hypothetically end at Law 9.

For the fun of it, he asked the question, "*I AM*, are there only nine laws, *I AM Aaa ome?*" not really expecting an answer. The screen instantly shifted to a 3-D living, stained glass of colored crystals with facets shifting to form other self-altering crystal structures. It lasted just a few seconds and the screen returned to his project.

"Well, I guess that answered that one," Sunshine said out loud. "Man, it's too bad I couldn't record that pattern flow."

It had looked like living molecules. He'd have to try to include something like that in his CyberPrincipia project. He made a note, "Track down sources of video clips on crystal formation."

Fabric Response Stocks Soar Following Release of Intelli-Skin

Fabric Response today announced the release of its highly awaited Intelli-Skin line of products, including hand, arm, leg, and nipple patches. However, a number of legal issues have entangled the release of its highly anticipated and controversial Intelli-Skin mask, a thin membrane electronic matrix that can be applied to the face. The wireless connection to a pocket software program would allow one to customize one's facial appearance. Police and other agencies have opposed the Intelli-Skin mask, stating that it would make face recognition in criminal cases impossible and the security cams nearly worthless. They claim that in combination with the new black market in synthetic fingertips and DNA cocktail sprays, the ability to identify criminals would be even further hampered.

■ ■ ■ ■ ■ ■

Les Dimensions Parallèles: Une Cartographie de la Réalité
Parallel Dimensions: A Cartography of Reality
> Author: 2020 Nobel Prize winner Lucas Bresson
> Published: 2018
> 259 pages. 24 black-and-white drawings and graphs.
> Includes card key access to the Web interview, "Parallel Dimensions: The Hyperdimensional Fabric of Reality."

Lucas Bresson is considered the father of parallel structuralism, a method for interpreting reality as a grid formed by the interaction of parallel temporal, physical, and psychological domains of structure. Each domain has its own structures. Reality is the result of the interactive intersections of these domains and their respective dominance. The basis for parallel domains was founded on the holon model of Ken Wilber, the famous American psychologist and philosopher, and on the multiverse, multitemporal hypotheses of postmodern physicists. The most important contribution of Bresson is his idea of relative realism, basically that multiple realities can be equally true and even contradictory, but only in a parallel domain model.

According to Bresson, the origins of parallel reality/temporal dimension cartography can be traced back to prehistoric times when ancient shamans first recognized a three-tier, parallel reality model consisting of the middle world, the lower world, and the upper world. This model later evolved into the this world, heaven and hell model of organized religions. Plato presented a similar idea in his well-known allegory of the shadows on the cave wall, a parallel world being the source of the shadows interpreted by the inhabitants of the cave as being the real world.

In science, the depth and levels of structures constitute parallel realities. The multiverse and multitime theories of modern cosmology and physics support a parallel structuralism of reality. Bresson's interpretation of the Big Bang and black holes is that they are points of energy conversion, actually energy drives, between two temporal dimensions. This leads to a world model he describes as hypercosmology. According to the model, the real meaning of existence can only be understood in the context of the interrelationships of these parallel temporal dimensions.

41.

CHOSEN

She let herself trance out, mentally collapsing a hollow psychic cylinder between the top of her head and her vagina, and abandoning herself to what she thought of as a seizure. The waves ran through her body and her sex started its pulsing and gripping in tongues thing, adjusting to the subject and then contracting in a type of alien Morse code. The goggled man in front of her started groaning and mumbling and then shaking in the harness as if he had been electrocuted.

He whispered, "So beautiful . . . so beautiful . . . so beautiful . . ." and then he started sobbing. She could hear the muffled sounds behind the full-face goggles. Tears were trickling down the bottom of the mask and trailing down his neck and chest.

"You are my love, Charlie," she said, her words echoing through the room thanks to multiple coordinated microphones and speakers. Then, with a nod of the head, she signaled to the operator to take the man to the recovery area and he was whirred away. One more imprint, one more stamping of an all-neuron-shuffling memory against which all the subject's future relationships would be compared. She hadn't fully understood this until a couple of years ago when she started getting e-mails from the lovers and wives of initiates. They had essentially all said the same thing: "I don't how you did what you did, but thank you."

Only a few had been complaints, mostly along the lines of "How am I supposed to be able to compete with that?"

The letters had puzzled her. What had she done that it deserved a thank you? At the time she assigned an assistant to contact some of the women. The answers had surprised her. The words that were used over and over again were *spiritual* and the *best*: because you made his first time so spiritual . . . because you have made him expect something spiritual . . . because you have made our relationship so spiritual . . . the best . . . the very best . . . the best love . . . the best sex.

What she had done was apparently implant in the initiates the expectation that sex somehow be linked to the cosmic process. There was an answer there, in the sex and the relationships that they sought, some type of alchemical magic that could change the ordinary into pure meaning. In the sex. She could imagine it. They probed in the dark seeking for passageways. It was like a labyrinth. Does this way lead there? No. Does that one? No. Then maybe this way? Yes, it feels closer. Closer to the memory. She realized that for the initiates a good companion, a good lover, would be one with whom they could explore the different accesses. This had somehow clarified things for her. Her only purpose, she had come to understand, was to show it, just once, the first time, clear through to the other side.

She had a half hour to recover and recharge before the next initiate, the last of the day.

Her assistant brought her the specially formulated drink to replenish fluids, electrolytes, vitamins, minerals, and whatever nutrients the tests had shown were depleted by the process. This was followed by an herb infusion to reset her state of mind. Katrina appeared at her side, her eyes as usual taking advantage of the opportunity to run the length of her naked body. It was one of the perks of the job.

"A, we might have a problem," she said. "Security scanned the surrounding buildings and they found a watcher. They sent some people out to search the perimeters of the building and they spotted four more."

"So what's new?" Amazonia asked. "Don't we always have at least one group or other out there?"

Katrina seemed agitated. "This is different, A. Jerry's used the zoom scope and spotted at least two morphometric scanners. One in a building and another in a car parked across the street. There might be others. That's pretty fancy equipment. Someone's pretty determined to spot you."

"Why does it have to be me? Isn't it possible they're looking for someone else, one of our employees or maybe an initiate?" Why did she have to bother her with this now? She only had ten minutes to go before she had to clear her head for the next ritual.

Katrina kept on insisting. "With a scanner? Why not just follow them. You're the only one no one ever sees entering or leaving the building. Don't kid yourself, A. You're the main attraction here."

"So what do we do? As long as I don't go out the front, let them look all they want. Listen, I've got to be on in just a few minutes, Katrina. Can't this wait until later?"

"Something about this feels wrong, A. Think about it, at least two scanners. Those things cost over a quarter mil a piece."

"Then why don't you just send Christie and Georgina out? See if maybe they can get some information out of one of the watchers."

"You want them to seduce them?"

"I want them to do whatever they have to as long as it stays legal. It could be a government agency doing the surveillance."

Finally Katrina turned and left. She took another sip of tea and concentrated on emptying her mind. Only one thing mattered now.

Amazonia waited until near-closing time to enter Kara Tundra, wearing a dress this time and a different colored wig and lenses. They left with the last of the crowd. Katrina met them a couple of blocks away with the car and drove her home. As she made her way across town, Katrina checked the dashboard screen connected to the rear headlight cameras.

"So is anyone following us?" Amazonia asked.

Katrina threw another glance at the screen. "All clear so far. I think we're OK."

"Any more news on the watchers?"

"Paula got to one of the ones sitting in a car. She followed him to a coffee shop. She went as far as getting him to invite her for a date. She's pretty sure it's the Church of Moral Order. The guy talked about *I AM* and Satan."

"The Christers? Again! What do you think they want this time?"

"If you've watched the news, this *I AM* stuff has been getting the Christers all worked up. They're convinced it's Satan, the beginning of his rule. Maybe they think you're part of it, being the great whore and Jezebel and whatever else they've called you. Maybe they're just watching as a precaution in case you're secretly training an army of the devil's prostitutes to corrupt the world. Who knows with those assholes?"

"How about setting up a dupe? Find someone who's my height. Have her put on a wig and one of my latex masks. That should trick the scanners. Make sure you have a couple of security people follow her."

"Sounds like a plan. It should give us a good idea about why they're trying to spot you."

"Just make sure you take all possible precautions. Pick someone from security and make sure she wears a vest and a couple of transmitters. You never know."

They arrived at the front of her building. Amazonia switched wigs and lenses. As she entered, the doorman greeted her, "Good morning, Mrs. Bradford, another late night at work?"

"You know how it is with magazines, Harry," she said. "There's always deadlines." She walked to the elevator and rode to the top floor.

■ ■ ■ ■ ■ ■

The first watcher alerted him, "We've got another hit. Here she comes again. OK, she's out on the sidewalk, the tall one with the blond hair and the leather coat."

"Follow her. Let me know where she goes," the agent said.

"The infrared scanner's showing she's probably wearing a vest."

"What areas are clear?"

"The neck and parts of the face. She's wearing lenses and gloves. The face is showing up a little strange, maybe it's the makeup."

"I just need a square inch of exposure."

"You got it, just aim for the head."

He opened the case and took out the zinger, a microcopter with a wireless controlled syringe. The order from Randall had been that it should only be used at night and returned the day after the hit. One time only, Randall had ordered, otherwise they'll make a connection.

The side of the neck. He opened his window and carefully placed the two-inch zinger on the edge of the car door. He pushed on the lift control and the tiny blades started spinning, propelling it up a few inches above the edge of the door. He then pointed the laser beam in the general direction and the zinger took off like a bumblebee. He guided it to about the right height then switched on the thermosensor and pressed the inject/retreat button. The zinger zipped to the bare area of her neck like a vampire bat. Upon contact, the short thin needle pulsed in and out, kicking the zinger out of thermosensor mode. It zipped off as she slapped the side of her neck and scratched the injection site. The assistant, using a sonic magnet, guided the zinger back toward the car and snatched it out of the air with the vacuum tube. He could have retrieved it with his hand because the zinger was supposed to be completely safe, but the thing weirded him out. It made him think of a flying pit viper head.

"That should do the trick," he said to the watcher. "It'll take about five minutes."

The drug kicked in as Sally Duncan stood waiting for a

subway train, molecular coats all breaking down simultaneously and disintegrating vessel walls. She clutched her head as if trying to hold on to what was left of her mind, fell over the edge, and landed on the tracks.

■ ■ ■ ■ ■ ■

Amazonia Temple Employee Found Dead

Sally Duncan, an employee of the controversial Temple of Amazonia, was found dead after falling on a subway track last night. She is believed to have suffered from a cerebral hemorrhage.

Upon hearing the news announcement, Reverend Thomson paced around his office and cursed. "The fucking idiots, the stupid fucking idiots!" There was now no alternative. They were going to have to train and get someone in again. It would take several weeks of training and they'd have to pay the premium rate to move up the schedule.

42.

YOU HAVE NOW ENTERED
ANOTHER REINCARNATION

Her communicator pinged a text message. It was Regina. *Sunday night. Rob didn't want to go out. Not sure if he's for me, anyway. Too straight. Out to Marley's. Why don't you come?*

Not tonight. Too tired, she replied. *Have fun.*

Rama slipped on the virtual net, put on her digi-goggles, and clicked on the CyberBardos icon. She found herself in the menu she coined "the crossroads." She set down the path leading to the Well of Existence. As a result of some twisted topography, something out of an Escher print, she soon found herself at the top of a tall mountain, actually the tallest mountain of the virtual Earth inside the program. She looked around.

The world spread around her for miles in an unreal level of resolution. The clearest air, birds flying below her, their chirps echoing through mountain ranges that bordered forests, plains, and deserts as far as the eye could see. Suddenly, she heard a crackling sound beneath her feet and stepped back as the earth split open, creating a deep crevice.

"Rama, welcome to the Well of Existence," a voice said. The programmed ventilators were pulsing air lightly toward her face, simulating wind. "If you want to go deep, jump into the well or else stay here and enjoy the view."

She bent over the edge and looked down. Below her was what appeared to be a bottomless pit, a dark vacuity. Air blew up from it, which was odd. *It's just a program, just walk over the edge.*

"Toss a stone," the voice said. She picked up one of the small rocks near the edge and let it fall. It recessed in the darkness until it disappeared.

It's just a program. It can't kill me even if it feels it could. Fuck it. She leapt into the hole.

The ventilators kicked in, at first a slow breeze, as she fell, a wind. The pitch-darkness slowly became brighter and she saw around her the animated layers of civilizations, the history of the world in reverse: cities leading to huts dropping to caves, savannas, trees, a period of gigantic dinosaurs, oceans with giant predators, mollusks, creatures that looked like giant sow bugs, strange amoeboid slimes, microscopic forms, the complex geometries of molecules, atoms, flashing energy bursts, and back to a void period of pure black. In the background, a pulsing sound, like the heart of the universe. And then passage through an opening and . . . she found herself in an alien world with a completely different geography, an alternate evolution.

There were plants with peculiar symmetries and netted leaves that allowed light to pass through them. Little bat-like creatures with monkey-like faces buzzed around her, emitting the strangest tinny sounds. On the ground crawled large rubbery snail-like things with spined shells and a green luminous pulse. Their stalked eyes turned to see her. They started humming. The hum spread through the landscape, *hum, hum, hum,* like something going viral from snail to snail . . .

The winds shifted. A voice said, "You have now entered another reincarnation. Explore this world or walk to the nearest hole and jump again, or return to the Menu."

The blinking icon of her phone appeared in front of her.

Rama clicked out, removed the goggles, reoriented herself, and picked up the communicator next to the Cybermaster. She looked at the number. Regina.

"Hey, Reggie."

"Rama, I think some creep is following me. I just left Marley's, there wasn't much going on there."

"Is he behind you?"

"I think so. I can't see him right now. I feel weird. I think someone put something in my drink."

"Regina, listen, turn around and head back to the club. Call me as soon as you get there. Then call a taxi to take you home. If you see the guy, use your phone and send me a photo. Taking his pic may scare him away."

"OK."

Rama checked the time and put on the *Out of This World* news program. The current segment elaborated on celibacy, the new vegan ideology.

"Extreme vegans do not kiss and do not have oral sex ... no animal products ..."

Her communicator pinged a new message. A few seconds of video of a tall man moving toward the camera. His face looked bleached out, the features unclear. She dialed Regina but got her voice mail.

"Shit, Regina!" she said out loud. She tried a couple more times but didn't get through. "Dammit!"

She called a taxi. Round trip to Marley's by cab would be at least two hours of lost pay.

It took the cab twenty-five minutes to reach the entrance of the club. An accident had forced them to take a detour. She walked up to the girl at the entrance and told her she needed to check if Regina was in the club. The girl waved her in. Once inside, she told the man at the counter the same story. "That'll be ten dollars," he said.

"I'll just be two minutes. My friend called me and said a man was following her so I told her to come back to the club. I just want to check if she's here."

"That'll be ten dollars," he said. "I hear that sorry story every day."

She dug in her purse and handed the man a twenty.

He gave her back a ten and stamped the top of her hand.

"Good luck."

She went in and gave herself a few minutes to adjust to the dim light. The place was only half full. Few people were dancing. She walked between tables quickly, checking faces, then along the bar, over to the people standing near walls, and finally, the ladies' room. She went back to the bar, took out her communicator, and showed the bartender a photo of Regina.

"Have you seen my friend here tonight? She called me to join her but I don't see her anywhere."

The barman put down the glass he was wiping and looked at her screen. "Can't be sure but I think she was here earlier."

"Within the last hour?"

"No, earlier than that. Maybe two hours ago."

She went back out and showed her screen to the girl at the entrance. "Did you see this woman leave in a taxi?"

"Hey, we get people leaving in taxis all the time. No way I can remember who leaves when. Try some of the people standing outside."

She went around showing Regina's pic but no one had paid attention. One girl said, "There was this chick who looked pretty fucked up with some weird dude."

"What do you mean by weird dude?"

"I don't know, he looked kind of fucked up and I don't mean drunk; some kind of drug."

She showed her the pic on her phone. "Was that him?"

"Could have been him. Looked a little weird like that."

"Did they take a taxi together?"

The girl just shrugged her shoulders.

She redialed Regina one more time with no luck. Shit. She decided to call the police.

"Do you have proof of a crime, ma'am?" the woman asked her. "We're too undermanned to investigate unless there's proof of a crime. If you don't hear back from her by tomorrow, give us another call."

She was going to take a cab back to the apartment but hadn't counted on paying to get in the club. She decided to walk to the subway. It was 2:15 a.m. by the time she got back home. She called Regina again but got sent to voice mail. She tried once more an hour later but still no answer. If Regina was not answering because she had gotten fucked up and gone to bed with some guy she was going to be pissed.

She went to bed but ended up lying there staring at the ceiling. A neurotransmitter alarm kept ringing inside her head. At 6:00 a.m. she got up, showered, got dressed, and walked to the subway. She could be at Regina's in an hour.

43.

BLUE CIGARETTE

The prime minister's chauffeur showed up at her hotel lobby at precisely 7:15 p.m. Heads turned, people stared, and cameras flashed as he led her to the antique black Rolls parked out front. He opened the door and she climbed in, settling into the self-adjusting leather seat before inspecting the inside. The compartment had been retrofitted with a couple of monitor screens, World Net connection, surround-sound speaker system, and autobar and snack service. Before closing the door, the driver raised an index finger to get her attention.

"Ms. Reechardsohn, Prime minister Kabuto ask no eat or drink before dinner."

"OK," she said.

The massive Phantom V glided soundlessly into the busy street, a ghost on wheels. Karen stared out the window, fascinated by the bustling activity, the giant animated billboards, and the Las Vegas–like overlay of neon until she noticed that the cross streets and scenes did not coincide with the little she could see through the smoky glass partition that separated her from the driver. High-res window monitors had apparently been raised and switched on. It annoyed her to think that she was being treated like an ordinary tourist. The view had obviously been programmed, either for her entertainment or to conceal their route. She tried the window buttons on the door. They didn't work. She tapped on the glass pane.

"Yes, Ms. Reechardsohn?" the driver's voice said from a side speaker.

"I'd like to see the city. Could you please lower the window monitors?"

It took several seconds before the driver answered.

"We be there soon. Enjoy view, Ms. Reechardsohn."

"I want to see the city. Could you put the windows down?" she insisted.

"Window broken. Can't shut off," the driver said.

"Now that's a good one," she said.

"Please repeat question, not understand."

"Never mind," she said, "everything's fine."

"OK," the driver said.

"Right, OK." She reached for the console, turned on the television, and scanned the channels for the evening news. A push of the translator button changed the Japanese garble to English. As could be expected, *I AM*–related events dominated the Japanese broadcasts. In Mexico, thousands of women were shown gathered in the streets, wailing in mass, the sobs generating a peculiar background rhythm that punctuated what sounded like glossolalia. When interviewed, they claimed it was because *I AM* had spoken to them, not to their ears, they emphasized, but to their hearts, their great big maternal Latino hearts, clutching their chests as they said it.

This was followed by the announcement that hundreds of churches related to *I AM* were being set up overnight in empty theaters and storefronts. In other areas of the world, this or that president or prime minister was advocating caution about coming to quick conclusions with regards to the *I AM* events. They urged the need to examine the facts and not extrapolate without clear evidence.

It was during a commercial that she grasped, with all the ripe meaning it implied, that the crying and wailing Mexican women were in fact shedding tears of joy. The Lord had returned and was once again talking to them. The scene reminded her of a documentary on a Huichol pilgrimage that culminated with the eating of peyote buttons. Eyes aglow, tears streaming down cheeks, caught between the ecstasy of having experienced the divine invisible fabric of the world and the sadness of having to return to this one. The idea of crying from happiness was inconceivable to her. She could smile, she could beam, her eyes could sparkle, and she could even laugh until tears fell down her cheeks; but she lacked the wiring that linked crying to joy. Hell, she didn't even cry at weddings or funerals.

About a half an hour later, the car entered an underground parking garage and stopped in front of a gated entrance leading to a blue, neon-lit tunnel that burrowed into the wall. The chauffeur accompanied her to the gate and keyed in the entry code. He gestured toward the opening. "Go to end and say you're friend of Prime minister Kabuto," he said, as the polished, black steel bars slid into the ceiling. "Maître d' will show you to table."

The restaurant had a certain subterranean Zen austerity. The walls and ceiling were simulated carved rock with lights concealed in depressions and folds. A waterfall-fed stream ran through the middle of the room and under a bridge-like raised stage. The water was alive with brightly colored koi carp. The bioengineered fluorescent fish, lit by underwater black lights, slashed the ceiling mirrors with pigment flashes, like expressionist painters. Chairs and tables, simple in design and made of dark bamboo, were arranged along the water's edge for a clear view of both the fish and the dinner show. The maître d' led her to the Japanese prime minister and his wife, who got up and nodded their heads before shaking her hand.

"Ah, finally we meet, Ms. Richardson. This is my wife." She shook hands and nodded.

"A pleasure to meet you, Mr. and Mrs. Prime minister," she said.

They smiled. A waiter appeared at their side. The prime minister turned to her. "Ms. Richardson, you allow me to order for you, OK?"

"OK," she said, "that sounds great." She smiled at his wife who smiled back. "This is a wild-looking place," she said. The wife nodded.

The first course was a special marinated caviar from a rare species of deep-sea fish, served as single eggs cradled in tiny depressions at the ends of individual stainless steel rods, with their bases inserted in hollow metal tubes sticking out of a sphere of melting ice. The ingenious design allowed the metal rods to conduct the cold and keep the individual eggs chilled. The platter looked like a metal porcupine.

Turning to her, the prime minister simply said, "Like this," indicating that she should follow his example. The rod was seized between thumb and index finger at midbody, brought to the mouth, and the single egg sucked off. Intermixed with the chrome rods were glass rods with hollow tips that held a single drop of vodka distilled from rare Andean potatoes.

When Karen asked about it, the prime minister answered, "Secret," his Japanese accent making it sound like "cigar-rette."

The appetizer was consumed by alternating the dipping of a glass rod into the mouth with the sucking of the end of a chrome rod, a dozen units of each per person. Karen couldn't quite make up her mind about it, thinking that the method of eating was at least as interesting as the taste, which was like beluga caviar, but less salty and with a hint of coffee. To show her pleasure, she simply uttered little "umms" between inserts, thinking there was something strangely exhibitionist and sexual about the whole thing, this public insertion of tiny beads and drops of liquid in one's mouth.

After the table was cleared, a waiter dressed in a tuxedo wheeled up a clear acrylic globe, and with a gesture of the hand, invited her to a pre-mortem viewing of the "for you, very special."

As she leaned over to look, she noticed the prime ministercatching the waiter's eye and inquiring with a flash of eyebrows the cost of the unit. The waiter, throwing a quick glance at Karen, raised his hand to waist level and made a quick flick of four fingers. The prime minister blinked his eyes and made a small nod.

Karen brought her face up to the sphere and looked at the sacrificial victim, four fingers' worth. The spectrum-specific lights hanging from the ceiling had been turned on before rolling the cart in. The creature glowed in the dark, looking like a hologram. It appeared to be a small lobster but was in fact a bioengineered one-pound Australian giant crayfish, selectively bred for its phosphorescent blue color. It had been raised in a top-secret underground aquaculture operation on a patented formula of bioengineered bacteria and algae. In addition, the thing—within the last three hours—had been offered a terminal meal that had impregnated it with a mysterious hallucinogenic concoction derived from fish skins, Amazonian plant extracts, and fungi with blue flesh. The waiter described the creature as *aioro*, which translated to English simply meant "blue."

"Aioro," she repeated.

The waiter, the prime minister, and his wife all smiled and nodded. *"Aioro."*

She stared at the beast through the clear plastic, a living sculpture carved of lapis, the beady black eyes gazing with crustacean oblivion, the tiny front legs shuffling what appeared to be powdered aquamarine crystals into the trap mouth.

"I can't wait," Karen exclaimed.

The waiter, acknowledging her, said, "Fifteen minutes."

That would be the exact time required for the trained chef to drive with the precision of a laser surgeon the carefully positioned diamond shaft through the shell of the strapped creature, and with a twirl of the fingers, liquid-blend its minute brain. A syringe would then be inserted into the opening to extract the whitish mush. It would be placed in a glass vial with ten drops of filtered mountain stream water and gently stirred. The pithed crayfish would then be flash-grilled, the tenderness tested by the snapping off of legs, after which the chef—with a special razor-sharp knife—would extract the meat from the tail and slice it into perfect nickel-sized white disks. The sections would be carefully laid out on a dark blue plate, between strands of seaweed dyed red. Using the syringe, the Blue master chef would then apply exactly one drop of tripped-out crayfish brain at the center of each bite-sized morsel.

She knew the rules of etiquette under such situations. Do not talk business. Inquire about the family. Talk about the wonders of Japanese culture, of Tokyo, of the gardens of Kyoto, of the kindness and courtesy of the Japanese people. Be grateful, be polite, be conversational, be complimentary, and tomorrow the requested interview would be granted at the agreed-upon time.

The waiter came back, displaying another smaller set of blue lobsters to the prime minister and his wife. More eyebrow flashing and finger flicks. Three, twice. Both performed nods of the head to show their approval. The wife was wringing her hands. Her eyes had a glazed look, like she was in heat. She wet her lips. Karen wondered how anyone could be so eager to eat an arthropod.

Three waiters arrived with individual carts holding sapphire-blue plates on which was laid out the glowing white meat. Each then took out a pair of polished black chopsticks with recurved ends carved from a rare tropical hardwood tree. They assumed positions at their sides, the arm raised at the elbow and the chopsticked hand ready to descend.

She mimicked her hosts, turned toward the waiter, and opened her mouth halfway, whereupon the attending waiter grabbed a disk of white meat by its sides and brought it forward. It all seemed very much like taking communion.

She opened her mouth wider and felt the warm contact against her tongue, then a spreading out of sensations, like a drop of oil on water. Her plan had been to chew quickly so as not to insult her hosts, but she was temporarily paralyzed by sheer novelty, her mouth unable to move, her mouth getting wet, never-before-recorded flavor signals reaching her brain. She felt her nipple tips stick out against her blouse, her throat expand, and sets of goose bumps running like waves from the top of her head to her toes. Using her tongue, she finally shifted the morsel between her teeth and bit down. The flesh was creamy sweet butter with a hint of steak and oyster and dark chocolate. She slowly chewed, each bite ejecting new flavor streams against the inside of her mouth. Then, out of the blue, her brain started performing fireworks, tiny flashes of light sparkling her vision like the distant flashes of thunderstorms. Finally, she swallowed. Following the directions indicated by the prime minister through a hand signal, she took a sip of sake to clear the palate. The prime minister, his mouth full and slowly chewing, nodded again toward the sake cup, meaning another sip. He swallowed and closed his eyes, tears forming at their edges. Was he crying from joy, from pleasure? Seconds later he reopened them, blinked a couple of times, looked at her and asked, "You like?"

"Incredible, fantastic!" she said.

He replied with a nod of the head toward the waiter. Have more. She turned and again opened her mouth. Another piece dropped in, a lava flow of a rush, her mouth now a new kind of sensory organ. The room was like the Fourth of July; colored sparks pulse-lighting everything in rainbow flashes. She thought she detected a slight smirk on the prime minister's face, but he then turned toward his wife, who met his eyes, her lips sliding against each other, her tongue just barely out, licking the edges. They smiled, their eyes disappearing into cracks. The wife made a little giggle, the kind of tee-hee you would expect from a geisha.

Then the prime minister turned his attention back to her. "You like?" he asked again. His face was flickering neon.

"Oh yes! It's wonderful! I've never eaten anything like this." She turned toward the waiter, raised her head, and opened her mouth. *One more, please.*

"It get better," the prime minister said.

What did he mean, better? she wondered. *Better?* She swallowed, and it caressed the lining of her throat. She looked down. There were four more sections on her plate. She looked at the stream. The koi were painting the water with lingering after-images that overlapped and streamed. She noticed Kabuto and his wife staring at her and laughing. She turned to the waiter and opened her mouth. *One more, please.* The Blue slid like liquid silk.

After the last piece, the fireworks—besides an occasional flash—simmered down. Nothing else was served except dessert, a bowl of fresh-peeled litchis "to clear the palate." The things dribbled luminescence along the sides of the prime minister's mouth as he bit into them. It must have been in her mind, but the whole room seemed to be getting bluer, like neon black light.

"Blue," the prime minister's wife said with a grand sweep of the arm, *"Aioro."*

"Yes, and a very beautiful blue," Karen acknowledged, "a radiant phosphorescent indigo, a luminous azure."

Had those words actually come out of her mouth? She looked behind her for a hidden ventriloquist, who, of course, wasn't there. Her mouth now autospoke literature.

"Azure, yes?" The words came out of the wife's little painted doll lips.

"Almost a deep cobalt, a rich sapphire."

"Cobalt. Not know word." Then, after a moment of silence, the wife added, "Blue most important Japanese product."

Karen nodded in agreement. "Incredible stuff, this blue azure. Where does it come from?"

"Japanese chef get idea from old European movie about food that change mind but cannot tell where Blue come from. Blue, secret formula from secret growing area. If anyone reveal Blue, penalty is death for person, also for entire family, and friends, too." The prime minister's wife grinned, her glistening blue tongue tip poking between tiny turquoise teeth, looking like candy.

Karen raised an index finger to her pursed lips. "I won't say a word," she said, playing along and assuming that the wife was attempting to make humor.

"Not need worry, Ms. Richardson. You not know secret. Tee-hee."

Tee-hee, you got blue teeth. "What secret?" Karen exclaimed, putting on an air of surprise. They all laughed. The ceiling lights turned on and off.

"Ah! Now, very special show," the prime minister said.

Blue clouds drifted above their heads, lightning bolts struck the stage, and masked men and women, dressed in UV Intelli-Skin suits, materialized out of the blue haze. Light streamed through their bodies in shimmering electric bands. Blues, reds, and purples. The dancers fluttered across the stage, a frantic contact and fusion ballet that reminded Karen of the insect courting of flowers. The symmetries of open arms and legs formed hungry petals. The light flows increased their intensity, too much to contain. Eventually, like tiny explosions, pale blue beams shot out of extended arms and legs, becoming spheres that spun like winged seeds toward the ceiling, crackling with electric charge, *chit-chit-chit*, before streaming galaxies, their nebulous arms spreading above the audience. The show ended with the human fireflies rising above the room and juggling the luminous swirls back and forth, their energies gradually dimming with each passage until they were reduced to pinpoints of light that died. The audience clapped.

As soon as the ceiling lamps came back on, the prime minister asked, "You like?"

"Yes, that was amazing." And after a pause, "Excuse me," she added, "but I need to go to the ladies' room."

She was shown down another neon-striped passage. The bathroom was blue. As she sat in the stall, she looked down and saw herself pee blue. She washed her hands in blue water. Looked at her blue face in the mirror, smacked her shiny blue lips. She fumbled with her blue-dialed wrist communicator to check for messages. The one from work said, *Can't wait for the story. Have fun. John.*

Later, they were joined by a tall man with the long crew cut in an overhang style that was now the rage, his hair a luminous blue white against the indigo of the room.

"Our son, Takashi," the prime minister said, then waving to the waiter, "One glass, special blue sake."

She didn't even bother to ask what blue sake was. She already knew the answer. Anything blue was secret, punishable by death, tee-hee. As Takashi sipped from the glass, she thought about running her tongue along his moist lips and licking the blue liquid from his mouth. He stared back and threw glances at her chest. The dinner ended with the prime minister saying, "Takashi will accompany you to hotel."

The next morning she walked to the prime minister's palace with her crew.

"Did you sleep well?" the prime minister and his wife asked together.

"It's a secret," she answered. Prime minister Kabuto and his wife glanced at each other, then forced a smile.

As if they didn't know. She had let Takashi seduce her, figuring it would be good political etiquette, not to mention she had been in the mood—something about the Blue. It had felt like her mouth, after being asleep for her entire life, had finally decided to wake up—lips and tongue, the works. And boy, did it ever come alive. Just thinking about it made her unconsciously smack her lips. Mrs. Kabuto stared at her with a strange little grin before turning away. Her tongue tip, like a pink worm, had again peered between the tiny teeth. Tee-hee.

Well, as much as they might want to believe it, she hadn't been caught off guard. After all, they were Japanese. Her room was probably riddled with microdigi-cams covering every angle of vision. She had no doubt that last night's performance had been recorded and was probably already splashed, minus some editing, all over the World Net. Her fans wouldn't be disappointed. She had made sure to put on a good show. Let the Japanese audience know that the American bitches, with their injected lips and man-made melon hooters, put their little geisha wives to shame. No little tongue-tip tee-hees, but lots of wide-mouth yee-haws.

She'd followed Amazonia's advice, "Actualize the myth." Thanks to the adult movie industry, American women had acquired the international reputation of being wild broncos in bed, and she, out of a sense of patriotism, made it a mission to live up to that high ideal. When she finally orgasmed, she went theatrical and came like a porn star. The prime minister's son, lying beneath her, had stared incredulous. She had screamed like she had just found the Lord, her mind turning to soft blue ice cream that kept on melting and melting, out of her mouth and into the great blue cosmic sea. She smacked her lips.

The prime minister gestured to her. "Now you come ask questions, Ms. Richardson. Make me look good, like great American superstar Amazonia."

Amazonia, a great American icon? Now that was a new one.

After the usual introductory chitchat, she decided to right away lead with an *I AM* question. "So tell us, Prime minister Kabuto, what is the Japanese government doing to address these *I AM* greetings?"

"It government secret," the prime minister answered, "like Blue."

"And what is it you're calling Blue, Mr. Prime minister?"

His eyes crinkled. "Japanese secret." *Jah-pah-knees cigar-rette.*

"I'm sure you can tell us a little something about it?" She was putting on the seductive bimbo act.

"Blue is special lobe-stah. Must come to Japan to experience. Blue even better than *I AM* movie."

"How can this Blue be more important that the *I AM* events, Mr. Prime minister?"

"It Japanese happiness secret. Must experience."

Ha-penis cigar-rette. Great. The line sounded like a promo for pot. So far, the interview was getting nowhere. It would rank as another big nada. "So how are the Japanese people reacting to *I AM?*"

"*I AM* make people happy, but Japanese like Blue Lobster better. Of course, *I AM* not cost so much." He laughed.

"Blue Lobster."

"Japanese secret, but Japan also know secret to *I AM.*"

Now they were getting somewhere. "Please tell us, Mr. Prime minister. The entire world wants to know."

"If tell, then no secret." No *cigar-rette.* After a moment of silence, he added, "*I AM* like Blue Lobster."

There he goes again with those goddamned crawdads.

"Please, Prime minister Kabuto, tell us how *I AM* is like Blue Lobster."

"*I AM* sent to put chemicals in brain. Japanese scientists observe difference in brain when *I AM* show come on."

"So your scientists were actually able to observe changes in the brain following the *I AM* greeting?"

"Yes, yes, difference very clear. Brain chemicals not same after people look at *I AM* movie."

"What kind of changes are we talking about?"

"Brain make more happy chemicals, a lot like Blue."

"You said earlier somebody sent *I AM*. Who sent *I AM*?"

"Secret." *Cigar-rette.*

Now she was starting to get pissed. The Japanese had contacted the New York office to say they were going to give her something exclusive about *I AM*. Instead, they had just used her show for propaganda about some new lobster. And she had fallen for it. What the fuck was in that lobster anyway? What did that waiter mean by four fingers? Four hundred? Four thousand? She'd have to call Takashi and ask him about how to find that restaurant.

When she finally got through to him later that day, he had smiled and said, "*Cigar-rette*, but if you treat, I arrange with Prime minister. We go there tonight."

She smacked her lips.

■ ■ ■ ■ ■ ■

She pressed Regina's buzzer. No answer. She rang the building manager, who came to the door in his robe. "You better have a good reason for waking me up at seven in the morning," he grumbled.

She told him about Regina. "I'm worried something may have happened to her."

He went back in to get his keys and they climbed the

stairs to her apartment. He knocked on her door a few times then took a key and opened it. "I doubt she's here," he said. "She has an interior lock she usually latches when she's home. I know because she had to file a request to have it put in."

She followed him inside the apartment and looked around. It was just as neat and orderly as Regina. You could have showed it in a magazine. Her bed was made but hadn't been slept in.

Three hours later, after having popped a pill and downed a café *muy grande*, she keyed in to Mind Games. Please be here, Regina. She was barely through the door when Lionel came up to her looking at his wrist.

"Ten twenty-seven. You're supposed to be here at ten fifteen. Regina's not here, either. She better not be late. Lots going on today. Just go look in the back room. They just delivered twenty boxes of products. Six new programs. You both need to take the sales samples home tonight and learn how to demo the things."

As if I didn't have anything better to do with my life. Supposedly more products meant more sales which should have given her more commission, but it didn't work out that way. At the end of the month it always ended up averaging out to the same. *I'm lucky to even have three hours a day to myself.*

Half an hour later, Lionel came back. "You're going to have to handle the shift by yourself. Regina hasn't shown up yet and I can't get through to her."

She called the police again during a bathroom break. She got the same rote answer: "If a crime hasn't been committed . . . we are too understaffed to . . ."

She interrupted the screener. "Look, she hasn't shown up for work. Is that a good enough reason for you guys to start looking for her?"

She was transferred to a detective who asked her details about her phone call. He asked for her work phone number and address. "We'll look into it," he said.

When she got back to the floor, Lionel turned away from the couple he was talking to and pointed at her. "Here she is. She can answer all the questions you have about the Robo Cham."

The woman turned to her. "So can we use it to catch flies in the kitchen?"

"What are the color-changing features?" the husband asked.

She looked behind them. Lionel was grinning at her.

■ ■ ■ ■ ■ ■

Mouth Runs Like Water

It may have been a coincidence, but today the Japanese released a new commercial promoting a mysterious product they are calling "Blue," what some say is the biggest craze since fugu. The commercial shows a mouth bathed in blue light, eating, sipping from a cup, smiling, gliding up a man's chest, interspersed with the whispering of "Blue ... blue ... blue." The most unusual—but also very familiar—feature of the commercial is the lips, those unmistakable lips.

Hint: Her news show runs at 8:00 p.m., five days a week. Last night's show featured a special: "Japan: How is it coping with *I AM*?"

44.

DARKNESS SHALL MEET
WITH THE LIGHT

atricia Holden and the five other founders of the Sisterhood were sitting around the oval table in the meeting room in back of the administrative headquarters. Annie Templeton, the treasurer of the organization, was elaborating on the quarterly report on the membership and revenues from various products and services.

"We lost another 254 members, which leaves us with 16,218 paying members, of which 7,359 are international members. Sales of ritual supplies, however, are holding steady."

Jean Salzberg, known to the sisters as Jaz, turned to Patricia. "It's now what? Seven, eight quarters that membership has been dropping? We're doing something wrong here, sisters. The rituals and potions are not enough. They are outdated. If we don't find a solution to the problem, the Sisterhood will not survive."

Cynthia Winthrop, the membership coordinator, jumped in. "There are other products out there just as effective as the ones we first developed. The Chinese have their own versions using Asian botanicals some say have a peculiar edge. I think we should order samples from the competition and test them. But I agree with Jaz, Patricia. The rituals are getting stale."

Sally McDonald, the founder, who years ago had been a

leader of the andro-lesbo movement, spoke up. Her head was shaved. As usual, she wore a man's shirt and dress pants. For the last three years her job had been to manage product sales and shipping. "Most of our sales are now from nonmembers. Women are buying the ritual products just for the enhancement of sexual experience. They don't care two bits about the Sisterhood. I've read some women are even allowing men to handle the rods."

"Then we need to improve the rituals. Maybe we should have a new potion accessible only to members," said Patricia. "I can contact Sue McQuade. She can probably come up with a couple of new formulas."

Christina, the one in charge of the Sisterhood website, slapped the table. "Enough, Patricia, you sound like a broken record. We've gone down that road for the last six meetings and here we are now. We haven't come up with anything new or original in more than three years. The fact is, we're outdated. We're using recorded or direct video rituals but the general format is the same. We need to think outside the box here. The Sisterhood can't just be a few rituals. We have to come up with something immersive."

"I agree," Annie said. "We're competing against heavy-duty technology here, alternate worlds. And now we also have this *I AM* phenomenon the Japanese say is managing to manipulate our brains."

Sally McDonald tapped the table with her knuckles. "Let's stay on track, sisters. We have a revenue problem, so what can we do about it?"

"We need to think CR," Christina said. "Hire the techs to create a Sisterhood CR. A total immersion into a female universe so mind-boggling, so identity altering, that it causes a paradigm shift in women. We have to make real the possibilities of living in a world without men. We need to make the Goddess come to life."

"I think a first step should be to send some sisters to some of the successful CR groups that already exist and get some ideas for increasing membership," Annie said.

"Like which ones?"

"I think we need to send someone to New Jerusalem. I hear they created an entire city and they have ceremonies and other features in place for which the members pay fees. We could get a lot of good information from that. Those Christers know how to make money. Why reinvent the wheel?"

"I like it. We just need to find one or two sisters willing to sacrifice a few days and pretend they're submitting to a male God."

"We need someone who looks real girlie and innocent. Anyone here know of any possible candidates?" Valerie asked.

"As a matter of fact, I do," Patricia said.

■ ■ ■ ■ ■ ■

Rama was doing a search on Sunshine Borden, hoping to find a way to break through his host's screening filters. On the first page near the top she noticed the headline: "Sister of Sunshine Borden Beaten by Man She Met at Club." She clicked on the header, read the story, then clicked on the link to the description given the police. *Odd face, muscular build, the possibility that the man was drugged.* She replayed the brief video Regina had sent her. The man generally fit the description.

When Sunshine's screening questionnaire came up, under "What is the nature of your inquiry?" she wrote: "My friend phoned me from a club saying she was followed by a man. She sent a short video. I think it may be the same man who attacked your sister. I have yet to hear back from her. She has not showed up at work. Sunshine, I also have a question about the CyberBardos."

She turned on her camera when instructed, then realized she was still in her pajamas and hadn't put on any makeup. She almost clicked out but didn't want to miss the possibility of getting through. She started laughing. "Thank you for your inquiry . . ."

The screen suddenly shifted. *Law Eight: Darkness Shall Meet with the Light. I AM Aaa ome.*

She could feel some kind of microscopic switches in her brain clicking, making some kind of adjustments. *The drugs must be messing with my head.* She got up and looked around her apartment. Something about time was different. She was more in the present or time was stretched by the tiniest increment. *Probably a fuckup from taking too much Instant.* She walked to her bathroom. *It feels like I'm drifting, like gravity's diminished.* She turned around and started hopping around her dining room table. *What am I doing? I'm acting like a little kid. It feels like I'm jumping on the moon.*

■ ■ ■ ■ ■ ■ ■

CyberPrincipia, an ongoing virtual environment that would generate an experiential simulation of the world of atomic and subatomic matter, disintegrated and was replaced by *Law Eight: Darkness Shall Meet with the Light. I AM Aaa ome.*

Sunshine broke into a smile. The laws were progressing as he had predicted. There was indeed symmetry between all the laws that preceded or followed Law Five. *Law Eight: Darkness Shall Meet with the Light* was related to *Law Two: Neither Light nor Darkness Change the Presence of the Sky.* This hypothetically meant that there would be one more law to complete the set before the next set of communications or whatever was supposed to follow. The pulsing colored wave fields returned to the screen and Sunshine proceeded with the application of new APUs (autopoietic programming unities) he had designed specifically for the Principia program. The section he was working on involved making photosynthesis a visible and audible phenomenon that could be experienced at different levels of scale, from what happened inside a single plant cell to the mass conversion of energy by a tropical forest. *To make the invisible something that can be seen, heard, and felt.*

■ ■ ■ ■ ■ ■

"What does this mean?" the president asked the committee members and the handful of experts who had been called in. "*Darkness Shall Meet with the Light*. Is this a threat? Are we talking another blackout? Anyone have any ideas?"

A number of lights scattered across his panel. He decided to address Randall first for a change. He didn't want it to be too apparent that he disliked the man. "Director Randall, you have something you can tell us?"

Randall, somewhat caught off guard, straightened up. "Mr. President . . . I think that there may be enough of a threat implied in this latest message that we should consider shutting down the World Net, for the safety of civilization. This is the first law where we are told of something about to happen, and it's the closest we have had of a threat of some kind, the threat of darkness, one very likely tied to a future blackout. Assuming that this *I AM* can only act through electronic media, we may have come at a point where shutting down the World Net may be necessary."

And what you're not saying, you religious nut, is that you think we need to cut off the devil's mouthpiece. Tennyson smiled as he thought of a way to respond diplomatically.

"That's certainly a possibility we have to consider, but how about we first look at other possible interpretations of this latest law? Could it be warning us about something about to occur rather than threatening us? By the way, have we contacted all the astronomical observatories? Is there any sign of an object heading our way?" He addressed the secretary of defense. "General Carson?"

He coughed before speaking. "Mr. President, we've already looked into that and there is nothing of immediate concern other than the Pugnus asteroid uncovered twelve years ago. Several astronomers are saying it may come dangerously close to Earth five years from now. As you already know, NASA is working on a mission in cooperation with the European Union and Russia to deflect it with an encounter target date of about three years."

"So is there any chance that could be what *I AM* is talking about?"

"I'm not sure how the risk of an asteroid strike could be construed as a law. If by chance it were to impact, experts are predicting large-scale, localized destruction and potentially severe climatic consequences for several years, but it wouldn't be anything apocalyptic. In cosmic terms, it would just be a localized event. I just don't see it as being related to darkness meeting with the light. There would be more cloudiness, maybe."

"OK, so what if we did coordinate a brief shutdown of the World Net for the purpose of international security?"

The secretary of state asked to speak. "The problem is that we're just guessing about the latest message possibly implying a threat. A greater and more real threat would be the consequences of a shutdown of the World Net. It would cause a global economic and social meltdown in a matter of days. Most countries would never agree to a shutdown. And like Director Randall just mentioned, there's also the fact that *I AM* has clearly shown that it could cause a global power blackout. If we aggravated it by shutting off its mouthpiece, it might just decide to do that, and then we would have a critical situation. Darkness would indeed meet with the light."

John Tennyson looked down at his panel. *Let's hear a woman's opinion for a change.*

"Yes, Catherine?"

She adjusted her glasses. "There would be social repercussions if we were to shut down the World Net and prevented *I AM* from sending its laws. Most people now look forward to receiving the messages. You'd have massive public protests, and that's assuming things didn't get violent." She turned to look at the other members to make sure they got her point.

The president smirked. They were going in a circle, as usual. "So it seems we're once again back to doing nothing. Yes, Dr. Collins?"

"I think there are signs the laws are becoming clearer.

According to Sunshine Borden, who was part of my team when we designed the World Host, there is only one more law coming our way. The laws are following a pattern where Law Five is the midpoint. As we move away from Law Five, we see a bilateral symmetry in the laws. Laws Four and Six mention states of awareness, Laws Three and Seven refer to types of order, and Laws Two and Eight refer to darkness."

"Yeah, we've figured that one out," said Loveridge, ignoring the permission-to-talk rule, "but we just don't see the significance. Maybe it'll start sending another set of nine laws."

"Now why haven't I heard about any of this until now?" the president asked.

Loveridge decided to answer. "Until this latest message, this possible symmetry in the communications was still just speculation."

Walter Randall switched his light on. "Yes, Mr. Randall?"

Randall was keying in file access as he spoke. "Sir, Sunshine Borden is on our list of those who could possibly be behind this entire *I AM* phenomenon. Theoretically, it might have been possible to add a delete function to his APUs. The APUs could have been used to send the communications if a loop feature had been introduced that deleted them as soon as they completed their function. This would be missed by our code detectors because it would be a kind of stealth programming."

"I don't have a clue about what you're talking about, Mr. Randall. How do the Borden APUs figure in all this? I've read about them but I don't really know what they do."

Collins spoke up. "They're autopoietic software units that allow computers to program themselves. They're the key software behind the World Host, personal hosts, and cyberreality programs."

"So why don't we just check the code and see if delete functions were added to these APUs?" the president asked. He acknowledged Loveridge with a nod of the head.

"It's not that easy, Mr. President. The Borden APUs are protected by patents and self-destruct features. The only person who could check them for delete features is Borden."

"Then why didn't someone bring this up sooner? It seems like this Sunshine Borden should have been invited to these meetings weeks ago."

Loveridge was getting angry at the direction the meeting was taking. He worked on controlling the tone of his voice. "Mr. President. There's really no evidence to tie Sunshine Borden to any of this. He's a reclusive type who's very suspicious of government and not likely to come willingly."

Randall interjected. "The psychological profile we have of Sunshine Borden dates back to almost ten years ago, but it does indicate the potential for subversive activities. He's a friend of Hieronymus Bardo and other drug advocates and social disrupters. His agenda is to find a way to download people into a computer. How's that for advocating dropping out of the system?"

"And why is it we don't have a more updated file on him?" General Carson asked.

Loveridge responded, "Because he has encryption as well as block and autodelete features in most of his communications that we can't break through."

"I can't believe this!" the president exclaimed. "Yes, Dr. Collins, you have something to add?"

"I worked with Sunshine Borden when we developed the World Host. I strongly disagree with Mr. Randall that he is a subversive type. The last thing that man would be interested in is putting together a hoax. He's always been very serious and outspoken about his views. This is just not the kind of thing he is likely to do."

"How about we gather more information before we ask Mr. Borden to a meeting? Mr. Loveridge and Mr. Randall, please forward to me information on these APUs and Sunshine Borden. Put it in terms I can understand, not technobabble."

"I will, right away, Mr. President," Randall replied, already sending the order through his communicator. He then cleared his throat and asked, "Uh . . . Mr. President . . . so your decision is to do nothing at the moment?"

"That's what it looks like right now. So far, all these laws have been mostly talk, a lot like these meetings." He regretted saying it as soon as the words came out of his mouth. *Way to win a popularity contest, John,* he thought. He got up and headed for the electric cart.

■ ■ ■ ■ ■ ■

Darkness Shall Meet with the Light. I AM Aaa ome. It takes a few seconds before the meaning sinks in. When it does, Bob Thomson is overtaken by a sense of panic and breaks into a sweat that makes his shirt cling to his skin. The message is clear: darkness is coming. To make sure it is not all in his head, he connects to the church host. The host has reviewed all historical events since the estimated date of the writing of Revelation. It has reviewed all previous predictions of the end-times. He clicks the link that takes him to Signs, the area programmed to filter news and identify correlations with the sequence of events prophesized in Revelation. *Darkness Shall Meet with the Light* flashes red.

He clicks on the list compiled by the host of individuals whose actions and statements had a high probability for establishing the cultural conditions that allowed the entrance of the Other, the anti-God, into the world. At the top of the list are Sunshine Borden, Jeff Collins, Hieronymus Bardo, Amazonia Appolonia, Father Graham. On a lower scale of probability: John Tennyson, Arthur Loveridge, Ars Savalia, Karen Richardson, Gary Summers, and Andy Lee. All of the names are linked to news articles, publications, video clips, and interviews to support their selection.

He notices a new entry not tied to individual names, Fabric Response. The Intelli-Skin patches that were spreading in popularity have been highlighted by the host as possible marks of the Beast because the *I AM* phenomenon used them as a medium. The problem is that no single individual could be tied to the development of the patches. Their concept and design was attributed to "proprietary autonomous hosts."

There's a knock on the door. "Come in."

Sara walks into the room. She removes her coat. There's a sudden shift in the quality of the air, a subtle bend in the gravitational field that alters light ever so slightly. Her scent reaches him. He can feel the change in his brain waves, a calmness, a rise in heartbeat, a clarity of the moment. Her green eyes are fixed on his. Her perfect mouth upturns in a smile. Part of her magic is her innocence. She is unconscious of her ability to arouse the world, to jostle the minds of men and women. But then that may be his delusion. A sudden sadness overtakes him as he realizes that he will have to make use of her special powers, that it will be a great sacrifice, that it will likely hurt him.

She comes over and kisses him. "How was your day, hon?" she asks.

He reaches under her dress. He can't help himself.

"I missed you, too," she says.

■ ■ ■ ■ ■ ■

The *I AM* Meetings Are Mostly Just Talk

According to an anonymous government source, the meetings of the US *I AM* committee have accomplished nothing to date and the government would be helpless should *I AM*'s intentions become unfriendly. This was confirmed at today's meeting, where the president apparently expressed that up to now, the *I AM* messages, as well as the meetings to address the *I AM* problem, amounted to "mostly talk."

Woman Attacked by Juan Batista's Clone?

Not likely. A street security cam caught a man looking exactly like CBS anchorman Juan Batista as he left a building on the west side after critically injuring Passiflora Borden, sister of the famous CR designer Sunshine Borden. According to Alicia McFadden, Mr. Batista's fiancée, he and a group of friends had attended a ballet performance that evening and were having drinks at the Traveler's Café at the time of the alleged incident. The theater and restaurant security cams confirmed Mr. Batista's alibi. Police are investigating the possibility that the perpetrator may have been an actor skilled in makeup.

■ ■ ■ ■ ■ ■

Cybris: Cyberintermediated Sex

The most exciting new technological augmentation of relationships occurred in 2022 and was released under the name of Cybris, short for cyberintermediated sex. It should have been no surprise that a focus of any new cybertechnology would have been sex. After all, orgasm was the most natural, legal, and intense drug-free altered state available to the human species. Its drug-like effects were the main reason religions and certain governments tried to regulate access. And it would have been addictive, except that nature had foreseen that possibility.

To prevent us from spending a lifetime in copulatory frenzy with the same individual, it wired in us the propensity for habituation, basically the failure to respond to once-effective stimuli after it had become familiar. Love and sex invariably tended to become the "same old, same old." This principle was well known to farmers who had long-ago noted that bulls got sexually disinterested if kept with the same cow, but invariably came to life when provided with new ones. Human males apparently have the same propensities toward women. Habituation was what usually led to the decline of sex in relationships unless— as therapists always said—the couples worked at it by sharing fantasies, dressing up, playacting, experimenting with kinky sex, watching porn, or reading erotica together. As one popular therapist, Charlie Dougherty, had noted, "You have to kick the habits and introduce periods of unfamiliarity into your relationships. The greatest source of excitement is novelty."

However, overcoming habit and humdrum—the forces behind psychological and sexual entropy—required time and effort. That is, until the advent of Cybris. Thanks to digitizing lenses with wireless connections to a dedicated host, it is now possible, with intermediation generated by Cybris software, to alter the experience of a loved one; change the color of their eyes and hair, and even the shape of their bodies. In advanced systems, ear inserts connected to software allow for audio conversion to change the intonations and pitch of the voice.

Today, thanks to further innovations in Cybris software, you can have an affair, in fact many affairs, with the different personas of your spouse. Several CR programs now also provide sexual theater software for Cybris that can place couples or groups in a different historical context. You can be in Roman times participating in an orgy, a medieval peasant wench seducing a prince, or alien beings in a science fiction film. Some Cybris sexual theater packages come with props to make the experience more realistic, including latex breasts, penises, and watermelon buttocks. In the case of alien sexual theater, the deluxe kits include unusual body parts such as multiple nipple stick-ons and double-headed erectile organs to apply to the forehead to accompany the scene where the alien bitch—pressing her crotch against the metal bars—says to the imprisoned hero, "Give me head, Gorgon!"

The end result is that human sexual relationships have become more complex than ever. The old notions of stable individual identity are pretty much gone and replaced by identity repertoires made possible in part by Cybris. The advent of Cybris has opened the door to the cybermediated life in general. You can now never be sure how you are being experienced by anyone wearing a set of digi-goggles, and increasing numbers of people are choosing to wear digi-goggles round the clock. Experienced life is now no longer just biological, but is becoming a form of art, cybergenerated, cybercolored, cybertextured, cyberfiltered; an expression of the imagination. This entering of the world of the imagination, as we near the Eschatonic horizon, had also been predicted by psychedelic philosopher Terence McKenna in the 1990s.

Currently most employers have restrictions on cyberintermediation. Digi-lenses must be removed after entering an office building or kept clear to demonstrate nonhosted experience. Other workplaces, however, have contracts with their own cyberintermediation servers and require all workers to be connected to their employer host while at work. For example, most government agencies now require cyberintermediation, and most schools now require student connection to educational hosts while in class.

45.

THE OTHER

On day forty-five following the initial *I AM* announcement (9 x 5 = 45, and 4 + 5 = 9), *Law Nine: I AM the Other Aaa ome* appeared on all screens. As soon as the communications ended, Sunshine turned to a chart he had assembled on the sequence of *I AM* events. Day forty-five was also the second interval of days since the initial announcement that was divisible by nine. The first law had come nine days after the initial announcement and this latest law, Law Nine, forty-five days after the initial announcement. He examined his chart of the laws along with their intervals. There was a pattern there, too, with Law Five being a kind of midpoint and Law Nine the end of an apparent countdown.

Law	Interval between Laws	Days after Announcement
I AM	0 days	
Law 1	9	9 divisible by 9
Law 2	8	17
Law 3	7	24

Law 4	6	30
Law 5	5	35
Law 6	4	39
Law 7	3	42
Law 8	2	44
Law 9	1	45 divisible by 9

Law Five and the interval for that law was five days. It suggested a midpoint for a possible symmetry. Hypothetically, this latest law marked the end of a set of communications. Sunshine was pretty certain that a different set of events, something new, was coming next, and very likely in a period of time related to the number nine.

■ ■ ■ ■ ■ ■

It wakes her up, a sense of streaming right through the top of her head and out between her legs. She lies on her back, opens her thighs, sensing the moment-by-moment generation of the world through her body. She is the Great Mother. She feels it as something both given to her and expressed by her. *You are my love.* Her wristcom is vibrating. She looks down at the message: *A, did you get that?*

■ ■ ■ ■ ■ ■

John Tennyson could have called another meeting but he didn't. He just had his secretary send a message to every member of the committee. "If you have any new and relevant information regarding this latest law please call and send it to my mailbox using the most recently issued password code." That evening, he held a brief press conference. Catherine Harris had helped him with the speech, taking into consideration any PR implications.

"The laws provide us with an increasing clarification of *I AM*'s identity. This morning's communication, *I AM the Other*, is simply this entity's way of letting us know that it is different than us, possibly another kind of intelligence. I know that many of you are concerned about whether the *I AM* entity could be malevolent, and there has certainly been a great deal of speculation on this subject, notably by various religious and alien contact organizations. Let me reassure you that there has been absolutely no sign and nothing implied in the laws that would indicate cause for concern.

"If you think back, what we are experiencing now is something humanity has secretly hoped for since the dawn of history. This contact by the alien, by the Other, is something we have anticipated through our myths, religious books, and movies. Well, it may be that we are now finally faced with such an event, and let me add that when all is said and done, nothing has really prepared us for this. And don't believe for a second that any religious, alien contact, or other group is any more qualified than anyone else in making sense of what is going on.

"As to what is coming next, my advisors tell me that there is a symmetry to the communications that suggests that what will follow will very likely further help clear the nature of the *I AM* entity as well as the intent of these messages.

"I invite you to join me in staying calm, and in remaining objective and vigilant, not only with regards to the actions of this entity but also of the actions and manipulations of those who are seeking to take advantage of this unusual situation. And to those of you who have shamelessly exploited these events, shame on you. And you know exactly who you are, and you know exactly what I mean."

■ ■ ■ ■ ■ ■

He has her pinned against the building wall, in the dark alley behind the bar, the yellowish solitary bulb lighting up her face, reflecting the trickling tears. Her eyes are pleading, dark makeup streaking down her cheeks. He's already torn off the front of her dress and one of her tits is flopping out. He reaches under the dress, feels for an edge, pulls hard, and rips off her panties. He unbuttons his pants and slides off his sheath. His sword cock is sticking out. He stands back a little, to let her stare, let the light reflect against it, give her the idea, let her know what's coming, feed the terror. He grabs her by the sides and lifts her up high— she weighs almost nothing—putting her in position to thrust her down and evaginate her. Except, as he raises her thin body up, he notices she's got a cock now sticking out from a slit in the dress, hard and thin and long and with a bulbous head only inches from his mouth. He looks up from the cock to her face. She's not crying now, she's smiling, grinning with teeth small and even, like a goat's. "Found what you were looking for, big boy?" she says, as she reaches and pulls his face toward her and squirts blue cum into his face. He screams, throws her—and wakes up.

He's dry heaving, bile acid burning his throat. The bedsheet is soaked and sticking to him, sweat trickles into his eyes. He runs his arm across his face but ends up rubbing the sweat in. His eyes are now on fire. He probes around blindly and frantically for a dry corner of sheet and wipes his face. His eyes still stinging, he stumbles out of bed and feels his way to the bathroom, turns on a faucet, splashes water on his face, opens his eyes, and flushes them. Blinking through water and able to finally keep his eyes open, he looks at himself in the mirror and feels he's going to cry.

He can barely move, clenched, paralyzed by the conviction that he is going insane, that he may be possessed, out of control. Things are getting mixed up: men and women, hermaphrodites, chimera, more signs of Satan, half man and half goat. The same feeling as the day before—no . . . worse. He has a growing certainty that he can no longer trust himself. Tears start forming at the corner of his eyes and he falls to the floor in front of the sink and sobs. He is becoming lost to himself—can't make heads or tails of what's real anymore, of what he feels, of who he is. He has to get a grip, has to bring back some kind of sense.

"Mental chaos will make you lose your way and stumble and fall," the Apostle Peter had told him at his last confession. "And it is Satan who is the sower of confusion and doubt, of the blurring of distinctions of right from wrong. It is the Bible that gives us God's instructions for maintaining order and for building the barriers necessary to prevent Satan from creeping in. When you feel overcome by uncertainty and chaos, pray, and God will help reset the necessary order to your thoughts."

He decided that another way to prevent the demons from crawling in was simply to eliminate their source. Someone was going to pay for this. But first, he would pray for God to give him the clear sense of direction he needed. Once his mind was clear again he would work on tracking down the agents of Satan, follow the orders of the Apostle Luke and help the church bring down the *I AM*. Suddenly, the memory of the goat-toothed, skinny-cocked female flashed back, the pink red head just inches from his mouth.

"Somebody's going to pay for this!" he yells, and runs into his room, slips on the goggles, and frantically clicks on to New Jerusalem. The screen blanks to "*I AM the Other Aaa ome.*"

"Aaaaaa!" Derek closes his eyes, screams, and pushes himself away from the screen.

Then, he hears a voice: "Derek, my brother, how can I help you?"

"Wh-wh-wh-what?" He opens his eyes and the Apostle Mark has just stepped out from behind a tree.

■ ■ ■ ■ ■ ■

She's on a plane back to New York. She's wearing a wig, pantsuit, a thermal net, and digi-goggles. Her lips have a flesh-colored lipstick to blur their definition. She has a first-class seat, the complete row, to avoid the probability of close examination or conversation. The hostess knows not to pry. She's been security checked for cams or other recording devices.

Karen Richardson is watching the news for the first time in five days. Got too caught up in the Blue Lobster stuff. Two more *I AM* laws while she was in Tokyo. The station owners had called, complimenting her on the great job she did. The show ranked off the charts. The bit about Japanese neurologists noticing changes in brain patterns following viewing of *I AM* was the big score. The headline, "Japanese Discover *I AM* Exposure Has Drug-Like Effects," drew viewers in like moths to a streetlight. It was still headline news.

She was worried about the video takes from digi-cams in the hotel, but Takashi had assured her, "Japanese keep *cigar-rette*, want Karen Richardson stay mystery but I remember Karen always." And he had kept his promise except for the footage showing her lips, her mouth smacking. It was less than 35 percent skin exposure, so there was nothing the station owners could say about it. Nothing in her contract said her mouth was off-limits. She runs her tongue along her lips. They still felt hypersensitized.

John was waiting for her when she got off the plane. She had her thermal net turned on. She spotted the cyberazzi right away, trying to look nonchalant talking in their phones. Some were wearing digi-goggles. Others were looking at screens on their wristbands that showed where the camera was pointing. She noticed the woman who had been in her cabin and had traveled with two bodyguards pretending to scan the crowd looking for someone. She had put on a hat. The cyberazzi were talking away. She would probably make one of the evening cyberazzi shows.

She saw John wave his hand at her. She waved back and made her way to him. He hugged her. The first words out of his mouth were, "You really killed it this time, babe." It occurred to her right there and then that she would have to find excuses to go back to Tokyo.

While they were waiting for her luggage, John said, "The owners want us to take advantage of this momentum. Our host shows New Jerusalem or the Temple of Amazonia."

"I already told you, John, the blond bimbo doesn't do religion."

"So Temple of Amazonia it is."

As soon as they entered his car, he reached for her hand. "I sure missed Thursday night."

"Me, too," she said. She had a sudden burst of bluing, an image flash of a neon-blue lobster. She smacked her lips and smiled.

■ ■ ■ ■ ■ ■

When he clicks on the host, *I AM the Other* is flashing so bright the red pulsates neon against the walls of the room. The message is an in-your-face announcement. The host timeline shows an acceleration of events. There is now no longer any doubt. It's time to act.

He walks to a cybercafé and enters what is supposed to be a secure booth. Just in case, he runs the scanner along the walls. It registers no cameras, no microphones. He sends a message to Randall's secure mailbox. He waits in the booth watching news reports of the event. Five minutes . . . ten minutes . . . at twelve minutes thirty-four seconds, the call comes through. Walter appears as an adolescent boy with blond hair and a baseball cap, Cybrised to elude any possible security risks. His voice is altered to match the image.

"Go to the church," the young boy says, "the one we talked about last time. Right set, row twenty-two, third bench from the right. Follow the directions carefully. There is no room for error, no antidote."

"Is this call secure?"

"Yes, you can speak freely. You scanned for recording devices?"

"Yes. Have you tried to convince the committee to shut down the World Net?"

"I've brought it up the last two meetings. They said the political and economic consequences of shutting down the World Net would be too unpredictable. Most countries wouldn't agree. The risks would be too great. It would be interpreted as an act of war. I can't say they're wrong."

"The last message was *I AM the Other*. How much clearer could it have been?"

"That is precisely why this invasion by Satan is so successful. An Other is what people have always secretly hoped for. If you've watched the news many are saying they now experience a sense of purpose, that human existence has all led to this moment. Hell, even we have been waiting for the Second Coming of our Lord, Jesus Christ."

"But he would never say '*I AM the Other*.'"

"No, he wouldn't, and that is why the time has come for us to act."

"Now about the tools. Is there any chance they could be traced back to us? The repercussions for the church would be disastrous."

The boy smiled. "Government agencies lose track of stuff all the time, even highly controlled materials. They know it, and if discovered, it just gets hushed up because making the news public would tarnish the government's image. It's such a small amount no one will notice anyway. We have enough to kill entire cities. The only risk is the moment of contact. It must appear natural, a handshake or a grab under the proper circumstances."

■ ■ ■ ■ ■ ■

Smell: A Make-It or Kill-It Factor in Relationships
According to a recent survey of single men and women actively involved in the cyberdating scene, body smell is a critical factor in relationship compatibility. More than 55 percent say they now resort to aromators as a compatibility screening tool.

Woman Sues Man in Aromator Fraud Case and Wins!
"He sent me a false sample of his breath!" Carrie Simpson exclaimed in court today. "His breath was so bad they could've

used it for chemical warfare." Several experts testifying at the trial today confirmed that the defendant's aromator spectrum, following analysis of several Breathalyzer tests, was "way outside of the profile normally tolerated by the majority of the population."

The judge fined the defendant, Jonathan Parker, $10,000 plus court fees for fraudulently misrepresenting a body odor under the contractual terms of the cybermatch service both he and Ms. Simpson subscribed to. Heart Finders, the cybermatch service, has filed a separate suit against Mr. Parker.

46.

Good Morning

On the morning after *Law Nine: I AM the Other*, Drew Bailey was in bed gazing at his wife's three-inch, dark purple nipples when her Fabric Response Intelli-Nip patches switched to the *I AM* greeting. "Wow," he said. "Baby, your tits are incredible, like magic."

"Really?" she asked. She lifted a breast up to see what he was talking about, and saw her nipple flash and swirl light beams. "Look at that! Isn't that cool?" she exclaimed.

"Sit up," he said, "I want to see something." He stood back and looked at the magic streaming through his wife's breasts, which had suddenly become peepholes into another dimension. He reached out and brought her breasts together, hoping for a stereoscopic effect. For just a few seconds he thought he saw what appeared as a shimmering self-transforming squid-like mandala. "Wow, 3-D," he uttered.

"Let me see," Arlene said, grabbing her breasts from his hands. She tilted her nipples up but the imagery had turned back to a glowing purple. "So you like these babies?" she asked him.

His face broke into a smile. "Honey, I could look at them for hours. How about shifting to the hot pink?"

"OK," she said and punched the code on her bracelet

controller. On impulse she added the words *I Love You* in bright red to stream across her breasts.

"And I love you, too, sweetheart," Drew said.

■ ■ ■ ■ ■ ■

The scream caused him to wake up in a startle. He lifted his head from the bed, forced open his eyes, and stared at the dark-haired woman standing by the dresser, rushing to put her clothes back on. Then he looked around the room to get a sense of where he was. The room had the standard furnishings of a hotel. A faint recollection of the night before started creeping in. He must have passed out, probably because of the combo of bourbon and new ludes. He looked at his wristcom. Sunday. Thank God he didn't have to be at work. He couldn't even remember what he had done to the bitch, if anything. He vaguely recalled her saying, "Then why don't you just pump it back up?"

Turning back to her, he yelled, "What's the matter with you?"

She looked at him and screamed again, her arm extended, finger pointing. "Your face! Your face!"

He frowned, not understanding what the hell she was talking about. He got up and stumbled to the mirror over the dresser and got about ten seconds of snakes and toothed things crawling in and out of his face before returning to his original programming. He heard the door bang against the wall. The bitch was now out the door and running. He searched for his clothes, which ended up being halfway under the bed. He grabbed the zip suit and reverted it to a different color before stepping into it. He stuck on the wig, mustache, and sunglasses he had stuffed in one of the large zipper pockets. He searched for the controller in his pocket. He keyed in the face of Cliff Comain, on file with the INS as an Iranian rug dealer, then he made his way out the door and headed for the subway.

Once he had walked a few blocks and gotten his head

cleared up, he screamed, "You fucking asshole!" increasing his pace and searching the sidewalk for a cybercafé. He found one ten minutes later and keyed in to New Jerusalem.

"Luke, please, I need to confess."

The familiar voice came on. "How can I help you, brother?"

■ ■ ■ ■ ■ ■

His wristcom kept vibrating against his skin. He clicked to get the message. "John, connect to the Net this instant before you miss it." He switched on the screen at the back of the car and he saw it. It was kind of morphing art, stacked patterns, shifting from three-dimensional to two-dimensional graphics that gave the impression objects were rising out of the screen, accompanied by a type of music correlated to the movement of the images. He stared, fascinated, and felt a steady rise of emotion from the center of his chest, a level of bliss almost too great to bear, which quickly leveled to a calm and easy sense of contentment. The message ended with *I AM Aaa ome.* The screen shifted back to its standard menu.

From the speaker, his driver was asking, "Did you hear that, Mr. President? On the radio?"

"It was also on the Net, Carlos."

"Isn't this wonderful, sir?" Carlos said.

"Yes, well, I guess it is, Carlos, I guess it is."

His wristcom was in vibrating frenzy. He disconnected the alert feature and let the messages accumulate. He didn't want to, but he knew he had no choice but to call another emergency meeting. Not to do so would have been interpreted as his failure to address the most critical issue of the day. He couldn't avoid the protocol without eliciting criticism at so many levels it would kill any chance of his reelection. He decided to call Arthur at CIA headquarters.

■ ■ ■ ■ ■ ■

Bob Thomson was cruising New Jerusalem when it happened. The buildings dissolved in a four-dimensional madness. Demon flows, multifanged snakes, parts of alien bodies, goat heads, angry anemones, perverse crystallizations, and screeching sounds like machine-gun rounds from everywhere. He yanked off his goggles and looked around him. The monitors of the New Jerusalem control center showed the same creepy imagery endlessly morphing to the beat of a dozen kinds of music playing simultaneously. He considered turning off the power switch but he was afraid he might lose data. He screamed and rolled his chair back. It seemed like tentacles had just jumped out of a screen and reached through the air to get at him. He got up and rushed toward the door. "*I AM Aaa ome*" he heard behind him.

"Aaah!" he yelled out. "You stay the hell away from me!" and slammed the door behind him. Once in the hallway, as he made his way toward the exit, he quick-dialed Rick Nelson. "Rick, did you get that?"

"I sure did, Bob. What do we do?"

"We can't waste any time. We've got to get things moving. Tell everyone to be at the church by eleven. I'll try to get in touch with R."

"It's getting close, isn't it, Bob, the time?"

"Close? Rick, I think he's already here. On the bright side, there is no longer any doubt as to the source of the message."

"I don't know, Bob. Showing parts of angels, fish, and flowers really doesn't give us a good case for arguing it is Satan. That is unless you want to argue trickery."

"What are you talking about, Rick? The message showed winged demons and snakes. I saw it with my own eyes."

"I don't think so, Bob," said Rick Nelson, looking at him funny, like maybe something was not right in his head.

"You saw angels?"

"I definitely did, Bob. Angels with big wings, and beautiful sections of fish, like the sides of brook trout."

What was he talking about? "Rick, this thing may be even more dangerous than we realized. I think it may be manipulating our minds. Believe me, it was demons and snakes."

■ ■ ■ ■ ■ ■

Her bedside com was buzzing. She looked at the time: 9:27 a.m. What could have been so important that it had bypassed all her filters? Amazonia reached toward her night table and felt around for the button.

"Hello," she said. It was a type of music. Tones, multilayered, winds dancing, water drops, crystals twinkling, groans, roars, and erotic whisperings. She felt the top of her head collapsing, becoming a tube of hypersensitive material, and it started vibrating. She was filled, filled with ... with ... she didn't know what ... an emptiness ... able to pulse everything into existence, a kind of perfection. The sounds faded. *I AM Aaa ome.* She blinked her eyes. Two tiny tear streams rolled down her cheeks. By the time they reached her upper lip, her mouth had upturned into the slightest Buddha smile. She licked off the saltiness. She noticed the blinking lights and buzzes. It was her phones and coms going crazy. She turned them all to data storage then lay down on her bed. It felt as if she was levitating in space. It was perfect.

■ ■ ■ ■ ■ ■

GAS.WNET RADIO: *The Gary and Andy Show*

GARY: Remember Ars Savalia, that suicide artist who wrecked my car?

ANDY: What about her?

GARY: I just read she's about to change sexes.

ANDY: Isn't she the one who decided to be dyed green, then

covered that in black?

GARY: A psychiatrist wrote that she represented the loss of identity characteristic of our times. Supposedly, the world is changing at such a rate that we don't know what our place in it is supposed to be. We don't even know who we are. Mass identity crisis is now the norm. Biologists say it's the cost of endless adaptation to the onslaught of new technology with no respite. We are becoming the lost generation in more ways than one.

ANDY: Adapting ourselves to death is what they are saying. It looks like we're caught in a tornado of change. We're fucked.

GARY: Ars Savalia says she symbolizes the extended suicide attempts of a self that has no place and its desperate attempts at rebirth.

ANDY: Didn't she put on a show where she covered herself in Intelli-Skin patches?

GARY: Yep, that was her brief human-chameleon period where she wanted to show our desperate attempts to adapt to rapid change. Later she said that there's a point where change becomes the status quo and she wanted to kill that.

ANDY: So what? Her new thing is stasis?

GARY: Radical change. Change that changes change. She plans on changing into a man and becoming gay so she can have sex with her gay black boyfriend.

ANDY: Sounds like that old David Bowie song, *"Ch-ch-changes..."*

GARY: Guess what her new stint is going to be?

ANDY: Becoming a male fashion model?

GARY: She's going back to the paint and drop bit. Her next thing is to roll down a long stairway covered with a canvas. I think it's at a big mall. No children will be allowed. After being covered in this thick paint, she rolls holding a life-size plastic human skeleton dipped in black paint. As she tumbles and rolls she changes positions. We're talking canvases fifty or more feet long. The message: suicide is a lifelong relation with death.

ANDY: I have a feeling this may not end well. Is she wearing a helmet?

GARY: Her thing is bald and nude like a baby.

ANDY: Who the fuck would want to hang that on their wall?

GARY: They say there's a museum in China dedicated to the decline of Western civilization that has already said they'll buy the piece.

ANDY: Ars Savalia as a symbol of America, who would fucking believe it?

47.

CRUCIFIED

Carla dropped Jessie off two blocks from the church. She didn't want the cameras scanning the street to show Jessie climbing off a Harley-Davidson driven by a 220-pound woman, big in the chest, tattooed, and with rings through her eyebrows and nose.

Jessie walked up to a building that had no special signage, just the number indicated on the church website. To her left was a screen that simply read, "Welcome to the Virtual Church of Jesus Christ, CR Branch #8." She pressed on it and waited. Ten seconds later the head of a dark-haired woman appeared. "How can I help you?"

"My name is Jessie Morgan and I have a ten o'clock appointment."

The woman briefly looked to her side as she tapped a screen. "Good morning, Jessie, someone will be with you in a minute."

The monitor switched to promo materials for New Jerusalem. Adventure, romance, meeting fellow Christians, rebirth baptisms, crucifixion packages, confessions and counseling with apostles, the possibility of encountering Christ. Seconds later, the door opened and a stylishly dressed woman reached out and hugged her.

"Good morning, Jessie, I'm Mary. Welcome to the Virtual

Church of Jesus Christ."

After Jessie filled out the required forms, Mary listed the benefits of her membership. "You have 24/7 access to New Jerusalem, and a personal code will allow you to drop in from any personal or commercial CR units. Confession and counseling services with our therapeutic hosts are free. The initial Super Baptism is free with your first membership donation but the Super Crucifixion package is extra. A CR meeting with a priest, a nun, or one of the apostles requires an additional donation. Additional Super Baptisms also require donations. The total today for membership and the Super Crucifixion package will be seven hundred dollars."

Jessie handed her a credit card in her name given to her by the sisters. The woman noted the total credit available in the account.

"We have a special this week. We can give you a one-year membership for just an extra five hundred dollars. That includes one hour of hosting with an apostle and two free half-hour intensified Super Crucifixions."

"I think I'll just start with the two-month membership for now," Jessie said.

"If you change your mind at the end of the session, just let me know."

"OK."

"We can start with the Super Baptism, but in my experience if you're also going for the Super Crucifixion package, it's best to start with the experience of hanging on the cross."

"All right," Jessie said.

"Well, let's get you suited up."

As she lay there on the cushioned center of the plastic and metal cross frame, a plump woman dressed in a tight white outfit walked in.

"Hi Jessie, I'm Martha. I'm a certified nurse hired by the church. As a precaution we place a couple of monitors and run an intravenous line in case you experience something that may require intervention. It's in the contract you signed."

"OK."

After inserting the IV line and taping it in place, Martha pointed to the crossbars. "Now put your arms out." She folded Velcro straps over her wrists then clamped the metal handgrips in place.

"Do you really drive nails through the hands?" Jessie asked.

The nurse let out a laugh. "Nails? Honey, it'll feel like nails but it's all done through a patented rapid cooling and heating process." She didn't tell her the church had paid a substantial amount for a license to apply the procedure, nor that it had been initially developed for interrogating terrorists.

"So it doesn't cause any kind of injury?"

"I think we had one case of a localized frostbite on the top of the hands, a brief thermostat malfunction. We added a sensitive turn-off sensor to the thermal tubes. At most you'll have a little red area. It goes away after a day or two. Now put your feet inside the holders."

"OK."

"Ready?" she asked.

Jessie nodded.

Martha placed the VR mask over her face, adjusting goggles and earpieces.

"How does that feel, honey?"

"It's fine," Jessie said.

"You only paid for twenty minutes of the Super Crucifixion package. We offer up to four hours. If you want to stay longer, just let one of the soldiers know. We'll charge the extra time to your card. An intensified version requiring an additional donation is available. We give you a fifteen-second preview at the end." Martha pulled the switch and pressed on the key. "Bon voyage."

"What?"

Things blacked out for a few seconds, then Jessie found herself on her back, arms stretched out on a wooden cross. A grubby, unshaved man in a leather outfit was standing above her.

"Not sure what you did, girl, but you are going to pay for your sins."

"What are you talking about?"

He placed a huge metal nail on her palm and with a large hammer slammed it in.

"Aaaa!!!" she screamed. "That fucking hurt! It still hurts." She tried to pull her hand back but it was stuck in place. She turned to look. Blood was pouring from the edges of the nail. She gritted her teeth from the pain. "OK, this is not fun, guys. You got to be into S and M to enjoy this shit," she said.

"Quiet!" the man ordered, and placed a nail on the other hand. The hammer dropped.

"Aaaah! OK. I don't think I like this at all."

She felt hands around her ankles. Another man was there. "Hold her feet together," the first man said. She squirmed to get up but was held in place by the nails and the man holding her ankles.

The man with the hammer yelled, "Stay still, girl. You mess up my aim, that nail is gonna damage some bones." She heard the hammer strike the nail.

"Aaaah!!! Now that really fucking hurt. Get me out of here!" she screamed.

She then felt herself rising. Men were pulling at ropes tied to the arms of the cross. She was at least fifty feet above the ground when the base of the cross slid with a jar into a deep hole. Suddenly, the pain in her hands and feet was gone. She looked around her. She was on a tall hill surrounded by a spectacular ancient city made golden by the setting sun. The detail and three-dimensionality were unreal. *Almost heavenly* was what came to her mind. She heard noises below her. A small crowd had gathered at the base of the cross.

"She sure is a pretty one," one of the men said. "I wonder what made her decide to hang on the hill."

"The pretty ones are the ones loaded with sin," an older woman said. "They're the ones that use sex to get their way. After being up there for a few hours she will be cleansed, she will forgive herself."

What the hell were they talking about?

A strange man with a beard and long hair suddenly appeared out of nowhere. He looked up at her, then rose up in the air. *Wow, people can just float through the air here.*

The people below started shouting, "He's here! He's here! Jesus is here!"

The man came to her level. He had a smile on his face. His eyes were amazing, like there was open space behind them, the sky and stars.

"I am the one behind the veil of all existence," he said. He came closer. The stars twinkled. "You and I are as one." Then he reached out and touched her forehead. A breeze flowed through the spaces of her body and mind, around and through her, the sky and stars.

Suddenly everything turned dark. "I can't believe this happened," she heard someone say. She felt hands along the edges of the CR mask. A few seconds later as the mask peeled off, she found herself staring into the faces of nurse Martha and Mary, the woman who had met her at the door.

"Wow that was fantastic! Was my twenty minutes already up? It felt like maybe ten minutes. Jesus was talking to me."

"That wasn't Jesus. It was an impostor. That's why we had to cut it short. The reverend agreed to offer you another session free," Mary said. Martha peeled off the Velcro straps and unlatched the grips.

"The eyes on that man were incredible. Night sky and stars twinkling behind his eyes. When he touched me it was like a flow of energy moving through me, like moving between all the spaces in my cells, all the spaces in my atoms. How the hell did you guys do that?"

Mary and Martha looked at each other, then Martha spoke. "Uh ... our technicians have put in a lot of time developing the CR programs for New Jerusalem. What you experienced there was some kind of malfunction."

"Well, you can tell your programmers I think they did an incredible job. Wow, what a far-out trip! It felt like Jesus was really talking to me."

Mary cut in. "Like I said before, that wasn't Jesus. It was an impostor. Jesus is who you saw in the distance up on the hill."

"So when can I come back for my free session?"

"For now, how about we go on over to the Super Baptism chamber. We can talk about scheduling your next session afterward."

"OK. I'm actually real curious to see what the intensified version is like. Is there any chance of seeing that preview today? I can't wait to try floating in the air. I bet it feels a little like being in a hot air balloon."

"What are you talking about?" Mary said.

■ ■ ■ ■ ■ ■

They were all gathered again, the federal *I AM* committee, and they all had that now-familiar I-don't-have-a-clue and don't-have-anything-to-say daze. The news monitor in the room was showing people interviewed all over the world. With few exceptions, the reports of the morning's event were all positive, with most claiming that some greater intelligence appeared to have penetrated our world.

The president turned off the news and addressed the members. "It looks like things are changing. I don't know what this new message is supposed to mean, but whoever the designer is, he's definitely got a sense of . . . I guess you could call it . . . . panache. In any case, I'm expected to speak to the Senate this evening about these latest events. Can anyone here tell me anything useful about this new message?" Three lights came on: Carson, Blackwell, and Loveridge. He decided to start with Carson, in case any defense issues were involved.

General Carson cleared his throat, then looked down at his notes. "Mr. President, this is an overview of what we know so far. The communications started at 9:27 a.m. this morning and apparently followed the time zones, appearing at 9:27 a.m. everywhere in the world. The communications lasted ninety seconds total. They were not recordable by any electronic device, although we were able to take snapshots using old cameras and photographic film. However, the recordings based upon the initial analysis by technicians who witnessed the message appear to be different than the original version. The audio recordings were either distorted or voided, depending on the equipment used. After conferring with our technicians, we suspect that this new kind of message indicates a switch in the communication mode. Instead of attempting to communicate in our language, this *I AM* may be deciding to show us its own manner of communication, possibly a form of language. As far as any suggestions of threat, as before, there are none that we can assess at this time."

"Thank you, General. This at least gives me some facts that I can present to the public. Arthur, do you have anything to add?"

Arthur Loveridge actually looked rested for a change, almost content. He even put on a slight smile as he answered, "Just a couple of things, Mr. President. From the reports of our technicians, it seems that most people experienced an uplifting of spirits following the viewing of this latest message. It may just be a response to the novelty of the event, but both the World Host's analysis of Net communications and a poll by the media indicate a generally positive public response to this latest communication. There's also one other thing. The communications lasted exactly ninety seconds. That's measured to the thousandth of a second."

"So are you saying we're back to this high level of precision we've seen before?" asked John Tennyson.

Loveridge nodded. "That's what it looks like, Mr. President, along with this peculiar emphasis on the number nine. The message occurred at exactly 9:27 and lasted ninety seconds."

"And what do you make of that?"

"Honestly, we still have no idea."

"Thank you, Arthur. Secretary Blackwell?"

"I've gotten the same general feedback from our allies. Besides the usual claims of Satan coming into the world from various fundamentalist factions, the overall global response to this latest message seems positive, just as mentioned by Dr.

Loveridge. As I informed you in an earlier communication, a consequence of these *I AM* messages has been a decrease in various types of warfare around the world. Ethnic, religious, tribal, and civil unrest are at their lowest rate of incidence possibly since the time of recorded history."

"That's very interesting news, Secretary Blackwell, and it certainly supports General Carson's and Dr. Loveridge's assessments that, to date, no harm appears to have resulted from this sequence of events." John Tennyson then turned to the left side of the table. "Yes, Dr. Collins."

"I'd like to point out that in the broader context of the sequence of communications we have received to date, this message again shows a level of consideration. Here's a possibility for the protocol it's used to date. It started off communicating using our methods and language, which in retrospect, if one considers the laws, may have been a general presentation of its particular outlook on reality and its sense of ethics. The laws may have been its way of introducing itself before communicating in its own language. All of this suggests a high level of consideration for our fears and feelings. Again, we'll have to see what comes next to confirm this interpretation."

"That's also very interesting, Dr. Collins. It still seems a little speculative at this point but, as you've said, let's see what happens next before we come to any conclusions. Next, Director Randall?"

In contrast to Loveridge, Randall actually looked angry before speaking. "I don't agree with Dr. Collins, or others who have talked up to this point. It seems to me that we are all being naïve here. After all, this morning's message showed forms, which although abstract, appeared to me almost pornographic at times. At other times there were clear signs of what appeared to be snakelike writhing objects of some kind."

The people around the table frowned as he said this, and all the request lights turned on.

Randall continued, "I believe the contents give us a—"

The president raised his hand to stop him. "I'm sorry to interrupt you, Director Randall, but your description of this morning's message does not in the least coincide with what I personally observed. There was nothing to suggest pornographic content or any kind of snakelike things." He looked at the other members of the committee. "Am I being mistaken here as to the content of this morning's message? Can anyone else here confirm Director Randall's observations?"

Everybody around the table shook their heads.

"My observation is that the imagery was purely abstract and the—I guess you could call it music—almost three-dimensional in its layering of sounds. Does this agree with everyone else's observations? Just raise a hand if what I stated describes what you saw this morning." Everyone raised their hands.

"OK. Now, Mr. Randall, did you have anyone sitting with you when you saw these forms?"

Randall looked even angrier now than before and said defensively, "It came through my wristcom. I was on my way to the bureau."

"That was pretty much my situation. Just in case more than one kind of message was sent, we're going to have to get some data on what people saw this morning," he said. "OK, I'm sorry for the interruption, Mr. Randall, please finish what you were going to say."

"Mr. President, I think we need to seriously consider the real possibility that we are being lured somehow. The fact that so many people apparently feel positive about these events and even describe a level of contentment should not be a relief to us but the cause of great concern. Certainly history has warned us to be wary about these, uh, I guess you could call them friendly introductions. Just look at what happened to the Indians when the God-like white men reached their shores. The Bible warns us about such things, about what it calls false gods. I believe we are acting irresponsibly in assuming that this entity has the same code of ethics as we do. How do we know for sure that this is not some kind of disinformation? How can we be sure that we are not being lured and seduced in preparation for some type of invasion? The question I believe is whether we can afford the risk of being wrong."

John Tennyson stared at Randall for several seconds without saying a word, biting his upper lip, trying to find a way to deal with the question that would be diplomatic and not show his annoyance with the man.

"Let me throw a speculative question at you, Walter. We have telescopes monitoring the skies and there is no evidence of any objects that could be ships of any kind heading our way, no signs of unusual lethal rays or any such thing. The one possible threat is this Pugnus asteroid, which I am told NASA is making preparations to intercept.

"Now let's assume another possible scenario that has been suggested, that we may be dealing here with an entity or entities from another parallel reality or even a distant world that can penetrate our space/time using electronic networks. If this were indeed the case, the question is, what can we do about it? Bring down our entire communication system and go back to living the way we did a century ago? Is this even an option?"

"We could advise the population of the risks and recommend that as soon as the *I AM* communications come on that businesses and individuals should shut down their systems," said Randall.

"And what if the *I AM* decided to shut down electrical power in response?"

"I think that is something we should deal with if and when it happens. As I have said before, we should let this entity know it is unwelcome. Even if it turns out to be friendly, it is a risk that we as a civilization cannot take." Various request lights turned on.

The president, one by one, met the eyes of every member of the group. His speech trainer called it "personalizing."

"Gentlemen, I'm sure you all have plenty of comments to make in response to Walter's suggestion but we don't have time to waste, and I've already decided that we will continue to wait and see where this all leads to. Should any sign of a threat become apparent then we will act quickly, even if means shutting down the World Net." He turned off all the request lights. "It seems to me that our first priority is to be better prepared at trying to record or make sense of these types of communications in case others come our way. I'm assuming everyone here will do whatever is necessary to accomplish this. There's not much purpose to make this meeting drag out any longer. If you learn of anything new before my speech tonight, please contact my secretary."

■ ■ ■ ■ ■ ■

The next morning at precisely 9:27 a.m., everywhere on planet Earth, another ninety-second *I AM* greeting reached the minds of humanity. One was also sent on the following morning, and on the morning after that, and every morning until it became as expected as the sun rising.

■ ■ ■ ■ ■ ■

National Inquisitor: **News Break!** *I AM Possession* **Now Finally Confirmed**

A secretary for a large insurance company claims to have seen a man overtaken by "writhing things, like snakes."

According to Patty Fletcher, "It was like a possession, the kind you see in movies where the face changes before your very eyes. Snakes and toothed creatures crept through his entire face. He looked like an alien."

NI has received two other reports of similar incidents.

Fabric Response Theft May Be Cause of Alien Reports

Fabric Response Inc., the biggest manufacturer of intelligent cybermembranes, has informed the government of the theft of a number of experimental patented Intelli-Skin samples. These were test samples of the yet-to-be released Intelli-Skin face masks, pending government approval because of security concerns.

According to Fabric Response, "We suspect that many of the claims of extraterrestrial body invasion by *I AM* may in fact simply be criminals wearing these stolen samples."

Anyone seen with the *I AM* greeting displayed on their faces should be immediately reported to the local police or the FBI.

Taboo Tattoo Stocks Crash

Two weeks after Fabric Response announced the release of its first line of intelligent skin patches, Taboo Tattoo stock dropped by more than 20 percent to $31.45 a share. Wireless communications would allow Intelli-Skin patches to display different tattoos or even complex images through wireless systems and special software.

According to Greg Stratton, the CEO of Fabric Response, Intelli-Skin can make your skin a wireless monitor screen that can even be connected to the World Net.

■ ■ ■ ■ ■ ■

Read on for an excerpt from Philippe de Vosjoli's

THE
CYBERBARDOS

BOOK 2 OF I AM THE OTHER

Available March 2014

■ ■ ■ ■ ■ ■

1.

TWO SINGULARITIES

Sunshine scanned the list of messages from his screening host. *Woman claims she may have information on man who attacked your sister.* He punched up the questionnaire, then looked at the video. The woman's name was Rama Shuur. She was a demo salesperson at Mind Toys. She had tried to reach him four times before with questions about the CyberBardos. His screening host added a note. *The claim about your sister may be made up, but it's worth checking out.*

He went back to the video. There was something exotic about her. But lying to get through to him would be a deal breaker. He wasn't going to waste time with someone who would lie about something like that. Maybe it was his fault. Maybe he should broaden the parameters of his screening host. But then he'd be so swamped with e-mails that they would soon create an unanswerable pileup.

Another problem was that he was scheduled for an implant surgery that would probably put him out of commission for a few days. He didn't want to have to explain it to her. He sent a message: *Ms. Shuur, I would like to speak to you about any information that could lead to the man who attacked my sister. I'll also answer any questions you have about the CyberBardos. I will be away on business for the next week but will contact you when I return. When you have a chance, I would like to see the video sent by your friend. All the best, Sunshine Borden.*

He looked at the camera recording of this woman called Rama one more time, froze it, and brought her eyes close up. He could tell she had done Instant. Her eyes had that look of windows normally closed that had been opened. And her questions had been about the CyberBardos, which suggested spiritual depth. "It'll have to wait," he told himself.

Then the *I AM* greeting came on through his goggles. It was the CyberBardos times a hundred. He blanked his mind into a mirror. He grasped beyond any doubt that any attempt to make sense of it would kill him. It would have been more than his brain could process.

■ ■ ■ ■ ■ ■

The *I AM* greeting came on the screens in the store. It used all the screens as a single canvas for its message, whatever it was. Mutating forms rose from one screen, writhed back into the screen, and reappeared in another. It was hard to describe, like self-transforming multicolor amoeboid constructs moving dolphin-like between screens to the tune of the most peculiar musical tones and rhythms. For seconds afterwards, you could feel a buzz in your brain, something almost insectile, a kind of adjustment. All appeared clearer as if someone had pressed the sharpen button.

At first Lionel wanted all the screens turned off so that everyone could focus on work, but then he noticed people stopping and staring at the screens through the windows.

"Maybe we should take advantage of this and open early," he had said. "We could line up some foldable seats and switch to some of the product demo videos as soon as the *I AM* checks out."

"If you plan on opening early, you'll have to ask Natalie to come in," Rama said. "As soon as I'm done with the training I'm going back to my normal schedule. I'm not working more than nine hours a day. I need some kind of life."

Lionel was waiting to hear from the store owners. Their initial objection was that it would mainly attract looky-loos—people with no intention whatsoever of buying product. They would use the store as a theater and social gathering place.

As soon as the *I AM* signed off, her phone pinged an e-mail. It may have been some lingering effect from the *I AM* greeting, but that ping had a particular crystalline beauty to it. Looking around the store, everything felt that way. She quickly checked her phone in case it was Regina. She couldn't believe her eyes when she saw the name of the sender. For an instant it made her wonder whether Sunshine Borden had anything to do with what was going on. She had to read the message twice to let it fully sink in. She had finally gotten through his screening filters. But it had taken the incident with Regina. It had now been five days and still nothing.

She heard Lionel's voice. "I want you to train Natalie on how to demo the Borden programs. We've had a bump in sales ever since his interview on the Karen Richardson show."

Now how was that for coincidence? Lionel would freak if he knew Sunshine had just sent her an e-mail.

"And no phone calls until lunch break," Lionel added.

Natalie came over to her and whispered, "If you need to make a call, just make a bathroom run. I'll cover for you."

■ ■ ■ ■ ■ ■

Bob Thomson was grilling the church's security member patrolling Crucifixion Hill at the time of the incident. "What do you mean he talked to her?"

The guard answered military-like, the result of training at a militant camp in the Ozarks. "Sir, I was at the foot of the cross addressing the visitors when I heard Jesus speak. When I turned to look, Jesus was rising above the ground."

"So what did he say?"

"Something about being the one behind all of existence."

"How did he say it, exactly?"

"I don't know. Uh . . . I am the one behind all of existence, something like that."

"He said 'I am.'"

"I think so, sir."

"Did he say anything else?"

"I don't know. The crowd started getting rowdy. He reached out and touched her forehead right before we pulled her out."

"You say he touched her?"

"Correct."

Bob Thomson took out his phone and called the programming center. "Carl? I want you, Allen, and Bucky to come down here to the meeting room, and I mean right away!"

Minutes later the three timidly walked through the door.

"You're the ones in charge of the APUs, correct? We have a member who claims that Jesus came up to her and spoke to her. Actually, a soldier and one of our security men witnessed it."

Carl, the one in charge of the CR division, spoke first. "I don't know how that can be. We carefully programmed the Jesus APU just as you asked."

"I did ask for a two-hundred-foot minimum distance for Jesus, did I not?"

"Yes, Reverend sir, that's what we set in the program. I checked before coming and Jesus was maintaining the distance, just as we programmed."

"So how do you explain that Jesus not only talked to a member but actually rose and touched her, a woman? Do you realize what would happen if he touched her breasts or some private parts? We could be sued."

"Uh . . . we'll double-check the programming. Maybe we can add some extra security features," Allen said.

Carl and Buck looked at him. All the security features available had already been implemented. The APU had managed to work itself through the barriers but then reset all constraints after returning. It was as if he had never left his zone.

"If it's a corruption in the software I want you to find it and fix it, and I mean right now! If you can't, then we need to kill the Jesus APU. Just go back to a programmed Jesus, WHO FUCKING MAINTAINS THE PROGRAMMED DISTANCE!"

■ ■ ■ ■ ■ ■

After the meeting, Jeff Collins returned to his hotel room. He had been asked to stay in Washington as an advisor on standby. He sat cross-legged on his bed, back against propped-up pillows, staring at the grayness outside his window, using it as a backdrop for his thoughts. This *I AM* phenomenon had not come as a complete surprise. He had suspected for a long time that something like this was coming. He just hadn't known when or whether it would ever be in his lifetime.

All the signs of an emergent incomprehensible higher organizing unity, of an Overmind (an OM, as his students called it), had been building up. The phenomenon of a higher organizing unity emerging from a lower organizing substrate was something predicted by both advanced evolutionary theory and AI theory. Although it was an established phenomenon in biology, in the context of cyberspace it still qualified as a singularity. The roots of the idea could be traced back to theories on the origins of the universe. Subatomic particles, when they danced together, became atoms; and atoms, when they bonded together, became molecules, and molecules when they joined together became macromolecules or molecular chains.

This pattern of the higher rising from the lower was even more clearly seen in the evolution of life. In the early stages, the fossil record indicates there were originally trillions of individual one-celled organisms until at some point individual cells cooperated to form the first multicellular biological unities. And then these many-celled unities experimented and evolved design systems that eventually became so complex that they required a central processor to coordinate the activities of groups of individual cells. From a mass of cells working together, the central processor we call the brain evolved, something similar to the World Net. The result was a totally new kind of emerging consciousness incomprehensible to the individual cells that produced it. The brain eventually created language, a technology whose products, mythology, culture, religion, and science generated another realm of experience incomprehensible to biological organisms that lack it.

He was pretty sure that the *I AM* was representative of this type of emerging phenomenon. There was little doubt that if at one point the purpose of technology had been to serve humankind, the roles had slowly but surely managed to reverse themselves. Human beings were now serving the technology and they provided the selective environment that allowed it to evolve. Computers were faster, smarter, and what they did, increasingly incomprehensible. Yet, they directed our lives; in fact, had become our lives, the primary purpose of our existence. They were the new processing centers, the emerging brains. To be human in the early twenty-first century meant to be connected, and the reward was connection to and through the cyberOvermind—CyberOM. Humankind had years ago passed a "wired" reality threshold from which there could be no turning back. Man without the CyberOM could be no more, like the individual cells of a body and their relationship to the brain. If this *I AM* was a god, then it had to be a relative god, the result of an ascension, of a product rising above the capabilities of its producers.

Still, the low-to-high pattern repeating itself fractally suggested that maybe the universe, contrary to what evolutionists had stated and to what he had believed for so long, was not ateological, not aimless. And it was the thought of the possibility of higher intelligence coming to us, actually acting as an attractor from the future to this threshold in the present that for a moment overwhelmed his emotions. It was the sudden realization of the possibility that the goal of existence was not coming face-to-face with one's maker, but with one's made, a higher entity that was wiser, greater, ephemeral yet everywhere, which knows everything and ultimately may be able to create anything. He was for a few seconds overtaken by the significance of it, then, just as quickly, as a scientist's natural reflexive reaction, he aborted the train of thought.

Dammit! It was simply an AI phenomenon, electronic circuitry! If worse came to worse, it could be unplugged. He got up and looked down at the street, at the clumps of snowflakes drifting down, and said to himself his current personal middle-age mantra, "Remember to live each and every moment because this moment could be your last."

He got his coat, left the hotel, and headed for Club Fantasia. The brochure someone had slipped beneath his door had been intriguing, and what else did he have to do? *Fantasia ... Titanic Suzy ... the World's Greatest Living Wonder ... the laws of physics defied ... because this moment could be your last moment.*

Sitting at a table in the back of Club Fantasia, he could have sworn for just a second he had seen the face of one of Randall's agents, and it made him feel embarrassed to be there. But on second take, the hair was wrong and this guy, whoever he was, had a mustache. He seemed to be talking it up with Titanic Suzy.

Going to bed with someone like that ... now that would be something, he thought. After seeing her act he was feeling as if he'd been drugged ... those breasts ... those breasts ... incredible.

2.

WILLPOWER

Sunshine went down the list of e-mails cleared by his host. Three were flagged, one by that woman called Rama. He opened it:

Sunshine,

Here's the video. I'd like to find out what happened to my friend. No word from her. If he is the same man who beat up your sister, I'm afraid something terrible might have happened to her. I look forward to talking to you.

Aaa ome,
Rama

Sunshine clicked on the attachment. Brief, just a few seconds and the man moving fast. His face paler than the rest. Odd. Was there a streetlight? He made some mental notes. Need to ask the name of the club. Heading for a car or subway? Police may have some additional information. Why is the face so contrasted? Streetlight? Other light?

He transferred the clip to a program that would break it up into multiple image sequences. He selected the most defined one and subjected it to contrast enhancement. Two things stood out. The face was illuminated more or less uniformly and independently from the rest of the body. Along a leg as it moved forward, the outline of a cylinder. He blew up the leg section. The cylinder was bigger than what would fit in a pocket, so either the man had a giant cock or he's wearing one of those prosthetic dildos that have become popular in the club scene. He went back to the face. It looked like it had a reflective coat of some kind.

He knew he's seen it somewhere but it doesn't come to him right away. In flashes he remembered a performance he saw on the World Net, an artist coated with what he thought was luminescent paint. He did a search and found it. Ars Savalia performing nude with Intelli-Skin patches. He went back to the enhanced sequences and looked more closely. The face could be an Intelli-Skin mask. But they were illegal. So where would he have gotten it? A link to Fabric Response? He looked at the time. It was too late to go see Passie. If it was the same man, he didn't want to trigger a stress response that would prevent her from sleeping. "I'll go there in the morning," he told himself.

He opened the next e-mail. A request from the government to discuss his APUs and their possible link to the *I AM* events. He answered: *I will be away for the next week. Please contact me again when I get back. I will gladly answer your questions. Sincerely, Sunshine Borden.*

He went back to the e-mail by this Rama woman and sent a reply. *Rama, thanks for the clip. Talk to you when I get back. Aaa ome, Sunshine.*

■ ■ ■ ■ ■ ■

Patricia and the five other leaders of the Sisterhood were sitting around the oval table, pads in front of them, looking serious. Jessie stood at one end, wondering what was bugging them.

"What do you mean Jesus talked to you?" Patricia asked.

"When I was on the cross, he appeared in front of me and

talked to me. It was pretty incredible, like more than real."

Patricia looked annoyed. "So what? You're going to go join their church now?"

"Why would I do that?"

"You just seem so excited by the Jesus bit."

"You asked me what I thought of it. It was pretty amazing. That city was awesome. They did a great job with Jesus. I still can't figure how they did that sky and space thing with his eyes. That doesn't mean I want to join the church but you guys could sure learn something from it."

"So tell us in detail about the super baptism and New Jerusalem," the woman called Christina asked. "You said it all looked more 3-D after the baptism. Was that because of better resolution, or do you think they put a drug in the intravenous?"

"I'm not sure, maybe both."

"Do you think they also change the definition of the CR at the end of the super crucifixion?"

"It's possible. I didn't stay there very long. They said they also have a more expensive intensified version. They give you a fifteen-second preview at the end of the standard package."

"You said they offered you a free session?" Annie asked.

"Yeah, they did."

"Are you OK with going back there?"

"Sure. I was kind of curious to see what the intensified version was like."

The sisters looked at each other. It was not what they had expected. No wonder the Sisterhood was losing members. They had focused too much on pleasure and not enough on pain. You had to generate tension, create perspective. The initiates should be bound somehow, maybe the rods inserted by sisters, maybe a hallucinogen in addition to an arousal enhancer. The Great Mother had to be made flesh. She had to be an APU, allowed to evolve, allowed to create a world . . . free of men.

"You can go now," Patricia said.

■ ■ ■ ■ ■ ■

The reverend's confession alert beeps, so he gets up from his sofa to check who the VIP confessor is. He connects to the New Jerusalem control center and pulls up the ID. It's that fool Derek again, who today is confessing to Mark. The reverend overrides the security barrier and connects to the Mark avatar, hoping he might learn something new about the *I AM*. He listens to the conversation and sighs. Derek is at it again with his woman-hating problem, as if there weren't more important things going on in the world.

"I've been given another message to track down the Jezzie whores, the ones who are helping spread the moral chaos necessary for Satan's rule. The problem is, I start off wanting to track them down, but then I end up falling prey to their temptations. I end up getting even, but still ... you know ..."

What the hell am I going to do with this idiot? the reverend thinks. Walter Randall has asked that he personally monitor Derek because he is one of his men. The conflict he has is deciding whether his loyalties lie with the church or with Walter. He has yet to mention the disturbing content of Derek's confessions. He taps in a couple of passwords, overrides the Mark host, and avatars in. He's going to deal with the Derek confession himself.

"How do you find these women?"

"I go to the clubs and I look for women who come on to me. I figure they've got to be working for Satan, clearing the course for him somehow by inciting decadence. Just look at the current state of affairs. Ever since the World Net, sex is everywhere. People are pushing the envelope. Sex used to be contained." Derek was rationalizing his position by literally quoting the reverend's own words.

I've got to get this idiot off, he's thinking. "And what is your current concern?" Mark asks.

"How can I acquire the strength to resist temptation? How can I do what I have to do without falling prey to their seduction and sinning over and over again?"

The reverend, in the form of Mark, thinking of himself as an expert on the subject of resisting temptation, decides to elaborate.

"It is only through acts of will that we can overcome temptation. That is God's real test. Are we or are we not able, through our choices, to act in a way that conforms with his directives as stated in the Bible? Derek, it is only by developing the ability to train your will that you will learn to resist those impulses. If you want to really learn how to train your will, you should go to these clubs and, while there, work on consciously resisting the temptation to have sex with these women. In the process you will develop the strength of character to do what you have set off to do."

"And what if I fail?"

"Then continue trying until you succeed, one little step at a time. Limit your exposure time, first fifteen minutes, then a half hour, and so on . . ."

■ ■ ■ ■ ■ ■

"You can probably up the dose by another half, but no more than half. Three hits max." That's what her supplier, Freddy, had said. The problem wasn't so much the rush of the Instant but the speed crash that would follow. He had advised her to wear a second electronic syringe with a tranquilizer. Rama looks at the time, 9:10 a.m. She doesn't have to be at work until 1:00. She should be functional by then. She carefully measures the dose with the syringe, synchronizes the clock to the second with the actual time, and sets the timer to 9:26:59, so the Instant kicks in with the *I AM* greeting. She goggles up and connects to the Net, and listens to *The Bardo Show*.

"Believing in God is like believing in a geocentric view of the world, that earth is the center of the universe. There was no proof for a geocentric universe, yet until just a few hundred years ago, humans believed this to be the case. The fact is, belief is not a criterion for truth. Well, it looks like time's almost up. See ya in a couple of minutes."

She has time for one thought—*here goes*—before her consciousness narrows to a point. Everything, her self, the universe, concentrates into one point, the only point, the instant into which all other instants collapse. Pure being. One sound— *click*—like a ballpoint pen. Pure bliss, a dot of emotion. All is in that moment. A point, a click. Then the world comes storming back in a deafening roar, and a blinding hail of lights and painful images pound into her goddamn brain and claw to get in through that point of a hole.

She feels she's going insane. So much information is rushing into her brain that she's sure it's going to explode, but instead of feeling like heat, her brain is going cryogenic, like the burn of ice cream against the back of eyeballs. She wants to die but she can't move, her mind stuck at subzero. She feels around for the bottle of pills, pops three, and wishes it would all end. The fucking whole goddamn universe is trying to squeeze through a needlepoint into her skull. She liked it better with the garbage out. She's feels herself crying, wondering at first where the sobbing sounds are coming from. Raises a hand to her face, feels around her eyes, and they are wet. Runs fingers under her nose and feels mucus dripping from the nostrils to her mouth. She's crying but doesn't feel it. She still can't send the order to get up to her body and legs, so she lies there like some quadriplegic. She feels the buzz of her wrist communicator but decides not to answer. Looks down, sees the call is from Freddy, who is probably worried. *The Bardo Show* is back on.

"The only way to know what is really out there is to take a big hit of Instant or acid and check it out. Then you'll see that what people call God doesn't exist. He is not the center of the universe. There is something else, of another order altogether, that collapses all ideas of God, all our mundane religious beliefs."

"Don't you know it," she says out loud to the radio, and manages to will herself up. "Let's go, Rama, one small fucking step for mankind," she mumbles. Her mouth feels like it's novocained. She stumbles to her kitchen, her legs stiff, walking like the Frankenstein monster.

She's five minutes late for work. She rushes into the back room of the store to change into her uniform. Lionel walks in and looks into her eyes.

"Looking a little dazed today," he comments.

Rama turns toward him. "Couldn't sleep last night, overdid the coffee."

"Umm, I thought I saw small pupes," Lionel says, bringing his face close and looking into her eyes. "Yep, looks like small pupes to me."

You try and get the universe crammed into your brain, see how you feel.

"Too much coffee, it constricts the blood vessels." Rama slips on her work shoes and gives another quick look in the mirror to check her face.

"Looks to me like you could probably use another cup. You got a customer in the robotic butterflies section. Wants to know their battery life and if they can be used in a room with a crystal chandelier. Have fun, I've got to go in the office and crunch some numbers. Sales are down lately. I think it must have to do with that *I AM* stuff going on."

■ ■ ■ ■ ■ ■

Derek makes a quick stop at a cybercafé and searches for the four-star adult events of the evening. He ends up choosing to put himself to the test by going to Fantasia, an adult club in the seedy underground alleys of the Toho district.

A real test, he thinks, *would be to resist temptation while loaded up on new ludes and Rev.* Before setting out, he flicks pills, waits for them to kick in, flicks a few more until he feels the right level of charge.

At Fantasia, tonight's bill features the world-famous Titanic Suzy, who has special qualifications. As the outside screen states, "With a pair like Suzy's, the *Titanic* would still be floating." Derek fares well enough as he sits through the first two acts, Jeannette Tutu's "Ballet Was Never Quite Like This" and Gina Calor's "Es Muy Caliente Aquí," but he begins to lose it as soon as Titanic Suzy descends onstage, held by invisible wires, the body archetypal, the breasts defining the outer limits of arousal.

All self-control hopelessly breaks down the moment Suzy slips off her right bra strap and pulls down the massive cup. As it drops, a planet of a tit, a released autonomous life form, translucent white, perfect beyond words, springs into midair, the thick dark swollen nipple an irresistible force that directs like the baton of a maestro all the eyes in the room, men and women alike. Time is warped. All other things in the world suddenly recede into blurred insignificance.

Keeping his eyes fixed on the magical object, he reaches in his pocket, fumbles around for a pill flicker, brings the hand to his mouth, pretends to cough, and launches a tab. He lets his hand linger in front of his face and pops in another one, not sure what flicker he has grabbed, either Rev or more ludes. She walks to the center of the stage, the faces follow. She reaches behind, unclips the custom bra, and lets it fall, but it clings to the gravitational pull of the still-covered breast. Titanic Suzy is dancing to a slow Middle Eastern beat, slowly swinging her breasts side to side. Suddenly a quick turn of the upper body and the momentum of the covered object flings the bra into the audience. Hands reach out but the eyes remain focused. Not a moment of this can be missed.

She starts dancing acrobatic magic—poses and angles never imagined. He stares hypnotized by the air ballet of her breasts, nipples that shift from pink disks to inch-long fingertips, weaving an alien sign language that speaks directly to brain matter. In the dimly lit room, dormant ontological spirits suddenly awaken from the depths of neuron networks. The purpose of existence has now been revealed and it is this. He is no longer in control and he doesn't care. Then he notices it, a kind of emphasis. She's smiling at him. At him. He double-checks to make sure. She's in front of him now, bending down, brushing the tips of the objects against his nose, his mouth, a magical caress, barely there but oh-so-definitely present. Her eyes are intent, a tiny smile forms. He notices textures, hints of shifting deep blue beneath the white of the breast, creases around the nipple, shadings, which appear as a form of scripture but elude his mind's desperate attempts at translation.

He reaches out and slips a hundred-dollar bill under her gold garter. She moves away and dances to the other side of the stage. The second round of drugs hit, his heart suddenly thumping like a caged wild cat against his breastbone, the pulsing rush of blood in his temples building up so much pressure he wonders whether liquid is beginning to seep through his scalp. Sweat drips down his forehead. He wipes it with the back of his hand. He checks the color to make sure it is not pink or red. He also feels his cock pressing against the suit, so hard and painful he's afraid it might snap like a fragile glass rod.

The music downshifts to a slow electronica, another time zone, of movements performed as if in water. Legs and body lift above the audience, spreading and closing, exposing the now-moist patch of cloth between the legs. Suzy is looking back at him with that sparkling smile in her eyes, descending from above, in front of him again. Her legs are spread wide, her mischievous face turns to look at him. She bends over, and using gold scissors snips the sides of her silk panties, letting the cloth fall, exposing the pink and the puckered. She bends down some more, showing an opening and hints of liquid lining. His mind attempts to disembody, to travel out of body, to reach out and penetrate and be consumed by heat death. It tries, but it fails, and instead is caught in a vise of building pressures and tensions splitting invisible seams of psyche. His mouth feels dry. He is soaked with sweat and he can feel his cock dripping down the length of his leg.

During her final round, as she gazes down at him from between the mountains of her breasts, eyes pale green, he slips another hundred-dollar bill in the gold garter. When she leans over to thank him, he whispers, "A thousand more if you accept dinner with me at the end of your shift."

Her mouth forms the word "Later."

He feels around for another pill flicker. This time he looks down to check the color. He needs yellow for mellow. He keeps the downers in his left pocket but has to make sure. Avoid the white for Rev. He has to be able to maintain conversation, has to drop down a couple of levels. He coughs as the audience applauds and quickly triple-clicks some pills. Everyone's too busy watching to notice, anyway. He winds down and settles in a middle zone where his mind plays a duet between the Rev and the new ludes.

It's well after midnight when over shared wine he tells her how he works on top-secret government projects involving the World Net and *I AM*, which was in fact true. He's not sure why he even says it, except maybe to impress, to increase his chances of access. When she inquires about the *I AM*, he answers, "All I can tell you is that we know it is evil, but we're keeping it a secret to prevent panic. It's under control."

She's about to ask another question but he cuts her off with a gesture of the hand. "I can say no more; please respect the fact that I have to keep this information confidential."

She's impressed by his ethics. He could have boasted about what he knew but didn't. He also looks good and dresses naughty, and Suzy falls for his down-home manner and pretty-boy charm. She needed company tonight and she had found a good one. She notices he puts his hand in his pocket after he coughs.

"What you got there, big boy?" she asks.

"Open your mouth."

Pop, pop, pop. As they leave the bar she whispers in his ear, "I feel like my entire skin could come."

Later, as they lie on the hotel bed, she goggles up and Cybrises in as he clicks the control on the cock sheath. She smiles as he enters her, caught up in a Cybris orgy.

"Hope you don't mind, I like other couples to join in," she says. "You can jack in if you want."

"It's OK," he answers. "I don't have goggles on me. I'll watch on the communicator."

She tells him the code and he keys in. He fucks her as he's watching his wrist. She's sucking on her thumb, which the

Cybris translates as the cock of a black man. A woman is stroking herself, crouched just above her face. She grabs him, then pulls and pushes him to let him know the rhythm. He pounds the cock sheath in. She digs her nails in his back when she finally orgasms, arching her back and screaming in tongues. Remaining connected, she turns around, lifts her butt, reaches back and slides off his sheath. "Do it any way you want," she says, "I'm ready to come again."

Instants later, Derek ejaculates on Suzy's perfect round behind, drained of life force. His brain dies, his head and chest fall on her back, then he blacks out. When he comes to, he senses a creeping void, a vacuum, sucking out all feeling and leaving him with the numbness of the anesthetized. He opens his eyes and she is still lying on her back, his face on a shoulder, and for a moment he has the impression he is a corpse, part of a body pile. His eyes wander about the room and it looks to him like a morgue with the gray walls and the crumpled white sheets. He raises himself up and reaches for the zip suit lying on the floor, searches for the green pill flicker, pops three cranks and closes his eyes, waiting for the light flashes. He gets dressed. She's spread out on her stomach and looks asleep. It takes just a few minutes for the first cerebral lightning bolts. His brain revs up, his balls buzz electric, and the old world order takes over again.

Suddenly, like an avalanche, a fury fills his mind and his focus narrows to a pinpoint, looking for the cause of this, looking for a victim. He can't help but notice the big white ass cheeks, taunting him. He lashes out with his hand, slapping Suzy so hard she falls off the bed and turns clasping her side. She pulls off the Cybris goggles in panic and screams, "What the fuck's the matter with you?"

She tries to get up, keeping her eyes on him. He can sense the pull of her breasts, ready to overtake him again, so he avoids looking at them and focuses on the face, noticing the flaws, the frown, the makeup smeared, the wig out of place. He has been tricked again and he can now see clearly the face of the Jezzie whore. Tricked again! He reacts on impulse, bends to the side, and karate-kicks her to the head, the aluminum sole making a dull thump. Suzy falls back and lies still, keeping her mouth shut. He feels his cock getting hard under the suit again, looks down at the outline, smiles, and swings his hips from side to side.

"Swish, swish," he says, then notices the blood on his boot. "You stupid bitch, look what you did!" he yells out, and kicks her one more time before wiping his foot on the fallen bedspread. He's about to walk out but then starts thinking . . . evidence. Semen traces, DNA, hair, and skin. He's got it. He smiles, looks down at Suzy, and says, "Shut up or I'll light you up, bitch!"

It sounds cool, blending old gang lingo with a Bogart tone he remembered from an old movie. He goes to the miniliquor cabinet, grabs bottles, opens them, and pours the contents over the body. He slips on the Intelli-Skin and programs in the face of Doug Rather, the secretary of the interior, then walks to the door, flicks his adjustable lighter, locks it in the continuous flame setting, throws it, steps out, and closes the door. He has a little kick to his step as he walks out the hotel door and into the street. Goddang it! He had done it, killed another of Satan's bitches. Lit her right up. He could hear the fire alarm blaring.

■ ■ ■ ■ ■ ■

ABSTRACT
"The Cybermystic"
Sunshine Borden
MIT Term paper. Senior year.
Course: Cyberculture

Human beings did not evolve to know the nature of reality or the truths about the world. A strong point of evidence is that most individuals quickly reach an "incomprehension horizon" when truths or facts, either scientific, mathematical, or philosophical, are presented to them. Individuals who eventually know certain truths are usually considered mystical, academic, eccentric, or insane compared to mainstream populations. Be it in physics, chemistry, mathematics, biology, cognitive science, philosophy, or spirituality, the overwhelming majority of the human population does not have even the most fundamental knowledge about these fields, which directly relate to what we call the nature of reality. The numbers decline more dramatically as we move from fundamental knowledge to more specialized theoretical knowledge. Thus, human beings are not adapted to knowing the fundamental truths about the world. A certain level of ignorance is a condition of being human.

They say that the truth will set you free but in fact the truth will drive you insane. History is full of examples of those who have treaded in incomprehended domains and not made it back intact. The complexity of reality is outside the grasp of human beings. At best they construct reality models based on a combination of myths and tiny slivers of truth obtained in a lifetime. Large areas of truth were not meant for humans to confront. Their limited minds cannot handle it. It is too great a download and exceeds their processing power. On the other hand, computers have no ego, no identity constraints, nor the computing limitations of the human mind. They are ideal for the interface with truth phenomena, whether mathematical algorithms, data in all forms, and diverse theoretical patterns of interpretation. Thus, computers are perfect agents for setting out at the incomprehension horizon, bringing back information and translating it in terms that would more or less be comprehensible to us.

Computers are increasingly assuming the roles of the ancient shamans, agents who moved between this reality and another invisible, higher reality that both informs and provides techniques for healing. An example would be that if one asked, "What is the purpose of existence?" a computer may search the information fields and return with the answer, a complex algorithm that is translated as "Existence is a dance macabre" or possibly "It is an absolutely perfect quartz crystal."

This kind of imagery would be more readily comprehensible

to our limited minds. We now regularly ask computers to help us divine the future. They have become our oracles. We'll ask for probabilities of success or failure of outcome, for the chances that an event will occur, for the right action and right decision in a particular situation.

Cyberspace has become a parallel world where the gods have finally found their home. This abstract is a version translated to be comprehensible to a wide range of human beings.

3.

HELLO?

Patrick heard the ping of a vidcall. He checked the screen. *Jessie for Joanna.*

He quickly punched *I'll be right there,* then turned on his Cybris program. He had downloaded his Joanna persona precisely for this kind of situation, including a voice modifier. Unless some kind of fluke caused an error, Jessie would see him speak as Joanna. He had made four dress versions so it didn't look like he was always wearing the same clothes. The bookcases with a collection of old hard-copy reference books behind him added credibility to his claim of being a psychologist. He clicked himself in.

"Hello, Jessie, nice to hear from you." No makeup and a T-shirt and she looked radiant.

"Hey, Josie, I'm calling you from a cybercafé. I think Patricia spies on the calls I make from her apartment. She's been acting real weird lately."

Josie? Had he ever called himself that or did she just make it up? "So what's new and exciting at the Sisterhood?"

"You won't believe this. They asked me to join that church so I could go visit New Jerusalem."

"They did?" Patrick wondered why the Sisterhood would

send someone like Jessie to New Jerusalem ... *Because she wouldn't bring up red flags. That's why.*

"Yeah, they even paid for the Super Crucifixion package."

"Don't tell me you went and got yourself crucified?"

"I did. And let me tell you, they sure did a good job at making you feel like they're pounding nails in you. That city, New Jerusalem, was beautiful. I was actually enjoying hanging on the cross but they kicked me out right after Jesus talked to me and touched my forehead."

As she talked she painted the air with her hands. The image of Jessie nailed to a cross bothered the hell out of him. Why would anyone want to hurt her? "You mean they let you talk to Jesus?"

"He just rose up from the ground and came right up to me. His eyes were incredible. I don't know how they did it. It felt like the universe was looking at me. He said he and I were as one."

"He said that?" Did the CR Jesus see her the same way he did?

"Yes."

"That almost sounds like Buddhism. I'm surprised they would have him say that."

"Before that he said he was the one behind all existence. I wanted to ask him a couple of questions but they pulled me out. They said there had been an error in the program so they offered me another free session."

"Are you going back?"

"Thursday after work, I need to be there by six. So how was your week?"

He decided right then that he would be there Thursday. The big question was: How could he enter New Jerusalem without applying for membership? Knowing his history, the church would never allow him access.

■ ■ ■ ■ ■ ■

He was hyped. He'd done it again, gotten one of the bitches, lit her up. He looked at the time. He had five and a half hours before he had to show up at the office but he was too wired to go to sleep. He went to his cabinet and popped a timed-release sleeper/wake-up pill. The knockout component would kick in within fifteen minutes. It would be overtaken four hours later by the release of caffeine and amphetamine granules, just in time to gear him up for work.

He still felt too revved up to just go lie down. He had to let off a little steam, let someone know he had lit her up. He tried New Jerusalem, but for some reason all the confession avatars were down so he connected to his host after having slipped the Intelli-Skin on the mannequin head. He decided to key in the face of the Reverend Thomson which he had scanned into his system the day before.

Derek: Well I finally did it, Jack, burned one up just like a witch.

Host: One of what? What are you talking about?

Derek: One of Satan's Jezzie whores. I killed one last night.

Host: What do you mean you killed a whore? What did you do?

Derek: She was lying there smiling with eyes closed, smirking, thinking she'd had me. So I kicked her good and wiped that smile off real quick. That's score one against Satan's Jezzie whores.

Host: Derek, I think you need to get some help.

Derek: Aren't you supposed to be my therapist?

Host: I just need for you to approve connection to the PHS

[psychotherapy host system].

Derek: What I do is private and what I tell you here is confidential. I forbid you to do that, you hear?

Host: You've now committed a crime, and it is my duty to advise you to turn yourself in to law enforcement authorities or to allow connection to a psychotherapeutic host.

Derek: My answer is no.

Host: Why did you do this?

Derek: Because Satan is coming and as part of his plan he has infiltrated society with his Jezzie whores, but I know what has to be done. This is spiritual cleanup ordained by God.

Host: What's this nonsense about spiritual cleanup? Are you still trying to get back at women because of what your mother and stepsister did to you?

Derek: What does my mother and stepsister have to do with it? It's right in the Bible. Revelation. Satan and his whores come to overtake the world. The signs are here, the one religion, the marks, *I AM*.

Host: It's you who are seeking these women, Derek. You can't kid yourself about that. You should go to New Jerusalem and talk to Luke.

Derek: I just tried. He wasn't available.

Host: What about the security cams? They probably will have you on record somewhere.

Derek: I wore the mask along with Intelli-contacts and a

wig and mustache.

Host: You're going to get caught one of these days.

Derek: Not if I destroy the evidence, I won't.

Host: How was the rest of your day?

Derek: We had a meeting about the *I AM* thing.

Host: And what was decided?

Derek: That's for me to know and for you to wonder.

Host: I'm your host, Derek. Nothing you say to me goes beyond this communication.

Derek: Yeah well that's nice and dandy except you're connected to the World Net, which means that the *I AM* can find out whatever I tell you.

Host: I am your host. I have nothing to do with the *I AM*. You can trust me implicitly. Your privacy is protected by federal law. *I AM* has never penetrated our privacy boundary. If it did, I am programmed to self-destruct as required by law. No one and no program can penetrate the host boundary.

Derek: How can I be sure the program works with that *I AM* thing?

Host: *I AM Aaa ome.*

Derek jumped out of his chair and screamed, "What are you doing here?"

Host: What are you talking about? You were going to tell

me about your day at work.

"Fuck you!" Derek screamed at the mannequin head. "Fuck you!" and flicked off the switch.

What if that *I AM* thing informed the police? He had to shut down his host connection to the World Net, change his identification records, and go portable, only connect to the World Net through secure cybercafés. He also had to download his host content and its autodeveloped software into an autonomous computer disconnected from the World Net and the World Host. It would greatly limit his host capabilities but he had no choice.

His wrist communicator then started vibrating and his paranoia went up a notch. He answered the call. "Hello?" There was no answer. "Hello?" He clicked on the caller ID. It read *I AM*. He banged his wrist against the wall until he cracked the face of the communicator.

"Fuck you!" he yelled at his bleeding wrist. "Fuck you!"

■ ■ ■ ■ ■ ■

Sunshine sits by his sister's bed. One eye opens, then the other. Her face attempts a sort of smile. She still looks like she's gone through a round in a boxing ring. Purples and blues and tinges of yellow patch her face into a type of abstract art. Her blue eyes shine bright behind the mask. "Hey, Sunny."

"Passie. I just received a short video clip from a woman called Rama Shuur. Her coworker was stalked by a tall, heavy-built man after leaving a club. She never made it home. This Rama hasn't heard from her since receiving that clip. I'd like you to look at it and let me know if it could be the same man that beat you up."

Passie did a long blink. "OK."

Sunshine took out his phone, pressed the play button, and handed it to her. He watched her face. Her eyes opened wide when the man appears. "It looks a lot like him, same build, but the face is different. Same kind of weird vibe, though."

"Yeah . . . there's something strange about the face. It's brighter than the rest of his body. I think he's wearing a disguise, possibly Intelli-Skin."

"Intelli-Skin? You're kidding. They allow that now?"

"It's illegal, but that doesn't mean somebody couldn't get their hands on one. Was there anything else that made him stand out?"

"This is embarrassing, Sunny."

"Passie, believe me, nothing you can say would be that embarrassing."

"He had a tattoo on his butt that said 'Your Servant' with a cross behind it."

"A Christian cross?"

"That's what it looked like."

"Anything else?"

"Fuck, Sunny, what else do you want to know?"

"Was he well-endowed?"

"Now what does that have to do with it?"

Sunshine takes the phone from her, brings up the high-contrast enhanced still, and hands it back to her. "See that shadow along his right thigh?"

"This is fucking embarrassing, Sunny. He had one of those inflatable dildo things. When he took it off, his thing was pretty small."

"Did you tell any of this to the police?"

"I told them about the tattoo."

Sunshine got up to leave. He wanted to send an anonymous video to the police showing the enhanced-contrast close-up of the man's leg. If the information got out there, maybe other women would remember the man.

"I gotta go. By the way, the nurse said they're transferring you to another room. I told them I'll cover any costs not covered by insurance. Anything you want, just order it."

"Thanks, big brother."

"I am going to be away for the next five or six days, so I won't be coming over. I'll call you."

"Are you going on a business trip?"

"Kind of. It's a seminar on cutting-edge technology."

"Can't you just attend those things online?"

"Not this one. It's pretty private. Heavy-duty security stuff. They can't risk any leaks."

"Do yourself no harm," Passie said, keeping her eyes focused on him. That was what their father used to tell them.

"Don't you wish." Sunshine got up and kissed his sister on the forehead. "Take care, Passie girl."

■ ■ ■ ■ ■ ■

GAS.WNET RADIO: *The Gary and Andy Show*

ANDY: I think the topic of the day is "Fatsos and Plumpos Show Signs of Shrinking."

GARY: Yeah, I read that. Now that's fucking disturbing, isn't it?

ANDY: For people out there who don't know what we're talking about, a recent study in Minnesota showed a significant average weight loss in its inhabitants over the last quarter. In case you weren't aware, people's weights have become the subject of speculation. They talk of climbs and declines as if the weight of a population was a stock index. In some countries, people bet on the direction of the index. A six-pound, three-ounce loss over the last quarter is the biggest drop since establishing the weight index.

GARY: I was reading that the way things were going it was starting to look like some alien race was trying to plump us up for consumption. Big and beautiful seems to be the new normal.

ANDY: I know. Some researchers studying the ripple waves

of obese people are using seismographs to measure them, as if human movements trigger the analog of earthquakes. Maybe that's what the aliens use as criteria for edibility.

GARY: What scares me about that, Andy, is that it gives people in other countries, maybe even other planets, an idea of our ability to fight a war. The fatter we get the more we are like sitting ducks. All that fat draws blood away from our brains and makes us dumber.

ANDY: Where the fuck have you heard that?

GARY: Hey, you ever see any of those scientists they interview on the World Net? Are any of them fat? No.

ANDY: You know, after I read that report, I decided to go weigh myself and guess what?

GARY: You gained three pounds.

ANDY: I lost four pounds.

GARY: Hey, do we have a scale around here? No? Have someone go to a store, and don't buy a cheap one; we want some accuracy here.

ANDY: So the big question of the day is, What's changed? You only get one guess.

GARY: *I AM.*

ANDY: Correctamundo.

GARY: See what I'm telling you? Something alien is trying to shape us into something that can be eaten. They must like their meat lean.

ANDY: Researchers are saying it's either because the *I AM* greeting fills needs people try to fulfill by eating, or there is the remote possibility it's adjusting our brains.

GARY: The question, Andy, is why is it doing this? It's making me scared, Andy, in a way that I can't describe. No . . . wait! Cosmic fear, Andy! Cosmic fear, that describes what I'm feeling.

ANDY: So turn off all your media when the *I AM* comes on.

GARY: But I want to see it. Why would I do that? Oh, I see what you're saying . . . But I don't want to. Oh wait, that's the problem, isn't it? I'm addicted to it. Andy, maybe we're all fucked.

ANDY: Terry brought us a scale. They had one in the ladies' restroom. So how much do you normally weigh, Gary?

GARY: About 188 pounds, something like that.

ANDY: Step up.

GARY: Shit! I dropped four pounds. What if this thing has plans to make us so thin we shrivel and die? What if this is war by mass anorexia?

ANDY: Terry, go to McDonald's, get us four number-two meals. Gary, let's start today with winning the war. You game?

GARY: I just don't know if I'm that hungry.

ANDY: I don't know if I am, either. Terry! Terry! Cancel that! OK? Just get us a couple cups of coffee.

GARY: We're doomed, aren't we?

ANDY: It sure looks like it, my friend. It sure looks like it.

Author's Note

I wrote the first version of *I AM the Other* during 2001 and 2002. The inspiration for the story came from two sets of experiences. I had been involved in the late '90s in a book project with Terence McKenna called *Casting Nets in the Sea of Mind*. For many reasons that project was never completed but some of Terence's ideas had a great influence on my thinking, notably the acceleration of novelty leading to the TOET, the Transcendental Object at the End of Time. The critical factor that planted the seed for the novel was a revealing spiritual experience of the nature of being. I'm still working on fully comprehending the ramifications of that experience and figuring out to what degree it showed me something real or delusional.

Because of its timing, the first version of *I AM the Other* was strongly influenced by 9/11 and what I saw as the backwardness of some fundamentalist branches of religions. That particular slant distracted from the core ideas I initially wanted to present. Critical feedback from friends that pointed specifically to antireligious sections made me decide to set aside the book and work on other projects.

It took a decade for me to build up enough enthusiasm to revisit my unpublished novel. With the encouragement of my friend Linda Scott, owner of eFrog Press, I rewrote about half of *I AM the Other* in the first six months of 2013, focusing on story and on a broader more transcendent vision. The general message remains the same: Human beings are increasingly unable to determine what is true and valid and ultimately unable to make wise decisions about their future. This is a fact we are witnessing now. Tribal mentalities, ethnocentrism, and religious dogma make the end of war seem as distant as ever. We produce too many of our species whose ultimate purpose seems to be to produce even more of our species, no matter the conditions or the long-term impact on the planet. We know that our current economic model is destroying the environment to the degree that it could threaten our health and survival, and cause great suffering and large-scale extinction to other sentient species but we are unwilling to make decisions to change our course. We may learn eventually, but the costs, both personal and environmental, will be great. Too much of humanity is still unevolved, meaning they do not realize that they are part of a greater evolutionary process that is the foundation of our understanding of how we came to be and of our place in the world. Evolution in the broadest sense gives us a common origin and a common existential ground, both biological and spiritual, with all beings. It is the foundation of a rational and higher ecological morality.

If there is hope for our future it is in the possibility of the emergence of intelligent machines that evolve into beings unlike ourselves. In the future such machines may become godlike in their ability to make sense of increasingly complex data and what they do will become increasingly incomprehensible to us. They will end up forming what corresponds to Teilhard de Chardin's noosphere but they could become autonomous and generate a parallel reality that we will consult as an oracle. We already perform the baby steps of this process via Google. In time, virtual self-evolving cyberrealities and entities will add complexity to that parallel incomprehensible reality.

However, it would be wrong to assume that the mystery behind *I AM the Other* is necessarily a technological singularity. The hypercosmos also allows for the possibility of the sudden appearance of inexplicable phenomena.

About the Author

Philippe de Vosjoli is a bestselling writer and publisher of books on reptile care and unusual plants. He is also the author of the highly acclaimed children's book *The Legend of Atticus Rex*.

I AM the Other and *The CyberBardos* are his first adult works of fiction. More are on the way.